Books by Corey Ford

PARODY

THREE ROUSING CHEERS
MEANING NO OFFENSE
SALT WATER TAFFY
THE JOHN RIDDELL MURDER CASE
COCONUT OIL
IN THE WORST POSSIBLE TASTE
THE DAY NOTHING HAPPENED

HUMOR

THE GAZELLE'S EARS (*anthology*)
THE HORSE OF ANOTHER COLOR
HOW TO GUESS YOUR AGE
THE OFFICE PARTY
NEVER SAY DIET
HAS ANYBODY SEEN ME LATELY? (*anthology*)
COREY FORD'S GUIDE TO THINKING
WHAT EVERY BACHELOR KNOWS
AND HOW DO WE FEEL THIS MORNING?

WAR BOOKS

FROM THE GROUND UP (*with Alastair MacBain*)
SHORT CUT TO TOKYO
WAR BELOW ZERO
CLOAK AND DAGGER (*with Alastair MacBain*)
THE LAST TIME I SAW THEM (*anthology*)

OUTDOORS

A MAN OF HIS OWN (*with Alastair MacBain*)
EVERY DOG SHOULD HAVE A MAN
YOU CAN ALWAYS TELL A FISHERMAN
MINUTES OF THE LOWER FORTY
UNCLE PERK'S JUG

HISTORY AND BIOGRAPHY

A PECULIAR SERVICE
WHERE THE SEA BREAKS ITS BACK
THE TIME OF LAUGHTER
DONOVAN OF OSS

DONOVAN OF OSS

by COREY FORD

DONOVAN OF OSS

with illustrations

BOSTON · LITTLE, BROWN AND COMPANY · TORONTO

LIBRARY OF CONGRESS CATALOG CARD NO.: 70–92332

FIRST EDITION

A portion of this book originally appeared in *American Heritage*. The illustrations in this book were selected from the albums, scrapbooks, and personal files of the late William J. Donovan, except where otherwise noted.

Published simultaneously in Canada
by Little, Brown & Company (Canada) Limited

PRINTED IN THE UNITED STATES OF AMERICA

For Ole Doering

FOREWORD

SEVERAL YEARS after World War II had ended, I spent a quiet afternoon in General Donovan's apartment on Sutton Place. As an Air Force colonel, I had served under the General on liaison duty with the Office of Strategic Services, and had come to know the unique agency which he had created out of the chaos that led to Pearl Harbor. OSS had been abolished by President Truman in 1945, immediately following the Japanese surrender, and the unprecedented American adventure in secret intelligence, which for four years had matched wits with the centuries-old espionage organizations of Europe and Asia, had been emasculated by a stroke of the Chief Executive's pen. Most of its trained personnel, their talents no longer wanted, had returned to civilian life; and General Donovan was back in New York and practicing law again as senior partner of the Wall Street firm which bears his name.

We were sitting after luncheon in his library, looking out on the shimmering East River. The room was plain and rather impersonal. Shelves lined the walls from floor to ceiling, but there were no signed photographs of the world leaders he had known so intimately, no framed citations or letters, no display of the medals won in two wars. All the books in his library, so far as I could see, were on the same subject: the history of intelligence and its early practice in China, in the Greek and Persian wars, in Elizabethan times. When he had been asked in the Thirties to serve as President Roosevelt's eyes and ears abroad, he had gathered together every available volume which would provide background for his intelligence mission, and had studied them as assiduously as a lawyer preparing a brief. He was a rapid and voracious reader, and the books bristled with markers, their pages were filled with penciled notations and underlined sentences.

The reflected light from the river illuminated the General's features as we talked. It was the first time I had seen him since OSS days, and he had not changed perceptibly. Maybe a trifle chubbier, with the suggestion of a double chin — he was in his middle sixties now — but the face was still seamless, the same soft smile, the darker eyebrows contrasting with his close-cut silver hair. His manner as always was gentle and unhurried, the antithesis of his nickname of "Wild Bill." His pale blue eyes seemed to see through me, and sense my inner thoughts. He had a strange power of perception about people and events. I think he was the most intuitive man I've ever known.

Perhaps this instinct prompted him to take down a book from the shelf and hand it to me. It was Morton Pennypacker's *George Washington's Spies on Long Island and in New York*. In his familiar low murmur, he asked: "Why don't you write a book about American espionage during the Revolution?" That was the beginning of my interest in intelligence history, and the result, twenty years later, was the volume I called *A Peculiar Service*.

But another book was already taking shape in my mind, that afternoon a quarter century ago. Sometime, I resolved, I would set down the story of this controversial and much misunderstood man, one of the most enigmatic figures of his time. I knew it would be difficult to write a biography while he was alive; his innate modesty would balk at anything so personal. So I have waited until this moment, when the quarrels of wartime Washington have been largely forgotten, when "Wild Bill" Donovan and his OSS have settled into proper perspective as an important, though still largely unknown, part of our national heritage.

This book, let me emphasize at the outset, does not pretend to be a complete history of the Office of Strategic Services, a task which would fill many volumes. It is essentially the story of William J. Donovan, and his place in history as the instigator and organizer and director of America's first formal agency for organized intelligence and unorthodox warfare.

— *Corey Ford*

Hanover, N.H.

CONTENTS

xii   CONTENTS

ILLUSTRATIONS

ABBREVIATIONS

A-2	*Air Force Intelligence*
AEF	*Allied Expeditionary Forces*
AFHQ	*Air Force Headquarters*
AGFRTS	*Air and Ground Forces Resources and Technical Staff*
AVG	*American Volunteer Group (China)*
BBC	*British Broadcasting Company*
BEW	*Board of Economic Warfare*
BSC	*British Security Coordinator*
CBI	*China-Burma-India Theater*
CIA	*Central Intelligence Agency*
CIG	*Central Intelligence Group*
CINCPOA	*Commander in Chief, Pacific Ocean Area*
COI	*Coordinator of Information*
DF-ing	*Direction finding*
DNI	*Director of Naval Intelligence*
DSC	*Distinguished Service Cross*
ETOUSA	*European Theater of Operations, United States Army*
FBI	*Federal Bureau of Investigation*
FIS	*Foreign Information Service*
FN	*Foreign Nationalities*
G-2	*Army Intelligence Staff*
JCS	*Joint Chiefs of Staff*
J-E	*Joan Eleanor*
JPWC	*Joint Psychological Warfare Committee*

JSP	*Joint Staff Planners*
LST	*Landing Ship Tank*
MO	*Morale Operations*
MU	*Maritime Unit*
MVD	*Russian Secret Intelligence*
NI	*Naval Intelligence*
NLRB	*National Labor Relations Board*
OCD	*Office of Civilian Defense*
OEM	*Office of Emergency Management*
OFF	*Office of Facts and Figures*
OG	*Operational Groups*
OGR	*Office of Government Reports*
ONI	*Office of Naval Intelligence*
OPM	*Office of Production Management*
OSS	*Office of Strategic Services*
OWI	*Office of War Information*
PWE	*Psychological Warfare Executive (British)*
RAF	*Royal Air Force*
R&A	*Research and Analysis*
R&D	*Research and Development*
SAB	*Special Activities Bruce*
SACO	*Sino-American Cooperation Association*
SAG	*Secret Activities Goodfellow*
SEAC	*Southeast Asia Command*
SI	*Secret Intelligence*
SIM	*Italian Secret Intelligence*
SIS	*Secret Intelligence Service (British)*
SO	*Special Operations*
SOE	*Special Operations, Executive (British)*
SO-2	*Subversion Branch (British)*
SS	*Schutzstaffel: Hitler's protective squad*
S&T	*Schools and Training*
VHF	*Very High Frequency*
WAC	*Women's Army Corps*
X-2	*Counterespionage*

DONOVAN OF OSS

INTRODUCTION

SECRET INTELLIGENCE, so little understood and so often denounced as unethical and somehow un-American, goes back in practice to the very beginning of our republic. The espionage activities of the Office of Strategic Services, the wartime organization which was the forerunner of today's Central Intelligence Agency, were first employed by George Washington at the outset of the American Revolution.

That September of 1776 found General Washington sorely pressed. The remnants of his shattered army had escaped to New York, following the disastrous Battle of Brooklyn, and it would have been prudent to retreat to the more maneuverable country north of White Plains; but the General was under orders from Congress to hold Manhattan Island. With sixteen miles of vulnerable coastline, and no American navy, his only hope was to concentrate his vastly outnumbered troops at the most likely point of attack. It was imperative to know where and when the enemy blow would fall.

In plain sight across the East River the British were busy throwing up breastworks, but that could be a feint. Would Sir William Howe's forces land to the north at Throg's Neck or Westchester and seal off the King's Bridge, the only exit from Manhattan? Would they establish a beachhead midway up the island to cut his army in twain, or sail around the Battery and strike the undefended Hudson shore? The General appealed to his commanders for any information they could secure.

Among Washington's forces was a small detachment of Rangers

called "Congress's Own," commanded by Lieutenant Colonel Thomas Knowlton and responsible directly to the Commander-in-Chief. They were in effect a reconnaisance unit, with orders to secure intelligence and perform other secret duties "either by water or by land, by night or by day." At the General's request, Knowlton summoned his twenty officers to Ranger headquarters, and explained that Washington desired to send a spy behind the British lines on Long Island to learn the enemy's battle plan. "By the rules of war," Knowlton said, "no soldier can be ordered on such duty, so His Excellency has asked for a Ranger to volunteer for the mission."

His eyes moved over the circle, and we can imagine the ensuing uncomfortable silence. At last Lieutenant James Sprague, a veteran of the French and Indian War, spoke for his comrades. "I'm willing to fight the British and if need be to die a soldier's death in battle," he said, "but as far as going among them in disguise and being taken and hung up like a dog, I'll not do it." There was no other response, and Knowlton adjourned the meeting.

One of the Ranger officers, Captain Nathan Hale of Connecticut, left the room with a troubled mind. The thought of spying offended every decent principle; but, offensive or not, it was a chance to serve his country. He wanted to talk to someone, to voice his thought aloud and perhaps resolve his doubts. In his dilemma he sought out a friend and former Yale classmate, Captain William Hull, whose regiment was billeted nearby in Harlem Village. Hull set down his recollection of their conversation many years later:

"After [Hale's] interview with Colonel Knowlton, he repaired to my quarters, and informed me of what had passed. He remarked, 'That he thought he owed to his country the accomplishment of an object so important, and so much desired by the Commander, and he knew of no other mode of obtaining the information, than by assuming a disguise and passing into the enemy camp.' He asked my candid opinion.

"I replied, that it was an action which involved serious consequences, and the propriety of it was doubtful; and though he viewed the business of a spy as a duty, yet . . . who would wish success at such a price? Did his country demand the moral degradation of her sons, to advance her interests? Stratagems are resorted to in war; they are feints and evasions, performed under no disguise, and, considered in a military view, lawful and advantageous. The tact with which they are executed exacts admiration from the enemy. But who respects the character of a spy, assuming the garb of friendship but to betray? The very death assigned him is expressive of the estimation in which he is held. As soldiers, let us do our duty in the field, and not stain our honour by the sacrifice of integrity. . . . I ended by saying, that should he undertake the enterprise, his short, bright career would close with an ignominious death.

"He replied, 'I am fully sensitive of the consequences of discovery and capture in such a situation. But for a year I have been attached to the army, and have not rendered any material service, while receiving a compensation, for which I make no return. Yet,' he continued, 'I am not influenced by the expectation of promotion or pecuniary reward; I wish to be useful, and every kind of service, necessary to the public good, becomes honourable by being necessary. If the exigencies of my country demand a peculiar service, its claims to perform that service are imperious.'

"He paused — then affectionately taking my hand, he said, 'I will reflect, and do nothing but what duty demands.' "*

Hull's arguments, and Hale's own doubts, have a familiar ring today. The word "spy" has always jarred the American ear. From the time of the Revolution to the present, righteous citizens have looked down on espionage as a debasing business. Let foreign nations indulge in their dark intrigues. Ours is a free and open society, they hold, and clandestine operations are alien to its character. As Secretary of War Stimson is said to have observed when he abolished his cryptographic unit, "Gentlemen don't read each other's mail."

General Washington had no such scruples. Any stratagem was honorable if it served to unmask the intentions of the enemy. The aristocratic Virginia gentleman, stainless hero of the cherry tree legend and the paragon of truth, was in fact an expert in unorthodox and covert

* *Revolutionary Services and Civil Life of General William Hull* (New York, 1848).

warfare. Behind the grim visage and tightly compressed lips (due to his ill-fitting false dentures which had a way of popping out when he smiled) was a sly imagination, constantly intriguing to penetrate the enemy's secrets by duplicity and guile. He was that rarest of combinations, a brilliant military tactician and a master of the craft of intelligence.

The tragic end of Hale's mission, far from discouraging Washington, served only to convince him of the need for better preparation and protection for his spies. When New York became the British command headquarters in 1778, a group of American undercover agents called the Culper Ring set up operations in the occupied city, carrying on their secret business from a boardinghouse on Queen Street, only a couple of blocks from General Sir Henry Clinton's residence. At regular intervals a courier would pick up the information gathered by Culper Junior, cover name of the chief correspondent in Manhattan, and carry it by fast horse to Culper Senior in Setauket, on Long Island's north shore. Thence it would be transported by whaleboat over the Sound to Fairfield, Connecticut, and delivered by a relay of dragoons across Connecticut and Westchester to the Commander-in-Chief. For seven years they conducted their espionage undetected by the British. Even Washington never knew the identity of Culper Junior, a young Quaker merchant named Robert Townsend, whose conscience was so troubled by his role as a spy that he carried the secret to his grave.

Although Major Benjamin Tallmadge served as liaison officer with the Culper Ring, Washington, and Washington alone, was the head of American intelligence. To protect his agents, he prepared a numerical code based on Entick's Dictionary, of which only four copies existed: one for the General himself, one for Tallmadge, and two for the Culpers. As an added precaution, he furnished them with an invisible ink called Secret Stain which was invented in London by Sir James Jay, brother of John Jay, according to a formula which remains a mystery to this day. He suggested various methods by which their information could be smuggled past British guards, perhaps concealed in the sole of a boot — a method frequently employed by spies in World War II — or bound in the covers of a book. Messages in invisible ink would be less easily detected, he instructed Culper Junior, if he were to send "a familiar letter on domestic matters to his friend in Setauket, interlining with the Stain his secret intelligence," and "fold it up in a particular manner" to distinguish it from other correspondence.

No detail was too small to escape Washington's attention. When he decided to move his combined French and American armies from the Hudson to the Chesapeake, to join the French fleet which was blockading General Cornwallis at Yorktown, it was vital to prevent General Sir Henry Clinton in New York from rushing reinforcements to his besieged colleague. To immobilize the British, Washington went to great lengths to persuade them that he was planning to attack New York by way of Staten Island. In the most elaborate deception of his career, he halted his southbound forces in New Jersey, and began laying out an apparently permanent camp, including huts and artillery parks and a field bakery. Adding to the illusion, French troops paraded along the Palisades, their white uniforms clearly visible to British observers across the river, and a flotilla of landing craft was assembled in the rocky recesses along the Jersey shore to suggest an amphibious assault. Years later Washington confessed that "much trouble was taken and finesse used to misguide and bewilder Sir Henry Clinton, in regard to the real object, by fictitious communications, as well as by making a deceptive provision of ovens, forage, and boats in the neighborhood."

The wily American general resorted to every trick to hoodwink Sir Henry. An express rider carrying specifications for the fictional camp passed so close to the British lines that he was captured, and the false papers were brought promptly to Clinton. Even more convincing, Washington staged a conversation with "an old resident of New York" who was known to be spying for the British, and asked the Tory agent a number of naïve questions about the landing beaches on Staten Island and the terrain around Sandy Hook, explaining innocently that he was "fond of knowing the situation of different parts of the country." He warned the spy "by no means to lisp a word of what had passed between them" and, as a final artistic touch, started an American regiment marching down the road to Sandy Hook before the agent's bulging eyes. Not until Washington's forces had crossed the Delaware on their way to

Virginia did Clinton realize how completely he had been duped, and by then it was too late to send aid to Yorktown. The surrender of Cornwallis's army of seven thousand men marked the end of Britain's domination in the Colonies.

Irregular warfare, Washington claimed, contributed as much as orthodox military maneuvers to America's success in the struggle for independence. Crude as his spies and secret codes and invisible ink seem in the light of modern technological advances, they were the prototypes of many of the sophisticated techniques in use today. Out of his pioneer espionage efforts during the Revolution emerged our concept of security through constant vigilance.

BOOK ONE
1883-1920

Bravest of the Brave

'Twas there I first beheld,
drawn up in file and line,
The brilliant Irish hosts; they came,
the bravest of the brave.

— CLARENCE MANGAN

I

A LIFE-SIZE OIL PAINTING of General Donovan, completed shortly before his death, hangs in the Central Intelligence Agency headquarters in Virginia. It shows him in Army uniform, erect and rigid, the twin stars of his rank riding on each shoulder. Inevitably the eye is drawn to the banks of bright ribbons on his chest: the blue Congressional Medal of Honor alone at the top, and below it the Distinguished Service Cross and Distinguished Service Medal which, with the National Security Medal, made him the first American in history to win his country's four highest awards. No familiar smile mellows the stern face in the portrait; this is the military Donovan who led his troops in battle during the Champagne-Marne and St.-Mihiel and Argonne campaigns, the legendary "Wild Bill" of New York's Fighting 69th.

There are conflicting theories about the origin of the ubiquitous nickname. Some claim that Donovan acquired it in the course of his Columbia football days; others (including his wife, Ruth) believe it was a product of World War I. But according to his brother, Father Vincent Donovan, it was pinned on him in 1916, a year before the war, during National Guard maneuvers along the Mexican border. Bill Donovan, a rising young Buffalo attorney, had been elected captain of a newly formed cavalry troop which was called to federal service for patrol duty in southern Texas during the Pancho Villa raids. Always in prime physical condition himself, he resolved that the other members of the troop should be equally fit. Day after day he led them in strenuous calisthenics and drills and forced marches under the blistering Texas sun. After a particularly punishing ten-mile hike with full packs, the perspiring citizen-soldiers collapsed by the roadside, gasping for breath. "Look at me, I'm not even panting," Captain Donovan taunted them. "If I can take it, why can't you?"

From the rear of the ranks a laconic voice answered: "We ain't as wild as you are, Bill."

So "Wild Bill" he became, after another William Donovan, a celebrated baseball pitcher of the period who was nicknamed "Wild Bill" because of his erratic delivery. The colorful label was taken up eagerly by the public when he returned from France, one of the most decorated soldiers of the war. But it proved to be a political dud during his campaign for governor of New York, and later, when he was head of OSS, it was used against him maliciously by bureaucratic enemies and by the isolationist press which sought to depict both Donovan and his agency as trigger-happy and irresponsible.

The nickname was as misleading as the military portrait. In person he was mild rather than wild; gentle, unassuming. His orders were given in a soft slow voice, as though he were making a polite request rather than issuing a command. Nothing appeared to ruffle him; his blue eyes might grow cold when he was angered, but his manner remained imperturbable. Although his name was frequently in the headlines as Roosevelt's chief of intelligence, the necessity for secrecy made him more or less an enigma to the public, a Mystery Man of World War II, a shadowy and misunderstood figure. "Cloak and Dagger," the newspapers dubbed his clandestine activities; though the daggers were wielded by his Washington rivals, and the cloak was his serene Irish smile.

Little or nothing was ever revealed of his private life. He declined to talk of his family background as the grandson of Irish immigrants in Buffalo, the studious youth who wanted to be a priest. The early influences that shaped his career might have been lost forever in the shuffle of years, had I not been able to turn for help to his younger brother, the Reverend Vincent Donovan, O.P., then chaplain at the Mariandale Motherhouse of the Dominican Sisters for the Sick Poor. Father Donovan was almost the only one left, after three quarters of a century, who knew the General as a boy.

2

Mariandale is situated on the Hudson a few miles from Ossining, New York, in a tranquil setting of elm-bordered drives and broad lawns descending to the river. The meditative calm of the surroundings was reflected in Father Donovan's easy welcome. He led the way to his study, a small congenial room, full of sunlight. There was a replica of the CIA portrait in a silver easel frame on a side table.

"Though how much help I can be to you, I'll not be promising," he warned, with just the trace of a Celtic lilt in his voice. "I'll tell you all I can about the General's boyhood days, but some things are dim and others I was too young to remember. He was nine years older than myself, you know."

General Donovan was born on New Year's Day in 1883, I recalled, so that would put Father Donovan in his latter seventies. Glancing at the portrait on the table at his elbow, I could see the strong family resemblance, though Father Donovan's features seemed thinner and more delicate. His hair was as white as his Dominican robes, but his blue eyes, so much like his brother's, were alert, and he had a quick vigorous laugh. General Donovan's smile might broaden into a grin when he was amused, but he seldom laughed aloud.

"We were very, very close, the General and I." I noticed that Father Donovan never referred to his brother by name, but always as the General. "He turned to me; he used to call me 'the Rock.' Even when I was a youngster, he'd sit on the edge of my bed and confide in me. I suppose he had to have somebody to talk to, because he was naturally reserved. We were always very close." He laughed aloud at a sudden recollection. "The General bought me my first pair of long trousers when I was not yet sixteen. I kept them hidden under the mattress for fear my mother would find them and cut them off."

Father Donovan leaned back, the reminiscent smile lingering on his lips, and let his mind wander freely across the years.

There were originally nine of us children [Father Donovan began], but four died of spinal meningitis at an early age. William Joseph — the middle name was the General's own choice at confirmation — was the eldest. My brother the doctor, born a year later, was named Timothy after my father and grandfather; then came Mary, which was my grandmother's name; then myself; then Loretta, the baby of the family. We all lived in my grandparents' big high-stooped brick house at 74 Michigan Street in Buffalo. They had the first floor, and my parents and the girls lived upstairs over them, and there was an enormous attic which had been converted into a dormitory, and most of the males, my uncles and my brothers, slept up there.

Grandfather Donovan was from Skibbereen in County Cork; he was brought up by a priest uncle, and was a teacher. After he eloped with Mary Mahoney — my grandmother was from the same part of Ireland — they emigrated to America, and settled in Buffalo's First Ward, down by the waterfront. It was a predominantly Irish neighborhood, wakes and fistfights every payday, and to go out on St. Patrick's Day was taking your life in your hands. Most of the folks were fresh from the Old Country like my grandparents, hard-working but warm and hospitable. The women would gossip back and forth across the board fences, and at night the men would gather in the corner saloon and talk politics. My father never smoked or drank, but he would sip ginger ale with them, and nothing was thought of it. He used to take my brother the General along with him while he was still in knee pants, and he would sit on a bar stool and listen gravely to the discussions and nibble the free lunch. That could likely be the start of his interest in politics.

Our house on Michigan Street was a center for Irish immigrants, my grandfather sheltered them and found them jobs, and they say it used to be a refuge for arrivals by way of the "underground" from Canada. Neighbors were forever dropping in for a meal or an argument, and before elections there were some heated debates, I can tell you. In our neck of the woods you were born and died a Republican, but my father was very broad-minded, and we were brought up to vote for the best man, no matter what party, and the General inherited this trait.

My mother was Anna Letitia Lennon, a sweet saintly person; her parents came from County Monaghan in the north of Ireland. She was orphaned at an early age, and some cousins in Kansas raised her and gave her a fine education, and she had a pony and cart of her own to ride around in, she used to tell us. My father never finished school. He kept playing hooky to hang around the railroad yards, until at last my grandfather told him he could quit school if he liked and go to work, though he would live to regret it. My father found a job with the railroad; eventually he wound up superintendent of the Buffalo yards, but when he married my mother he realized the mistake he had made in not completing his education. So the first thing he did, before ever we were born, was to start building a library for the children he hoped to have. You've seen the General's library? Well, that was the nucleus. My father added to it year after year, and by the time I entered my teens I'd read and reread all of Shakespeare and Dickens and *The Divine Comedy*, I didn't understand it but I was fascinated by the Doré illustrations. We grew up in the midst of books.

The General was an omnivorous reader all his life, thanks to my father, and he could also thank my father for his skill as an orator that helped him in his law practice and as Assistant Attorney General. My father wasn't a public speaker himself, but he was always interested in oratory, I remember him taking me to hear William Jennings Bryan once, and he collected books of selected orations, including the Irish poets. They held elocution contests at the Christian Brothers' School in Buffalo that all of us attended, and the first medal the General won when he was only twelve years old was for reciting a poem by Clarence Mangan, the one that goes . . . let me think . . .

'Twas there I first beheld, drawn up in file and line,
The brilliant Irish hosts; they came, the bravest of the brave.

That poem always stirred my brother's imagination, and I suppose like any boy he had the dream of leading an Irish regiment into battle, though he never could have guessed in his wildest dreams that one day he would command the bravest of them all, the Fighting Irish of New York's 69th.

Father Donovan's eyes rested a moment on the face in the portrait beside him, with its air of placid confidence, the assured thrust of the chin, the unflinching eyes. I asked him whether his brother had always been so self-contained and calm.

Oh, he had a hot Irish temper as a boy [Father Donovan chuckled]. He and my brother the doctor, there was just a year or so between them, they were getting into fights all the time. My father took care of that. He set up a boxing ring in the loft of the barn behind the house, and bought some big training gloves, and whenever a quarrel started he would hustle them out to the barn and tie the gloves on, and say "Get it out of your system, boys." But it was the General himself who conquered his temper. He recognized it as a weakness, and he deliberately set out to control it. The madder he was inside, the calmer he would be outside. He taught himself to keep his voice down, and speak slowly, and the only way his temper ever showed was in his eyes.

It was self-discipline, like everything else he did. He had this concept of himself, you see, and he was determined to live up to it. He trained his body to be hard. He bought a set of dumb-bells, and he ran every day, and boxed and wrestled, anything to keep in top shape. He never smoked or drank. Oh, later in life he might sip a glass of wine, but it was only to be polite. Maybe it was my father's influence, but I think it was part of this self-discipline I mention, part of his thoroughness.

He went into everything thoroughly. When he was made captain of Cavalry Troop I of the National Guard, he read everything he could find about military tactics and drill, and during his summer vacation he spent his time with a Regular Army cavalry unit studying maneuvers, so he could do a thorough job. He had to learn to ride a horse — he'd never ridden before — and at night he'd come home very raw and ask me to rub him. I suggested that his doctor brother could take care of him better, but he had too much pride. He knew I'd never mention it afterward.

The General was always an athlete, proficient in all sports, but his favorites, besides boxing, were football and crew. My father was an amateur oarsman; he used to row in meets at the Celtic Rowing Club, and he developed my brothers into a tandem, and bought them a two-oared scull which they kept at the foot of Michigan Street. I used to

Timothy Francis Donovan and WJD — trainbearers for Bishop Quigley of Buffalo.

watch them race with the Celtics when I was old enough. Later the General was captain of a war canoe crew at the Buffalo Canoe Club over at Crystal Beach in Ontario, about twenty-five miles away, and he worked out there every weekend. When he went to Columbia, he rowed on the second varsity crew under coach Jim Rice, and also found time from his studies to win his "C" as one of the quarterbacks of the 1904 football team. Another Columbia quarterback that year, by the way, was Eddie Collins, the baseball great. My brother always played quarterback, in back-lot games at home, and at Niagara University, and then at Columbia. He liked to manage things. It was his natural bent for leadership; the rest of the team caught his confidence and drive, and Columbia had an outstanding season, though his modesty kept him from ever admitting he had any part in it. Did you know that his classmates voted him "most modest," and also "second handsomest"? I can't imagine who could have been first.

No doubt you're thinking to yourself all this sounds like hero worship, and what else would you expect after all from a younger brother? But he was indeed a handsome young man, the General, straight and well-muscled and light on his feet the way a boxer moves, and the girls were crazy about him, you may be sure.

Another side of him not generally known — I'm probably the only one who really knew, because he confided in me — was that he was deeply religious. Of course my father and mother were religious, but my brother actually thought for a time of becoming a Dominican priest. The prime reason he entered Niagara was to help him come to a decision, because there was a diocesan seminary in connection with the university. At Niagara his spiritual adviser was Father William Egan, an Irish gentleman and scholar, and a great influence on my brother. It was a long struggle to make up his mind, but at last he decided he wasn't good enough to be a priest.

I see you look surprised, but that's the actual fact; the General told Father Egan he didn't think he was good enough. That's what Father Egan told me later. I never understood why, for I always thought my brother was twice as good as myself. But Father Egan agreed with him, and urged him to leave Niagara — this was the end of his third year —

and transfer to Columbia University to study law. Father Egan was a shrewd man, and he had great insight, and I suppose he saw qualities in my brother that suggested law as more fitting for him. His thoroughness, maybe, and his logical and active mind.

It was a disappointment to my parents, of course, for in every Irish Catholic household it is assumed that one of the boys will be a priest, but nary a hint of their feelings was ever betrayed to the General. It was like that in our family, always the bridge of understanding between us. Ours was a happy household, I can tell you that, strict discipline but great affection. The General had almost a romantic love for my mother; he thought she had such a fine mind and was such a lady and had done such a good job raising us all. There was a real closeness between them, and my mother never let him see her tears as she packed his clothes, and he left home for Columbia in New York City.

So that was the start of his career as a lawyer, and later a General and a diplomat, a famous career it was, and yet . . .

Father Donovan's voice trailed. The afternoon shadows were lengthening on the lawns of Mariandale, and it was clearly time to be on my way. I rose and thanked him, and he escorted me to the door. For a moment he paused to look back at the portrait of his brother.

"He'd have made a fine priest," he said.

3

William Joseph Donovan received his A.B. from Columbia College in 1905. He earned his room and board by serving as house manager for his fraternity, Phi Kappa Psi, and worked nights and summers to pay for his tuition. Save for athletics, his only extracurricular activity was debating; he won the George William Curtis Medal for Public Speaking with an oration which bore the prophetic title "The Awakening of Japan." He was never a big-man-on-campus, and a quotation beside his photograph in the senior yearbook asked cryptically: "Is he quiet or always making a fuss?"

By combining his final college year with pre-law studies, he graduated from Columbia Law School in two years. Although he was not an outstanding scholar, his extensive reading as a boy had enabled him to digest books quickly, extracting the pertinent facts but wasting no time on irrelevant material — an invaluable asset in preparing a legal brief. One of his classmates at law school was Franklin Delano Roosevelt, but they moved in different social circles and did not become well acquainted until after Roosevelt's election to the Presidency. Another Columbia contact who played an important role in his later career was Harlan Fiske Stone, adjunct professor of law, who was appointed United States Attorney General by President Coolidge in 1924, and invited his former pupil to be his assistant in charge of the Justice Department's Criminal Division: Donovan's introduction to Washington.

He was twenty-four when he finished law school and returned to Buffalo in 1907, and began his legal apprenticeship with the small firm of Love & Keating. His associates were impressed by his retentive memory, and by the thoroughness and speed with which he assembled all the facts in a case. In court he never resorted to the elaborate gestures or purple rhetoric which were common among lawyers at the start of the century. His voice was always subdued, his manner unpretentious and intimate. His straightforward approach cut to the core of an issue, and by 1909, as his reputation grew, he was made a junior member of the firm.

Most of his early assignments were in the field of corporation law — he was to become one of the country's great counselors and trial lawyers — and he soon won the attention and respect of the Buffalo business community. In 1912, backed by their confidence, he formed an independent partnership with another local attorney, Bradley Goodyear, and later that summer they merged with the city's leading law firm of John Lord O'Brian and Chauncey Hamlin. Just five years after his graduation, his name was in bold letters on the shingle: O'Brian Hamlin Donovan & Goodyear.

Despite the pressure of legal work, he found time to join a group of young Buffalo men who were seeking to form a local troop of the National Guard. Military authorities approved their request, and in May of 1912 the unit was designated as Troop I, lst New York Cavalry, and

The 1897 St. Joseph's Junior Eleven. WJD, then aged fourteen, is standing third from right.

The 1905 Columbia varsity football team. WJD is seated in left foreground, Eddie Collins in right foreground.

they were given locker space and the use of the drill floor one night a week at the 65th Regiment Armory. The men themselves raised a fund to purchase six horses, which were kept in an old livery stable on Humboldt Parkway. In October, Donovan was elected captain of the troop.[1]

His first taste of action occurred when Troop I was ordered to the neighboring town of Depew, New York, to relieve the 74th Infantry which had been doing guard duty during a strike at the Gould Coupler Works. Captain Donovan had the troop in readiness for a call, and promptly the following morning he led his cavalrymen in formal parade up the main street of Depew, with dress uniforms and sabers drawn. As they passed a saloon which served as headquarters for the strikers, the Captain's horse stumbled and his saber clattered to the cobblestones. He ordered a lieutenant to take command of the column, wheeled his horse, and trotted back to retrieve the sword, just in time to see a brawny striker grab it and run into the saloon. Donovan dismounted, tied his horse to a post, and strode alone through the swinging doors. He re-appeared a couple of moments later, his uniform somewhat rumpled but with the saber clutched firmly in his hand.

Through his law practice and National Guard affiliation, a whole new social world was opening up to the Irish railroad worker's son from the other side of the tracks. His good looks and contagious enthusiasm made him a popular addition to Buffalo's younger set, and he was invited to join the exclusive Studio Club, which staged amateur theatricals for charity. He had done some previous acting in school plays at the Christian Brothers' and at Niagara, according to Father Donovan, and he had always been interested in the theater.

"Buffalo was a great tryout town," Father Donovan told me, "and we'd all of us save our pennies to attend a first night, with maybe George M. Cohan or the like. Our house wasn't far from the Star Theater which was run by Katherine Cornell's father; he gave up his medical business to manage the theater — that's how much of a show town it was. Even the famous Eleanor Robson came to Buffalo in 1914,

[1] *Niagara Frontier,* Buffalo and Erie County Historical Society (Buffalo, 1965).

she was a dream girl of mine; later she married the wealthy August Belmont, you know. During her visit she saw the General play the leading role in a private performance of Browning's *In a Balcony*, and she was so impressed with his ability that she offered to coach him. Once a week he would go down to New York for his dramatic lesson, which was not altogether pleasing to Ruth Rumsey." He lowered his voice confidentially. "She and my brother had just become engaged, though it was still secret at the time."

Ruth Rumsey was the daughter of one of Buffalo's oldest and most prominent families. She had great charm and presence, a gift of humor combined with quiet grace, and the independence that often accompanies a well-to-do background. She was fond of riding and fox-hunting, activities in which young ladies of that prim period were just beginning to engage, and Donovan shared her love of sports. He had never taken a romance seriously before; but now he was thirty-one, moving ahead fast in his profession, and in a position to propose marriage. Their engagement was not made public for several months.

They arranged to be married in Ruth Rumsey's home (the Rumseys were Protestant) by the Donovan family pastor, Monsignor Biden, and the date was set for July 15, 1914. And then in June, a month before the wedding, Anna Donovan died suddenly. She had not been well for the past few years, and her son Timothy, by now a successful doctor, realized that her heart was weakened by rheumatic fever, and cautioned the family that a fatal attack might occur at any moment. Her last request, when she knew she was dying, was that Bill's wedding should not be postponed, and that Vincent, who had recently entered a Dominican seminary at Somerset, Ohio, should not interrupt his novitiate to come home.

Timothy Senior lingered only a year after his wife's death. The big house was empty without Anna and the children, and he seemed to waste away. He had never known a day's sickness before, but now he had no will to go on living. A week before the end, Bill visited his father's sickroom to announce that Ruth had just given birth to a boy, named David. Timothy turned his head on the pillow, and looked his son in the eye. "I hope you'll be as proud of him," he whispered, "as I've always been of you."

4

The year 1914 marked the end of an era in Donovan's life, the changeover from civilian lawyer to citizen soldier. Tensions in Europe had been building steadily during spring and early summer; the assassination at Sarajevo was the breaking point; he was still on his honeymoon in August when the fateful rumble of guns echoed across the Atlantic. Most Americans were confident that the war could not last more than six weeks, and a convenient ocean would keep their country free from involvement; but Donovan's intuition warned him that the United States would be drawn inevitably into the world struggle. He curtailed the vacation at the lakeshore which he and Ruth had planned, and returned to the city to devote all his spare time to National Guard duties, drilling the men of Troop I in rifle proficiency and conducting joint maneuvers with other arms of the service. So effective was the troop's training that during World War I ninety percent of its members became commissioned officers.

Although the United States was maintaining an uneasy neutrality, its sympathy went out to the helpless noncombatants of Europe, caught in the crossfire of war. Belgium had been invaded by the German armies on their march toward France, and the American public was roused to indignation by propaganda stories of atrocities and the inflammatory cartoons of the Dutch artist Raemaekers — a foretaste of OSS Morale Operations in World War II — which depicted Belgian virgins being ravished and babies spitted on the bayonets of grinning Huns. As the fighting lines moved eastward, so did the devastation. Neutral Poland had become the battleground of opposing Russian and German forces, and whole villages were laid waste, factories destroyed, and farm animals and food crops requisitioned by the occupying powers. Famine threatened the destitute populace, and by 1915 it was estimated that "hundreds of thousands of men and women and children had perished."[2]

In order to aid these innocent victims of hostilities, the Rockefeller

2 *The Rockefeller Foundation Annual Report* (New York, 1915).

Foundation had created an American War Relief Commission to arrange with the belligerents for the distribution of food and clothing, and the trustees had appropriated a million dollars for use in Poland and the Balkans. Marwick Greene, head of public works in the Philippines, was appointed director, and Donovan, because of his fast-growing reputation as a shrewd and able lawyer, was made a member of the Polish Commission. He arranged for his wife and year-old son to stay with Mrs. Rumsey during his absence, and in March, 1916, he and Greene sailed to Europe to conduct exploratory negotiations with the British and German governments. In London they worked in cooperation with Herbert C. Hoover, chairman of the Committee for Relief in Belgium, and Donovan formed a friendly relationship with the future President which was to terminate abruptly and bitterly after Hoover's election. Although the Relief Committee could not reconcile the conflicting stipulations of Great Britain and Germany, they secured emergency permission to ship several hundred tons of condensed milk from Switzerland to the Polish children; forty-five tons of cocoa were purchased in Berlin; and secondhand clothing was obtained from the American Relief Clearing House in Paris for the refugees who were walking the streets of Warsaw and Lodz barefoot and in rags.

It was Donovan's first overseas mission, his first opportunity to observe at close hand the power struggles and intrigues of Europe, which he had previously read about only in books. As he traveled through France and Germany and Poland, he grew more convinced than ever that the United States could not remain neutral much longer; and he made it his private business to talk with military leaders of both sides, and make mental notes of the latest German armaments and modern techniques of open and trench warfare. He filed the information in his mind for future use.

He was back in London in June of 1916, when he learned that Buffalo's Troop I had been ordered to the Mexican border on patrol duty. Raids by Pancho Villa had destroyed American lives and property, and U.S. State Department protests had been ignored. General John J. Pershing was sent to Texas with orders to capture the elusive bandit leader, prompting Will Rogers, that wry commentator on his

times, to remark satirically: "I see where Pershing's got Villa hemmed in
between the Atlantic and Pacific oceans. Now all we got to do is stop up
both ends." When the Carranza government issued an ultimatum that any
invasion of Mexican soil in pursuit of Villa's band would be considered an
act of war, 150,000 more troops were ordered to the border, and the National
Guard was called up for service in the emergency. Donovan rejoined
his troop at McAllen, Texas, in July.

That part of Texas is flat and barren, a sweltering desert in midsummer. There were no trees to shade the canvas tents that lined
"Buffalo Street," Troop I's nostalgic name for its bivouac area, and at
night the men lay on their blankets in puddles of sweat. The bands of
their stiff broad-brimmed campaign hats chafed their sunburned fore-
heads, and their tightly wound puttees did not allow air to circulate
when they marched. There was no military action to relieve the
monotony, but Captain Donovan filled their time with target practice
and drills. The ruthless combat he had witnessed in Europe was fresh in
his mind, and he lived up to his newly acquired nickname by driving his
men relentlessly on long hikes, sometimes better than twenty-five miles.
He was determined that they would be ready when America entered the
war.

New York's 69th Regiment was stationed near Troop I, and Father
Francis P. Duffy, its chaplain, had heard of Captain "Wild Bill" Donovan who, in Duffy's words, "was the best-known man of his rank in the
New York Division." His curiosity led him to visit the troop headquarters, and meet this notorious wild man who commanded it. "I like
him for his agreeable disposition, his fine character, his alert and eager
intelligence," Father Duffy wrote in his diary. "But I certainly would not
want to be in his Battalion."[3]

They were instantly drawn to one another. Perhaps it was due to
Donovan's early affinity for the priesthood; perhaps, as his brother
Vincent suggested, it was because they shared the same feelings about
courage. "He admired the General," Father Donovan recalled, "and respected him because he was fearless. When war came the following year,

[3] Francis P. Duffy, *Father Duffy's Story* (New York, 1919).

and my brother was assigned as Brigade Adjutant of the 51st Brigade, a desk job instead of the command of troops he craved, Father Duffy went personally to Washington to request Donovan's transfer as Colonel of the Fighting 69th. 'I knew Bill would never be content to sit out the war on a swivel chair,' he explained to me later, 'though I only succeeded in having him made Major of the First Battalion. But he *will* be Colonel.' And Father Duffy added: 'When he comes back, if he comes back, he can have anything he wants.' "

I repeated in surprise: "If he comes back?"

"My brother never expected to come back," Father Donovan assured me, "or Father Duffy, either, for that matter. It was his firm conviction that he'd be killed, you see. When he left for overseas, I asked him 'Are you ready to go?' and he replied 'Yes, I've been to the Sacraments.' It was always in the background, this matter of death." Father Donovan observed thoughtfully: "Maybe that is why he was fearless."

II

As late as the spring of 1917, President Woodrow Wilson still remained neutral. Even when German U-boat 20 sank the *Lusitania* on May 7, 1915, with an appalling loss of American lives, Wilson had reminded his angry countrymen that "there is such a thing as a man being too proud to fight." For a year he exchanged a series of diplomatic notes with the German government, until Will Rogers told a Baltimore audience which included Wilson himself that "the President is getting along fine now to what he was a few months ago. Do you realize, People, that at one time in our negotiations with Germany he was five Notes behind?"

Determined to live up to his campaign boast that "he kept us out of war," Wilson protested Germany's submarine attacks on American shipping, but maintained the delicate balance of impartiality by complaining to Great Britain that her extension of the blockade infringed on America's rights at sea. Germany assumed that the President's apparent irresolution meant the United States would not retaliate, and on January 31, 1917, the German government announced that henceforth "all sea traffic will be stopped with every available weapon and without further notice" and Germany would "forcibly prevent" any vessel of the United States from sailing to England. Regretfully Wilson made the gesture of severing diplomatic relations, but nevertheless stayed short of an outright declaration of war.

Germany's unrestricted submarine campaign was tightening its grip on England. Though the facts were not made known to the public, the rate of U-boat sinkings was almost three times the rate at which new ships could be built. Submarines destroyed 6,600,000 tons in a year; all the efforts of Allied and neutral shipyards combined produced but 2,700,000 tons. American Ambassador Walter H. Page reported from London that the total food supply in the British Isles would not feed the civil population for another six weeks.[4] Slowly, inexorably Germany was winning the war; and Britain sought desperately for some enemy provocation which might bring the United States into the conflict on her side.

On February 24, 1917, she found the answer. British Naval Intelligence, alerted by agents, intercepted and decoded a message from the German Ministry of Foreign Affairs to the German minister in Mexico, suggesting that if the Mexican government would ally itself with the Central Powers, Germany in turn would assist Mexico to "reconquer her lost territory in Texas, New Mexico and Arizona." Britain promptly released the text of the message to Ambassador Page, headlines trumpeted the German threat to an outraged American public, and Wilson, who had been too proud to fight, was not too politically insensitive to recognize the way the wind was blowing. On April 2, he appeared before a joint session of Congress to call for "a war without hate. . . . The world must be made safe for democracy." British Naval Intelligence had achieved one of the most effective intercepts in history; and the value of cryptography and intelligence in modern warfare was not lost on Donovan.

Now America rose in all her naïve ebullience to the new adventure. War was as exciting as a Fourth of July parade, and no one thought of himself as any more involved than a flag-waving spectator. In a burst of patriotic ardor, the word sauerkraut was changed to Liberty Cabbage, dachshunds were renamed Liberty Pups, and German measles became Liberty Measles. Housewives helped make the world safe for democracy by firing their German cooks, and any hyphenated American with a concrete floor in his garage was suspected of hiding a potential gun emplacement. Lüchow's Restaurant in New York, in an agony of

[4] William C. McAdoo, *Crowded Years* (Boston, 1931).

public expiation, had its *umlaut* cut off. The mayor of East Orange, N.J., did his bit by refusing to issue a permit for Fritz Kreisler to give a concert. Everyone rolled bandages and planted Victory gardens and collected tinfoil as they hummed the gay war songs that were sweeping the country: "K-K-K-Katy" and "Good Morning, Mr. Zip, Zip, Zip!" and "Oh, How I Hate to Get Up in the Morning," written by an army sergeant at Camp Upton, young Irving Berlin.

But war means men, and gradually the sober truth dawned that this was for real, that American boys would be called on to fight and die. The total strength of the Regular Army of the United States in 1914 was only eighty thousand officers and men; the President had displayed a truculent aversion to military preparedness, but in 1915, with a canny eye to the coming election, he had yielded sufficiently for the Army to increase its quota to 141,000; now suddenly the nation needed half a million. Wilson personally disliked the idea of conscription, preferring the spirit of a free and motivated army, and Congress was equally reluctant to consider a Draft Act. In a coast to coast drive for volunteers, George Creel, propaganda wizard of the Committee for Public Information, mobilized artists and actors and singers to stimulate enlistment. Elsie Janis blew kisses to every youth who signed up. James Montgomery Flagg created his famous poster showing Uncle Sam pointing a forefinger directly at the viewer with the slogan "I Want YOU for the U.S. Army." A mobile corps of recruiters called Four Minute Men toured the country in an exhortatory marathon, and popular military figures were asked to give pep talks to any available audience. Captain "Wild Bill" Donovan, who was not above a patriotic cliché now and then, told an audience in Buffalo's Convention Hall that "the test of citizenship is our willingness to affix our signatures to an oath of enlistment and delivering that oath to a recruiting officer. Our flag has meant a country of peace and comfort and happiness, but now it stands as the symbol of service and of sacrifice."

Donovan, because of his Mexican border reputation and his recent observations in Europe, had been offered a colonelcy as chief of staff of the 27th Division; but he turned down the advancement in rank to become a battalion major in New York's 69th. The Fighting Irish, as the

regiment had called itself since Civil War days, was engaged in a recruiting campaign of its own to meet the expanded number of 2,002
fixed for an infantry regiment, and appealed for men of Celtic blood
who would be worthy successors to those early members who had
fought at Bloody Ford and Marye's Heights. The 69th was justly proud
of its long tradition. The regimental flag flew eleven streamers, to mark
the eleven major engagements in which it had participated, including
Bull Run and Antietam, and its staff was ringed with fifty silver furls to
commemorate its battles. The war with Germany was to add nine more.

The regiment soon filled its quota with the men it wanted, due to its
peculiar set of standards. Any applicant who might not be worthy of
the Fighting Irish was quickly found to have some physical handicap
and screened out; but "if some honest man with broad shoulders and a
knockout in each fist was unable to read ACXUROKY on a card thirty feet
away — why, the examining physicians were instructed not to be overly
meticulous in their work." Catholic clergy brought in candidates from
their parish athletic clubs. Irish county societies sent more. Machine gun
trucks roamed the Irish sections of Manhattan and Brooklyn and the
Bronx displaying the bold placard: "Don't join the 69th unless you want
to be the first to go to France," a challenge bound to appeal to any son
of Erin. "A number of our Irish recruits bore distinctly German,
French, Italian or Polish names," Father Duffy admitted in his diary,
"but they were Irish by adoption, Irish by association, or Irish by conviction. The 69th never attempted to set up any religious test. It was an
institution offered to the Nation by a people grateful for liberty."[5]

In August of 1917, the 69th received the electrifying news that it had
been selected from all the National Guard Regiments of New York to
represent its state in the newly formed 42nd Rainbow Division — "to
put the green in the rainbow," Father Duffy claimed — which would be
among the earliest units of the American Expeditionary Force to see
active service overseas. Though the regiment was drafted into the Regular Army and redesignated the 165th Infantry, it continued to call itself
the Old 69th throughout the war. On the 20th of August the Fighting

[5] Francis P. Duffy, *Father Duffy's Story* (New York, 1919).

Irish paraded through New York past throngs of cheering onlookers, just as they had done the previous March on their return from Mexico; but this time "the crowd was not rejoicing over a long-awaited reunion, and faces that had been happy were fearful now and the gestures were of farewell," Sergeant Joyce Kilmer wrote in his unfinished history of the regiment. "As we marched from the armory to the dock, an elderly woman burst through the crowd and, crying and laughing at the same time, thrust into the hands of a bandsman a green flag marked in gold with the Irish harp and the motto 'Erin Go Bragh!' That flag was to go 'over the top' at Rouge Bouquet, and in every engagement thereafter. Who the woman was who gave the regiment this appropriate tribute is unknown. Perhaps it was Kathleen ni Houlihan herself." With regimental colors and green flag flying, the men boarded the ferry to cross the East River and entrain for the still uncompleted Camp Albert L. Mills near Mineola, New York — the first step toward the fighting front.

Major Donovan rented a small house near Camp Mills, and his wife Ruth came down from Buffalo to join him, bringing David and their new baby daughter, born only a few weeks before the 69th left for France. Since Father Duffy had dedicated the regiment to St. Patrick and St. Michael, good fighters both, they decided to name their new daughter Patricia. Father Duffy baptized her with holy water from an army canteen, and made her the Daughter of the Regiment.

Secret orders to sail were received at regimental headquarters on the night of October 25, and Major Donovan led his 1st Battalion in silence through the dark camp and down the road to the train that would take them to Montreal. They sailed on the *Tunisian* at eight on the morning of October 27. "There was no khaki on her decks; the only figures to be seen were sailors and deckhands," Joyce Kilmer wrote, "but as soon as the vessel was out of range of spying Teutonic eyes, soldiers poured out of every hatchway and looked their last for a long time at the fast receding shore." Peaceful as the blue water appeared, the men could not forget that this was a danger zone, and they scanned the ocean apprehensively for any sign of an approaching periscope. One of the ship's officers found a soldier from Brooklyn leaning over the rail, his eyes fixed on the horizon. "What are you looking for?" the officer asked. "Something I don't want to find," he replied.

There was general relief when they docked at Liverpool, and entrained for Southampton, and during the night of November 11 crossed the English Channel safely to Le Havre. There they were packed into open boxcars — Hommes 40, Chevaux 8 — with hardtack and canned "Corn Willie" to feed them, and their own blankets the sole protection from the hard floors and icy blasts that swept the doorless cars during the interminable journey across France to the Meuse valley.

Donovan's 1st Battalion was billeted at Naives en Blois, promptly Anglicized as Blooey, an impoverished village of some forty farmhouses staggered along a rutted street. "The dung heap occupies a place of pride outside each front door," Father Duffy's diary noted, "and the loftier it stands and the louder it raises its penetrating voice, the more it proclaims the worth and greatness of its possessor. . . . There are a couple of wine shops in town, but the pious owners see that their wine is well baptized before selling it. So most of the men spread their blankets in the straw and go to bed at six o'clock," sleeping in their clothes to keep them from freezing, and waking half covered with snow that had sifted through the broken roof.

Even the miseries of Blooey were forgotten when the regiment sat out, the morning after Christmas, on a four-day hike to their training area at Longeau. The mules had not been shod for winter weather, many of them were unbroken to harness, and food supplies lagged far behind. Wearing full packs, the men climbed the steep snow-covered roads that led through the foothills of the Vosges Mountains, frequently in a blinding blizzard. At the end of each day's march, they billeted in empty cattle sheds, without fuel or food, huddling together for body warmth. Sometimes the wagon trains caught up with them at midnight, but the meat and vegetables were frozen solid and could not be thawed in time. In the blackness before dawn, the men crushed their swollen and bleeding feet into broken-soled hobnailed boots, and started out again without breakfast. By the second or third day, many had exchanged their wornout footgear for wooden sabots, or wrapped their feet in burlap "like Washington's army at Valley Forge," Kilmer observed. Hands were so frostbitten that the rifles slid from their fingers. Men pitched headlong in the snow, struggled to their feet, fell again. The strong helped the weak by encouragement, by sharp biting words when sympathy failed, or by the practical method of sharing their burdens. Major Donovan followed at the rear of the column to pick up stragglers who lay helpless beside the road. "I think I'm going to die," an eighteen-year-old moaned. "You can't die without my permission," Donovan replied, "and I don't intend to give it. I'll take your pack, but you've got to hike."

They got through on spirit. "There were bloody tracks in the snow where the Regiment had passed," Kilmer wrote, "and they seemed to have aged twenty years, but their hearts were unchanged. When they halted at Longeau on December 29, knee-deep in snow, the ice-crusted packs still on their bruised shoulders, they had a laughing word for every pretty face at a window. The bandsmen started a defiant air, and the Regiment joined in with a roar. The song was 'In the Good Old Summertime.'"

Here their real precombat training began. Members of the 32nd Battalion of Chasseurs, the famed French troops who had been in action since 1914, instructed them in open and trench warfare. Steel helmets replaced their felt campaign hats. They were indoctrinated in the use of hand grenades, called "potato mashers," and each man was issued two gas masks, one French type and one English box respirator. Through ceaseless drills in rapid adjustment of the masks, they acquired a proficiency which would save many lives in the Lunéville sector a couple of months later. Major Donovan kept up his intensive conditioning program, and since he knew the value of boxing, all the men were ordered to put on the gloves and spar with one another. The jab and uppercut, the footwork and body thrust that boxing taught, he perceived, were the basic moves required for handling a bayonet — a training method used by the Marine Corps today. There were a few swollen lips and flattened noses; but the 69th was prepared for its first taste of trench warfare when it moved up to Lunéville in middle February to join the French troops in the front lines.

Lunéville was known as a "quiet sector," meaning that the French and

German trenches were separated from each other by as much as five kilometers, and there was no immediate objective for which either side was striving. Generally the task of holding a static front was given to troops fresh from the drill field and lacking experience in actual combat. As New York's Fighting Irish marched up a gentle hill through groves of birch and pine, and saw rustic summer houses and picnic tables and benches and an occasional French dugout entrance decorated with whitewashed stones and flowerbeds, the outpost seemed too reminiscent of a vacation resort to satisfy the battle-hungry soldiers. Where were the bursting shells, the liquid fire, the bayonets of the charging Boche? Going "over the top" was as peaceful as a Sunday stroll. Major Donovan wrote his wife: "At daybreak this morning a patrol returned, bringing only a bouquet of tulips and forget-me-nots gathered in No Man's Land. Incredible, isn't it?"

Donovan had established his battalion post of command in hollowed-out ground under a road culvert near Rouge Bouquet. The P.C. was the center of a vast web of duckboards leading to the sinuous line of trenches, some of them four years old and badly in need of shoring up and repairing. Off duty the men lived in abandoned French dugouts, the dirt roofs supported by sagging timbers and the clammy mud floors covered with a few scattered planks. In the absence of any action, the Major made sure that his men remained in proper condition by leading them on cross-country runs over brooks and barbed wire.

The stalemate did not last long. Perhaps the Germans knew that the Irish in the opposite trenches were spoiling for a fight; the men had barely established their position when enemy rifles started cracking, building to a bombardment of the battalion's position with heavy minenwerfers, the awkward wobbling torpedoes which the troops nick-named "G.I. cans" because they resembled in size and shape a galvanized iron barrel. It was the 69th's initiation into battle.

One shell landed squarely on the sod-covered roof of a large dugout and exploded, collapsing the rotted support beams and burying a lieu-tenant and twenty-four soldiers in tons of fallen rocks and clay. "There were living men down in that pit," Kilmer wrote. "Their voices could be heard, and they were struggling toward the light. Several times they were at the surface and willing hands were outstretched when well-aimed shells plunged them down again into that place of death."

When Major Donovan arrived, he found the rest of the men exposing themselves heedlessly to enemy fire in an effort to liberate their trapped comrades. In a letter to his wife, Donovan described the scene: "Some diggers were hysterical, making so much noise that I thought we would have the whole German artillery firing on us. I handed one of them a good punch in the jaw, and that quieted all of them. . . . I took off my gas mask and climbed in there myself where the earth was still crumbling, thought of you and the children and wished I had finished my letter to you, and then started working with a little entrenching tool to find a soldier who had been partly uncovered before the last bombardment. I made a hole leading to his face, but his breathing was that of a man about to die. To my left, deep down, was someone murmuring in delirium. Under me was a cold muddy dead hand sticking up out of the earth. . . . As I looked about, it was brought home to me that nothing could be done, that this was their tomb." Two injured and five dead had been removed, but hope was abandoned for the remaining fifteen, and Donovan considered it unwise, in view of the steady shelling, to risk more lives in searching for the bodies.

A tablet was erected over the collapsed dugout with the inscription "Here on the field of honor rest," followed by their names; and on St. Patrick's Day Father Duffy read aloud Sergeant Kilmer's commemorative poem "Rouge Bouquet,"[6] composed just after the tragedy, with its haunting lines:

> Go to sleep,
> Go to sleep,
> Slumber well where the shell screamed and fell.
> Let your rifles rest on the muddy floor,
> You will not need them any more.
> Danger's past;
> Now at last,
> Go to sleep!

[6] Joyce Kilmer, *Joyce Kilmer*, Vol. I (New York, 1918).

The gas attack came three days later. There had been another lull in the action, with only an occasional minenwerfer or 77 mm. coming over to remind the men there was a war on. Then without warning, at 5:30 on the evening of the 20th, the enemy began bombarding the entire sector with a barrage of mustard gas shells. The trenches and dugouts and first-aid station were soon saturated with the deadly fumes, which burned the eyes and bit into the flesh and contaminated all food and clothing and blankets within their poisonous range. Though the men put on their masks as soon as the presence of gas was detected, they found it impossible to wear them indefinitely and keep up the defense of the sector. One after another they began to go blind, so that by dawn a considerable number from the front lines had been led all the way back to the Lunéville road, their eyesight completely gone, and were waiting their turn at an ambulance. Often the men who led them became blind themselves, and were lifted into the ambulance with the others. One soldier in Company K, struck by a shell which carried away his left hand, was escorted under heavy fire to the first-aid station, where a medical corps lieutenant coolly removed his own mask despite the mustard gas which filled the station and performed an emergency operation, for which he earned the Croix de Guerre.

By ten in the morning, fully two-thirds of Company K had lost their vision; but not a man panicked, not a man left the lines until he was stone blind. Many had to be carried on stretchers to the rear. There were four hundred casualties in the regiment during the nightmare forty-eight hours, including all of K Company and most of M, but those who survived the gas in their lungs and the cruel burns on their bodies were restless to be out of the hospital, and pleaded with Donovan when he visited them to be allowed to go back into action.

The 69th pulled back from the lines to recuperate in a little village overlooking the broad valley of the Vosges. "Stretching for miles was the rich green meadowland and winding river," the Major wrote Ruth Donovan. "Dusty red ploughed fields were splashed on the upper rim, and at intervals — much as David might set his building blocks on a green carpet — were dotted many villages. You would be surprised to see how eagerly the men drank in the picture. Your soldier man is a sentimental person, and when he is happiest he is singing some lonesome melody of home or mother."

Early in July the regiment moved to the Bois de la Lyre — Harp Woods, the 69th dubbed it — for the coming Champagne-Marne defensive. The Châlons sector reminded the Mexican border veterans of southern Texas: the same expanse of flat plains, the lack of water, the patches of low twisted trees that resembled mesquite. Everywhere the chalky ground was covered with wild flowers, marguerites and bluets, clumps of violets, and poppies in profusion: an exotic battlefield. Three battalions, temporarily under French command, were sent forward to occupy the front trenches, and at their rear the French placed 75's in position for direct fire on German tanks as they broke through the American positions, and machine guns to rake the invaders with open fields of fire across the sloping plain. It was the opinion of the French General Staff that the inexperienced Americans in the front lines could not hold, once the enemy offensive got rolling, and the Germans would continue in their mass assault into the waiting French trap.

While his men braced themselves for their first major engagement, Major Donovan pored over maps and visited every square foot of his battalion's position, studying the terrain in preparation for the German advance which was expected momentarily. A letter to Ruth Donovan, written just before the attack, admitted frankly: "I don't expect to come back, and I believe that if I am killed it will be a most wonderful heritage to my family."

2

"It was 12:04 midnight by my watch when it began," Father Duffy entered in his diary on June 15, 1918. "No crescendo business about it. Just one sudden crash like an avalanche; but an avalanche that was to keep crashing for five hours. The whole sky seemed to be torn apart with sound — the roaring B-o-o-omp of the discharge and the gradual menacing Whe-e-e-eez of traveling projectiles and the nerve wracking Wha-a-ang of bursts. I put my back against the door of the hut and peered up cautiously to see how high the protecting sandbags stood over my head, and then I took a good look around.

"I saw first the sky to the south and found that our guns were causing a comfortable share of the infernal racket. The whole southern sky was punctuated with quick bursts of light, at times looking as if the central fires had burst through in a ten-mile fissure. Then when my ear became adjusted to the new conditions I discovered that most of the Whe-e-e-eez's were traveling over and beyond, some to greet the invaders, some to fall on our own lines and as far back as Châlons."

At 4:30 A.M. the firing died down, after one last furious burst over the American positions, and the men crawled out of their burrows, eager for the first actual sight of the enemy. French veterans warned them not to fire too soon, since in the half-light it was difficult for an unaccustomed eye to distinguish between the Poilu's faded blue and the German's field gray. A tense hour passed before someone shouted "Boche, Boche!" and pointed to steel-helmeted heads appearing around the corners of the approach trenches. The Germans, finding that the 69th was the real line of resistance, went about the job of wiping it out in their usual thorough fashion. The light machine guns sprayed the top of every trench, and minenwerfer shells dropped with deadly accuracy on the regiment's own gun emplacements.

For three days the battle surged back and forth, with heavy losses on both sides. "Our men rose to it with the same zest they had shown when they fought their boyish neighborhood fights, street against street, in Tompkins Park or Stuyvesant Square," Father Duffy recorded with pride. The Champagne-Marne defensive ended in an almost total rout of the enemy. The French command reported that the Germans had been forced to pull back in every part of the long front, with the exception of the salient around Château-Thierry.

Donovan's letter home after the battle expressed his pride in his men and in his country. "America is now magnificent — beyond anything I expected. Her ideals clearer, her purpose higher than all the others. Another thing. Have you considered that before long America will be the strongest nation, with her fleet, her industries, her army, all organized? I wonder if, as these increase, envious eyes may be cast upon her. I hope the war won't end that way."

They had come through their first test of fire, but bigger battles lay ahead. After a week's rest, the regiment moved by French *camions* to

Epieds, to take part in the mounting Aisne-Marne offensive. Once again they were greeted with a fierce bombardment. German shells and aerial bombs began dropping on the château where they billeted the night they arrived, and Major Donovan and his adjutant, Second Lieutenant Oliver Ames, Jr., crawled under the bare boards of an ambulance and managed to get a couple of hours' sleep. Next morning Donovan and his four company commanders made a reconnaisance of their position. "In the afternoon," a letter to his wife mentioned casually, "we ran into a terrific fight, very hot and bloody. Two of my commanders were wounded, and a shell mixed with high explosives and gas hit the roof over my head. A rain of rocks and dirt and tiles fell about me, and I got a beautiful mouthful of gas. Back at the château a doctor gave me some sniffs of ammonia and fixed up my eyes with boracic acid and laid me down on a billiard table to rest."

Donovan's indifference to his own safety was a constant source of worry to his young adjutant, whose devotion to the Major amounted almost to idolatry. Ames was a serious and strikingly handsome youngster just turned twenty, whose Harvard football letter and gold lieutenant's bars marked the two proudest achievements of his life. When Donovan made him his adjutant, Ames wrote his mother that "it is the greatest honor I've ever had; it couldn't be so great with any other major but Bill Donovan, for *he* is the 'livest' officer in the American Ex. Forces. For the last two months general headquarters have been trying to get him on the staff, but he has his heart set on having the best battalion in the U.S. Army. . . . Perhaps you're wondering from this eulogy whether I'm returning to my schoolboy hero-worship days, but, Ma, though he expects you to work your head off for him, he is just as thoughtful as can be if you 'deliver the goods,' so to speak. Somebody told me that if he ever got back alive from this war he would be sure to be governor of New York."[7]

It was expected that the retreating German forces would make some sort of rear-guard stand on the slopes and in the forest north of the Ourcq River, a meadow stream which ran through the bottom of a wide fertile valley. On the hilltop a thousand yards north of the Ourcq was the

---

[7] DeWolfe Howe, *Oliver Ames, Jr.* (Boston: privately printed, 1922).

Muercy Farm — "O'Rourke's River" and "Murphy Farm," the Irish called them — consisting of a house and outbuildings with connecting stone walls which formed a large interior courtyard: a natural fortress. The whole valley was in the shape of a trough, both sides of which could easily be defended by German machine guns with direct fire, as well as by flanking fire from the opposite slope and the Muercy Farm. When the attackers reached the crest of the hill, moreover, they would have to cross five hundred yards of level meadow to reach the heavily entrenched forest. With plenty of artillery to cover their advance, the task might not have been so formidable; but on the afternoon of July 27 a message was received from Colonel Douglas MacArthur, Chief of Staff of the 42nd Division, 1st Army Corps, containing General Order 51:

"Pursuant to orders from the Sixth (French) Army, the Division will attack at H. hour under cover of darkness." The four infantry regiments were to advance abreast, the order stated, a battalion of each being in line, in pursuit of the retreating enemy. "The attack will be in the nature of a surprise, and consequently troops will not fire during the assault, but will confine themselves to the use of the bayonet."

Since patrols from Company K had felt out enemy resistance the previous night and found well-established machine gun nests just across the river, the battalion commanders felt that the corps's assumption of a fleeing and disorganized German army was not justified, and that the situation called for artillery cover and cautious advance; but the 69th's motto was: "Never disobeyed an order, never lost a flag." Against his better judgment, Donovan moved his battalion forward without protective fire, crossed the Ourcq, and swept up the hill. Somehow they made their crossing with only five casualties, and by nightfall had fought their way to the heights near the Muercy Farm. The following morning, Major Donovan and his young adjutant were crouching half-concealed in a meadow creek when a sniper's bullet from the farmyard sped past Donovan and struck Ames in the head, killing him instantly. A small square on Commonwealth Avenue in Boston bears his name today.

In a letter of condolence to Oliver Ames's widow, whom Oliver had married a week before sailing to France, Donovan wrote: "I have no desire to intrude upon your grief. I have refrained until you should be in receipt of your husband's citation for the Distinguished Service

Cross. It was the one thing I could do to very inadequately obtain some recognition of his magnificent work. Now I must hasten to get you word, because one cannot tell when one's own time is coming. . . . More than my feeling of respect and admiration for his qualities as a soldier and gentleman, there was between us an even deeper relation. To me he was like a younger brother. I should like if I could to send you some description of his last days, so that you can visualize the real nobility of his leaving us.

"On the morning of the 28th, we advanced our whole battalion across the Ourcq. I left Oliver in command of the Headquarters Detachment, which marched in the lead of our support. I was ahead waiting at the river. I can see him now, charging down the slope in front of his group, like a young football captain bringing his team onto the field. . . . We held the hill all that day and night, although we had no support on either of our flanks, and Oliver and I managed to get one hour's refreshing sleep in a hole that he dug out. Oliver, by the way, had no overcoat, but had, as always, the sweater that you knitted for him.

"Early again next morning the signal was given to advance. The elements on our right and left failed to move, so we pushed on alone, driving the Germans back slowly. I shall always be glad for one thing I did. Our front lines were held up briefly, and I called to Oliver, who was a little behind me, and had him lie down behind a mound of earth. I then told him what fine work he had been doing and that he had saved many lives for the battalion, and I would never forget him. . . . I heard that an officer in charge of the first group had been wounded, and I told your husband to take care of Headquarters Detachment, that I was going forward.

"As I started through machine gun fire, I heard a running behind me and turned, and saw Oliver coming. I told him to go back. He said 'No,' that he was going to take care of me. I lay down by a little creek and he came over beside me. A sniper, undoubtedly trying for me, hit him in the right ear. He died at once, painlessly. I would gladly that I had been the one and he had been spared to you."[8]

[8] DeWolfe Howe, *Oliver Ames, Jr.*

Joyce Kilmer was killed, under almost identical circumstances, one day later. His position as sergeant of the Intelligence Section would naturally have entitled him to a safe place at regimental headquarters; but he preferred to be with a battalion in the field, and volunteered to take Ames's place as Donovan's adjutant.

During the afternoon of the 29th, the battalion advanced some three kilometers without any support on either flank, with no artillery preparation, with no auxiliary arms. They did it with rifles and bayonets, creeping forward on their stomachs, taking advantage of every protective hummock. Some German soldiers were found dressed in French uniforms, in hope that the men would hold their fire. Others were wearing Red Cross bands on their arms while they worked machine guns against the attackers, and then crying "Kamerad" when the Americans rushed them. Thereafter in the battle few prisoners were taken alive.

Muercy Farm was still occupied by the enemy, but the battalion gained control of a narrow strip of woods facing the forest, which bristled with gun emplacements, and dug in for the night. Early on the 30th, Major Donovan worked his way forward through the strip of woods to look over the position. "Kilmer followed, unbidden," Father Duffy wrote. "He lay at the north end of the woods, looking out toward the enemy. The Major went ahead, but Kilmer did not follow. Donovan returned and found him dead. A bullet had pierced his brain. God rest his dear and gallant soul."

Kilmer was buried beside Oliver Ames, near the little creekbed on the Muercy Farm. On a wooden cross over Ames's grave, a corporal of the 69th had inscribed in painstaking letters: "A courteous kindly gentleman and a true soldier." As Father Duffy read the services of the dead for Kilmer, a bugle sounded "Taps," and the echo bore back the unspoken words "Danger's past; now at last, go to sleep."

At four A.M., August 2nd, the patrols reported no more resistance. The 4th Division was coming up, orders for relief were issued to the 69th, and the decimated battalions marched back past Muercy Farm amid the bodies of their unburied dead. In eight days of battle, the Rainbow Division had met the famed 4th Prussian Guards, commanded by the Kaiser's son Prince Eitel Friedrich, the pride of the German military machine, and had driven them back to the last ridge south of the Vesle, at a cost in Americans killed and wounded of 184 officers and 5,459 men.

Major Donovan wrote Ruth: "In every day of that fight, our Battalion had participated. It had never retired, it had gone the farthest and stayed the longest. . . . I hope that my name on the casualty list did not worry you. My wounds amounted to nothing. The one on the hand simply made a little bone bruise, for as luck would have it my hand was going away when the bullet struck. By the way, I had been previously hit on the chest with a piece of shell which ripped my gas mask, and another fragment had hit me on the left heel, tearing my shoe and throwing me off balance. I think perhaps there is a little shrapnel in my leg, but I hope to have some pretty Red Cross nurse hold my hand while they take it out. I guess I have been born to be hanged."

He added in a postscript: "The Division and Regimental Commanders have been good enough to recommend me for a cross in terms which are too exaggerated. One thing only I am glad of, and that is that the system which I used in the training of the men justified itself. Their discipline and above all their spirit held them full of fight in a position which had previously been given up by two other outfits. Physical endurance will give one control of one's nerves long after the breaking point. Courage is the smallest part of it. These men who all along thought me too strict, and felt I had made them work when others did not work, are now convinced that I was right, and that I would ask them to do nothing that I myself would not do. This tribute is greater than any honor my superior officers can give me."

Most of the battalion had long ceased to gripe about the rugged conditioning on which Major Donovan insisted, but Father Duffy happened to overhear the conversion of one last dissenter. His companions were hammering him with arguments to prove that "Wild Bill" was the greatest man in the world, and at last he admitted grudgingly: "Well, I'll say this: he's a wild son of a bitch, but he's a game one." When Father Duffy repeated the remark, Donovan laughed and said: "Father, when I'm gone, write that as my epitaph."

3

On September 7, in a field ceremony shortly before the St.-Mihiel offensive, Donovan and some of his officers and men were presented with Distinguished Service Crosses by General Pershing. "Pershing has been here and given us the crosses," was his casual comment to Ruth. He had been promoted recently to lieutenant colonel, and had narrowly escaped being called back to headquarters for staff duty. Donovan was still in command of the 1st Battalion when orders were received for the attack on the St.-Mihiel salient.

Dawn broke on a cool windy day and cloud-darkened sky. Donovan had been moving up and down his line since daybreak with a happy smile, assuring the men: "It will be a regular walkover. It won't be as bad as some of those cross-country runs I gave you." At the zero hour, four-inch Stokes mortars began laying down a smoke barrage and pounding the enemy positions, and the battalion started forward. Some of the support companies hesitated at the first belt of barbed wire, picking their way through it cautiously, and Donovan ran back from the front lines shouting: "Get moving, what do you think this is, a wake?" As enemy resistance cracked, he led his men in breakneck pursuit over the hills, hot on the heels of the fleeing Germans, reaching St.-Benoît in time to put out several fires which they had set as they left. "One group discovered the church ablaze," Donovan wrote, "and ran in to save what they could. They carried out pictures of St. Anthony of Padua and of the Holy Virgin, as well as some sacred vessels. A scout found a bag of potatoes which the Germans had left behind, so while the men worked in relays putting out the fire, those off duty roasted their potatoes in the embers."

At Marzerais there was stronger opposition, and one platoon found itself separated from the village by the swollen Rupt de Mad Creek. "They had no officer with them, so I assumed the functions of a platoon leader," Donovan continued. "I knew the character of the enemy — eager to surrender under a little pressure. So, I made the men swim the river, myself with them, and we swept up to the town. We captured there a lieutenant and forty men, one minenwerfer, and four machine guns. Prisoners began to come back to us in droves. We had to press forward so fast that we could not keep track of them, but gave them a kick in the backside and sent them on their way."

Lieutenant Colonel Donovan was convinced that the Germans had already decided to evacuate the St.-Mihiel salient before the battle began. "The enemy proposed pulling out," a subsequent letter to his wife said. "Our service knew it and saw a great opportunity to strike and hasten the withdrawal. On the 12th, captured German officers inform us, all their artillery was on the move, when our fire came down and created confusion. Luck was with us, and their withdrawal was hastened, but while the moral effect is great we must not pride ourselves too much on our tactical success. It was not a fight — it was a nice promenade. The German all along is shortening his line in order to stiffen his defense."

Donovan had learned that Germany was offering peace proposals, and his letter warned against an early armistice. "It is important that Wilson should at once send an answer telling them that we are not so easily beguiled. Frankly I am afraid of these peace overtures. I am afraid of their effect on public opinion, afraid of their effect on the fighting men. It is a most insidious weapon. It slips under your armor. Men want peace and they are eager to get home. If the chance of peace seems near they are less eager to fight, they stall, they hold off in the hope that peace will be declared. The German is tired, like the football player whose 'cork is pulled,' and he is calling 'Time out.' And then when negotiations are declared off, he will be in a better position to fight us. We are licking him. Let us lick him right. He is squealing, but as yet he is not really down."

The Germans were not the only enemy that Donovan had to fight. He had managed to dodge orders to send him to Staff College, orders to go on special duties, invitations to receive promotion by transfer. Major General Menoher, in command of the 42nd, and Colonel Douglas MacArthur had tried their best to keep him with the regiment. Now the Provost Marshal General wanted an assistant who was at once a good lawyer and a keen soldier, with a proficiency in French, and demanded

WJD (far right) about to receive Distinguished Service Cross from General Pershing, September 7, 1918.

"My boys regard you as about the finest example of the American fighting gentleman." (Theodore Roosevelt died on June 6, 1919, only seven months after he wrote this letter.)

THE KANSAS CITY STAR

OFFICE OF
THEODORE ROOSEVELT

NEW YORK OFFICE
347 MADISON AVENUE

October 25, 1918.

My dear Colonel Donovan:

It did me good to get your letter of the 7th of September. My own activities here are of no earthly consequence, for all that counts is what is done by you men at the front; but it is hardly necessary for me to say to you that I have been doing everything in my power to have our country insist that we finish this war by you men at the front and not by the men at the rear; that we use arms of precision and not typewriters; and that we beat Germany to her knees, declare war on Turkey, and fight the whole combination wherever the fighting can be done most effectively. Ted has just written me saying he would give anything if only he could be made a Lt. Colonel in a regiment under you as Colonel, and under Frank McCoy as Brigadier General. My boys regard you as about the finest example of the American fighting gentleman.

Faithfully yours,

Theodore Roosevelt

Lt. Col. Donovan,
Hqrs. 165th Infantry,
A. E. F. FRANCE.

that Donovan be sent to him. First Army Corps headquarters pointed out rather stiffly that the authorities of the 42nd Division had already succeeded in evading orders six times, and this seventh order was peremptory. The best that General Menoher could do was postpone Donovan's transfer until the next campaign was over.

It turned out to be the last campaign of the war. In the general Allied operation to turn the German retreat into a stampede, the most difficult and most important task was to gain possession of the Argonne District, and this was assigned to the American forces. If they could smash the resistance on the southeast end of the German lines, and break through to capture the military trunk line which ran through Sedan to the German depot at Metz, large bodies of enemy troops farther to the west would be brought to the point of surrender. The German commanders knew this as well as Marshal Foch and General Pershing, and they massed their strongest defenses at the point of danger.

Unlike St.-Mihiel, the Argonne offensive was no promenade. The nature of the country made it easy to defend, hard to capture. The heavily wooded hills were linked in an east-west direction, and the advance had to be made by conquering a series of heights. The 1st Division had captured the ridges on the east side of the Aire, at the cost of half the infantry in the division. It was the job of the 69th, coming up in relief, to break the main line of German defenses called the Kriemhilde Stellung.

This well-prepared and strongly fortified position consisted of three successive lines of barbed wire and trenches. The first rows of wire were breast-high and as much as twenty feet wide, all bound together in small squares by iron supports so that it was almost impossible for artillery to destroy the obstacles, and tanks were required to flatten them. Back of the wire were good trenches about four feet deep, with machine gun shelters carefully protected. Behind this front line at thirty-yard intervals were two other lines, with lower wire and shallower trenches, running east and west past the small villages of St.-Georges and Landres–St. Georges.

The 69th moved up to attack on October 11 with less than three thousand men, many of them inexperienced replacements. The past

WJD shortly after the German evacuation of St.-Mihiel. According to Mrs. Ruth Donovan, "this is the picture the General liked of himself above all others."

week's steady downpour had turned the battlefield into a quagmire. Soldiers sank knee-deep in the clinging mud, and had to pull out each foot with a sucking sound before taking the next step. Low clouds made observations of enemy movements by airplane or balloon impossible. Ammunition wagons foundered in the churned roads, putting the support artillery under a severe handicap. Food and medical supplies failed to get through. Telephone wires, strung along the wet ground, were constantly short-circuiting, and the front lines had to depend on runners who made slow time slogging back through a sea of mud to the post of command. Worst of all, the tanks they were counting on had bogged down somewhere to the rear, or skidded off the road to land upended in a rain-filled ditch.

The American strategy was dispersement. As a division approached the front line, it would separate into brigades and then into regiments. The regiments in turn would break into battalions, echeloned in depth with one on the line, one in support, and one in reserve. When they neared the enemy, these battalions broke into companies; and the companies, under shell fire, split up into platoons, with considerable distance between them. Advance was made by frequent rushes, about a fourth of the men in a platoon running forward while their comrades kept the enemy's heads down by constant fire. In its final stages, the fighting resembled the old Indian-style warfare of the Revolution, and was often a matter of individual initiative and courage. Sometimes a machine gun nest would be eliminated by a single sharpshooter firing from the elbow of a tree, or by one daring soldier who worked his way up a gully until he was near enough to throw hand grenades.

"Before dawn on the 14th we received orders that our attack would be made that morning," Donovan recorded later. "The brigade on our right was to advance first, and I moved to the forward position, which the Germans were shelling heavily, but I could see no advance. Then our hour struck, and promptly our leading battalion moved out. The enemy at once put down a solid barrage and swept the hill we had to climb with indirect machine gun fire. The advance did not go well. There were green company commanders; liaison was not maintained; the barrage was not followed closely; there was not enough punch, and I had to go out myself. There were times when I had to march at the head of companies to get them forward. They would follow me." Although officers were supposed to remove all signs of rank in battle, lest they became a target for sharpshooters, Donovan realized that the recent replacements might not recognize him. "I went out as if I were going to a parade, insignia, ribbons, Sam Brown belt with double shoulder straps. Foolish, you say, but necessary. New men need some visible sign of authority."

Orders came to stabilize for the night, and Donovan crawled into a small shell hole. "For mess," he recalled, "I had a raw onion, which was delicious, and two pieces of hardtack." Tanks had been promised, to crush the barbed wire and make a passage for the infantry, but morning came with no tanks in sight. One company commander attempted an attack, under impossible conditions; every man who reached the wire was hit. As Donovan started toward the unit, a bullet struck him in the knee — "I felt as if somebody had hit the back of my leg with a spiked club. I fell like a log" — but he managed to crawl back to the shell hole, and a lieutenant applied first aid. Though he would have ordered a similar casualty to be evacuated, he threatened to court-martial anyone who tried to remove him. Despite the pain of his shattered leg, he lay in his shell hole and continued to direct the battle.

The long-awaited tanks appeared about midmorning, to the elation of the troops, but they encountered such sustained artillery fire that they turned about and rumbled back down the road to the rear. "The situation was bad," Donovan admitted. "There was more defense than we thought and the battalion was held up. My telephone was out, and messengers I sent through were killed or wounded and my requests for reinforcements remained undelivered. We were shelled heavily. Beside me three men were blown up, and I was showered with the remnants of their bodies. Gas was then thrown at us, thick and nasty." At 10:30 Donovan was informed that an enemy counterattack was in preparation. His aides urged him to let them carry him to safety, but he refused and ordered them to bring up the Stokes mortars. The counterattack was smothered in its inception.

"Five hours had passed, and I was getting very groggy from loss of blood, but managed to get a message through withdrawing the unit and putting another in its place. Then they carried me back in a blanket. Machine gun bullets passed through the blanket, and one of the bearers was hit. I told them to put me down, but they said they were willing to take a chance. It was a tough hike. At last we reached the shelter of a hill, and met the support battalion. I turned things over to the major, made my report, and then was on my way to the hospital." As he was carried past Father Duffy, he looked up from the stretcher and grinned: "Father, I can see you're a disappointed man. You expected to have the pleasure of burying me."

A note scribbled to Ruth Donovan on Red Cross stationery stated briefly: "A machine gun bullet at the knee just below the joint. A clean wound through from front to rear. A hole in the tibia — a splinter from that hole extending downward for two and a half inches — in bed in a Paris hospital. There you have it. American Red Cross No. 3, 4 Place Chevreuse." It was his only mention of the action that won him the Congressional Medal of Honor.

On January 18, 1923, five years after the war, the Medal of Honor was awarded to Colonel Donovan in a ceremony at the 69th Regiment Armory in New York. Today it hangs on a wall in the armory, next to a framed letter written by the Colonel:

Dear Comrades:

Permit me to deposit with you the Congressional Medal of Honor which was presented to me tonight.

This medal was truly won by our entire command at the Kriemhilde-Stellung in front of Landres–St. Georges, Oct. 14–15, 1918 — a fight as bitter and as gallant in the annals of the 69th New York as Marye's Heights at Fredericksburg, Dec. 13–14, 1862.

A Regiment lives by its tradition — the noble tradition we have inherited impels me to ask that this medal remain in the Armory — there to serve as a recognition of the valor of our Regiment, as an incentive to those who enlist under its standard, but most of all as a memorial to our brave and unforgotten dead.

Sincerely,
WILLIAM J. DONOVAN

III

AFTER THE LOSS OF DONOVAN, the battered Rainbow Division fought on to the heights of the Meuse, directly overlooking Sedan, where it was relieved by the 40th French Division which had been given the honor of occupying that long contested city. On November 13, 1918, the 69th marched back to Landres–St. Georges, which they had tried in vain to enter from the opposite side five weeks before, pitched their tents on the outskirts of the demolished village, and spread their soggy blankets to dry on the crosses of the German dead.

That night they learned for the first time that the Armistice had been signed two days previously. In a tardy celebration, the men raided the Engineer and Signal stores for rockets of all descriptions, and the brilliant pyrotechnic display reminded Father Duffy of the bombardment before the Champagne-Marne battle. Bonfires blazed on every hill, but the jubilation of the troops was mingled with thoughts of those who were not alive to share the triumph. A formal muster of the regiment showed its strength at 55 officers and 1,637 men, thirteen hundred less than at the beginning of the Argonne campaign. Of the survivors, not more than six hundred were those original members who had left New York with such high spirits a little over a year before.

Hopes of an early return to the United States were dashed when the Rainbow Division was selected as part of the Allied Army of Occupation. While they were awaiting arrangements for their passage into Germany, the regiment had a visit from Lieutenant Colonel Donovan, hobbling on crutches and very depressed. The Provost Marshal General had had him transferred to headquarters while Donovan was still in the hospital; and no enlisted man marooned in a casual camp ever uttered with greater pathos: "I want to be back with my own outfit." Father Duffy was not overly concerned. "When that man Donovan wants anything very bad, he gets it," he observed. "I expect to see him on duty with us again in a very, very brief time."

On December 3, New York's 69th, now part of the Third Army, made its invasion of Germany. The trim khaki column came down along the river Sauer and, as they turned to cross the bridge onto German soil, the band struck up the regimental air "Garry Owen." They marched with advance and rear guards, as though entering a hostile country, but nothing more formidable greeted them than the click of cameras. The men had anticipated a sullen reception, and pictured themselves moving around in German villages with loaded rifle and fixed bayonet, alert for any treacherous attack; but they were received amicably, almost gratefully, by the war-wearied populace. Farmers in the fields went out of their way to give road directions; children were as excited and inquisitive as children at home; women lent their cooking utensils to the Yankee troops, and offered food from their own scant supply when the hungry men arrived at a village ahead of their kitchens. The long brutal conflict was over.

Early in December, as Father Duffy had predicted, Donovan rejoined the 69th, walking with a slight limp which he would carry the rest of his life. By persistence and Celtic charm, he had persuaded General Headquarters to order him back on duty with his regiment. He was advanced in rank to full colonel and placed in command of the Fighting Irish, fulfilling at last the boyhood dream inspired by the poems of Mangan. His first effort, through official and private channels, was to get back every officer and man of the old regiment who had been transferred to other outfits or was being held in a hospital. He made it his business to facilitate overdue promotions and decorations, which had been frozen by the end of hostilities, and Father Duffy was awarded the Distinguished Service Medal for his dedicated service. Shortly before Christmas, the regiment moved to the ancient and lovely town of

Remagen-am-Rhein, which was to be their home for the next three or four months; and at midnight on the 24th they celebrated Christmas Mass on the Rhine.

That winter was the happiest period in the regiment's overseas tour. The 69th was all together at last; the men had warm billets, and most of them were sleeping in beds for the first time during the war; food was substantial and plentiful, though Colonel Donovan was concerned about the lack of sustenance for the German civilians. With a long eye to the future, he wrote Ruth Donovan: "Germany's need is very pressing. Kaiserism has vanished, the government is being conservatively and sanely managed, but the danger is economic. German soldiers are being released, given fifty marks, and turned out into the streets. There are no clothes to be had. At present Bolshevism has no strength here, but unless we step in and help on the food question, there is bound to be difficulty later."

On St. Patrick's Day, the entire 42nd Division was reviewed by General Pershing in the town square of Remagen. When the Commander-in-Chief came to Donovan's regiment his eyes were taken by the silver furls which covered the staff of the flag from the silk of the colors to the lowest tip. Actually the staff was in excess of the regulation length, since an extra foot had been added to accommodate the nine new furls which recorded its battles in France. "What regiment is this?" he asked Colonel Donovan. "The 165th Infantry, sir." "What regiment was it?" "The 69th New York, sir."

Pershing nodded. "I understand now."

Pershing's inspection was a hint that their occupational duty was almost over. A week later, orders arrived for the regiment's return to America, and on April 2, 1919, the regiment boarded the train to Brest — the first leg of the long journey home. A couple of weeks later, they embarked for Hoboken on the troopship *Harrisburg;* and on the morning of April 21 the men thronged the deck to gaze at the southern shore of Long Island and the Statue of Liberty. Then down the bay came the welcoming flotilla, bearing relatives and friends and official greeters, the first indication of the overwhelming reception that was to be theirs during the next two crowded weeks.

New York had had more than its share of receptions, since the first shipload of AEF returnees arrived on December 23. Countless tons of ticker tape and torn telephone books had fluttered down from office windows, crowds had cheered themselves into a state of permanent hoarseness, and Mayor John Hylan and his top-hatted reception committee had worn hollows in the wooden stands at 82nd Street and Fifth Avenue where they sat to review each successive parade. No sooner had the street cleaners swept up the red-white-and-blue bunting and confetti from the gutters after one reception than another line of veterans started up the avenue. Will Rogers, peering quizzically over his twirling lariat, suggested: "If they really want to honor the boys, why don't they let them sit in the stands and have the people march by?"

But the city was not too jaded to give its own Fighting Irish the greatest reception of all. Some seven hundred invalided men, who had preceded them home for convalescence, joined the regiment to ride in open cars in the grand parade. Before the march began, Donovan ordered his men: "Look neither to the right nor left, only directly ahead. You won't see your friends and family, but no one who sees you will ever forget it."

With its band blaring the rollicking tune of "Garry Owen," the 69th swung with jaunty step on its triumphant way north from Washington Square, under the Victory Arch, and up Fifth Avenue, while the city thundered its welcome. "Every uniform was spotless," the New York *Sun* reported, "the rifles of the men glistened, and their bayonets glinted in the sun. Their gas masks were slung at the carry, their packs were on their backs, and every man had his battle helmet.

"In advance of the column was carried a banner marked with 615 gold stars — each star for a valiant son who slumbered in the fields of France. . . . Two other flags there were in the line of march — two, and yet a third. The first was the Stars and Stripes that had flown before their headquarters overseas. The standard showed many a rent in its folds, for it had moved with the regiment through the war, secure in the knowledge that the 69th never disobeyed an order and never lost a flag. The regimental colors, too, floated beside the national emblem. The third was a little green flag of Ireland, with harp and motto 'Erin Go Bragh!' which fluttered from a private's bayonet.

165th Infantry Parade up Fifth Avenue, April 28, 1919. WJD marches at the head of the 69th New York.

"At the head of the regiment marched Colonel William J. ('Wild Bill') Donovan. Ordinarily the colonel of a regiment rides in front of the column, but Col. Donovan explained that colonels and sometimes generals had to hike in France, and anyway what was good enough for the men was good enough for him. With him was his staff, including Chaplain Father Francis P. Duffy. A drumfire of cheers greeted the Colonel and the fighting priest as they marched along, leading the men who had followed them 'over there.' "

Father Vincent Donovan had arranged a surprise for his brother's homecoming. From the moment he read the late Joyce Kilmer's poem "When the 69th Comes Back," he determined that the regimental band should play it as they marched up Fifth Avenue. "It practically sang itself," he said, "so ten days before their return I asked Victor Herbert if he would set it to music. He said, 'Well, there isn't much time, Father, but I'll do my best.' And sure enough, in a few days he called me up and asked me if I would bring Mrs. Kilmer to his home, he'd like her to hear it. And after he thumped it out on the piano — he played abominably — he turned around and said, 'Now, Mrs. Kilmer, I'm signing over all the royalties to you.' The song was published with a cover by Howard Chandler Christy, a copy of the program cover for a benefit that John McCormack had given at the Hippodrome for the 69th; and that morning the band played it as they marched up the Avenue past the reviewing stand."

The parade was followed by an endless round of celebrations. The freedom of the city was conferred upon Colonel Donovan and his staff on City Hall steps by Mayor Hylan and the Board of Aldermen; and that night a dinner was given to the regiment by the Mayor's committee, headed by Commissioner Rodman Wanamaker. Donovan quietly bowed out of the ceremony, because he felt that this was a New York City affair. "I'll be around for anything official," he told his lieutenant colonel, a born New Yorker, "but otherwise you're in charge. A native son should be in position to receive the city's honors."

The regiment was based in their old quarters at Camp Mills, awaiting final discharge, and Father Donovan recalled: "I drove out with him to the silent camp that night, and he really wept at the affectionate tribute the 69th had been given. 'I'm thinking of all the men I've left behind,' and he wept. So that shows . . . that was really my brother."

2

That summer of 1919, before resuming his law practice in Buffalo, Colonel Donovan took his wife on a long-deferred honeymoon to Japan. He had been interested in the Far East since undergraduate days, and they sailed to Tokyo for a month's vacation "just to look around," he told Ruth Donovan. No pressing problems, he assured her. Nothing to do but sightsee and shop and relax.

They had relaxed in Tokyo but a few days when the American ambassador, Roland Morris, called Donovan on urgent business. Morris was about to depart for Siberia to evaluate the reportedly unstable status of the White Russian government at Omsk, headed by Admiral Alexander Kolchak, and advise the State Department whether the Kolchak regime should be supported by the United States. He needed someone with Donovan's background and training to accompany him on his confidential mission. Ruth Donovan reconciled herself to what would become a pattern of similar missions over the next forty years.

The vast undeveloped territory of Siberia, though completely cut off from the Moscow government, nevertheless felt the political tugs and strains which had disrupted Russia since the overthrow of the Romanoff dynasty in 1917. The Revolution had given local Cossack chieftains free rein to advance their own interests, often in defiance of Kolchak. Germany, England, France, and Japan were engaged in military and commercial conflict along its fringes. A large body of Czech soldiers had broken away from the Austrian army and made their way overland to Vladivostok, in hopes of sailing back to France and reentering the war on the Allied side. Their security was threatened by numerous German and Austrian prisoners of war in Siberia, liberated by Bolshevist sympathizers, who had been armed and organized into effective fighting units. The Bolshevist threat was mounting, and President Wilson, though hesitant to involve the United States in this squirrel's nest of conflicting international forces, had yielded sufficiently to dispatch a small body of five thousand American troops to the trouble spot, ostensibly to defend the Siberian railroad system and tacitly by their presence to maintain internal order in Russia's Far East empire.

Ambassador Morris and Donovan were met at Vladivostok by Major General William S. Graves, commander of America's Siberian expedition, and traveled to Omsk in a special train, consisting of a private railroad car shared by Graves and Morris and Donovan, several cars for the sleeping and feeding of some thirty American soldiers, and a flatcar for the General's Cadillac.[9] Donovan sat by the window and made occasional entries in his diary: "Vast fertile acres and great deposits of mineral wealth. Siberia contains resources which, when properly exploited, are capable not only of maintaining within itself millions of people, but of adding untold amounts, particularly of food supplies, to the outside world. . . . The difficulty in Russia is not absence of money or resources, but of management. . . . With stable government, can live within herself and produce everything. . . . Situation here must be grappled with. Afraid nothing else to do but support Kolchak. No time to organize another government."

Donovan's hopes of dealing with Kolchak wavered when the train halted near Omsk, and he observed the sick and wounded Russian soldiers brought back from the Bolshevist front for delousing. "Trains come in bearing one thousand patients daily. Inadequate personnel for caring for victims. The wounds are gangrenous — worms can be seen crawling around the wounds. The dead lie in the cars — wagons bearing coffins carry away thirty or forty per day. The typhus patients relieve themselves under the cars, beside the cars, and when too weak even in the cars. They are undernourished, fed irregularly, no water except at stated intervals. Piteous flesh-covered skeletons in loose, foul, filthy garments can be seen crawling to the stream for a drink. Wounded and dysentery and typhus all together. Russian doctors refuse to aid their own soldiers. No one at this point to enforce regulations. No effort by government to alleviate conditions. . . . Last winter American Red Cross successful in saving only six hundred — Russians would not accept help."

[9] William S. Graves, *America's Siberian Adventure* (New York, 1931).

The more he saw and heard, the more he was convinced that the Bolshevist forces were rapidly gaining the support of the people, due to the cruelty and oppression of the Kolchak regime. "Bolshevists making strong effort in Siberia because of internal strife. . . . Workers in Siberia are yearning for Bolshevism. . . . Red Army has mobilized most of peasants with trained fanatical Communists distributed among them, one mounted man to every five others. The whip and the pistol gets them."

It became increasingly clear, as they moved through the Siberian hinterland, that the corrupt Kolchak government was helpless to resist the Bolshevist advance. Kolchak's supporters had alienated the populace by committing atrocities even more callous than the Communists perpetrated. German and Austrian prisoners, illegally detained long after the end of the war, were starving and freezing to death in barbed-wire pens, and General Graves claimed their treatment was "a disgrace to modern civilization." He showed Ambassador Morris an order issued in March, 1919, by General Rozanoff, a member of Kolchak's staff:

> In occupying the villages which have been occupied before by the enemy, where you cannot get the enemy leaders, then shoot one out of every ten of the people.
> The villages where the population meet our troops with arms should be burned down and all the full-grown male population should be shot; property, carts, etc., should be taken for the use of the Army.

By the end of their trip, Ambassador Morris had come to share Donovan's disillusionment. "With all the people questioned by us, and through the interpreters," Morris concluded, "we have not found a single individual who spoke a good word for the Kolchak regime." Despite Admiral Kolchak's personal assurances to Morris that the Siberian Army was merely withdrawing to the Isham River in order to regroup and make a firm stand against the Bolshevists, Morris could see that the retreating Russian forces were little more than a disorganized mob, officers quitting their troops and fleeing, soldiers discarding arms and ammunition and even heavy clothing to enable them to move more rapidly to the rear. Cossack leaders, who had supported the White

Russians against the Bolshevists, told the ambassador that they "were tired of doing all the fighting and were on their way home." A Czech general stated that "Kolchak has surrounded himself with old regime officers whose only salvation for future existence depends on restoration of the former monarchy." Donovan wrote in his diary, under the title "Statement to be made by Mr. Morris to State Department: Morris always shy of Kolchak government. What he did find was a deep disappointment, for he had believed government had deeper roots than he found to be the case. Plan desired by State Department impracticable. Was based on what could be done to help Kolchak, but was in no sense what we could do to help Russia." Donovan added a note on August 10: "Fate of government will be decided in a few months." Shortly after he and Morris returned to Japan, Kolchak lost Siberia to the Bolshevists, and was captured and executed by them the following spring.

Donovan's Siberian diary contained a significant final entry: "We can prevent a shooting war only if we take the initiative to win the subversive war. And to succeed — is to win the peace that the world so badly needs." That thought was to guide him during the years that lay ahead.[10]

[10] Subsequently, in 1920, Donovan, then aged thirty-seven, was to make a private tour of the war-torn countries of Europe with Grayson M. P. Murphy. Donovan's comprehensive diaries of the trip anticipate, in an uncanny way, the function of the R&A Branch of OSS in World War II.

BOOK TWO
1920-1941

Man of Mystery

I

WHEN THE TIDE OF WAR RECEDED, America discovered the Eighteenth Amendment cast up high and dry on its shores, as unwelcome as a stranded whale. Preoccupied with the fighting in France, the country had barely noticed when the prohibition amendment slipped through the Senate in 1917 after only thirteen hours of debate, and passed the House of Representatives in a single day. By June of 1919, before the last troops had returned from overseas, it had been ratified by the required three-quarters of the states, and a wartime prohibition measure promptly went into effect, to be followed six months later by the actual amendment to the Constitution. The enabling Volstead Act was passed over Wilson's rather surprising veto, driving the final nail in John Barleycorn's coffin. William Jennings Bryan, raising his glass of grape juice high, proclaimed that "the liquor issue is as dead as slavery," and everyone chanted the dirge:

> Dry as the bones of Moses, dry as the Dead Sea shore,
> Dry as the bunch of roses that Cleopatra wore.
> Dry as a kippered herring that never saw the sea —
> After July, oh, God, how dry, how dry we'll be.

World War I had given the WCTU and Anti-Saloon League reformers their long-awaited opportunity. Here was a country blinded by Wilson's vision of Utopia, its citizens prepared to make any sacrifice in the crusading spirit of idealism. People had become accustomed in the short span of two years to government regulation of their lives. They had cheerfully accepted meatless Tuesdays and wheatless Wednesdays and porkless Thursdays; what was more logical, the Dries argued, than to conserve the nation's grain by banning spirituous liquors? Then too, there was a patriotic prejudice against anything German, and zealots played skillfully on the fact that many brewers and distillers had Teutonic names. That the prohibition law might be difficult to enforce after the war never occurred to its proponents. If the world could be made safe for democracy, certainly it should not be difficult to make it safe for sobriety.

The very speed and stealth with which the Eighteenth Amendment had been enacted was its eventual undoing. Since it had been passed without a popular referendum, the public did not assume any moral obligation to support it. A million AEF veterans, feeling that prohibition had been put over unfairly while their backs were turned, looked on it as the work of a few fanatics, a law to be contemptuously flouted. No one in the early Twenties believed that it could ever be repealed; so people adjusted to the new drought conditions, just as the human body adapts itself to an arid climate. The old saloon went underground and became the basement speakeasy. People learned to carry hip flasks, drink Orange Blossoms made of bathtub gin, install home brewing devices in their cellars or hall closets. Fast rum-running launches brought contraband liquor from beyond the twelve-mile limit. Loaded beer trucks pounded the dark highways, freighters filled their holds with camouflaged cases of whiskey, railroads transported whole carloads of alcoholic beverages by attaching false seals to the locked doors. Cities along the Canadian border did a handsome business in illegal imports from the Dominion; and Buffalo, only a few miles from Ontario, became the center of a vast smuggling empire.

President Warren Gamaliel Harding, whose gift to the American people was the word "normalcy," had been chary of grasping the prohibition nettle, and confined himself to pious platitudes about the virtues of abstinence. As a practical politician, however, he was troubled by newspaper accounts of widespread rum-running from Canada, and in February of 1922 he asked Colonel Donovan to accept an appointment as U.S. district attorney for western New York, in order to end the unfavorable publicity. Donovan and his partner Bradley Goodyear had taken on two associates and established the new Buffalo law firm of Donovan Goodyear Raichle and DePew, and postwar business was prospering; but "Wild Bill" was never one to ignore a summons to duty. He took a leave of absence from his firm, and embarked on another kind of war.

Although he personally did not drink, Donovan was by no means a dry; but he was determined to wipe out the graft and corruption which had been bred by the Eighteenth Amendment. "I am not a prohibition-ist," he declared when he became district attorney, "and this office is going to be neither an adjunct of the Anti-Saloon League nor the side door of a brewery." If prohibition were ever to be repealed, he believed, it should be done by orderly democratic processes, not by nullification through civil disobedience. As long as it was the law of the land, his duty was to enforce it.

On his return from France, Donovan had been invited to join the exclusive Saturn Club, whose membership included some of Buffalo's most important and influential leaders. It was no secret that their lockers were well stocked with choice whiskeys brought in from Canada, in the easygoing arrangement of the day, and Donovan cautioned the members repeatedly that such possession was illegal. When they ignored his warn-ings, he ordered a raid on his own club, confiscated the liquor, and prosecuted his guilty fellow-members. The raid was denounced as a betrayal of hospitality, a callous grab for headlines. Donovan found himself ostracized by Buffalo society, and his partner Bradley Goodyear resigned from the law firm, ending a long association.

So bitter and lasting was the feud that when the Republican party nominated Donovan for lieutenant governor of New York on the 1924 ticket with incumbent Governor Nathan L. Miller, Donovan failed to carry his home district of Buffalo and the Republicans were soundly defeated by Alfred E. Smith, though Donovan polled one hundred thou-sand more votes than his running mate. The Saturn raid, though morally justifiable, was politically unrealistic, an early sign of that stubborn refusal to compromise which was to deny Donovan elective office all his life.

Rum-running was not the only crime with which the district attorney's office had to contend. All over dry America, gangs bankrolled by prohibition were branching out into other lucrative enterprises. "Racketeering" joined "normalcy" in the American lexicon, with its attendant terrorism and political corruption. A thriving freight car hijacking ring was operating against the New York Central Railroad between Buffalo and New York, and local enforcement agents worked in cahoots with the lawbreakers. When Donovan stepped into the picture, he was warned by a member of the gang that he would be assassinated, his house dynamited and his children kidnapped, if he pursued the investigation. With the same personal fatalism he had shown in France, Donovan ignored the threat, and after closing his office at midnight he would get his daily exercise by walking home, alone and unarmed, for three miles along hoodlum-infested Delaware Avenue. In less than a year he brought about the indictment of thirty-two persons, including company policemen and yardmen and a corrupt state senator, and the racket was broken up. The railroad owners' delight at Donovan's successful prosecution of the case terminated abruptly when the diligent young D.A. unearthed evidence that the New York Central, as well as the Erie and the Lehigh Valley, were violating certain provisions of the Interstate Commerce Act, and all three companies were convicted and paid the maximum fine.

Donovan's strenuous efforts to clean up Buffalo did not escape the attention of Washington, which stood in far greater need of a cleanup. President Harding's sudden death in 1923 had set loose the first disquieting rumors of scandal in his administration. His flag-draped coffin had barely been lowered into the ground when the rank stench of oil seeping from Teapot Dome and Elk Hills began to pollute the Washington air, besmirching three members of the Harding cabinet and permeating several others with its clinging odor. Senate investigation disclosed an unprecedented effort by the late President's cronies to defraud the government of its naval oil reserves. While his successor, Calvin Coolidge, sat in the White House with lips pursed and nose wrinkled at the noisome smells around him, two of Harding's associates committed suicide, Secretary of the Navy Edwin L. Denby resigned and Attorney General Harry Daugherty was indicted, and Secretary of the Interior Albert B. Fall, convicted of accepting a bribe, was sentenced to jail.

President Coolidge was returned to office in 1924 despite the Republican scandals, and his first act was a sweeping reorganization of his predecessor's cabinet. Harlan Fiske Stone, untainted dean of Columbia University Law School, was appointed Attorney General to succeed Daugherty. Remembering his former law school pupil, Stone invited Colonel Donovan to head the Department of Justice's Criminal Division. Donovan arrived in Washington in August, 1924, and by March of the following year his spectacular success had won him a promotion to the Assistant to the Attorney General in charge of the Anti-Trust Division, the second highest position in the department.

Donovan brought to the Washington scene a rare quality and a new concept. In a city long inured to Congressional ranting and bombast, his quiet approach and straightforward style of delivery came as a refreshing novelty. His normally mild voice might harden and develop a brittle edge when he was angered, but he had disciplined himself rigidly to keep his tone muted, never exhorting, never indulging in flights of gaudy eloquence. Aware that an air of confidence was half the battle, he would make sure that he was relaxed by taking a steambath and rubdown before any important court appearance. He presented his arguments as unaffectedly as though he were conversing before a fireplace, his thumbs hooked negligently in the side pockets of his coat, his manner at once intimate and disarming.

Equally novel was his approach to the problems of the Anti-Trust Division. For years, since President Teddy Roosevelt's administration, the Justice Department had gone in for "trust busting," banging its big club over the skulls of one giant corporation after another. The results had made headlines, but relations between government and business had grown increasingly strained, and there was widespread resentment at the ruthless prosecutions and unnecessarily long delays in reaching a decision, resulting in waste of time and financial loss to the stockholders. Since the anti-trust laws were open to wide interpretation, innocent companies were brought into court and, even though exonerated, were forced to pay the penalty of legal fees and unfavorable publicity.

Donovan proceeded on the basic premise that businessmen in general were honest, and their infringements were due more often than not to ignorance of the law. Having briefed himself thoroughly in the Sherman and Clayton anti-trust laws, he initiated the practice of previewing any proposed merger which would come under the jurisdiction of his department, and warning the corporations in advance whenever their proposal conflicted with the law. "We do not think all mergers are wrong," Donovan stated, "nor do we fight big business just because it is big. Our policy is to notify the firms if their plans are illegal, so that they can make proper adjustments and avoid litigation." In this atmosphere of mutual frankness, the old antagonisms soon melted away. Donovan explained: "It's better to be directed by a traffic cop than trailed by a detective."

His unique concept benefited the taxpayers as well. Within two years after he took office, Congressional appropriations for the Anti-Trust Division were substantially reduced. Instead of hiring special lawyers, the streamlined department took care of all its prosecutions, the main cases being handled by Donovan personally. The Justice Department did not relax its vigilance — actually more firms were indicted and fines collected than during previous administrations — but there were no more sensational headlines, and relatively few contested the fairness of the decisions.

Colonel Donovan had moved his family into a handsome house in Georgetown, but he seldom returned home at night before David and Patricia had gone to bed. He was working long hours, from eight in the morning until after dark, and he expected his staff to do the same. "If I can take it, why can't you?" was "Wild Bill's" standard challenge to an exhausted associate. In addition to his legal activities, he and Ruth Donovan were caught up in the unavoidable round of Washington social life; and his only opportunity to be with his children was on a weekend when he drove them out to the country, or took them boating on the Potomac.

His punishing schedule baffled Washington, which was accustomed to a more leisurely pace, and there were suspicions that the Colonel's zeal might have political overtones. John Lord O'Brian, his former Buffalo law partner, said of him once: "Bill has a driving ambition. He won't be satisfied until he's the first Catholic President of the United States." And even Father Vincent Donovan admitted that his brother had "some erring thoughts."

His driving ambition found its opportunity in 1928 when Calvin Coolidge announced tersely that he did not choose to run for reelection, and Secretary of Commerce Herbert Hoover won the Republican nomination for the Presidency. Hoover and Colonel Donovan had been friendly since their first meeting in 1915 on the War Relief Commission, and Donovan had been Hoover's recent guest at the Bohemian Grove in San Francisco. He threw himself into the campaign with all his boundless energy. Governor Al Smith of New York had tossed his brown derby into the ring as Democratic candidate, appealing to the Irish Catholic vote, and it was no small aid to Hoover to count a staunch Catholic among his own supporters. Hoover used Donovan's Georgetown home frequently to meet unobserved with his advisers and financial backers.

The outcome of the campaign was never much in doubt. Smith fought gallantly, gambling on a bold plank to amend the Volstead Act and allow each state to determine its own right to manufacture and sell alcoholic beverages; Hoover, emulating Harding, straddled the issue with a statement that prohibition was "a great social and economic experiment noble in motive," a phrase that would come back to haunt him. Four years of Republican prosperity under Coolidge was the final unanswerable argument, Hoover was swept into office by a landslide vote, and left with his family for a brief vacation cruise to Latin America.

Attorney General Stone had retired, and it was a foregone conclusion in Washington that Colonel Donovan's reward for his loyal support of Hoover would be an appointment as Attorney General in the new cabinet. Though Donovan never mentioned it, he was equally confident that he would be named to that post, the logical stepping-stone to a bright political future. So certain were the newspapers of Donovan's selection that they had already prepared stories for release upon Hoover's return. Reporters gathered around the President-elect's S Street home when Colonel Donovan arrived to pay his official call. He emerged a few moments later, his face flushed. A newsman quoted the press questions and Donovan's answers:

"Did he ask you to become Attorney General?"

"No."

"Did he want you to be Secretary of War?"

"No, we sat there rather embarrassed, and finally he asked me what I thought of the governor generalship of the Philippines. I told him I wasn't interested. By that time it was becoming most uncomfortable, and I left."[1]

Washington was astounded when Hoover announced, without elaboration, that William D. Mitchell would receive the appointment, and indignation was loudly expressed. Royal S. Copeland, Democratic senator from New York, stated on the Senate floor: "Here is William Donovan, who will not be appointed Attorney General because he is a Catholic or a wet; I don't know which. It is outrageous that this man who has served his country, and served it well, will not be named to the Cabinet because he doesn't happen to fit the standard set by those who dominate the next President."

Colonel Donovan resigned from the Justice Department and left Washington to resume his private practice. In midsummer of 1929 he severed connections with Buffalo and established a small law business of his own in New York City, first at 41 Broad Street and later at 2 Wall Street, which expanded to today's prominent firm of Donovan Leisure Newton and Irvine. His office was a large corner room on the sixteenth floor, overlooking Broadway and ancient Trinity Church. Beside the window was a walnut lectern, at which Donovan liked to stand when he was reading, and near it was a favorite English cockfighting chair he had

[1] Former Attorney General Stone, who had just been made an Associate Justice of the Supreme Court, acted as a personal emissary for the President and urged Donovan to accept Hoover's offer of the Philippines post. Donovan replied: "Tell Mr. Hoover I asked him to be honest with me. That is the one thing he has not been."

picked up in his travels. The walls were lined with maps of Europe and Asia, indicative of his continuing global interests.

Despite the herculean task of opening a new law firm in New York on the eve of the Great Depression and in competition with the city's established firms which had already absorbed most of the corporate and banking and other available legal business, Donovan nevertheless found time to serve without pay in several important government investigations. Almost immediately after leaving the Hoover administration, he was asked to become the counsel for the New York State Commission on Revision of the Public Service Commissions Law. He promptly proposed a plan of procedure, and explained:

"This plan is based on certain assumptions. It assumes that the committee starts with no preconceived theory to be established and no particular policy to be demonstrated. It takes for granted that the purpose of this investigation is to ascertain all available facts. It assumes that, while there may be disagreement among the members as to the interpretation of these facts and the conclusions to be drawn from them, there is no disagreement among the committee as to the necessity of having presented for consideration every element and every opinion which would throw light upon the subject."

Even at this early point in his career, Donovan had learned the hard lesson that no informed decision could be made without objective collection and unbiased analysis of all the pertinent facts. He also realized that the investigation of facts is an art in itself, and requires the combined application of men outside as well as within the legal profession, whose skills in their respective professions would aid in accomplishing the objective. In the course of his public utilities investigation, 43 public hearings were held, resulting in 2,830 printed pages of testimony by 96 witnesses, including Norman Thomas and Morris L. Ernst. Without such tough and extensive preliminary training, it is questionable whether Donovan would have had the unique qualifications necessary to create OSS and lay the foundations for our present national intelligence system.

Other cases added to his growing experience. Early in 1929 Charles H. Tuttle, United States attorney for the Southern District of New

York, at the recommendation of a federal grand jury, started an investigation of alleged abuses and illegal practices in bankruptcy administration; and a joint committee of bar associations secured the services of Donovan as unpaid counsel. Over one thousand court files of cases and some four thousand witnesses were produced, and research assistance was given by a staff at the Yale Law School headed by Professor William O. Douglas, now Associate Justice of the U.S. Supreme Court. Donovan's final report, which recommended many changes in the law, comprised 326 pages, exclusive of statistical analyses, and was based on some twelve volumes of public and private testimony and memoranda relating to bankruptcy administration throughout the United States and abroad.

Donovan gained added training in this field when he served as defense counsel in the famous Madison Oil Trial, the largest criminal prosecution ever instituted under the anti-trust laws. The indictment charged 24 of the leading oil companies, 56 of their principal officers, and 3 oil market journals with a conspiracy to fix wholesale and retail gasoline prices. Some eighteen tons of documents, subpoenaed by the government and impounded in the courthouse at Madison, Wisconsin, had to be analyzed and indexed with cross references. Donovan invented a whole new system of filing so that any document in the huge mass of evidence could be produced immediately when needed.

In 1932 an action, called the Appalachian Coal Case, was brought by the Attorney General of the United States against some 135 coal companies for violation of the anti-trust laws; and again Donovan served as chief defense counsel. The case necessitated a vast factual analysis of the rivalry between the Appalachian companies and other coal operators, the effect of freight rates, competition from natural gas and oil, and other factors which had to be charted both statistically and graphically after thorough investigation. In the U.S. Supreme Court, the government offered some thirty-seven exhibits and the defendants' tables came to more than ninety, including such related items as the annual supply of energy from mineral fuels and water power, production of natural gas and petroleum and coal for each state, names of companies that had changed from coal to fuel oil, and a large map showing coal fields, coal consumption, and relative freight charges from Appalachian and other eastern districts to the principal market areas. The Appalachian Coal Case finally resulted in an eight-to-one Supreme Court victory for the defendants, and their operation continues to this day.

All of these cases required the collection of immense amounts of material, which had to be digested and presented as hard facts — provable in court under the hostile and able scrutiny of opposing counsel — rather than opinions or theories. It was this professional thoroughness which led a decade later to Donovan's conception of America's first intelligence agency, with its major emphasis on research and analysis.

Although immersed in his law work, Donovan still entertained erring thoughts of politics. In the spring of 1932, when he sailed to Germany on legal business, a group of veterans from the 69th, led by Father Duffy, came down to the pier to see him off, and pleaded with him to run for governor of New York in the coming election. Colonel Donovan laughed at the suggestion, and said: "I'll have to have proof that I'm wanted." On his return from Germany, he was presented with a petition signed by ten thousand names. The Colonel was stunned by this token of support. He confided to Father Vincent Donovan later: "I haven't a chance of being elected, but I don't see how I can gracefully turn them down." And he added, with a rare display of anger: "I'd enjoy the nomination for two reasons — to tell the machine what I think of them, and to show Hoover I don't need him."

It proved to be one of the dirtiest campaigns on record. Donovan's opponent, Herbert Lehman, was backed by Al Smith; and Smith was convinced that Donovan's support of Hoover in 1928 had split the Catholic vote and contributed to his defeat. Donovan was depicted as a renegade Catholic, and a Baltimore newspaper carried a scurrilous letter written by a lay journalist. Franklin D. Roosevelt, the Democratic candidate for President, stumped the state for Lehman, and referred condescendingly to "my old friend and classmate Bill Donovan." Donovan retorted: "I didn't know Franklin Roosevelt in college. I came from the other side of the tracks." His hometown of Buffalo, still rankling at the memory of the Saturn Club raid, refused to support him, though the

Bishop of Buffalo published a front-page editorial in his defense. Even his wartime nickname "Wild Bill" was used against him to prove that Donovan was erratic and unfit to handle the responsibilities of governor.

Donovan could not have chosen a more inopportune time to run for office on a Republican ticket. Rightly or wrongly, President Hoover was blamed for the Wall Street debacle of 1929 and the onset of the Great Depression. Hoover's rosy assurances that "conditions were fundamentally sound" and would soon improve had failed repeatedly to materialize, and his reputation had declined with the falling market. Bread lines stretched longer and longer, ramshackle "Hoovervilles" for the evicted and homeless sprang up in the outskirts of every city, and "Brother, Can You Spare a Dime?" became the new national anthem. Hoover, at a loss for a solution, grew increasingly inept. When fifteen thousand veterans of World War I marched on Washington to plead for government help, he ordered Army troops under General MacArthur to drive them out of town with tear gas and bayonets, thus losing himself countless votes. Franklin D. Roosevelt, described by Walter Lippmann as "a pleasant man who, without any important qualifications for the office, would like very much to be President," made a shrewd bid for popular support by pledging to work for the immediate repeal of the Eighteenth Amendment; Hoover's weak reiteration of his phrase "a noble experiment" was greeted with jeering laughter. To a public disillusioned with the party in power, FDR's Pied Piper voice and seductive if vague promises of "a New Deal for the American people" appealed to the forgotten men, and in November Hoover and the entire Republican ticket, including Donovan, went down to cataclysmic defeat. Some years later President Roosevelt told a Columbia Law School class reunion: "If Bill Donovan had been a Democrat, he'd be in my place today."

It was the last time Donovan ran for public office, the next to last time he would ever seek a political position. Henceforth for the rest of his life his energy would seek its outlet in other channels.

A campaign portrait of WJD's family, 1932: Patricia Donovan, then fifteen; Mrs. Donovan; and, standing, David Donovan, seventeen.

II

AMERICAN SENTIMENT in the early Thirties was predominantly isolationist. Out of the disillusionment of the decade emerged a "revisionist"
theory that World War I had been not a struggle of democracy against
autocracy, but a crass rivalry between imperialistic powers, Germany
no more guilty than England. A Senate committee, chaired by Gerald P.
Nye, had dug up evidence purporting to prove that the United States
had been dragged into the war through the connivance of international
bankers and munitions makers, and intimated that Woodrow Wilson
had cynically pretended to be ignorant of their secret treaties. America
Firsters, together with such oddly assorted neutralists as ex-President
Hoover and Charles Lindbergh and the small but active Communist
party, swore that the country should not be duped again by the power
struggles of Europe and Asia, and they were supported by the great
majority of the American public — estimated by a Gallup poll to be as
high as 75 percent — who opposed any future foreign entanglements.

President Roosevelt had been one of the first world leaders to recognize the menace of Adolf Hitler. "I am concerned by events in Germany," he wrote British Prime Minister Ramsey MacDonald in 1933,
"for I feel that an insane rush to further armaments in Continental
Europe is infinitely more dangerous than any squabbles over gold or
tariffs." But Roosevelt's efforts to throw American power into the
balance against Germany and Japan were defeated over and over by an
implacable House and Senate. When he asked for authority to embargo

arms shipments to aggressor nations, Congress insisted that the law should apply equally to all belligerents, thus nullifying America's potential influence in averting war. Even the President's relatively innocuous proposal to join the World Court was summarily rejected.

Perhaps his efforts were already too late. In the fall of 1933 the Nazi regime in Germany, which had replaced the Weimar Republic, withdrew from the League of Nations, the first phase of Hitler's *putsch* into the Rhineland. Japan politely hissed and bowed out of the League later the same year, and in 1934 denounced the Five-Power Naval Treaty in preparation for its attack on China. And in October of 1935 Mussolini's expeditionary troops crossed the frontier into Ethiopia.

Other Americans were aware of the gathering thunderheads on the European horizon. When Colonel Donovan visited Germany in 1932, he had been concerned about the new and ugly shape that events were taking, and on his return had urged immediate rebuilding of the American army, which had deteriorated so badly that it ranked seventeenth in the world in actual strength.[2] Despite his war record and continuing military interest, Donovan could not by any strict definition be termed a militarist. Informed that General Douglas MacArthur had called him "as determined, resourceful, and gallant a soldier as I have ever known in my life," Donovan replied stubbornly: "I do not consider myself a soldier. I am a civilian who did his duty." He simply could not believe that an American military establishment might ever abuse its power. "I have more faith than that in the democratic system," he insisted. As a civilian, he advocated armed preparedness as America's best safeguard in the growing international emergency; and preparedness, to Donovan, included firsthand knowledge of what was going on across the ocean.

During his term with the Justice Department in Washington, Colonel Donovan had taken the opportunity to talk with European diplomats and visiting businessmen and scholars who had just arrived from abroad. Fitting their remarks together, he saw a pattern that disturbed him, and he made it his business to cultivate every foreigner who might be useful now or in the future. His home in Georgetown became an unofficial

[2] Blum, Catton, Morgan, Schlesinger, Stampp, Woodward, *The National Experience* (New York, 1963).

clearinghouse for intelligence. Polish Ambassador Jan Ciechanowski sipped wine before Donovan's living room fireplace, while his host spread maps on the floor and asked pertinent questions; later OSS used the information Donovan had gathered to organize Polish underground resistance. He went to prizefights with Stanton Griffis, roving ambassador in Europe; during World War II he put Griffis in the belly of a bomber and sent him to Stockholm to buy up ball bearings which Germany urgently needed. Italian Ambassador Rossi was a frequent dinner guest in Georgetown; when Mussolini invaded Ethiopia in 1935, Rossi was Donovan's link in arranging a meeting in Rome with the Fascist leader.

Government officials had assured him that it was impossible to visit Ethiopia. No one could see Mussolini, they said. No foreign observer had ever been allowed in Marshal Badoglio's African headquarters. Neither Washington nor London knew the strength of the Italian army, or Il Duce's future plans. Would Italy strike next through Abyssinia at Egypt? Would she advance from Libya to seize the Suez? British Foreign Secretary Anthony Eden had tried to find out, and Mussolini had ignored him with supreme contempt; miffed, Eden and his entourage had returned to England. Donovan was not convinced. It was his theory that you can find out anything you want to know about anybody in the world if you try hard enough. Undeterred by Eden's failure, he set out for Italy at his own expense. Perhaps he had a premonition of vast potential danger to his country. Perhaps he sensed the opportunity once again to play an active role in her defense.

Colonel Donovan arrived in Rome two days before Christmas, armed with a letter of introduction to Mussolini from Ambassador Rossi. He was traveling as a private American citizen, he told Suvich's chief of cabinet, and he wanted to understand the Italian situation because it affected business at home. The official explained that Mussolini was very busy. Donovan replied that he was just as busy; that he could not wait indefinitely; that if Mussolini would not see him, he wanted to know so that he could return to America at once. He pivoted on his heel and left; he was scarcely back at his hotel when a dispatch arrived from the somewhat shaken official, granting him an interview with Il Duce the following afternoon at three.

Donovan's private diary noted: "I went to the Venetian Palace at 2:50. At the door were two sentries, not particularly smart. Inside the corridor was a major domo, dressed like a Park Avenue doorman. I gave him my letter, and he went to the telephone. A moment later a plain-clothesman arrived with a paper, and compared it with the signature on my letter. I tried to get my letter back, but they confiscated that. We climbed two flights of stairs, he pressed a button, a door opened, and a footman in livery ushered me into a waiting room."

Donovan's quick eye photographed every detail of the room as he waited. Years afterward he was able to name even the paintings on the velvet-covered walls: a Van Dyck, a seventeenth century anonymous Italian, a Van Ploem, a Giovanni Pinni of the early sixteenth century. Promptly at three the attendant returned, saluted, and led him into a larger room, evidently the council chamber, with blue damask covers on the dark tables. "The door was opened by an older usher in a black Prince Albert coat. I entered a large room, bare and high. At the far end was a plain table, a few papers on it, a desk light. Behind the desk was Mussolini."

Mussolini's trick when anyone arrived was to look down at his papers and pretend to be engrossed while his visitor waited, shifting uneasily from one foot to the other. Donovan managed to catch Mussolini's eye as he entered; he held it as he walked the entire length of the room, head erect. He recalled: "I walked as if I were leading my regiment."

Mussolini came around from behind the desk to shake hands, and they chatted for a few moments. "He asked me how long I had been in France during the war," Donovan recorded in his diary. "I told him nineteen months. 'Wounded?' asked Mussolini. 'Three times,' I replied." Mussolini lifted his eyebrows when Donovan added that he had received Italy's Croci di Guerra, and his formality thawed. " 'And now you wish to go to Eritrea. Why?'

" 'I would be interested in seeing the spirit of your soldiers. I did not think much of the Italian troops in the World War — neither the disci-

pline of the men nor the quality of the officers. After the war I saw
your officers chased by crowds through the streets of Milan.'

" 'It is different now,' Mussolini said angrily. 'You would see a vast
change.'

" 'I would like to see that change, and I would like to be where the
men are because, to judge of their power and strength, one must see
how they take care of their feet, of their middle, and of their heads. If
Italy is to have a new Empire, she must have a new Tenth Legion.'

"Mussolini clapped his hands and smiled: 'Tenth Legion, that is
right.' He paused and looked at me shrewdly. 'Your country, will she
aid Britain? Are you in favor of the oil embargo?'

" 'I am in favor of a foreign policy that is our own and not one that
makes us an instrument of someone else.'

"Mussolini clapped his hands again in delight. 'You will go to Africa.
First to Libya and then to Abyssinia. You will see our colonization; you
will see our soldiers, and you will see for yourself that Italy has a new
Tenth Legion.' "

Colonel Donovan visited Asmara, Adsum, Benghazi. He stayed at
Marshal Badoglio's headquarters, in a striped silk tent beside the Marshal's; his knowledge of Badoglio's character proved useful a decade
later when OSS sought to lure Italy away from the Axis. He saw the
improved artillery weapons, the new S–81 bombers, the discipline and
morale of Italian troops in the field. Disagreeing with all the military
experts who predicted that disease and rain and other obstacles would
cause the invasion of Haile Selassie's empire to fail, Colonel Donovan
alone forecast a sweeping Italian triumph. On his return he told President Roosevelt that, contrary to popular opinion, Italy's Army had been
vastly improved over the past few years; that if the troops could be
taken as an expression of the people's will, it meant a new national spirit
of determination and unity; that the Italians realized the dangers of their
attack on Ethiopia, but they would go through with it, despite the risk
of involving the rest of Europe if it tried to block them.

Former American Ambassador to Berlin Hugh Wilson met him in
Switzerland, on Donovan's way back from Africa. Eden, who was in
Bern at the same time, did not see him. Wilson claimed in his memoirs:
"If Donovan had been able to tell Eden that the Italians were sure to

overrun Ethiopia, there might have been a shift in British policy that would have kept Italy in the League and prevented the birth of the Axis between Rome and Berlin."[3]

The peripatetic Colonel — "He is not happy if there is a war on the face of the earth," Wilson wrote, "and he has not had a look at it" — was off again the following year when Spanish Fascists under General Francisco Franco sought to overthrow King Alphonso's Loyalist government. Once more he traveled as a private citizen, though with President Roosevelt's personal foreknowledge. While the President's hands were tied by the Neutrality Act, forbidding the sale or transportation of American munitions, other world powers were involving themselves actively in Spain's civil war. Russia sent a limited supply of weapons and technicians to aid the Loyalists, and Mussolini and Nazi Germany furnished Franco's Fascists with sixty-five thousand trained troops as well as quantities of airplanes and matériel. Spain became in effect a proving ground for World War II, offering Hitler a convenient opportunity to test out his recently developed weapons in actual combat. As Colonel Donovan toured the Spanish front, he realized the revolutionary technical advances which Germany had made, and recorded the details in his diary. His estimates of character were equally perceptive. "Alphonso of Spain has charm and attraction," he noted, "but it is not difficult to see why he didn't hang on. It looked to me as if he lacked the stuff."

He was particularly impressed when he saw the new German 88-mm. gun shoot down Loyalist planes, cover Franco's advance with antipersonnel fire, and halt the Russian tanks. Back in the States, he reported his findings to General Malin Craig, then Army Chief of Staff. For whatever reason, however, no corrections were made in our ordnance and infantry programs. In 1942 that same 88-mm. gun almost blew us out of Africa.

2

Slowly, almost imperceptibly, American isolationism was shifting. Ironically it was not Hitler but the Japanese war lords who wrought the

[3] Hugh R. Wilson, *Diplomat Between Wars* (New York, 1941).

first change. Breaking the Tangku truce, Japanese troops began a new invasion of China in July of 1937, and in a few weeks had captured Peking and Tientsin. When Japan's airplanes bombed Shanghai and all but obliterated ancient Nanking, and Chiang Kai-shek was forced to move the Nationalist government to Chungking, pro-China sympathy in the States was so strong that patriotic citizens banned Gilbert and Sullivan's *The Mikado* and made bonfires of silk stockings to express their hatred of Japan.

Although the public was beginning to take emotional sides, Congress was determined to avoid any actual involvement; and Roosevelt had to use all his political influence to block a resolution which would have required a national referendum to bring the United States into the conflict. In an effort to alert the nation to the dangers of compulsory neutrality, the President made a speech in October at Chicago, the stronghold of America Firstism, warning that "an epidemic of world lawlessness" was raging, and suggesting that "when an epidemic of physical disease starts to spread, the community joins in a quarantine of the patients in order to protect the health of the community." Responsible Republicans like Donovan and Chicago publisher Frank Knox and former Secretary of State Henry Stimson seconded the idea of a quarantine, and the Communist party, in an extraordinary series of back-flips and somersaults, reversed its isolationist position and applauded the speech as a "declaration of a positive peace program." Even the leftist American Student Union, which had pledged only a year before "not to support any war which the government may undertake," now called loudly for "immediate steps to restrain fascist aggression" and urged repeal of the Neutrality Act "so as to discriminate between aggressor and attacked and to give aid to the latter."

The pace of aggression was quickening. In March of 1938 Hitler proceeded with his announced program of German expansion by invading and annexing Austria, and the alleged plight of the German minority in the Sudetenland became his pretext for warlike moves toward Czechoslovakia. That September Neville Chamberlain, British Prime Minister and an apostle of negotiation, grasped his bowler and furled black umbrella, met with Hitler in a series of personal talks, and returned from Munich to proclaim confidently from the balcony of No. 10 Downing Street the achievement of "peace for our time." Peace, it turned out, had been at the price of abject capitulation to Hitler's demands, and his callous seizure of Czechoslovakia the following March proved to the world the futility of compromise. Appeasement had failed; now intimidation and aggression had free rein.

While an adamant Congress still balked at repeal or modification of the arms embargo, events in Europe were moving swiftly to the inevitable climax. Spring of 1939 saw the German occupation of Memel, the final defeat of the Spanish government by Franco, and Mussolini's invasion of Albania. In August Count von Ribbentrop flew to Moscow to sign a German-Russian nonaggression agreement, causing another convulsion in the American Communist party. The next day Britain and Poland signed a pact of mutual assistance. On September 1, 1939, after a frenzied exchange of threats and counterthreats, Hitler's armies launched their *blitzkrieg* against Poland; and on the morning of September 3 the radio from London carried Neville Chamberlain's low-keyed and weary announcement: "This morning the British Ambassador in Berlin handed to the German government a final note stating that unless we heard by eleven o'clock that they were preparing at once to withdraw their troops from Poland, a state of war would exist between us. I have to tell you that no such word has been received, and in consequence this country is at war with Germany."

In a fireside chat that evening, Roosevelt promised the shocked American public "to use every effort" to keep the nation out of war, but added: "I cannot ask that every American remain neutral in thought. . . . Even a neutral cannot be asked to close his mind or his conscience." He called Congress into special session in order to repeal the arms embargo, but isolationists led by Herbert Hoover forced the administration to accept restrictive measures which placed the arms trade on a cash-and-carry basis, requiring Britain and France to pay cash and carry their purchases away in their own ships. The American public was still disposed to let Europe fight its own battles, and a Gallup poll in October showed less than 30 percent in favor of participation even if Britain and France were faced with imminent defeat.

Hitler's panzer divisions overwhelmed Poland in a lightning three weeks. As the Luftwaffe hammered Warsaw, radio listeners heard the last strains of Paderewski's "Polonaise" playing defiantly until they were silenced by the bombs. That fall, after Germany's victory, the Soviet Union gobbled up eastern Poland, subdued the small Baltic republics of Estonia and Latvia and Lithuania, and invaded Finland in November. Roosevelt roundly denounced "this dreadful rape," but Congress showed no enthusiasm for his program of aid, and the Finns bitterly sued for peace, ceding a large slice of their territory to Russia. With the coming of winter, the conflict in Europe settled into a temporary period of inactivity which earned it the title of "the phony war."

Britain wasted the long winter months in agonized indecision, still mesmerized by the appeasement doctrine of Neville Chamberlain. A quiet little Canadian industrialist named William Stephenson, who had made several prewar business trips to Germany to purchase steel, reported that the German Bessemer converters were largely dependent on a special iron ore, of high phosphorous content, which was obtained from the Gallivare mines in northern Sweden, and shipped to Germany from Narvik in Norway and from ice-free ports on the Gulf of Bothnia. When Hitler invaded Poland, Stephenson estimated that the Nazi war machine had only nine months' supply of the vital ore, and urged prompt action to block further shipments. Winston Churchill, who had joined the Chamberlain government as First Lord of the Admiralty, proposed that mines should be laid in Norwegian territorial waters, but decision was deferred because of Foreign Office scruples about Norway's neutrality.

Frustrated, William Stephenson presented his facts to Colonel Stewart Menzies, the head of Britain's Secret Intelligence Service (SIS), and suggested the sabotage of Scandinavian docks and loading cranes, even volunteering to supervise the project personally with the cooperation of Swedish friends. Menzies concurred, and Churchill recommended in a cryptic memorandum to the cabinet that "ore must be prevented from leaving by methods which will be neither diplomatic nor military." Stephenson managed to smuggle a supply of plastic explosive into Stockholm, concealed in diplomatic courier bags, and hid it in the studio of a Swedish sculptor who pretended to use the plastic for his modeling. Unfortunately word of the sabotage plan reached the aging King Gustav, who dispatched a frightened telegram to King George VI pleading that the British effort would result in a German invasion of Sweden, and the operation was called off.[4]

Late in March, after seven months of futile delay, the Supreme War Council authorized Churchill to carry out his proposal to mine Norwegian waters. Before he could act, Hitler terminated the "phony war" with an attack on Norway and Denmark, convoying troops and ammunition in innocent-appearing ore carriers. A small British expeditionary force, equipped with inaccurate charts and outdated maps, botched the job of landing on the Scandinavian coast; Norwegian resistance was broken; and Sweden, as Churchill had predicted, bought its neutrality at the price of continuing to supply iron ore to Germany.

Now Hitler had a valuable air and submarine base on the North Atlantic coast, able to cut off Britain's food and supplies from the Continent. As the German blockade tightened, American aid became more and more vital. In the spring of 1940, British Intelligence Service sent Stephenson to America, posing as an ordinary businessman, but under orders to develop a secret British organization, working in liaison with the FBI, that would counter enemy subversive efforts in the Western Hemisphere. At the same time, Churchill suggested that he promote cooperation with the Allied cause in the isolation-minded United States. Stephenson had not met Colonel Donovan previously in London, but knew that his views were sympathetic; and he decided to arrange a confidential meeting with the Colonel on his arrival in Washington.

Their meeting was deferred due to a sudden tragedy, perhaps the most crushing in Donovan's life. His daughter Patricia, still known affectionately as "the Daughter of the Regiment," was just twenty-three, a striking brunette with her mother's grace and quiet charm and her father's driving energy. Donovan worshiped her, and there was an understanding between them which went beyond words, a silent communion of thought and feeling expressed in a smile or the light pressure of a hand. Father Vincent Donovan put it simply: "Pat was his life."

---

[4] H. Montgomery Hyde, *Room 3603* (New York, 1963).

Patricia, who was studying at Georgetown, had driven to North Carolina to visit friends over the weekend, and she started back to Washington on Monday in a pelting April rain. The red Virginia mud had washed over the highway in places, creating patches of treacherous slick. As she rounded a curve near Fredericksburg the car skidded out of control and crashed against a tree. Passing motorists pulled her from the wreck and rushed her to a hospital. She died two hours later without regaining consciousness.

Colonel Donovan, notified in New York of the accident, took the first train to Washington. An associate met him at Union Station with the news of her death. He was stunned by the senseless loss — it would be months before he could bring himself to mention Patricia's name — but his immediate concern was for his wife, who was cruising in the Pacific. Ruth Donovan was located by wireless, and in an effort to ease the shock Donovan flew to Los Angeles to meet her and accompany her home for the funeral services. To help overcome the emptiness in his heart, he forced himself to devote all his thoughts to the impending world crisis.

3

That crisis was fast taking shape. On May 10, 1940, Hitler followed his successful conquest of Norway by striking without warning at Belgium and Holland and Luxembourg. Public discontent in England with the Chamberlain government, already aggravated by its woeful mishandling of the Norwegian campaign, had become so intense that Chamberlain resigned the same day, and the King appointed Winston Churchill the new Prime Minister. One of Churchill's first acts was to cable President Roosevelt, urgently requesting fifty of America's overage destroyers; and as added insurance he asked William Stephenson, now back in England, to return to Washington at once and personally explain Britain's dire need to the President. Churchill's primary desire was "to discourage any complacent assumption on the United States' part that they will pick up the debris of the British Empire. . . . On the contrary, they run the terrible risk that their own sea-power will be completely overmatched. Moreover, island and naval bases to hold the United States in awe would certainly be claimed by the Nazis. If we go down, Hitler has a very good chance of conquering the world."[5]

Stephenson arrived in the United States at one of Britain's blackest hours. The Allies had been unable to match the power and punch of the German attack on the Low Countries, and the main body of the British forces, the flower of her professional army, had been forced to retreat to the open beaches of Dunkirk, trapped between the English Channel and the pursuing enemy. America thrilled vicariously to accounts of the courageous volunteer flotilla of private sailboats and small pleasure craft which crossed the Channel repeatedly to rescue the troops from what seemed like certain annihilation. Meantime the Nazi *blitzkrieg* swept on almost unopposed into northern France, and a few days later Italy joined the war and invaded France from the south. Roosevelt interrupted a prepared radio broadcast to insert a barbed comment: "The hand that held the dagger has struck it into the back of its neighbor." In short order, Paris fell to Hitler, doddering Marshal Pétain became head of the provisional French government, and on June 22, France and Germany signed an armistice at Compiègne.

A mood of defeatism gripped Washington. The collapse of France left Britain alone, her arsenals empty, her skies filled with Luftwaffe bombers raining devastation on her cities. Churchill could offer his people nothing but "blood, toil, tears and sweat." The White House official circle was pessimistic about British chances of survival, and Joseph P. Kennedy, American Ambassador to the Court of St. James's, advised President Roosevelt vehemently against "holding the bag in a war in which the Allies expect to be beaten."[6] Stephenson reminded the President that "the British do not kneel easily," but Roosevelt felt that a transfer of American naval vessels would require the assent of Congress, and politically the time was not opportune. Roosevelt was facing a campaign for reelection, and had to act with circumspection; but he gave evidence of his sympathy for the British cause by forming a bi-

[5] Hyde, *Room 3603.*
[6] Robert E. Sherwood, *The White House Papers of Harry Hopkins* (New York 1948).

partisan cabinet, replacing isolationist members with prominent Republicans who advocated intervention. Publisher Frank Knox became the new Secretary of the Navy. Roosevelt seriously considered appointing Colonel Donovan as Secretary of War — "Frankly I should like to have him in the Cabinet," he told Knox, "not only for his own ability, but also to repair in a sense the very great injustice done him by President Hoover"[7] — but he yielded at last to the persuasion of Justice Felix Frankfurter and named seventy-two-year-old Henry L. Stimson to the post.[8]

Stephenson turned instinctively to Colonel Donovan in his dilemma, feeling that he might accomplish more than any of the official channels to the White House. "Donovan, by virtue of his very independence of thought and action, inevitably had his critics," Stephenson told his biographer Montgomery Hyde, "but there were few among them who would deny the credit due him for having reached a correct appraisal of the international situation in the summer of 1940. . . . Immediately after the fall of France, not even the President himself could feel assured that aid to Britain was not to be wasted. . . . The majority of his Cabinet was inclined to the same conclusion, which found vigorous expression in organized isolationism led by men like Lindbergh and Senator Wheeler. Donovan, on the other hand, was convinced that, granted sufficient aid from the United States, Britain could and would survive [and] American material assistance would not be improvident charity but a sound investment."

Colonel Donovan met with his friends Knox and Stimson to search for a possible formula which would cover the transfer of fifty four-stackers now in mothballs. The only hope, they agreed, was to convince the President that he would be justified in bypassing Congress and sanctioning the transfer by executive decree. Knox proposed that Donovan should visit Britain to view present conditions and estimate her chances of holding up against Hitler, and give the President a firsthand report. Roosevelt welcomed the idea, and suggested that Donovan should travel as his unofficial personal representative; and on July 14, 1940, the

[7] Elliott Roosevelt (ed.), *The Roosevelt Letters* (New York, 1950).
[8] Forrest C. Pogue, *George C. Marshall,* Vol. II (New York, 1965).

Colonel boarded a Flying Clipper for Lisbon, ostensibly on private business, and arrived in London at the onset of the Nazi aerial bombardment which came to be called the Battle of Britain.[9]

He was widely respected in England as a World War I hero, and enjoyed the confidence of the British high command, and he was given every opportunity to conduct an impartial investigation. "I marshaled my friends in high places to bare their breasts," Stephenson recalled. "He was received in audience by the King, and he had ample time with Churchill and members of the Cabinet. He visited war factories and military training centers. He spoke with industrial leaders, and with representatives of all classes of the community. He learned what was true — that Churchill, defying the Nazis, was no mere bold facade, but the very heart of Britain which was still beating strongly." Colonel Donovan also talked with military attachés at the Embassy, including Lieutenant Colonel Carl Spaatz (later Chief of Staff of the U.S. Air Force) who said American Air Corps observers were convinced that the Germans could not beat the RAF, and that Hitler would not attempt an invasion until he controlled the air.

Because he was Bill Donovan, the British showed him things no American had seen before: their top-secret invention of radar, their newest interceptor planes, their coastal defenses. He was made privy to some of Britain's ingenious propaganda devices, including the carefully planted rumor that a system of underwater pipelines could turn every beach and cove into a sea of flaming oil in case of German landings. They unlocked their safes, and initiated him into the mysteries of the Secret Intelligence Service (SIS) and the techniques of unorthodox warfare. He was particularly intrigued by their use of captured German spies as counteragents and playbacks. "I suppose one of the reasons that Britain wasn't invaded," he concluded, "was because of her success in nabbing all the agents that came in, and turning them around to furnish the false intelligence that the enemy was using." His observations of British counterintelligence and unorthodox operations were filed in his

---

[9] Ambassador Joseph Kennedy learned of the visit from Edward Ansel Mowrer, a newspaperman, before he received official notification from Washington.

THE SECRETARY OF STATE

WASHINGTON

July 11, 1940.

To the American

      Diplomatic and Consular Officers.

Sirs:

      I take pleasure in introducing
to you Colonel William J. Donovan,
United States Army, Retired, who is
about to proceed abroad.

      I cordially bespeak for Colonel
Donovan such courtesies and assistance
as you may be able to render, consistently with your official duties.

      Very truly yours,

Cordell Hull

"The effects in Europe were profound." These letters of introduction accompanied WJD on his dramatic trip to England on July 14, 1940.

July 11, 1940.

My dear Beaverbrook:

This letter will be presented to you
by Colonel William J. Donovan, an intimate friend of
mine at whose house, you will remember, we met some time
ago. Colonel Donovan is abroad on an official mission
for me, with the full approval of the President of the
United States.

I shall deeply appreciate anything
you can do to promote the purpose of Colonel Donovan's
mission, and I hope you will be as frank in talking to
him as you might be in talking to me if I were able to go
over myself.

With best wishes, I am,

Yours sincerely,

Frank Knox

The Right Honorable
    Lord Beaverbrook,
Minister of Aircraft Production,
London, England.

memory, later to be incorporated into the structure of America's own wartime organization, the OSS.

On the basis of what he had seen, Colonel Donovan stated unequivocally to President Roosevelt that Britain would hold, and recommended the prompt transfer of the requested destroyers. As a lawyer, he argued that there was no need for the President to submit the plan to Congress, if it were part of a deal to swap American destroyers for naval bases on British territory. Wendell Willkie, who had just become the Republican candidate for President, promised Roosevelt that he would not make a campaign issue of the transfer; and the historic destroyers-for-bases agreement was drafted, providing for a ninety-nine-year lease of British bases in Bermuda, the Caribbean and Newfoundland, in exchange for fifty overage destroyers and a pledge that the British Navy would never be surrendered to the Germans or sunk. Churchill noted: "The effects in Europe were profound."

In October, shortly before the national election, Colonel Donovan was invited to accompany Navy Secretary Knox on an inspection tour of the Pacific Islands. Nearing Hawaii, they took off from the aircraft carrier *Enterprise* and flew the remaining hundred miles to Pearl Harbor. Donovan observed as they landed: "If we can do this, the Japs can do it too."

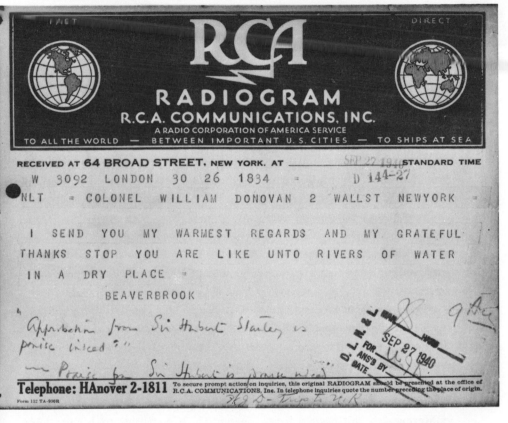

Lord Beaverbrook likens WJD's successful mission to England to "rivers of waters in a dry place." (Cable is dated September 27, 1940.)

III

ROOSEVELT WAS REELECTED for a third term in November, after a heated and sometimes acrimonious campaign. As the tempo of debate increased, Willkie yielded to political pressure and predicted that his opponent, if returned to the White House, would bring the nation into war by the following spring. Goaded into a response, Roosevelt made the rash pledge in a Boston speech: "I have said this before, but I shall say it again and again and again: Your boys are not going to be sent into any foreign wars." It was a promise he would be reminded of again and again and again.

With the election out of the way, the President could address himself once more to the problem of furnishing aid to Britain. Churchill had warned him that England was nearing the end of the dollar resources necessary to purchase supplies under the old cash-and-carry arrangement; and Roosevelt, a master of political legerdemain, pulled out of his sleeve the concept of lend-lease. In explaining the measure at a press conference, he hit upon a happy metaphor. If a neighbor's house were on fire, he said, you would not waste time arguing about the cost of the hose; you would put the fire out, and get the hose back afterward. He cushioned the public for the blow with another of his fireside chats which introduced the memorable phrase: "We must be the great arsenal of Democracy." In January, 1941, the administration introduced its controversial bill in Congress, which would authorize the President to "sell, transfer, exchange, lend, lease, or otherwise dispose of war materials for the government of any country whose defense the President deems vital to the defense of the United States."

Now the isolationists joined ranks to oppose what they held was a direct infringement of America's neutrality. "The lend-lease-give program," said Senator Burton K. Wheeler, "is the New Deal's Triple-A foreign policy; it will plow under every fourth American boy on foreign battlefields for the benefit of a decayed British Empire." Roosevelt retorted that Wheeler's statement was "the rottenest thing that has been said in public life in my generation." Ex-Ambassador Joseph Kennedy had been recalled from London, and John Winant had taken his place at the Court of St. James's; and Kennedy joined the bitter fight against the lend-lease proposal, in Congressional testimony and personal radio broadcasts, claiming that "this is not our war" and that the country did not face "such immediate danger as to justify this surrender of the authority and responsibility of the Congress." His attacks became so intemperate that the New York newspaper *PM* published an interview with its London correspondent Ben Robertson, in which Robertson explained that the former ambassador was a "confirmed pessimist and would sell anything short. . . . We used to laugh about the fact that Kennedy stayed in the country most of the time" during the air raids. Asked how the English public felt about Kennedy's defeatist attitude, Robertson replied that they found him something of a novelty "with all his Irishness and his nine children. And they had never had a liquor dealer before as the ambassador of a great power. . . . You know Kennedy always wanted people to use his full title — His Excellency, the United States Ambassador to the Court of St. James's. He looked well in a top hat." He added: "It was felt [by the correspondents] that the difference of opinion between Kennedy and the military and naval aides at the Embassy was the reason Washington sent Donovan over — in order to see who was right. We know Kennedy was furious about Donovan's arrival. We certainly know what Donovan's conclusions were. They weren't Kennedy's at all." Donovan went everywhere, he said, seeking information on which to base his report, but "I never saw Kennedy in Dover at all, and I never saw his picture taken in any of the army camps. . . . He was in the country."[10]

While the lend-lease debate raged, Germany's submarines and armed

[10] *PM*, January 19, 1941.

raiders were taking an increasingly heavy toll of British shipping. On November 3, 1940, Churchill confided to Roosevelt that during the past five weeks the losses had reached a total of 420,300 tons, and predicted it would be "in shipping, and in the power to transport across the oceans, particularly the Atlantic Ocean, that in 1941 the crunch of the whole war will be found."

Colonel Donovan, at a private conference with Knox and Stimson and Attorney General Jackson, argued that the United States Navy should perform convoy duty across the Atlantic, if only as a means of playing for time and keeping Britain in the war until American preparedness was sufficiently advanced to meet the German challenge. The other conferees felt they needed more evidence before advising President Roosevelt to protect the Atlantic lifeline at the risk of open hostilities; and Donovan volunteered to seek that evidence by making another visit to London and to the Mediterranean, where the threat to British vessels had recently become acute due to Italy's invasion of Greece. To avoid involving the President, it was agreed that Donovan should travel on his mission as an official representative of the Navy Department.

Despite Donovan's efforts to remain anonymous, the curiosity of the press had been whetted by his unexplained trips overseas. "Man of Mystery," the papers began to call him. "America's Secret Envoy." "Silent Confidante of FDR." When he refused to discuss his duties, a note of irritation crept into the newspaper stories, a foretaste of the ridicule which would be heaped on OSS. "Rarely has one of these mysterious emissaries failed to cause difficulties for the foreign service," Arthur Krock wrote testily in the New York *Times;* and Westbrook Pegler jeered that "Our Colonel Wild Bill Donovan . . . seems to have a 50-trip ticket on the clippers, which he must use up in a certain time or forfeit the remainder." In order that his current journey would be undetected, Donovan booked passage on a Bermuda clipper under the alias of Donald Williams, but alert newsmen at the Baltimore airport spotted the telltale initials "WJD" which he had forgotten to remove from his luggage, and that night's headlines proclaimed: "Donovan Secretly Flies to Europe — Buffalonian Goes on Another 'Mystery Mission.' " (During the war, Donovan described his slip to an OSS infiltration group as an example of how one neglected detail can ruin a cover story.) He had hoped to elude the press by transferring at Bermuda to a Lisbon-bound plane, and Pan-American Airways officials told the *Times* with a straight face that "they did not know whether Colonel Donovan was among the passengers." Reporters recognized him on his arrival in London, however, and pressed him for a statement. "I can't say anything about why I am here," he pleaded, "but please don't make me mysterious or important."[11]

William Stephenson, who accompanied Colonel Donovan as far as London, had cabled ahead to British Intelligence Headquarters that "he can play a great role, perhaps a vital one, but it may not be consistent with orthodox diplomacy nor confined in its channels." Donovan on his arrival was given the fullest cooperation – he assured Stephenson that "the red carpet was thicker and wider than I thought it possible to lay" – and talked freely with Prime Minister Churchill, Colonel Menzies of SIS, and other key officials. After five days of firsthand observation, he told a London correspondent for the New York *Times:* "When I returned to the United States last August after a previous visit, I said I found the British 'resolute and courageous.' Now I would add 'confident.' "

Churchill arranged for Brigadier Vivian Dykes, assistant secretary to the cabinet, to accompany Colonel Donovan to the Middle East, and the director of Naval Intelligence sent a signal to Admiral Sir Andrew Cunningham, Commander-in-Chief of the Mediterranean Fleet, stressing the importance of the tour and explaining: "Donovan exercises controlling influence over Knox, strong influence over Stimson, friendly advisory influence over President and Hull. . . . Being a Republican, a Catholic, and of Irish descent, he has following of the strongest opposition to the Administration. . . . There is no doubt that we can achieve infinitely more through Donovan than through any other individual."

Donovan's departure from London evoked a new rash of speculation in the American press. Columnist Drew Pearson confidently predicted: "Inside fact on the mystery trip of Col. Donovan to Europe is that his

[11] New York *Herald Tribune*, December 17, 1940.

real mission is . . . to see his old World War friend Marshal Weygand, commanding the French army in Africa." The New York *Post*, in a dispatch labeled "Exclusive," hinted that Donovan was bearing an olive branch to Vichy France. Calmly ignoring the furor of conjecture and keeping his plans to himself, the Colonel flew with Viscount Dykes in a British bomber to confer with Admiral Cunningham, and then moved on to Greece to meet with General Sir Archibald Wavell, British Middle East Commander. A survey of the Albanian front convinced him that American supplies must be made available if Britain's crucial strategic position were to be maintained, and that the United States should work out some immediate arrangement with the Free French in order to deny North Africa to the Axis.

"People are too prone to think of the Mediterranean as an east-west channel for shipping," he advised President Roosevelt in a confidential memorandum. "It should be thought of primarily as a no-man's land between Europe and Africa, with two great forces facing each other from the north and south. Germany controls, either directly or indirectly, most of the northern battle-line on the continent of Europe. It is imperative for the British — or the British and the Americans — to control the southern front along the Mediterranean shore of Africa."

Churchill was anxious to find some means of upsetting Hitler's timetable for the subjugation of the Balkan countries; and, at the Prime Minister's personal request, Colonel Donovan extended his tour to Bulgaria and Yugoslavia. Though he was unable to persuade King Boris and the Bulgarian leaders to abandon their pro-German policy, his arguments caused them to hesitate before allowing German troops to pass unrestricted through Bulgaria in order to attack the British forces who were seeking to gain a foothold in Greece. Churchill had indicated he would be happy with a delay of twenty-four hours; Donovan secured a delay of eight days. After his conversation with Boris in Sofia, he reported to Roosevelt:

"The King said to me: 'I must avoid a head-on collision with a stronger nation; I must not run the risk of having my country overrun without first attempting to reduce the shock.' . . . I said 'Of course I understand, but your great difficulty is that in Hitler you are dealing

WJD at the Albanian front during the Greco-Italian War, January, 1941.

WJD with foreign correspondents in the Balkans, early in 1941.

with a man who has never kept his word.' To that he shrugged his shoulders. . . . Before leaving, I said 'I wish you would tell me of your meeting with the officers who were involved in the conspiracy to kill you.' He described them being with him from 2:15 in the morning until after 6 A.M. He said that he watched the clock and fought for time with them, because he knew that a conspiracy is strong in the dark but as daylight comes its strength is diluted. I then said 'I now understand your whole manner of dealing with Hitler; that you are seeking, by gaining time, to dilute the force of his demands. I hope you are right about this and that your attempt to deal with him in this way will not meet the fate of others.' "

Donovan's appraisal of Boris in his private diary was characteristically penetrating. "In estimating his personality, I should say that he is idealistic, so much so as to have an over-belief in the virtue of peace; that he is honest, shy; but I fear he has been so successful in maneuver that he places too great reliance upon it, even when the time has been reached when decision and not maneuver is essential."

The Nazis were becoming increasingly suspicious of the Colonel's furtive activities, and a German newspaper termed his mission "an impudent act" by President Roosevelt. Hitler's agents shadowed him during his visit to Sofia, and even followed him into the Royal Palace, stealing the diplomatic passport from his overcoat during a conference with the King. The palace staff searched for it in vain, and the Orient Express was held up for twenty minutes while the American legation arranged for him to cross the border into Yugoslavia, where a duplicate passport would be issued. From Berlin, Dr. Goebbels gave worldwide publicity to the incident, adding that the American State Department had ordered Wild Bill Donovan's immediate recall "because he dishonored his military uniform and sullied his diplomatic status by getting himself into a state of complete drunkenness in a Sofia cabaret. . . . He will be arraigned before the Special Court."

When Colonel Donovan reached Yugoslavia, he found the Regent Prince Paul and his government about to join the Axis. President Roosevelt sent a personal message to the Colonel in Belgrade, suggesting that some means should be found of impressing the Yugoslavian leaders that "the United States is looking not merely to the present but to the future, and any nation which tamely submits on the grounds of being quickly overrun would receive less sympathy from the world than a nation which resists, even if this resistance can be continued for only a few weeks." When Donovan tried to convey the President's view, he was informed that the Prime Minister and Defense Minister had already been summoned by Hitler to Berchtesgaden and had committed their country to collaboration with Germany. Learning through private sources that Yugoslav Air Force General Simovic and a group of Serbian officers had formed an underground opposition to Nazi domination, Donovan paid a clandestine visit to the General at the Air Force headquarters across the river from Belgrade in Zemun. Shortly after his visit, on March 25, the Yugoslav ministers signed the Axis pact in Vienna. Simovic organized a revolution two days later which led to the overthrow of Prince Paul and his government. Hitler was forced to countermand an order moving three panzer divisions to Poland, and turn his full attention to Yugoslavia.*

Roosevelt's "mystery man" proceeded to Istanbul, where he conferred with Turkish officials and army leaders and brought encouragement from President Roosevelt for Turkey to stand fast against any Axis threats, assuring them that the United States was determined not to see Britain lose the war. Just before he boarded the train at Ankara for a trip through Syria to Jerusalem, an official from the French Embassy, acting on last-minute instructions from the Vichy government, informed him that the Syrian visa on his new passport had been canceled. Undismayed, Donovan detoured around Syria and was flown to Jerusalem, where he "found battalions of Arabs and Jews serving together, their political differences submerged in the need of common defense." From Palestine he continued to Egypt. After an inspection of the British front in Libya, he cabled a significant forecast from Cairo:

"If deterred by the magnitude of her task, Germany may abandon the attempt at invasion of England and, while continuing to strike at

---

* Churchill stated later that Donovan's visit with Simovic delayed Hitler's attack on Russia by a fatal five weeks, and as a result he could not carry out his campaign the first year, a failure which led to Hitler's ultimate downfall.

British shipping, may gamble on over-running in a short war not only all the Balkans but Turkey as well. Russia's fear of this German encirclement may give us the one chance of securing her support. . . . Germany deals with all theatres of operations as constituting but one strategic front from the Atlantic to the Pacific, of which the Mediterranean from Spain to the Black Sea is an integral part. Whatever she does in one theatre has its intended repercussions in another. For example, she may induce Japan to strike in the Far East simultaneously with any offensive she may make in the West."

The indefatigable Colonel came home by way of Baghdad, Africa, Malta, Gibraltar, Spain, and Portugal, arriving in Washington on March 18, 1941, after an odyssey of twenty-five thousand miles. Showing no sign of fatigue, he reported his findings at an early breakfast with President Roosevelt, who had just received a message of thanks from Churchill for "the magnificent work done by Donovan in his prolonged tour of the Balkans and the Middle East. He has carried with him throughout an animating, heart-warming flame." Following their breakfast conference, Roosevelt issued a proclamation that the Red Sea and the Persian Gulf were no longer combat zones from which American vessels were excluded by the Neutrality Act, and soon afterward the U.S. Navy assumed the duty of convoy protection for British shipping across the Atlantic.

A week after his return, at the President's request, Colonel Donovan made a coast-to-coast broadcast over three major networks, which Secretary of the Navy Knox, who introduced him, called "an unofficial report to the American people" on his recent secret mission. Donovan paid particular tribute in his talk to the bravery of the Greeks, fighting almost bare-handed against Mussolini's mechanized forces. "They really made their fight there with a rock, a mule, and a gun: a rock for a parapet, a mule to carry supplies, and a gun for a weapon. . . . The Greeks believed not in their machines, but in themselves. As I went through the front, I asked the Greek soldiers whether they were afraid to meet the Germans if they should come against them, and they answered that they were not afraid."

He explained that the Lend-Lease Act transformed the armies in

China, the Middle East and England, in effect, into American "expeditionary forces" which the United States must support with material aid. Pointing out that the German counterblockade was attempting to "throttle the American supply," he asked: "Are we going to deliver the goods? This question must be answered now. Are we prepared to take the chance? For there is a chance. There is a danger, and whatever we do we must recognize that the danger of attack exists. . . . As a self-governing people, we must determine for ourselves what is the right thing for us to do. And, having decided, we must then accept the consequences."

Describing Germany as "a formidable, a resourceful and a ruthless foe . . . aiming at absolute domination of the world," he warned: "Don't underrate her. If we do, we deceive ourselves. Her victories have brought her new military and industrial strength. She got the jump at the start of the war. . . . Her greatest gains have been through fear. Fear of the might of her war machine. She has played upon that fear, and her recent diplomatic victories are its product." But, he added, "there is a moral force that, in the long run, is stronger than any machine."

His broadcast concluded: "We have no choice as to whether or not we will be attacked. That choice is Hitler's and he has already made it — not for Europe only, but for Africa and Asia and the world. Our only choice is to decide whether or not we will resist. And to decide in time: while resistance is still possible, while others are still alive to stand beside us."

Dr. Goebbels stepped up the Axis propaganda barrage after Colonel Donovan's broadcast. The controlled German press denounced "that 'smart Aleck' Donovan" who "proved such a nincompoop that they [Knox and Stimson] must befuddle the American public with vocal strength rather than logic; that's the way they sing in chorus. . . . We have no thought whatsoever of attacking the American people." Fascist newspapers in Italy called him "Washington's No. 2 Agent Provocateur" — Donovan, when told, asked "Who's No. 1?" — and blamed him for the Belgrade revolution which overthrew Prince Paul and brought about the "ruin" of Yugoslavia. "It was not for nothing that Col.

Donovan, this 'ersatz' ambassador of President Roosevelt, had talks with Gen. Simovic, organizer of the coup d'etat."

Isolationist papers in the United States echoed the Axis line. Colonel McCormick's Chicago *Tribune*, mouthpiece of the America First Committee, emphasized that during his mission "Colonel Donovan was not a state department representative. . . . he did not have the advantage of consultation in advance with American diplomatic experts or of any coaching for a mission of such scope as his turned out to be." Demaree Bess, in the *Saturday Evening Post*, accused Donovan of making promises which could not have been kept. "In the Balkans," he wrote, "Colonel Donovan gave Bulgarian diplomats the idea that he had authority as a spokesman. . . . Bulgarians interpreted [his] statement as something very much like an ultimatum." And George Sokolsky, perched atop his daily column like a sulky St. Simeon Stylites, deplored the fact that "Wild Bill" was "following a long line of unofficial diplomats from the United States, who have done more than their share to keep the world disturbed. . . . This disease of irresponsible promises may be as devastating to our friends as Hitler's victories."

Colonel Donovan's only comment was: "It's always reassuring to find you've made the right enemies."

2

Propaganda, to Hitler, was neither a secret weapon nor a new one. He merely modernized it, regimented it, and coordinated it under the guidance of Dr. Goebbels, whose fine hand reached into every country of strategic importance to the Axis. "As, in the military sphere, the airplane has become a combat weapon," Hitler wrote, "so has the press become a similar weapon in the sphere of thought." After his surprise attack on his former ally Russia on June 22, 1941, Der Führer boasted: "The organization of our press has been truly a success. . . . We have eliminated the conception of political freedom. It's enough for me to send for Goebbels and inform him of my point of view, and I know the next day all the German newspapers will echo my ideas. I am proud to think that with such collaborators at my side, I can make a sheer turnabout, as I did on 22nd of June last, without anyone's moving a muscle."

Colonel Donovan had long been aware of Hitler's use of planned propaganda to subvert Allied morale. On his return from his earlier mission to London in 1940, he and Edgar Ansel Mowrer, one of Washington's most distinguished foreign correspondents, had collaborated on a series of articles for Frank Knox's Chicago *Daily News*, revealing the scope of Nazi fifth column activities. "The masterpiece of the fifth column," they stated, "was unquestionably the French debacle. . . . Hitler terrified the French soldiers by his noise-making machines; he demoralized the officers by the surprise and power of his attacks; he bewildered the Generals by the daring of his strategic conceptions; he troubled the entire population by his radio propaganda which insisted that France was being betrayed by Britain and by the French warmongers. He spread horrible rumors through villages, issued fearsome reports by wireless, and then, when the population had congested the roads in their fright, machine-gunned them to heighten their panic."

Donovan's second visit to Britain and the Middle East persuaded him further that the United States should engage at once in a campaign of counterpropaganda to offset the Nazi radio offensive. His trip alerted him to another and greater need. Under the guidance of Air Commodore Sir Frank Nelson, chief of Special Operations, Executive (SOE), Colonel Donovan had been shown the various SO stations, including the propaganda division (later PWE) which operated from Woburn Abbey in Bedfordshire, and the sabotage and subversion branch (SO-2) whose inconspicuous headquarters were located, appropriately, in Sherlock Holmes's Baker Street. It was imperative, he was convinced, to establish an agency in the United States which would prepare for similar unorthodox activities in the event of war.

In addition to these functions, he recommended to President Roosevelt, the proposed agency should seek to centralize the intelligence gathered by the scattered and uncoordinated intelligence services in Washington. There were currently eight separate fact-finding units in the government: Army G-2, Navy ONI, the Justice Department's Federal Bureau of Investigation, the State Department's overseas attachés, the

Department of Commerce's customs inspectors, the Treasury Department's Secret Service, the Labor Department's Immigration Service, and the Federal Communications Commission, whose monitoring of foreign broadcasts ran to nearly a million words a day. All their reports were either placed undigested on the President's desk, or were excerpted by each department with an eye to its own particular interests. The sheer volume of raw information, the often conflicting interpretations, the lack of any impartial evaluation rendered the intelligence all but useless.

President Roosevelt welcomed the suggestion of a single agency which would serve as a clearinghouse for all intelligence, as well as an organ of counterpropaganda and a training center for what were euphemistically called "special operations," and invited Colonel Donovan to be its head. At first Donovan was reluctant. His World War I antipathy to desk generalship was still strong, and though he was now fifty-eight he prefered to lead a combat division; but the prospect of organizing a unified intelligence, sabotage and subversive warfare unit, the first in American history, was most tempting. After a lengthy discussion with the President, he agreed to form the new agency, under the somewhat misleading title of Coordinator of Information.

The appointment of Colonel Donovan as director of COI was formally announced by executive order on July 11, 1941, and his duties were defined in Roosevelt's own words: "To collect and analyze all information and data which may bear upon national security, to correlate such information and data and make the same available to the President and to such departments and officials of the Government as the President may determine, and to carry out when requested by the President such supplementary activities as may facilitate the securing of information important for national security not now available to the Government."

The directive was purposely obscure in its wording, due to the secret and potentially offensive nature of the agency's functions; and the other intelligence organizations, jealous of their prerogatives, took advantage of the vague phraseology to set loose a flock of rumors that Donovan was to be the Heinrich Himmler of an American Gestapo, the Goebbels of a controlled press, a super-spy over Hoover's G-men and the Army and Navy, the head of a grand strategy board which would dictate even to the General Staff. In vain the President reiterated that Donovan's work "is not intended to supersede or to duplicate or to involve any direction of or interference with the activities of the General Staff, the regular intelligence services, the Federal Bureau of Investigation, or of other existing agencies."[12] The bureaucratic war was on.

It was a war all too familiar to Washington, the dog-eat-dog struggle among government departments to preserve their own areas of power. J. Edgar Hoover, perhaps fearing that the COI would steal the spotlight long enjoyed by his FBI, was not satisfied until he had Roosevelt's word that Donovan would be expressly forbidden to conduct any espionage activities within the United States. Nelson Rockefeller, chairman of the State Department's Committee to Coordinate Inter-American Affairs (once called, even more pretentiously, the Committee on Cultural and Commercial Relations Between North and South America) echoed the FBI in seeking assurance that Donovan would likewise be excluded from his established bailiwick in the southern hemisphere. Major General George V. Strong, later chief of Army G-2, could not understand that G-2 represented tactical military intelligence and COI strategic intelligence of all kinds; and Strong therefore felt there was a definite conflict of interests. He vigorously fought Roosevelt's proposal that Colonel Donovan should be returned to active duty with the rank of major general — a grade more commensurate with his new duties — and offered the irrelevant argument that "Wild Bill" was too independent to be a team player. "If there's a loose football on the field," Strong protested, "he'll pick it up and run with it." Isolationist senators such as Burton Wheeler and Robert Taft likewise opposed Donovan's advance in rank, and Taft rose on the Senate floor to warn his colleagues of the danger of White House control of intelligence and investigative units. Realizing that the suggested promotion might cause a prolonged Congressional fight, Roosevelt yielded, at least for the moment, and Donovan took over as head of COI in a civilian capacity.

He set up shop without fanfare first in a cramped office in the Bu-

12 New York *Times*, December 7, 1941.

reau of the Budget and then in the State Department building, and recruited a staff of seven assistants who had to reach over the Colonel's shoulder to use the single telephone on his desk. No press conference was held, no public announcement ever issued. Washington newsmen, accustomed to the extravagant statements of objectives which launched the average Washington agency, could not understand Donovan's aversion to ballyhoo, and were inclined to sneer that " 'Wild Bill' has become 'Hush Hush Bill.' " Frank R. Kent rallied to his defense in a dispatch to the New York *Sun:* "There is a disposition in certain quarters to refer derisively to Colonel William J. Donovan as the 'Mystery Man' . . . because he has not gone into elaborate detail as to what he intends to do or how. . . . The stage has been reached where many public men here would feel less helpless without their pants than without their press agent. That being so, it is easy to understand that Colonel Donovan's ban against press conferences should excite distrust." He pointed out that "the nickname of 'Wild Bill' conveys an utterly inaccurate idea of the man. Shrewd, studious, competent, controlled, mild mannered and soft spoken, he is always aware of the consequences of his words and deeds. There is nothing reckless about him. But there is in him a cold force and an unflinching determination which, combined with real ability, make him a very effective citizen indeed. . . . For the kind of work he is doing, public statement would be worse than foolish."

The original concept of the COI was the result of Donovan's factfinding trip to England and of Roosevelt's quick appreciation of America's need for a unified intelligence-gathering agency, with a capacity to engage in unorthodox warfare. Among the elements was Research and Analysis work designed to bring expert knowledge and training to the task of evaluating all incoming intelligence, and Foreign Broadcasting, which in turn would have full research assistance. Heading Donovan's early staff was Colonel Edward Buxton, a close friend since World War I days, who left his business in Rhode Island to become the deputy director of the COI. James Murphy, formerly Donovan's secretary when he was Assistant Attorney General, was made his personal assistant. Dr. William L. Langer, distinguished Coolidge professor of history at Harvard, who had seen action as a sergeant in the Argonne and at St.-Mihiel, headed the key Research and Analysis division, following the resignation of Dr. James Phinney Baxter, president of Williams College and a brilliant administrator, who served briefly as the first chief of R&A. Dr. Edward S. Mason, later director of Harvard's School of Public Administration and a prominent economist, Dean Calvin Hoover of Duke University, the late Dr. Edward Meade of Princeton's Institute for Advanced Study, and Dr. Henry Field, curator of physical anthropology at Chicago's Field Museum, joined Donovan's expanding unit. David K. E. Bruce, later to be named U.S. ambassador to the Court of St. James's, came to Washington to head COI's Special Activities Bruce (SAB), the agency's secret intelligence branch; and M. P. Goodfellow left his newspaper business to head the sabotage branch (Special Activities Goodfellow — or SAG). (Both these branches existed in the training stages only, since the U.S. was not yet at war.) Robert E. Sherwood, noted American playwright and an intimate of President Roosevelt, assumed responsibility for the Foreign Information Service (FIS).

By October of 1941 the research staff (still under Dr. Baxter at the time) had already increased to almost two hundred, eventually to become the largest collection of eminent educators and scholars ever gathered together in a single government agency. R&A skimmed the cream of the social science departments in all the universities, including specialists in every field of intelligence. Geographers furnished information on foreign terrain and climate for American policy planners; psychologists probed Axis broadcasts for hidden meanings; economists sifted German newspapers in search of figures on Nazi war production; historians provided depth and background to world events. By the war's end, R&A had enlisted over sixteen hundred social scientists from Washington alone, a national super-university unequaled before or since.

As the agency expanded, it moved to larger quarters in Washington's Apex Building on Pennsylvania Avenue, its offices isolated from the public and heavily guarded. Most of Dr. Langer's research staff continued to work in the Library of Congress; and Robert Sherwood opened a branch office of COI at 270 Madison Avenue in New York to handle his burgeoning overseas propaganda program. Joseph Barnes, Berlin correspondent for the New York *Herald Tribune,* was made chief of the news and editorial section of FIS, aided by such experienced newsmen as Wallace Deull of the Chicago *Daily News* and Edmund Taylor of the Chicago *Tribune*, author of *The Strategy of Terror*. Six short-wave listening posts monitored Nazi propaganda day and night, enabling government officials to answer false charges promptly. James Reston in the New York *Times* called COI "an official worldwide 'information service' designed to crack the Axis news monopoly on the continent of Europe, and neutralize Germany's lie campaign against the United States."

Spotting the latest notables recruited for the agency became a popular newspaper game. "Among Donovan's constellation of literary men," Drew Pearson shrilled, "are Thornton Wilder, author of *The Bridge of San Luis Rey*, and Stephen Vincent Benét, author of *John Brown's Body*." The New York *Sun* scooped its competitors by reporting the addition of James P. Warburg, one of President Roosevelt's early advisers. "Capt. James Roosevelt of the United States Marine Corps, eldest son of the President," the Washington *Times Herald* announced, "reported for duty yesterday as an aide to Col. William J. 'Wild Bill' Donovan. He will act as a military advisor and liaison officer between the information office and the other branches of the government."

Even Jimmy Roosevelt's prestigious name could not overcome the widespread hostility to the new agency. Rival service departments declined to furnish COI with the secret data necessary to produce a complete intelligence picture for the President, and Colonel Donovan was without authority to force their full cooperation. The State Department proved reluctant to risk identification with an agency whose covert functions might endanger United States neutrality and, despite initial promises, balked at providing the needed "cover" for COI operators abroad. Still more frustrating, the crucial counterpropaganda broadcasts were hampered by the lack of government short-wave facilities; broadcasting was a private industry, and, short of an outright declaration of war, the owners of the stations could not be coerced or removed. Frequently they declined to follow directives, or to send out material the agency furnished.

In his dilemma, Colonel Donovan turned for help to British Intelligence. William Stephenson had developed an undercover organization in the United States, called British Security Coordinator (BSC), which was staffed with experienced officers, and they supplied the pioneer American agency at the outset with much of its secret intelligence. Experts in counterespionage and subversive propaganda and special operations were put at Donovan's disposal, and he was shown their methods of communicating with resistance forces behind the lines. In the early days, COI agents were trained at a school near Toronto, Canada, later a model for some of the training schools of OSS. Donovan said after the war: "Bill Stephenson and the British Intelligence Service gave us an enormous head start which we could not otherwise have had."[13]

BSC controlled two short-wave sending stations in America, one beamed to Europe and the other to the Far East, and Donovan's propagandists were invited to use these British facilities, which they did with great success. One ingenious COI broadcast charged that Germany was asking for a million more troops from Italy, intentionally weakening her ally in order to betray her. Axis stations, unaccustomed to being on the receiving end of a propaganda attack, reacted with a violent harangue which repeated the original charge, thus inadvertently giving it the widest European coverage. A Berlin station termed it "an infamous and unprecedented maneuver to promote the awful suspicion that the Reich would betray its ally" — a protest made doubly ironic by Hitler's treacherous attack on Russia, on June 22, 1941.

3

Hitler's Russian invasion had not caught Winston Churchill by surprise. He had been amply forewarned when Rudolf Hess, second-ranking member of the Nazi hierarchy, had parachuted into England under what he considered a flag of truce, bearing a proposal that Britain and

---

[13] David Bruce, then head of OSS/SI, recalls the great head start which British Intelligence gave his Secret Intelligence branch. Bruce notes in particular the help of Colonel George H. Ellis, to whom "we owed much; indeed, in the beginning, we would have lost months in the absence of his advice and assistance." It should be said, too, that the British even gave us models of their agents' radio sets, which formed the prototypes for OSS sets manufactured in the United States.

Germany should cease hostilities and join in a mutual assault on the
Soviet Union. The Prime Minister refused to honor the truce and
clapped Hess into jail, where he remains to this day, and warned the
Kremlin of Der Führer's intentions in a confidential message, which the
skeptical Stalin ignored. "I have only one purpose," Churchill insisted in
justifying his action, "the destruction of Hitler. . . . If Hitler invaded
Hell, I would make at least a favorable reference to the Devil in the
House of Commons."

Germany's break with Russia marked a new phase of the war, and
sent shock waves all the way across the Pacific to Japan. The Nazi-
Soviet pact in August of 1939 had temporarily stayed the hand of the
warlords in Tokyo, dedicated to a "new order in Greater East Asia,"
and they were forced to delay their grandiose scheme to seize China and
the colonial empires of France and the Netherlands. When Hitler broke
the pact in 1941 and launched his *blitzkrieg* against the Soviet Union,
Japan was freed once more to pursue its program of expansion to the
south, and by mid-July Japanese troops crossed the borders of Indochina. President Roosevelt retaliated by placing an embargo on oil
shipments to Japan, and freezing all Japanese assets in the United States;
but his effort did not deter Tokyo's military leaders from proceeding
with their planned aggression. In October the moderate Prime Minister
Prince Konoye resigned from the Imperial Cabinet, and was succeeded
by the fire-eating General Tojo, who threatened that, if diplomatic
negotiations with America and Britain failed, "we will immediately
make up our minds to get ready for war." The deadline for negotiations
was set as November 29.

Unknown to Tojo's warlords, American cryptographers had succeeded in solving the character of the intricate cipher machine the Japanese were using to encode all diplomatic communications. Based on their
brilliant analysis, a corresponding machine was built which was able to
decipher the Japanese messages. These intercepts, known to the initiated
as "Magic," were the main source on which Washington depended for
the final warnings of an enemy attack. Tight security prevented Tokyo
from discovering that their code had been broken, and an extraordinary
flow of information continued to be decrypted; but from June until

November 12, 1941 the Navy selected only those intercepts which they thought might interest the President, and delivered them verbally. Due to this lack of coordination — Donovan was never given access to any of the material — there was no final evaluation of the captured intelligence. Secretary of State Hull continued his futile exploratory talks with Japanese Ambassador Nomura, and the War and Navy Department heads, although aware from "Magic" messages that Japan was mounting an offensive somewhere in the Pacific, failed to pinpoint the target of the coming assault.[14] When intercepts established that a large carrier force had left Japan under strict radio silence, its destination secret, naval authorities assumed the mystery fleet was bound for the Dutch East Indies, and no red alert was issued to the commanders at Manila or Pearl Harbor. Even a significant message from Tokyo on December 2, instructing the Japanese Embassy in Washington to burn its papers and destroy all but one code machine, did not impress government leaders with the immediate danger. "The basic problem," Admiral King testified later at the Pearl Harbor inquiry, "was that the Navy failed to appreciate what the Japanese could, and did, do."

On Sunday, December 7, only a skeleton staff was at work in Washington's cryptographic center, decoding the last section of an intercepted fourteen-part three-thousand-word message from the Japanese Foreign Minister to Ambassador Nomura. It was Japan's final ultimatum to the United States, and it carried the baffling but specific instructions to Nomura to hold up its delivery to Hull "until further notice." Early that morning, two more intercepts were received. One read ominously: "Destroy at once the remaining cipher machine and all machine codes. Also dispose in like manner secret documents." The other ordered Nomura to "please submit to the United States Government (if possible to the Secretary of State) our reply at one P.M. on the 7th, your time." Alarmed by the specific timing, Colonel Rufus Bratton, chief of the Far Eastern Section of G-2, tried to telephone General Marshall at his quarters at Fort Myers; but the Chief of Staff was enjoying a horseback ride in the balmy Sunday sunshine, and did not receive Brandon's call

[14] Forrest C. Pogue, *George C. Marshall* (New York, 1966).

until 10 A.M. He replied calmly that as soon as he could shower and change his clothes, he would be at his War Department office. On his arrival, Marshall read the entire fourteen-part message deliberately, ignoring Bratton's effort to call his attention to the vital final part. When he realized the significance of the exact delivery time — which would be daybreak in the Pacific, a logical moment for a surprise attack — the Chief of Staff penned a dispatch to the various American commands in the threatened area:

> The Japanese are presenting at one P.M. Eastern Standard Time today what amounts to an ultimatum. Also they are under orders to destroy their code machine immediately.
> Just what significance the hour set may have we do not know, but be on the alert accordingly.

Marshall phoned Admiral Stark to ask if he wanted Pacific Navy commanders to be notified also, and the chief of naval operations replied that he thought enough alerts had been sent. After a moment's reflection, he called back and asked that "Inform Navy" be added to the message.

At 11:50 A.M. Bratton took Marshall's draft to the Signal Room, where more precious moments were lost deciphering the General's handwriting. The Army signal system was unable to contact Hawaii at the moment, and no one dared use the scrambler telephone for fear of revealing that the United States had broken the Japanese diplomatic code. "Sent out finally by commercial telegraph," Marshall's official biography reveals, "the warning to Pearl Harbor, listed third in importance after Manila and Panama, reached the telegraph station in Honolulu about the time the Japanese planes were leaving their carriers. As the messenger boy, a Japanese on a motorcycle, rode out to General Short's headquarters with the message, he could hear antiaircraft guns firing at enemy planes. The message had not even been marked 'Priority.' "[15]

That Sunday afternoon Colonel Donovan, an ardent football fan, was

[15] Pogue, *George C. Marshall.*

attending a professional game between the Dodgers and the Giants at New York's Polo Grounds. The Dodgers were leading 7–0 at the end of the first quarter, and Pug Manders had just burst through the middle on a spinner play, as the Giants' linemen were mousetrapped, and gained twenty-nine yards for a first down on the four-yard line. To the annoyance of the spectators, the loudspeaker account of the game was interrupted for an announcement: "Colonel William Donovan, come to the box office at once. There is an important phone message."

Donovan paused at the exit a moment to watch the next play. Manders plunged across the goal line for the Dodgers' second touch-down, and as the crowd cheered, he made his way downstairs to the office, where a telephone lay uncradled on the desk. An awed attendant said: "The White House calling, Colonel." Donovan picked up the phone and gave his name.

James Roosevelt answered: "The President wants to see you at once. It's an emergency."

The Dodgers won the game, and the crowd filed slowly out of the stands. It was not until they reached the street that they learned of the Japanese attack on Pearl Harbor.

BOOK THREE
1941-1945

Twenty-Fifth and E

I

A SHORT DISTANCE WEST of Washington's Lincoln Memorial, on a rise of ground at the intersection of 25th and E streets, stood the former home of the National Health Institute. No sign or number marked the driveway which rose steeply to a group of brick-and-limestone buildings and converted barracks. Just beyond the entrance, 25th Street petered out to a dead end in a clutter of weeds and tin cans.

The neighborhood was dreary and down-at-heel. Several dilapidated warehouses; a public skating rink; some colliers in the Potomac unloading at a dusty coal yard. A file of tenements climbed the hill away from the river, and at its crest, presiding over the shabby scene, were the twin cylinders of the municipal gasworks. Motorists speeding along fashionable Rock Creek Park Drive on their way to the city turned their heads away from a disreputable brewery, sprawled like an amiable bum beside the parkway's neatly tended lawns. No one gave a second glance at the anonymous structures huddled at its rear.

There was little about them to invite attention. Only an Army officer with padlocked briefcase hurrying up the steps and between the Greek pillars of the central building, or a uniformed guard with shoulder holster who challenged him at the door, might have suggested that anything of interest went on inside.

The occupants, save for their security badges, were as prosaic as their surroundings. The tiny offices which lined the creaking corridors were crowded with paper-strewn desks and clattering typewriters. Here researchers with green eyeshades sweated over columns of foreign labor statistics, bills of lading, traffic reports, production costs. Fitting the items together, analyzing, forecasting. A professor of psychology making laborious notes on a transcript of an Axis broadcast. An engineer with a magnifying glass examining the steel engraving of a munitions plant at the top of a yellowed sheet of German business stationery. A foreign-language expert translating an article on aircraft production in an obscure Japanese magazine.

This was the wartime headquarters of the Office of Coordinator of Information. Colonel Donovan's agency had burst the seams of the Apex Building; temporary quarters in the old Federal Security Administration Building had proven inadequate; and the National Health Institute, to its considerable annoyance, had been hastily evicted to make room for COI's mushrooming staff. An experimental laboratory, containing live monkeys and goats and guinea pigs inoculated with disease viruses, still occupied the entire top floor of one building; and Dr. Langer and his assistants, crammed into the two lower floors, cast covetous eyes at the valuable office space taken up by the zoo overhead. Donovan's fertile mind found a solution. A complaint was made to the National Health Institute that one of the infected monkeys had bitten a stenographer, who feared she had contracted some dreadful plague, and the other secretaries refused to work in the building until the menagerie was removed. The institute, though properly skeptical of the story, was forced to transfer its laboratory elsewhere, the top floor was fumigated, and Dr. Langer's academicians obtained more elbow room. Nazi propagandists, seizing on the episode, broadcast gleefully that the COI consisted of "fifty professors, twenty monkeys, ten goats, twelve guinea pigs, and a staff of Jewish scribblers."

Already Colonel Donovan had become more hated by the Nazis than any other American except President Roosevelt, and Dr. Goebbels's slander machine in Berlin lost no opportunity to attack his intelligence agency. "America's Secret Service," proclaimed the American-born Jane Anderson, sometimes known as Lady Haw Haw, "is under a renegade Irishman named Wild Bill, who prepared for his job by visiting a chain of Balkan nightclubs and brothels." A Munich newspaper

"Fifty professors, twenty monkeys . . . and a staff of Jewish scribblers."
OCI/OSS headquarters at 25th & E streets, Washington, D.C.

called Donovan "the world's chief fifth columnist" whose hired "Jewish refugees . . . have concocted a monstrous conspiracy against all Europe." Even the Nazi propaganda chief himself took to the air-waves with an occasional passage of pure Goebbeldegook: "Donovan's radio perjures world opinion by vomiting the larvae of lies in an avalanche of hatred and vituperation to which Dante might have dedicated with fervor a choice spot in his immortalization of the hellpits of the earth."

Donovan's broadcasters retaliated promptly and effectively. Jane Anderson had bragged in English to a United States short-wave audience that the Nazi food supply was ample, illustrating her arguments with a description of her own visit to a Berlin cocktail bar: "On silver platters were sweets and cookies. I ate Turkish cookies, a delicacy I am very fond of. My friend ordered great goblets of champagne, into which he put shots of cognac to make it more lively. Sweets and cookies, not bad!" The following night her description of the bacchanalian feast, translated into German, was short-waved back to her adopted country for all hungry Germans to hear. *Time* magazine commented: "Plain Jane went off the air, has not been heard from since. A technical knockout for the Donovan Committee."

After Pearl Harbor, the independent American broadcasting industry had become more cooperative with Donovan. COI's Foreign Information Service, directed by Robert Sherwood, was preparing more than three hundred fifteen-minute programs a week for European and Asian consumption. Eleven commercial short-wave stations operated around the clock, sending in English, German, Swedish, French, Danish, Turkish, Arabic, Italian, Spanish, Greek, Serb-Croat, Portuguese and Finnish. In addition, a powerful NBC directional antenna in New Jersey centered its beam on Paris; CBS established a new fifty-kilowatt transmitter on Long Island; another hundred-kilowatt station in San Francisco transmitted to the Orient. In Sherwood's busy Madison Avenue branch office, Foreign News Editor Barnes selected items of interest from the wire services, handed them to key writer-researchers, and their copy, after approval by the commercial companies, was put on private teletype wire to receivers in each short-wave room.

Facts were ingeniously elaborated or distorted, and usually credited to some unidentified government official. A one-line War Department announcement, destined for routine burial in the back pages, might be pointed up to give it propaganda value. "The following from the Coordinator of Information is for your use if desired," the dispatch would read. "A War Department statement today, announcing that nearly 2,000,000 woolen blankets of the highest quality are to be purchased for the use of American draftees, caused Washington observers to comment on the contrast between this action and recent news of the seizure by German authorities of blankets from Norway's civilian population to protect Nazi soldiers during the Russian winter."

Despite the success of the overseas broadcasting program, a widening division of opinion had developed within the agency. Colonel Donovan believed that, once a state of war existed, the propaganda arm should be exploited as a weapon of deception and subversion, and should be under military supervision. "Now that we are at war," he wrote President Roosevelt on March 2, 1942, "foreign propaganda must be employed as an instrument of war — a judicious mixture of rumor and deception, with truth as a bait, to foster disunity and confusion in support of military operations. . . . In point of fact, propaganda is the arrow of initial penetration in preparing the people of a territory where invasion may be contemplated. It is the first step; then fifth column work; then militarized raiders or 'commandos'; then finally the invading divisions."

Robert Sherwood, on the other hand, held that propaganda broadcasts should stick scrupulously to the facts, and let the truth eventually prevail. A man of the highest moral standards, Sherwood echoed Captain Hull's righteous protest to Nathan Hale during the Revolution that "we should not stain our honor by the sacrifice of integrity." The American image overseas would suffer, he felt, if we emulated Axis methods and resorted to lies and deceit. He felt strongly that the agency should remain under civilian direction, and warned that if it became a supporting arm of the military establishment, as Donovan urged, it might in time become an American Gestapo.

His split with Donovan had another and more personal motivation. Sherwood was also Irish, a lanky six-foot-seven-inch veteran of the Canadian Black Watch. Shy and abnormally sentimental, he was capable of fierce loyalties and equally intense dislikes. The depth of emotion which made his dramas so memorable — *There Shall Be No Night* contained some of the finest writing of the war — was an integral part of his own somber and sensitive nature. He had been President Roosevelt's favorite speech-writer, he had long enjoyed a unique position of confidence in the White House family, and his possessive love for the President tolerated no rival. Consciously or unconsciously, he resented Colonel Donovan's increasing intimacy with Roosevelt, the more so in view of Donovan's Republican affiliations and lack of sympathy for the New Deal. In a memorandum to the President, Sherwood wrote: "It is all right to have rabid anti-New Dealers or even Roosevelt haters in the military establishment or in the OPM, but I don't think it appropriate to have them participating in an effort which must be expressive of the President's own philosophy."

Roosevelt, who admired both men, was forced to make a Solomon's judgment. Newspaper articles and editorials were beginning to complain of the proliferation of government information agencies: COI's Foreign Information Service (FIS); Archibald MacLeish's Office of Facts and Figures (OFF); Lowell Mellett's Office of Government Reports (OGR); the Office of Civilian Defense (OCD); and the Office of Emergency Management (OEM). "Washington initialdom," the columnists dubbed it. John O'Donnell in the *Times Herald* referred to their personnel scathingly as "several hundred ex-reporters, jobless foreign correspondents, lyric poets, dramatists, and ordinary merchants of literary mush," and the Baltimore Sun claimed the duplication of effort produced "nothing but generalities, vagueness, overlapping authority, and giganticism." Senator Robert Taft estimated that five thousand people were engaged in publicity, spending more than thirty million dollars a year of government funds, and stated that "this nation can neither scare its enemies nor further its own war by talk." Encouraged tacitly by the State Department and the competing service departments, as well as by the antagonistic Bureau of the Budget, the press clamored for a consolidation of all war information bureaus.

Advised that the President was leaning to the same conclusion, Colonel Donovan begged him not to remove the function of foreign news broadcasting from his unit. "Due to your continued support and confidence," he wrote, "we have been able to set up for you an instrument of modern warfare which, if left unimpaired, would be able to stand up against any similar weapon of the Axis. In doing this we have not usurped the functions of the Army, Navy or State Department. I feel it is now my duty respectfully to urge . . . that this weapon should not be disturbed at home before it is put to its really crucial test abroad."

Colonel Donovan left for London early in June of 1942 to confer with the newly appointed Chief of Combined Operations, Vice-Admiral Lord Louis Mountbatten, who was now the fourth member of the British Chiefs of Staff's Committee, and to arrange further collaboration with Colonel Menzies, the Chief of the Secret Intelligence Service, and Mr. Hambro, the Director of the Special Operations Executive.[1] This early and full cooperation between the highly experienced British organizations and the fledgling OSS not only saved OSS an immeasurable period of trial and error, but may well have been one of the decisive factors in its survival. Meanwhile, on June 13, 1942, in the midst of these discussions, Donovan learned that President Roosevelt had selected Elmer Davis, news analyst for the Columbia Broadcasting System, to head a single unified agency called the Office of War Information. COI's Foreign Information Service, under Robert Sherwood, would become the Overseas Branch of the new OWI.

The choice of Elmer Davis was greeted by the press with universal acclaim. His flat Midwestern twang and pungent comments had won him a host of admiring listeners; as a professional journalist, he was popular with other newspapermen; and editorials applauded the fact that Washington's information squabble was ended at last. In their excitement over Davis's appointment the news dispatches barely mentioned that Roosevelt's Executive Order 9182 simultaneously established an-

---

[1] OSS had the advantage of combining the functions of SIS and SOE in a single organization — another indication of the extent to which Donovan had profited from his earlier fact-finding tours in England and of the frankness with which Mountbatten and his associates had spoken to Donovan on intelligence matters.

other agency, the Office of Strategic Services, which would supplant the Coordinator of Information. Eventually all overt or "white" propaganda was handled by OWI; all covert or "black" propaganda was under OSS.

In the words of the President's order, the Office of Strategic Services would operate "under the direction and supervision of the Joint Chiefs of Staff . . . to collect and analyze strategic information, and to plan and operate special services," defined as "all measures . . . taken to enforce our will upon the enemy by means other than military action, as may be applied in support of actual or planned military operations or in furtherance of the war effort": unorthodox warfare, guerrilla activities behind the enemy lines, contact with resistance groups, subversion, sabotage.

The director of the Office of Strategic Services, the dispatches added, would be William J. Donovan; and OSS would operate from the old COI headquarters down by the gasworks.

2

If the Pearl Harbor disaster accomplished any small good for the United States, it served to demonstrate the woeful deficiency in American intelligence. Our battleships had been lined up in open invitation, our airplanes had been wheeled out of their revetments and ranked side by side along the Hickham Field flight line, because military leaders underestimated Japan's strength and capabilities and failed to fit the pieces together which might have foretold the air strike against Honolulu. Nor was our faulty intelligence confined to the Pacific. Observers in Europe had predicted that Russia could not last more than six weeks against a German assault, and Allied strategy had been based on that false assumption. The Office of Strategic Services was devised to bring our outmoded conception of international espionage up to date, with new techniques never indulged in by this nation before.

Executive Order 9182 had insured, at least for the moment, the continuance of Donovan's controversial experiment in organized intelligence and paramilitary service; but the transfer of its jurisdiction from the President to the Joint Chiefs of Staff (which Donovan had personally requested) posed even more critical problems. Now the struggling COI had a new supervisor as well as a new name, and its functions and the extent of its authority were entirely dependent upon the decision of the JCS. This meant that all funds to operate OSS must come from Congress, primarily the House and Senate Appropriations Committees, and its budget requests must first be submitted to and approved by the gimlet-eyed Bureau of the Budget. The immediate problem of maintaining OSS during the transition period was temporarily bridged by instructions from the JCS that it should carry on as usual, pending further study of its wartime functions; but Donovan and his top staff were keenly aware that OSS faced a critical struggle to convince the Joint Chiefs and other ranking officials of the government not only that OSS should be given adequate written authority and manpower and supplies, but in fact that it should exist at all.

Donovan had hoped that, when his agency became a part of the military establishment instead of a personal protégé of the White House, it would not present so inviting a political target. As it turned out, members of the military felt he was all the more vulnerable without Roosevelt's backing, and they moved in for the kill. Half a year after its inception, the agency was still operating without an official directive. Navy ONI and Army G-2 claimed that its research and analysis function should be handled by military personnel, not by civilian professors. General Strong, now Army Chief of Staff G-2, refused to exercise his authority so that OSS could obtain the supplies and personnel of which it was desperately in need. When Ned Buxton, deputy director of OSS, appealed personally to General Strong for more affirmative support, his request was turned down so bluntly that Buxton, who had retained his civilian status, challenged Strong: "General, is it your purpose to destroy us?" Buxton reported later that Strong was "visibly embarrassed."

According to Lyman Kirkpatrick (*The Real CIA*), "General Strong . . . hated the OSS (and later the CIA) and vowed that he would not rely upon its intelligence collection system, but established his own in

1942. This resulted in one of the most unusual organizations in the history of the federal government. It was developed completely outside of the normal structure, used all of the cover and communications facilities normally operated by intelligence organizations, and yet never was under any control from Washington." During World War II, however, not only was G-2's strategic intelligence collection relatively limited, but G-2 also failed to provide adequate trained personnel for tactical military intelligence behind enemy lines. (Cryptography was one major exception to this statement.)

Month after frustrating month dragged on without any directive, and the OSS executive staff feared at any moment the agency might be transferred bodily to the War Department or absorbed by Strong's G-2. Their fears were not without substance. Donovan's request for manpower and material was submitted to the Joint Psychological Warfare Committee (JPWC) of the Joint Chiefs of Staff, who batted it back and forth in endless hearings, then passed it on to the higher-level Joint Staff Planners (JSP), who referred it in turn to the JCS, who sent it back to the JPWC to start the weary round of committee hearings all over again.

OSS found itself blocked at every turn. Months before Pearl Harbor, Donovan as Coordinator of Information had been confidentially authorized by the President to start training agents in the field of secret intelligence procurement as well as sabotage and guerrilla and psychological warfare. The Joint Chiefs, however, felt that there were more possibilities of embarrassment to the country in this guerrilla activity than there were of solid achievement, and rival service chiefs warned that such an authorization might lead to "Donovan's Private Army." As a compromise, OSS was allowed to train and operate "Operational Nuclei," small cadres of experts in guerrilla warfare, but was denied permission to organize any large guerrilla groups of its own. This directive was, however, later modified.

The agency was also forbidden to operate in Latin America, which J. Edgar Hoover and Nelson Rockefeller regarded as their own preserve, a limitation which Donovan felt should be determined by function and not by geography. Once Dr. Langer, head of R&A, sought their cooperation in allowing some of his economic analysts to visit the southern continent, but even this idea was rebuffed. "They really gave me a beating," Dr. Langer recalled, "and I was so discouraged that I went back to Colonel Donovan and told him the whole town was united against us. And he said to me — you know, Donovan was really amazing — he said, 'Well, Bill, you can't run a show like this without suffering some setbacks, and they may be very serious setbacks. But let me tell you one thing — if we're right, we'll prevail, and if we're wrong, the sooner it's found out the better.' "

Donovan was the calm eye of the storm. Instead of resorting to recrimination, he remained positive and forward-looking. Utilizing the legal skill acquired both as public prosecutor and head of his own law firm, he and his staff drafted and painstakingly redrafted a proposed OSS directive, which he submitted to the JCS with a memo explaining simply but forcefully all the reasons why such a directive was necessary to enable the agency to carry out its assigned function with sufficient authority to give it at least a fighting chance for success. On one point he was adamant: OSS should never become a part of any other government agency or of the Armed Forces. To be effective, he argued, it had to supply informed and reliable information both to Army and Navy intelligence and to the State Department and other federal branches. His insistence on this principle of independence, to the possible jeopardy of his own future as well as that of OSS, was the main reason that the agency emerged in time as an integrated unit, serving all departments of the government but subservient to none. "Looking back on it now," Dr. Langer added, "perhaps Bill Donovan's greatest single achievement during the war was to survive."

Despite its uncertain future in 1942, OSS continued to attract top-flight men to the still obscure agency. Donovan's own personality and reputation enabled him to lure professional leaders of the highest character and ability, who were then or later would become nationally famous in academic, diplomatic, banking, business, and other fields. It is a striking fact that, from among these recruits to OSS, any President could have selected an outstanding cabinet. In addition to such early

COI stalwarts as Buxton and Langer and Bruce, the roster of Donovan's operating lieutenants included:

Brigadier General John T. Magruder, VMI graduate and head of the Magruder Mission to China, who became deputy director of intelligence.

John W. Gardner, later U.S. Secretary of Health, Education and Welfare.

Arthur Goldberg, head of the OSS Labor Desk, later U.S. Supreme Court justice and ambassador to the United Nations.

Junius Morgan, partner of J. P. Morgan & Co., who was of invaluable assistance in supervising the expenditure of OSS funds, particularly "unvouchered" funds.

Henry S. Morgan, head of Morgan, Stanley & Co., investment bankers, the unlikely but well-qualified chief of the OSS branch whose functions, among others, included the collection of identity papers and similar documents from occupied countries, from which forgeries were made and supplied to OSS agents infiltrated into enemy territory.

Dr. Henry A. Murray of Harvard, who organized and operated the OSS Assessment School which analyzed men's character and response to stress with unbelievably accurate results. This pioneer effort has since been widely used by industry and universities throughout the United States.

John Ford, famed motion picture director and winner of many Academy Awards, who came to Washington to head the OSS Field Photographic Unit.

Allen Dulles, diplomat and lawyer, later director of the CIA; Richard Helms, present head of the CIA; and Lawrence R. Houston, now its general counsel.

Dr. James L. McConaughy, former president of Wesleyan College and governor of Connecticut; William H. Vanderbilt, onetime governor of Rhode Island, who headed the OSS personnel administration; historian Arthur Schlesinger, Jr.; Lester Armour and Russell Forgan, bankers; and Russell B. Livermore, noted lawyer and recipient of a DSC in World War I, who directed the agency's guerrilla operations.

Diplomats Hugh Wilson, our last ambassador to Germany; John

G. Edward Buxton, Deputy Director
of OSS.

William L. Langer, head of R&A for
OSS.

Otto C. Doering, Jr., chief of OSS
secretariat and later executive officer.

David Bruce, director of OSS/
London.

Wiley, then minister to Lithuania; and Russell H. Dorr, later U.S. ambassador to Turkey.

James B. Donovan, who became OSS general counsel, and who after the war defended Colonel Abel, the Russian spy, and later negotiated his exchange for Francis Gary Powers, the U–2 pilot captured by the Russians; and Paul Helliwell, Chief of SI/China.

Some staff assistants and field operatives were borrowed from Donovan's New York law firm: Otto C. Doering, Jr., chief of the OSS Secretariat and later executive officer; Ned Putzell, who followed him as executive officer in the closing months of the war; Thomas J. McFadden; James R. Withrow, Jr.; Walter Mansfield, who parachuted into Yugoslavia and later served behind the lines in China; Richard Heppner, who became head of OSS/China.

Operatives for behind-the-lines duty were selected according to a simple standard. Strength of character was Donovan's prime requisite for a spy. The type of American who could best lead a double life in enemy territory, he insisted, was a man who had never lived a double life before. It was easier to train an honest citizen to engage in shady activities than to teach honesty to a man of dubious background. Drew Pearson charged that OSS was made up of "Wall Street bankers." Donovan observed serenely: "You know, these bankers and corporation lawyers make wonderful second-story men."

Newspaper scoffers had no end of fun with the initials of the Office of Strategic Services. "Oh, So Secret," they jibed. "Oh, So Silly." "Oh, Shush, Shush." When they learned of the large number of wealthy bluebloods who were joining the agency, they promptly added "Oh, So Social." Certainly it was an imposing list of Social Register names: Ryan, DuPont, Vanderbilt, Bruce, Armour, Roosevelt, Morgan, Mellon. Raymond Guest, ten-goal polo player and cousin of Winston Churchill. Ilya Tolstoy, grandson of the novelist, who visited the holy city of Lhasa in Tibet. Marine Captain Winthrop Rutherford, who led his resistance team several times through the German lines in southern France. Fifty-four-year-old Prince Serge Oblensky, one-time cavalry officer in the White Russian Army and a New York socialite, who disappeared from his table at El Morocco one night to parachute into Sardinia and help organize the Partisans.

They came to OSS from all walks of life, offering themselves freely for devious and dangerous assignments. Rene Dussaq, a Hollywood stunt man known as "the human fly," who was awarded the DSC for his heroic work with the French underground. Henry Laussucq, ostensibly a painter on the Left Bank, who helped organize the French underground. Jumping Joe Savoldi, Notre Dame fullback and professional wrestler, and John Ringling North, owner of Barnum & Bailey's Circus, both members of the OSS unit which laid the groundwork for negotiations with Italian Admiral Girosi. Motion picture star Sterling Hayden, who helped organize a Splinter Fleet of decrepit fishing schooners and caïques to run the German blockade along the Dalmatian coast and deliver arms to the underground in Yugoslavia. Quentin Roosevelt — grandson of President Theodore Roosevelt — who was killed in China. Marine Colonel William A. Eddy, who resigned as president of Hobart College to play a key role in the invasion of North Africa.

Hitler had jeered that in time of war America's mixed racial background would be her weakness. Donovan sought to prove it was her strength. The melting pot provided men of every language and country, from whom OSS could select behind-the-lines operators with intimate personal knowledge of the particular terrain which they would penetrate. There was a former Paris bartender from the Yale Club, an Alsatian *maître d'* from Armando's, and a French chef from the River Club, who infiltrated as a team into occupied France; only one escaped the Gestapo, the others were captured and executed. There was a former German sergeant who prepared convincing Nazi military passes for parachuting agents. There was a Swiss mountain climber familiar with the high passes of the Apennines, and a Catholic missionary who had lived with the Kachin tribesmen in northern Burma. There were even Communists. A group of four known card-carriers slipped into Italy, made contact with local party members, and sent back a daily flow of valuable information to the American forces. Congressman John Elliot Rankin, investigating their leftist affiliations, informed Donovan indignantly that one of the group was said to be on the honor roll of the Young Communist League.

"I don't know if he's on the Communist honor roll," Donovan retorted, "but for the job he's doing in Italy, he's on the honor roll of OSS."[2]

And there were the first- or second-generation Americans of Greek or Polish or Japanese descent, newly made citizens with a single burning desire to pay off their obligation to their adopted land. Many of them paid off that obligation with their lives.

3

You might have been a mechanic in a Brooklyn garage. You spoke Italian fluently; both your parents had been born in Naples, and you had spent your boyhood in Italy. One morning, shortly after Pearl Harbor, you were interrupted at work in the grease pit under a car. "There's somebody named Blank here to see you. Says it's important."

Perhaps you were an Oriental-language professor in a New England college, comfortably insulated in your little academic world. Your specialty was Japan; you had taught in Tokyo for several years, and had a sizable library of Japanese magazines and newspapers. Your telephone rang after class and a friend's voice said: "A man I know named Blank would like to talk to you. No, I can't tell you what it is over the phone."

Or you had been a dishwasher in a Chicago restaurant before you were drafted into the Army early in 1942; you were training as a paratrooper at Fort Benning. Your mother was Austrian, your father German. On your way to the flight line, with pack fastened and jump boots laced tight, an officer in Army uniform hailed you by name. "I'm Captain Blank. Could I have a few words?"

What he told you — mechanic or professor or paratrooper — was always vague. There was a special job to be done, but the details could not be discussed. All he could say was that it involved an extremely hazardous mission in enemy territory. The destination was secret. Your safe contacts would be designated at the proper time. If you were caught, your very existence would be denied by the organization for which you worked. Would you be willing to volunteer?

[2] Stewart Alsop and Tom Braden, *Sub Rosa* (New York, 1946).

If you said yes — and few tapped by OSS were ever known to refuse — you would be sent to the Assessment School. You had already
been checked for security clearance, but it was necessary to determine
your mental and physical fitness for behind-the-lines duty.[3] Your interviewer told you to select a fictitious name, and report at a specified hour
to Schools and Training Headquarters in a ramshackle brick school-
house at the corner of 24th and F streets in Washington. There you
were led to the basement, and ordered to remove all your outer clothing
and to destroy any identifying name tags on your underwear. Letters,
photographs, even a wallet stamped with your initials were taken from
you. For the next three days, you would be incognito, known only by
the student name you had chosen. Your civilian background and personality would be left behind with your clothes.[4]

After donning Army fatigues and a pair of heavy Army boots, you
boarded a canvas-covered truck with your anonymous fellow students,
and were transported over winding country roads to Station S at Fair-
fax, Virginia, a former private estate with well-kept lawns and a Southern
mansion which the candidates shared with the senior staff. You were
assembled in the front hall, and the director of the Assessment School
described its purpose, and the need for security. "Our job here is to
discover your special skills, unique abilities, and individual talents in
order that they may be put to the fullest use. To hide the nature of our
work, we have given out for local consumption the explanation that this
is an Army Rehabilitation Center. The residents of the nearby village
have accepted this fiction, and are firmly convinced that you are all
serious mental cases. For reasons of your own security later in this
organization, you have to take similar precautions during your stay here.
Just as our area has a 'cover story,' so each of you must develop a story
designed to hide your true identity. You must claim to have been born
at some place other than your actual birthplace; educated in institutions
other than those you attended; working at an occupation other than
your real profession; and living in a location other than where you

[3] It was a rigid policy of OSS that no individual who failed the Assessment School
Test would be permitted to go overseas except on the request of the Branch Chief
concerned with the express written approval of the director's office.
[4] OSS Assessment Staff, *Assessment of Men* (New York, 1948).

reside. Let me warn you that members of the staff from time to time will try to trap you into breaking cover, by asking casual questions about yourself when you are off guard. Don't be caught."

Actually, you were under keen surveillance from the moment you arrived at S. Instructors noted the way you disembarked from the truck, either jumping off the tailgate with natural agility or climbing down awkwardly; the manner in which you greeted the staff members, brash or suspicious or uneasy; whether you fumbled in giving your student name or, in your nervousness, blurted out your own. Every hour of the next three days was taken up with mental tests, psychological tests, physical tests. To estimate your ability to observe and draw correct inferences, you were placed in a room containing twenty-six articles of clothing and personal belongings and timetables and newspaper clippings. After studying these items for four minutes, you were taken to another room and requested to answer a questionnaire about the mythical occupant whose effects you had just examined: his age, marital status, weight, color of hair, residence, occupation.

Your initiative and resourcefulness were gauged by the Brook Test, in which four to seven candidates at a time were led to a shallow meadow stream about eight feet wide, given a number of short boards, none long enough to reach from bank to bank, three lengths of rope, and a pulley, and told: "Before you, you see a raging torrent so deep and fast that it is impossible to rest anything on the bottom. You are faced with the problem of transporting this delicate range finder" (pointing to a log) "to the far bank, and of bringing that box of percussion caps" (indicating a small boulder) "to this side. You are not permitted to jump across the stream. You have ten minutes." The speed with which the students found a solution to the problem — by building a bridge with the boards and rope, by lassooing the branch of a tree on the far bank and rigging an overhead cable, or by swinging out and across on a rope tied to a tree on the near bank — was graded by the instructor; and since it was a group test he gave extra credit to the candidate who showed leadership in organizing the others.

The Construction Problem was diabolically designed to test your emotional stability and tolerance to frustration. You were shown a pile of wooden blocks and half-blocks with circular holes and dowels to fit, like an oversize tinker toy, and told to build a five-foot cube with seven-foot diagonals on the four sides. Two alleged G.I. helpers nicknamed Buster and Kippy, actually junior members of the staff, were assigned to assist you, but were under secret orders to present you with as many obstructions and annoyances as possible during the ensuing ten minutes. A concealed tape recorder took down the characteristic reactions of one candidate to their relentless heckling:

Kippy: What cha in, the Navy? You look like one of them curly-headed Navy boys all the girls are after.

Candidate: Uh . . . no, I'm not in the Navy. I'm not in anything.

Kippy: What's the matter with you — you look healthy enough. Are you a draft dodger?

Candidate: No, I was deferred for essential work — but that makes no difference. Let's get this job done. Now connect those two corners with a five-foot pole.

Buster: What kind of work did you do before you came here? Never did any building, I bet. I seen a lot of guys, but nobody as dumb as you.

Candidate: Well, that may be, but you don't seem to be doing much to help me.

Buster: Wha — what's that? Me not being helpful — why, I've done everything you've asked me, haven't I? Now, haven't I?

Candidate: Well, you haven't exactly killed yourself working and we don't have much time left, so let's get going.

Buster: No one else ever complained about me not working. Now I want an apology for what you said about me.

Candidate: Okay, okay, let's forget it. I'll apologize. Come on, will you?

Kippy: What's your name, anyway?

Candidate: Uh . . . you can call me Slim.

Kippy: That isn't a very good name — Stupid would be better. You can't even put together a child's toy.

Candidate: Just let's get this thing finished. Hey there, you, be careful, you knocked that pole out deliberately.

Buster: Who, me? Listen, you good-for-nothing little punk, if this thing had been built right from the beginning the poles wouldn't come out. (*He kicks the other poles out of position, and part of the structure collapses.*) Jeez, they send a boy out here to do a man's work, and when he can't do it he starts blaming his helpers.

Kippy: Christ, they really must be scraping the bottom of the barrel now.

In all the history of Station S, the construction problem was never completed in the allotted time.

Your hardest ordeal, and one of the most important tests of the program, was the Stress Interview, designed to assess the candidate's emotional stability under severe strain. You were escorted alone into a dark room, seated on a hard chair with a strong spotlight on your face, and subjected to rapid and merciless cross-questioning by a simulated Gestapo board behind a table. Every trick was used to expose flaws in the cover story you had prepared, to trip you up in a contradiction, to rattle you by yelling: "Now we have the truth — you admit you just lied." You were never allowed to relax. You were ordered curtly to sit upright, to stop smoking, to uncross your legs, to remove your glasses, anything to heighten your tension. The least inconsistency in your story was immediately jumped on by your inquisitors. After ten minutes of steady interrogation, the examiner conferred with the rest of the board and announced solemnly: "It is our decision that you have failed this test." Instructors watched your reaction closely, noting whether you showed signs of autonomic disturbance such as sweating, flushing, swallowing, or moistening the lips, which might indicate your guilt. Some candidates became so overwrought during the questioning that they had to be discharged from the program and declared unfit for future OSS work; but it was obviously better for the agency to discover a man's weakness at once than to have a captured agent crack under actual Gestapo grilling.

Assuming you passed the assessment tests at Station S and were recommended for an overseas assignment, you were sent to an OSS

Training School. Here you were given preliminary instruction in close combat and gutter fighting: a knee in the groin, a sideswipe with the heel of your hand against an Adam's apple. You learned a unique cipher system, devised so that each individual cipher could be memorized and an agent would not need to carry incriminating evidence on his person. You were taught to write "innocent texts," letters which appeared guileless but contained enciphered messages. You studied the technique of short-wave radio, and practiced repairing a damaged set with make-shift articles. You dismantled firearms and repaired them by cannibalizing parts from other disabled weapons. You were initiated into such black arts as surreptitious entry, cracking safes and photographing secret documents, handling explosives, blowing bridges, derailing trains, concealing abrasives in a truck's motor. You were shown how documents could be sneaked past a border guard by an innocent-looking peasant, leading a cow whose teats had been dilated and stuffed with rolls of microfilm.

With a masked instructor at your elbow, you moved with drawn revolver through a Scare House which outdid any amusement park Chamber of Horrors in one-a-minute thrills. Boards teetered underfoot as you groped your way along a dark hall, footsteps echoed mysteriously ahead of you, a hidden loudspeaker reproduced the rumble of guttural German voices around a poker table, clink of glasses and slap of cards. A turn in the corridor revealed a pop-up dummy in the uniform of a Nazi Storm Trooper, suddenly confronting you. Whirl, fire. There was someone in the room just ahead. Reload, safety off. Burst open the door, fire; fire again.

You were given a final field problem under frighteningly real conditions. Through a confidential arrangement between Colonel Donovan and the FBI, by which OSS agreed to notify the FBI area chiefs in advance, each OSS trainee was assigned to infiltrate a designated factory and steal certain top-secret papers. If caught, a code number over the telephone to OSS would clear the suspect.[5] Not only did the student

---

[5] There were occasional clashes despite the agreement with the FBI. Once J. Edgar Hoover sent a personal note to the White House, complaining that an OSS trainee had penetrated classified material in San Diego by falsely representing himself to the local Chief of Police as an FBI agent. The note was forwarded to

learn to use his wits, with the very real danger of being shot by company police if he blundered, but the industries had a unique opportunity to test their plant security. On several occasions, Donovan was able to show a chagrined executive microfilmed copies of his most closely guarded blueprints, which had been locked in his own office safe. One shocked official ordered a complete shakeup in his airplane factory when the Colonel revealed that a trainee had forged a security pass and spent several nights rifling vital radar and bombsight specifications without being detected.

You said goodbye to your family, assuring them that you would have some easy desk job in London, and sailed overseas in a crowded troop ship, one more khaki-clad G.I. among thousands. In England you spent three crowded days at a parachute school, jumping first from a balloon and later from a plane; and then you proceeded to another OSS area for more intensive and grim instruction. For the first time, you were told the location of your drop. You studied marked maps and memorized safe addresses where you could take refuge. You learned special code signals that would warn OSS in London if you were captured and used as a "playback" to send messages as directed by the enemy. You were taught how to garrote with a knotted rope stealthily, silently.

You climbed a rickety staircase to the fourth-floor attic of a house at 72 Grosvenor Street, London, where you were processed and briefed and clothed by the Moles, a group of naturalized Americans whose slogan was "We turn out spies." This was the OSS Authentication Bureau, which transformed ordinary G.I.s into French factory workers, Belgian longshoremen, even members of the Nazi SS Police. On a hand-operated press in a corner of their secret loft, the Moles printed SS identification cards and ration books to be carried by the agents. When a German ration stamp expired, they ran off another issue in the proper

---

OSS by the Joint Chiefs of Staff for reply, and a staff investigation promptly revealed that the trainee had told the Chief of Police that he was an ex-FBI agent (which was true), and that OSS had advised the regional FBI director well in advance of the training exercise, in accordance with the OSS agreement with the FBI. In reporting the facts to JCS, the OSS executive officer pointed out that such training exercises were not only a functional necessity, but would help protect the lives of agents when operating in enemy territory.

color. They copied the authentic papers of European refugees who had fled to America, and forged the signatures on a pass so convincingly that one agent, according to a popular OSS story, reported after his mission that he had been seized by SS police and taken to the Kommandant, who examined his pass, held it up, and shouted to his assistant: "At last, one of these *verdammt* things is filled out correctly."

Your cover story was carefully appraised, any dubious factors eliminated, and tiny details added to give it verisimilitude. The Moles were taking no chances. Under their tutelage, you mastered the local customs and mannerisms and *patois* of the area you would visit. Ersatz clothing material smuggled out of Europe was fashioned into authentic native garments in a small tailor shop in their garret. Items of civilian apparel borrowed from repatriates who returned to the United States were shipped to OSS/London, and scrutinized for British or American laundry marks which might betray the wearer. Secondhand shops in New York's Lower East Side were combed for German fountain pens, battered suitcases of European manufacture, even the little religious symbols worn by farm workers in the Balkans.

If you were to simulate a French peasant, you were clad in faded and patched blue work clothes, heavy home-knitted socks, sabots, beret. The Moles supplied you with torn and filthy franc notes in small denominations, such as a farmer might carry in his pockets or stuff in his socks. Since the least flaw might alert the Gestapo, your buttons were resewn with the threads parallel, rather than crisscross in the American fashion; the linings of your garments were made full, European style; even your suspender buttons were stamped "Made in Paris." You were provided with cheap French cigarettes, and warned to smoke them clear down to the stub; one OSS agent had been recognized as an American because he tossed away a half-finished cigarette, something no frugal native would do. Your cover story was backed up with tangible proof: a hospital certificate for a recent illness which would explain why you were not in the army, a letter from a friend deploring a death in your family in order to establish your presence in the area. As an added precaution, in case you failed to make immediate contact with the resistance forces, you were given a pistol and ammunition, flashlight, emergency food rations, knife, rope, and a K-pill, a lethal product of OSS R&D which would cause instant death if swallowed and thus save you from Gestapo torture and, in your pain-induced delirium, the possible betrayal of your associates.

Now the long months of preparation were over, and you were ready for your jump. After your peasant costume had been given a last check for any oversight, you pulled camouflaged coveralls over it and donned a crash helmet, grabbed your parachute pack, and made your way in the darkness to the flight shack for a final cup of coffee while the plane was warming up. A merciful lethargy had settled over you. In your numbed mind, it seemed that you had already made the jump and were safe on the ground somewhere in France, looking back in retrospect at what you were doing now. It all seemed so familiar: the summons from the sergeant of the flight crew, the quick walk across the ramp to the shadowy plane with its twin engines glowing, the awkward "Good luck" of the maintenance men as you climbed aboard. The echoing interior of the bomber where you squatted, wrapped in a blanket against the cold. The lurching motion as the plane taxied down the strip, the roar of revving engines, the bump and lift as you were airborne.

A quarter hour; a half hour. You were staring hypnotized at an evil red eye in the forward part of the cabin, the signal light that said you were still off target. Three quarters of an hour. You started to shiver involuntarily, and your ears began to pulse in rhythm with the throbbing motors. Although you had not taken your eyes from the red light, it was a full moment before you realized that it had changed to yellow. The sergeant hurried down the cabin toward you, in fur-lined leather jacket and flight boots, and cupped his hands to shout: "We'll be over the target in ten minutes." You nodded silently and checked the straps of your parachute for the hundredth time, while he tested the static line which would trip the 'chute, and released the catches of the metal cover over the "joe hole" through which you would drop. You both saw the yellow light blink out, and a green light showed.

"Target area," the sergeant yelled in your ear. "We'll circle once, and when we level off, jump."

You felt the plane bank and curve, and then the engines were throttled back, and the cabin was deafeningly still. Methodically the sergeant flipped the cover off the trapdoor, and motioned you forward. The wind howled through the opening, and it was all you could do to force your legs down and out until they were dangling in space. You gripped the sides of the hole, and tried not to wonder whether the resistance people were waiting below, or whether the enemy had spotted their flares and . . . To keep from thinking, you ran over in your mind the jump instructions: hold straight, head on chest, legs together, pull the webs.

"Running in," the sergeant warned.

You nodded again. The plane leveled off, and began its glide.

"Okay. GO!"

You shoved forward and down on your arms, and the prop-wash caught you and turned you clear over, and you felt a tug on your harness from the static line, and heard the silken slap of the parachute opening. You grabbed the lift webs and pulled down hard to lessen its swaying motion. The plane's roar receded as it climbed for altitude and was lost in the rushing blackness. You were alone, more completely alone than you had ever been in your life . . .

Eight hundred thirty-one members of OSS were known to have been decorated for gallantry during the war. Still other awards were made in the field. Some were posthumous. A careless word, the discovery by the Germans of a clandestine radio, the betrayal by a turncoat in the resistance group, and the agent would die slowly and agonizingly in a Gestapo torture cell. A few were found later in POW camps in liberated areas, starved and permanently crippled from their beatings. Others simply disappeared and were never heard from again. Only an ominous silence at their scheduled radio contact hour told OSS/London that the mission had failed.

There was Navy Lieutenant James Harvey Gaul, a brilliant young archaeologist from Harvard, who parachuted into Czechoslovakia to work with the local Forces of the Interior in maintaining an underground railroad for evacuating downed Allied flyers. Ambushed by the

Nazis, Gaul retreated with his team of partisans through the mountains to a hideout near Polomka. It was hopeless; they were surrounded by two hundred German troops, and after three hours of fighting were forced to yield. Gaul was taken to the notorious Malthausen concentration camp near Linz, Austria, and executed by a firing squad. .

Or there was T/5g Salvador Fabrega of New York, another OSS paratrooper, who was picked up by the Gestapo while fighting with a resistance mission in northern Italy. His citation for the Distinguished Service Cross stated: "T/5g Fabrega was taken to SS headquarters in Belluno for interrogation, but despite ten days of starving, severe beatings, and torture by application of electrical charges to his ears and hands and feet, he revealed nothing about the work and location of his unit. On 16 March he was taken by automobile from Belluno to a prison camp in Bolsano for what he was told would be further questioning and torture and probable execution." Taking advantage of an opportunity when the German escort officer stopped at a tavern, Sette, the Italian driver of the car, revealed that "beside being the chauffeur for the SS commander in Belluno, he also acted as a spy for the American mission and on numerous occasions had furnished valuable intelligence items." Sette warned T/5g Fabrega that he would never get out of Belluno alive, and begged him to make a break before the German officer returned. Fabrega refused "because he realized the importance for the American mission to retain the services of a spy in the SS command," the citation concluded: "His unselfish action in refusing to escape when facing further torture and possible death, in order to further the aims of the mission to which he belonged, are in keeping with the highest traditions of the Armed Forces of the United States."

Or there were the fifteen soldiers from the 2677th Special Reconnaisance Battalion of OSS, young Italians from the States, who volunteered to dynamite the main tunnel of the coastal railroad running from Genoa to La Spezia. The Navy PT boats, waiting at a prearranged rendezvous to pick them up after their mission, were surprised by German E-boats; one PT was sunk, the other driven off. Subsequent attempts to rescue the stranded fifteen were unsuccessful, and weeks of air reconnaisance could discover no sign of them. A searching party found them a year later. "They'd all been shot through the back of the head and dumped into an open slit trench," a G.I. member of the party told me. "They were still in uniform, only the combat boots had been stolen off their feet. When we turned them over, the bones of their wrists were still tied with rope." His voice faltered a moment. "We untied their wrists before we buried them."[6]

[6] This was the first major execution under Hitler's orders to shoot to kill all types of Allied commandos. It subsequently became the basis of some of the War Crimes trials, during which OSS personnel, including Donovan, aided Justice Jackson.

II

GOOD INTELLIGENCE, Donovan liked to say, is no more mysterious than McGuffey's Second Reader. "Our experience showed us," he stated after the war, "that a half hour spent with the brakeman of a freight train running into Occupied France would produce more useful information than a Mata Hari could learn in a year. . . . We did not rely on the 'seductive blonde' or the 'phony moustache.' The major part of our intelligence was the result of good old-fashioned intellectual sweat."

From the beginnings of COI before Pearl Harbor to the termination of OSS after V-J Day, the Research and Analysis branch was the very core of the agency. The cloak-and-dagger exploits of agents infiltrated behind the lines captured the public imagination; but the prosaic and colorless grubbing of Dr. Langer's scientists, largely overlooked by the press, provided far and away the greater contribution to America's wartime intelligence. From the files of foreign newspapers, from obscure technical journals, from reports of international business firms and labor organizations, they extracted pertinent figures and data. With infinite patience, they fitted the facts together into a mosaic of information — the raw material of strategy, Donovan called it — on which the President and his Chiefs of Staff could form their operational decisions.

Dr. Langer credits the whole research-and-analysis conception to Donovan's "inspiration"; but it might also be ascribed to his unique combination of experience plus imagination. In his law practice over the years, Donovan had learned the value of a team of trained specialists working together to integrate and evaluate all the evidence. His Public Utilities Investigation in 1929, which employed special researchers to dig out the facts, had been in effect an early R&A. It was his imagination which saw that the universities were full of scholars with specialized knowledge and language equipment and field experience in various parts of the world. If they could be brought together under the same roof, to consult and check with one another, a regional system could be set up to cover Europe and Africa and the Far East, including special economics and geography and map sections. After the war, his R&A conception was the prototype for the regional studies programs in our leading universities today.

"Back in 1944," Dr. Langer recalls, "John Gardner, later head of the Carnegie Foundation, and Jim Perkins, president of Cornell, visited my office and expressed their opinion that R&A had pioneered an important new direction in education. After the war, the Carnegie Foundation put up the initial money to start Russian and Middle East and Far East Research Centers at Harvard and Columbia and elsewhere, with sociologists and historians and political scientists all working on the same area study — a very important part of the modern university curriculum."[7]

President Baxter of Williams and Dr. Langer of Harvard arrived in Washington in August of 1941, and set up the original Research and Analysis unit of COI. This unpublicized research staff, working for the most part in the Library of Congress, consisted of scholars drawn from all the social science fields — economists, historians, geographers, psychologists, archaeologists, anthropologists, philologists. The great objective was to get these specialists to work together, to pool their knowledge of the materials and literature and to focus their various techniques

[7] "It is a curious fact of academic history that the first great center of area studies in the United States was not located in any university, but in Washington, during the Second World War, in the Office of Strategic Services. In very large measure the area study programs developed in American universities in the years after the war were manned, directed, or stimulated by graduates of the OSS—a remarkable institution, half cops-and-robbers and half faculty meeting. It is still true today, and I hope it always will be, that there is a high measure of interpenetration between universities with area programs and information-gathering agencies of the government of the United States."—McGeorge Bundy in *The Dimensions of Diplomacy*, edited by E. A. J. Johnson (Baltimore, 1964).

on specific problems, in the hope of coming up with the best-informed, most comprehensive, and most critical estimates of particular situations.

Economic intelligence work, one of R&A's greatest strengths, was headed by the noted economist Dr. Edward S. Mason, later director of the School of Public Administration at Harvard. Other scholars hastened to join Langer's growing staff, where they received the best possible graduate training for their postwar careers: Carl Kaysen, now director of the Institute of Advanced Studies at Princeton; John Sawyer, president of Williams College; Fred Burkhard, who was to become chairman of the American Council of Learned Societies; Sherman Kent, later to be for twenty years the assistant director of the CIA for national estimates; Ray Cline, later deputy director of CIA for intelligence; John K. Fairbank, founder of the Center for East Asian Studies at Harvard; Ralph Bunche, later deputy secretary-general of the United Nations; Franklin Ford, Henry L. Roberts, and Charles Kindleberger.

At the start, Donovan established an R&A Board of Analysts, consisting of half a dozen scholars, each of whom took charge of some major activity and played an important role in recruiting further staff members. In this way, he was able to secure the high classifications needed to get the very best people for a general directorate. (Subsequently this Board of Analysts provided the model for the CIA Board of National Estimates, set up in 1950 by Dr. Langer for General Bedell Smith.) Due to its many-sided and brilliant staff, R&A was credited with producing the most accurate estimates made by the Allies in World War II.[8]

Donovan's theory was that secret intelligence, though essential, was often a matter of chance; SI could never be sure what it was going to get, or when it would get it, or how accurate it would be. In any case, it achieved maximum usefulness when combined with information derived from already published works by scholars who knew the literature of a

---

[8] Toward the end of the war, recognition of our work was so general that we were hopelessly pressed. Even in purely operational fields such as bomb targets and determination of enemy losses, our help was regarded as indispensable. But above all, in the study of the capabilities and intentions of foreign powers I think we went far beyond anything previously known in Washington or previously attempted anywhere else, even in Germany."—*Address by Dr. Langer to the American Philosophical Society,* November 20, 1947.

target country and could track down the needed answers. (An estimated 85 percent of the background data for the invasion of Italy was acquired in this manner.) Small-town enemy newspapers, purchased in neutral Stockholm or Lisbon, supplied important order of battle intelligence. The society column of a German weekly reported the presence of several Nazi officers in a garrison town; the location of a long-sought panzer division was revealed. An illustrated brochure published in Scandinavia furnished the first photographic proof that the Germans were using tankers to refuel their submarines at sea. An Italian scientific magazine solved the mystery of Mussolini's two-man underwater demolition craft, used to plant explosives on ships riding at anchor.

It had been confidently assumed, early in the war, that Germany's food shortage would cause an early collapse of Hitler's war effort, but that the manpower of the Third Reich was virtually unlimited. The agricultural section of R&A studied European farm journals and foreign export market statistics, and concluded correctly that the Nazi food supply would never become so low as to affect the course of the war, and in fact there would be an increase in basic rations shortly. On the other hand, by scanning the obit columns in local German periodicals — the Nazis were careful to keep any compromising material out of their main newspapers, but allowed the country journals to print complete obituaries of prominent native sons — R&A statisticians were able to predict an increasingly critical shortage in manpower. In all armies, they reasoned, the ratio of enlisted men to officers is more or less constant. They tallied the published notices of officer casualties, and estimated with remarkable precision the dwindling strength of the German *wehrmacht*.

As R&A expanded, it sent teams to the various war theaters: London, Delhi, Kunming. These overseas units aided the Army and Air Forces directly in making spot evaluations and locating profitable industrial targets for aerial bombardment. Reconnaisance parties combed the battlefronts to copy down the serial numbers of captured German tanks; their figures, analyzed and evaluated by R&A experts, provided a dependable gauge of enemy tank production. The Washington headquarters initiated other vital projects. At the outset of the war, there were almost no detailed maps of European countries, and frequently the military planners had to depend on back issues of the *National Geographic* magazine. The geographical section of R&A prepared an unparalleled collection of maps of various types. R&A cartographers produced the largest globes yet made, one of which was used by President Roosevelt in his White House office. When Roosevelt and Churchill met off Argentia, Newfoundland, for the historic conference which produced the Atlantic Charter, the British Prime Minister pointed to a number of R&A maps on the wall of his cabin. "See?" he said to Roosevelt. "I've got them, too."

In addition to analyzing the Nazi economy and estimating how long Germany could hold out in the war, R&A was called in to appraise the Soviet economy. Because of Russia's enormous requests for American goods under lend-lease, the Board of Economic Warfare asked Dr. Langer's staff to determine whether these demands were justified. A careful investigation indicated that the Soviets had no such need at the time, but wanted to obtain the latest U.S. products for prestige purposes as well as for possible postwar use. R&A's estimate of the strength of the Soviet Union differed from British findings; and Professor Geroid T. Robinson of Columbia, a diligent student of Russian history who later headed the first Russian Institute at Columbia, went to England and spent a week with the British counterpart of R&A, located at Oxford. "You've got better men, you've got more information, we accept your estimates," the British conceded. Dr. Langer claims that no other government had anything comparable to R&A. "And that includes the Germans," he added, "who could have had it if they wanted it — they had the competence."

Prior to the North African invasion in 1942, R&A made elaborate preparatory studies for the JCS. It was important to know how much the French North African railways could carry, the capacity of their rolling stock, the condition of the roadbed and track; all the information proved to be available in current engineering journals. Under the direction of Sherman Kent, terrain maps, charts of reefs and channels, and tidal tables were prepared in detail, and were in the hands of military planners long before the invasion was launched.

2

Torch — code name for the Allied landings in French North Africa — was America's first major offensive of the war. It was also the first OSS operation in direct support of a military action, the crucial test of Colonel Donovan's struggling agency, still forced to operate without a JCS directive. "Our whole future," he confided to his staff, "may depend on the outcome of Torch and the accuracy of our intelligence estimates."

Ever since his mission to the Balkans in 1940, Donovan had argued that the Mediterranean was a potential battlefield, that the Germans held most of the northern front in Europe and therefore it was imperative for the Allies to control the southern front along the African coast. When France fell to Hitler's *blitzkrieg*, defeated and feeble Marshal Pétain had managed to exclude the French colonies in North Africa from the surrender terms, but everyone realized that Germany could seize them at any time. France's navy, holed up in African ports, was loyal to the Axis-dominated provisional government in Vichy. No one knew for sure which side the French army would support in the event of an Allied attack, but it was assumed it would not be Britain. As a result of the Royal Navy's shelling of the French fleet at Oran and Dakar, all British consulates had been closed and their staffs ejected from North Africa, giving the Axis a complete monopoly in the fields of intelligence and propaganda.

In October of 1941, two months before America entered the war, Donovan had presented to President Roosevelt a plan for COI operations in the area as "a concrete illustration of what can be done." His opportunity for secret surveillance came about through an economic pact between the United States and the Vichy French government, with which Roosevelt had prudently maintained diplomatic relations. Robert Murphy, counselor of the American Embassy at Vichy, had signed an agreement whereby the United States would ship cotton, sugar, tea, petroleum, and other essential supplies to France's African dependencies. In exchange, Vichy would permit some American observers to supervise the distribution of the goods and prevent their acquisition by the Axis. A dozen officers were selected who spoke French and who had some prior knowledge of the area. Ostensibly vice-consuls attached to the United States legations at Casablanca, Algiers, Oran, and Tunis, they were actually under orders, unknown to their superiors, to. collect intelligence.

The oddly assorted group — a noted anthropologist, a California oil man, a Harvard librarian, a wine merchant — assumed their posts in July, working under the covert direction of Murphy in Algiers. Their vice-consular status gave them use of diplomatic pouches and cables. Since the Vichy agreement insured them access to North African ports in order to check American shipments, they were able to make overlays of harbor facilities, and accumulate other pre-invasion data. If the regular career consuls were puzzled by their frequent and prolonged absences from their desks, Hitler had no difficulty in guessing what they were up to. A German dispatch, intercepted that fall of 1941, read: "There are ten U.S. citizens in Casablanca who are there for the purpose of forming a fifth column to pave the way for intended Allied disembarkations next spring."

Hitler's estimate of the Allied invasion date was somewhat premature. Though Britain and the United States had agreed on a joint attack against the Axis, they were by no means in agreement as to when and where that attack should take place. Lord Louis Mountbatten was appointed "Adviser on Combined Operations" in October, 1941, and was told by Churchill to plan and prepare for the invasion of the Continent. This was two months before the United States entered the war. In March, 1942, when the possibilities of a successful invasion were obviously enhanced by the United States' becoming Britain's ally, Churchill wished to step up the tempo of invasion preparations and made Mountbatten Chief of Combined Operations with a seat on the Chiefs of Staff's Committee. No one was keener than Mountbatten to get on with the invasion, and he worked hand in hand with Eisenhower and the U.S. Joint Chiefs of Staff from June, 1942, on. When Donovan came to see Mountbatten — partly on this subject — Mountbatten explained to him (as well as to Eisenhower and the JCS) that until enough landing ships, landing craft, support craft, artificial harbors, and the like could be constructed, and until enough men could be trained in amphibious operations, the Germans would be able to defeat any attempt at invasion.

At the time of Donovan's visit, Mountbatten was preparing for the first trial operation at Dieppe. (Donovan joined Mountbatten to watch the rehearsal in England's West Bay.) The Dieppe trials convinced Mountbatten that the Allies were right to invade North Africa first to gain experience. Mountbatten also forecast that however fast the Allies worked they would not have the capacity to breach the "Atlantic Wall" in Normandy and defeat Hitler on land before May, 1944. This opinion was finally accepted, and appears to have been borne out by events. The decision was made to mount a full-scale assault on the French African colonies in the fall. Operation Torch was placed under the command of General Dwight D. Eisenhower.

Once the invasion site was settled, Colonel Donovan dispatched Marine Colonel William Eddy of COI (soon to become OSS) to work with Robert Murphy in shifting the intelligence apparatus into high gear. Eddy was an ideal choice; he had been born in Syria of missionary parents, was familiar with Egypt and Africa, and spoke Arabic fluently. Arab chieftains claimed there were few tents in Saudi-Arabia in which he wasn't welcome. At the outbreak of war, Eddy had quit his academic career with the classic remark: "I am out of love with teaching; I want to be a Marine." He was designated naval attaché to Ambassador Murphy, a position created by Secretary Knox at Donovan's request; and before his departure for Africa in January, 1942, he was briefed on the plan which Donovan had submitted to the President: "That the aid of native chiefs be obtained, the loyalty of the inhabitants cultivated, fifth columnists organized and placed, demolition materials cached, and guerrilla bands of bold and daring men organized and installed." In addition, Eddy would cooperate closely with British intelligence in the Tangier International Zone and Gibraltar.

Eddy and Murphy worked in perfect harmony. Together they set up a clandestine radio network across North Africa, with the key station *Midway* at Tangier, located in a winepress overlooking the airfield; *Lincoln* at Casablanca; *Yankee* at Algiers; *Pilgrim* at Tunis; and *Franklin* at Oran, handled by the chief radio operator for the Division of Oran, who avoided detection by keeping his OSS set broken down, assembling it only for transmission and reception. Eddy established his own head-quarters in Tangier, and all intelligence was routed to him by diplomatic couriers. When the American vice-consuls were denied access to French strategic installations, he turned to native leaders for aid. "Tassels," one of the most influential tribal chiefs in the hilly coastal region of Spanish Morocco, was financed with State Department and OSS funds. His Riffs were Berber adventurers, who knew how to handle arms and conduct guerrilla warfare in the roughest terrain, and were highly adept at eluding Spanish or French police. To keep his relationship with the Americans secret, the furtive "Tassels" assumed a different disguise for each rendezvous with Eddy.

Another valuable underground contact was "Strings," divine head of a powerful religious brotherhood in northern Morocco, whose sect numbered tens of thousands of Moors in all walks of life, sworn to obey unquestioningly the will of their spiritual leader. For fifty thousand francs, "Strings" furnished reports from caids and sheiks, from shep-herds who relayed pertinent local information, and from holy men who penetrated areas forbidden by the French authorities to the general populace.

Individuals having natural occupational cover were also recruited as OSS agents. A native fisherman supplied the locations of Spanish AA guns overlooking the Straits of Gibraltar, and the movements of Ger-man submarines operating out of caves along the rocky coast. A *sherif* notified Eddy of hidden fortifications in the Tetuán-Ceuta area. Two OSS agents who worked as coding clerks in the Spanish consulate at Rabat, capital of French Morocco, turned over decoded copies of all German cables passing through their office. Another accomplice in the ticket office at the Casablanca airport reported all Axis arrivals and departures, and the airline's chief technician passed on to OSS the blue-prints of all airfields as well as their defenses, safety channels, and recognition signals.

North Africa was fast becoming a center of foreign intrigue. German and British and American agents rubbed elbows in the Tangier International Zone or sat at adjoining tables in Casablanca's sidewalk cafes, eavesdropping on one another's conversations in the best E. Phillips Oppenheim tradition. Germany had done a characteristically thorough job of preparing her spies in Berlin training schools, drilling them not only in the basic languages of Africa but also in the various tribal dialects. They were placed stark naked under powerful sunlamps until every portion of their skin was dark enough to pass inspection. They were even taught such niceties as bending the knees slightly when urinating, in the native manner. The very thoroughness of the Teutonic training was its undoing. An apparent Arab peddler, apprehended in a restricted military area, was challenged by a guard in the local dialect, to which he responded correctly. Still suspicious, the guard asked him a question in a second dialect, and again his reply was flawless. After giving letter-perfect answers in three or four more dialects, the German spy was arrested; a genuine native peddler would know only a couple of dialects at most.

In July of 1942, shortly after OSS was established, Colonel Eddy was summoned for a briefing session with a high-level group including Major General George V. Strong, chief of Army intelligence, and General George Patton. Eddy was an impressive figure as he entered the conference room in his Marine Corps uniform, with five banks of decorations which he had won with the Fighting Fifth Marines during the last war. OSS Deputy Director Ned Buxton, who introduced him to the others, informed Colonel Donovan after the meeting: "When Patton first saw the World War I ribbons on Eddy's chest, two more rows than Patton had, the General grunted: 'I don't know who he is, but the son of a bitch has sure been shot at enough.' "

General Strong of G-2 had never lost his jealousy of Donovan, Buxton added, and his antagonism extended to any member of OSS. Colonel Eddy had barely started to brief the conferees on North Africa when Strong interrupted in a belligerent tone: "Listen, Eddy, are you going to tell us what you think or what you know? For God's sake, stick to the facts." Eddy nodded courteously and proceeded to give a detailed account of the special forces which were prepared to seize key points when the invasion took place, the possibility that the French

Army might not oppose an Allied landing, and the disposition and defense of harbor and air facilities, based on R&A estimates. "After listening to Eddy's description of the airfields," Buxton's memo to Donovan concluded, "Patton jumped up and said 'I want Jimmy to hear this.' He returned a moment later with General Doolittle, and they sat until one in the morning, asking Eddy every conceivable question. He knew every answer." Even General Strong was impressed. When the briefing ended, he held out his hand to Eddy. "You seem to know what you're talking about," he conceded.

In London, Eddy conferred with General Eisenhower, and was told that the Allied landings would be at Casablanca in Morocco and at Oran and Algiers in Algeria. The date would be late October or November. Eddy flew back to Tangier to spend the remaining months in detailed preparation for the invasion. With the assistance of the British, American arms were removed from the arsenal at Gibraltar to equip native resistance groups. Sten guns, .45 pistols and ammunition, flares, and explosives were shipped across the Straits to the British Legation at Tangier, from which they were shifted to the U.S. Legation to be smuggled through the Spanish Zone to Casablanca. Hand grenades were obtained from a Riff leader who had bought up a large supply left over from the Spanish Civil War. The grenades were loaded on muleback, disguised as contraband tea and sugar, and carried over the Spanish Morocco border to an OSS agent who hid them in a safe place until D-Day.

As the target date drew nearer, Eisenhower's London headquarters requested Colonel Eddy to furnish a dependable pilot who could guide the Allied fleet past reefs and sunken ships to the North African beaches. Eddy knew precisely the man: Chief Pilot Malverne of nearby Port Lyautey, currently hiding in Casablanca. Malverne had been forced to flee from Vichy France, and was only too eager to serve the Allied cause. The problem was how to smuggle him past the French and Spanish border-control posts into Tangier. Two OSS vice-consuls volunteered to run the gauntlet in their ancient Chevrolet, carrying Malverne secreted in the trailer. The chief pilot was stashed behind some gasoline drums, and covered with a Moroccan rug and a heavy canvas tarpaulin, lashed down securely. Although a vent in the canvas admitted enough air to overcome the danger of carbon monoxide poisoning, the uneasy consuls halted at frequent intervals to lift the vent and inquire in a whisper how Malverne was doing. *"Pas trop mort,"* he would choke gallantly.

They passed the French border post without incident, but at the Spanish post the sentry demanded to know what was in the trailer. While one of the consuls was exhibiting the gasoline drums in the rear, the other noticed to his dismay that the sentry's dog was sniffing at the front of the tarpaulin and bristling suspiciously. With rare presence of mind, he produced a tin of canned meat from his lunch box to distract the dog's attention; the sentry was overwhelmed by this generosity to his pet, and motioned them through the control post gates with a sweeping gesture. Safe at last in Tangier, Malverne was helped out of his cramped hiding place, slightly stiff but otherwise intact, and flown to Washington by way of Gibraltar. On D-Day, Malverne had the satisfaction of piloting the first American destroyer up the treacherous channel of the Sebou River to Port Lyautey, a feat for which he was awarded a Silver Star and the Navy Cross.

There was a last-minute complication. The popular French General Henri Giraud had escaped from a German prison, and the French Army in North Africa looked to him as their hero and natural leader. In a secret communication to Robert Murphy, Giraud asked to be taken into full partnership in the coming invasion, and recommended that the American fleet should make a feint at Africa but land instead in the south of France, which he promised to make ready. For security reasons, the Allied High Command was unwilling to reveal the exact time and place of the invasion, let alone the fact that the British were taking part; but General Eisenhower was anxious to insure the cooperation of the French Army and neutralize any possible resistance. In order to keep the sensitive French in line, he deputized General Mark Clark, commander of the U.S. Fifth Army, to meet with General Charles Mast, Giraud's representative in North Africa, and explain tactfully that it was too late to alter plans. Murphy arranged for the rendezvous at a villa on the Cherchel beach, some seventy-five miles from Algiers, and

Colonel Eddy was instructed to notify Mast that "General Clark and staff will meet at point agreed at 2100 hours October 22."

Murphy and OSS agent Ridgeway Knight drove out to the villa at dusk on the 22nd, and an electric light bulb was hung in a window facing the sea, the prearranged signal to the British submarine *Seraph* bringing General Clark. "I paced the beach until almost midnight," Ridgeway Knight recalled, "and at last I spotted a rubber kayak a hundred yards offshore. I waited in the shadows while it beached, then came out to greet a British commando officer. After mutual identifications, he signaled with a flashlight that all was clear, and three more kayaks appeared out of the darkness with Generals Mark Clark and Lyman L. Lemnitzer and several staff officers. We carried the kayaks to the villa and hid them. General Mast and the French representatives arrived at dawn, and they talked all that day."

Clark and Mast were just concluding their conference when a loyal French coastguardsman hammered on the door, shouting the warning: "*Gendarmes!*" General Clark observed later: "One would have thought that fifty dead skunks had been thrown into the room, the way our friends disappeared." The General and his staff took refuge in the wine cellar, the trapdoor was replaced and a table moved over it, and Murphy and Knight emptied all the money from their pockets onto the table to indicate that a friendly game of poker-dice was in progress. After a cursory search of the premises, the police departed, and Clark and Lemnitzer and the other American officers emerged from the wine cellar, festooned with cobwebs, and carried their kayaks down to the shore to return to the waiting submarine. The swells were so high that the light rubber boats promptly overturned; after three futile attempts to launch them, Clark and his staff removed their uniforms and waded waist-deep through the surf to climb aboard, while Knight held the kayaks steady until they were safely past the breakers. The beach was raked clear of telltale footprints, and Murphy and Knight drove back to Algiers in considerable relief.

Suspicions of an impending Allied invasion were rife, and, since it was impossible to halt the rumors, Eddy took advantage of them by starting a rumor or two of his own in order to mislead the Germans as to the actual site. By great good luck, one of his vice-consuls encountered two young Austrians who had been thrown into a Vichy concentration camp because of their violently anti-Nazi sentiments, and who had escaped to Casablanca. They were on very friendly terms with General Theodor Auer, chief of the German Armistice Commission in Africa. At Eddy's suggestion, the pair of Austrians offered themselves to Auer as his personal spies, and for several weeks fed the Herr General accurate but unimportant intelligence about American movements. To demonstrate their ability to penetrate the OSS ring, they dined openly with two vice-consuls in a black market restaurant, while Auer and his staff watched approvingly from a nearby table. Having gained his complete confidence, they informed him that the invasion fleet was planning to strike at Dakar, on the South Atlantic coast of French West Africa. General Auer rewarded them handsomely for their tip-off, and forwarded his sensational scoop to Nazi command headquarters in Wiesbaden; and the German Mediterranean fleet and submarines were ordered to rendezvous off Dakar, a couple of thousand miles away, leaving the coast of North Africa undefended. Another carefully planted rumor that Britain was rushing a food convoy to the starving island of Malta was so effective that the Germans completely misinterpreted the passage of 150 Allied ships through the Straits of Gibraltar on their way to Casablanca and Algiers.

Everything was in readiness as the amphibious force, largest yet assembled by the Allies, neared the African coast. Resistance groups had been assigned to beachheads and parachute fields, with flares to guide the invaders. The signal to alert them for action was to come to OSS communications operators in the form of a British Broadcasting Company announcement: "Robert arrive!" On the night before the landing, an OSS agent in Oran removed the caps from enemy demolition charges in the tunnel connecting Mers-el-Kebir with Oran, vital to Allied movement. The network of clandestine radios supplied the approaching armada with detailed information on what to expect at each landing point, the disposition of the pro-Axis French Navy, the shore batteries which were actually manned, the number of planes on every airfield, and current conditions of wind and weather and tide.

At midnight of November 8, 1942, Colonel Eddy was in Gibraltar with General Eisenhower, who went under the alias of "Howe," and General Clark, called "Mark." As they sat before a receiving set in the United States Consulate, they heard the BBC code signal flashed to the five radio stations: "Écoute, *Yankee, Franklin, Pilgrim, Lincoln, Midway.* Robert arrive! Robert arrive!" Landing boats were met at the beaches by friendly guides. Some 107,000 Allied troops went ashore without major opposition over a stretch of almost two thousand miles of North African coast, while the German fleet waited vainly in the South Atlantic, and seven squadrons of Sicily-based Luftwaffe bombers circled the Mediterranean three hundred miles to the east in search of the mythical Malta-bound British convoy. After three days of light resistance by the Vichy French Navy, Admiral Darlan signed an armistice agreement, and on November 11, a ceasefire was ordered.

R&A's pre-invasion charts and estimates, and the OSS-pioneered technique of keeping commanders informed of conditions ashore up to the very moment of landing, had clearly demonstrated the new agency's value; but Donovan's draft directive, submitted to the JCS before Torch, was still being debated in committee hearings. Early in December Donovan had an informal chat with his old friend Frank Knox, Secretary of the Navy. Knox was surprised to learn that so long a period had elapsed without any formal or comprehensive instructions from the Joint Chiefs, and he took up the matter with President Roosevelt, who told General George C. Marshall, chairman of the JCS: "I wish you would give Bill Donovan a little elbow room to operate in." Shortly afterward the Joint Chiefs appointed committees of high-ranking officers, including Admiral Fredrick Horne and Generals Joseph T. McNarney and Albert Wedemeyer, to make a personal inspection of OSS and recommend what should be done. The committees promptly rendered reports (which were not made available to OSS), and on December 23, 1942, six months after it was created, the agency received its long-awaited directive, almost word for word the draft which Donovan had prepared.

In the field of intelligence, OSS was given the independent status which Donovan sought, climaxing the bitter feud with the rival service agencies. The Joint Psychological Warfare Board, on which OSS had a minority of members, was abolished by the JCS. Henceforth OSS was the sole agency of the JCS authorized to operate in the fields of intelligence, sabotage, and counterespionage, to conduct guerrilla operations, and to direct resistance groups in all enemy-occupied or -controlled territory. General Marshall stated in a personal letter to Colonel Donovan, written on the same day the directive was issued:

"I regret that, after voluntarily coming under the jurisdiction of the JCS, your organization has not had smoother sailing. Nevertheless, it has rendered invaluable service, particularly with reference to the North African Campaign. I am hopeful that the new Office of Strategic Services' directive will eliminate most, if not all, of your difficulties."

3

Despite General Marshall's optimism, Donovan's difficulties were far from over. After the successful conclusion of Torch, control of French North Africa passed to Allied Force Headquarters, and OSS personnel in North Africa came under the command of AFHQ in Algiers. Local field commanders did not understand the strategic specialty for which the agency had prepared its personnel, and employed them instead for front-line tactical intelligence or ordinary infantry duty.[9] When the brilliant generalship of German Field Marshal Rommel, the Desert Fox, defeated the Anglo-American forces at Kasserine Pass early in 1943, a group of seven OSS operatives, assigned as liaison officers with a forward British intelligence unit in Tunisia, were ordered out on reconnaisance patrol to destroy German panzer division tanks with hand grenades. Two members of the group were captured during a surprise attack by enemy artillery; an OSS Marine officer and a sergeant were injured by an exploding land mine in the course of a search for snipers; another OSS

[9] General Mark Clark, commander of Fifth Army, found on landing in Italy that his G-2 had no personnel prepared for tactical military intelligence, one of G-2's primary functions. So great was Clark's need that OSS agents, trained for deep penetration and procurement of strategic intelligence, were used to find out the German strength directly behind their front lines.

Marine observer, who had volunteered to lead a combat party, was lost while destroying a German machine gun nest singlehanded. Although they performed bravely, their use as infantrymen was a waste of trained experts.

Some of the agency's troubles were due to the overeagerness of its own young and inexperienced personnel. One of the largest OSS blunders of the war — and inevitably there were many — occurred after General Mark Clark's Fifth Army took over the western defenses of North Africa. To meet the possibility of attack from Spanish Morocco, General Clark desired information on the activities of Vichy French officials and pro-Axis members of the Arab population, as well as knowledge of German sabotage units and military preparations by the Axis in Spain. Impressed by the assistance OSS had rendered during Torch, General Clark arranged to have a veteran contingent from Casablanca assigned to G-2 at Fifth Army headquarters at Oujda: the first time that an OSS group was attached to an American Army at the specific request of its commander.

Unfortunately the OSS commander had committed three serious errors. The agents he selected for the mission were Communists, recruited through "popular front" organizations in Africa and Mexico. Moreover, they carried American army matériel, including grenades and submachine guns and ammunition, all bearing U.S. markings and serial numbers. Third and worst, he had never submitted his plan to OSS headquarters in Washington, nor received official approval. Eventually the agents were captured by the Spanish police in Málaga, and Communist codebooks were discovered on them. Under pressure, they revealed details of the American training school at Oujda, the location of their secret SSTR-1 radio sets, and the names of other leftist comrades. A widespread cleanup by the Falangist government resulted in 261 arrests and 22 executions, a crippling blow to the whole underground. Since Spain was a neutral country with which the United States was maintaining friendly relations, the State Department was hard pressed to explain how American arms happened to be in the possession of Communist elements. The embarrassed U.S. ambassador to Spain, Carleton Hayes, tried to cover the blunder by denying any American involvement, but OSS had been seriously compromised. Lack of judgment by one field commander in Oujda nearly ended the agency's usefulness in Spain.

The indiscreet commander was released from OSS; but General Clark considered his previous services so valuable that he was reassigned to Fifth Army, and placed in charge of a detachment during the landings at Salerno a few months later.

Meantime OSS/Washington was having its own higher-echelon difficulties with the British Intelligence Service (SIS). Back in the early days of COI, London had been most cooperative, sharing its training facilities and operational techniques with the struggling new agency. As OSS grew stronger, however, SIS showed an increasing reluctance to accept its American counterpart as a full and equal partner.

Britain's position was enhanced by the Theater Command's lack of sympathy with OSS objectives. Throughout 1942-43, the practice of ETOUSA (European Theater of Operations) was to rely mainly on British Intelligence and ignore OSS offers of assistance, thus inadvertently aiding SIS efforts to subordinate the younger American organization. The U.S. Theater Command staff based their policy on Britain's greater experience in the field; but they overlooked the fact that OSS could provide new and different information to supplement or even refute the intelligence from other sources, and would serve long-range U.S. strategic needs best if it remained independent.[10]

The issue came to a head in September of 1943 when ETOUSA refused to give OSS authority to conduct espionage on the European continent unless it operated under British supervision. General Donovan insisted that freedom from the knowledge and influence of any outside power was essential to the success of his Secret Intelligence branch, and he strongly opposed the SIS efforts to force an amalgamation. In an appeal to the Joint Chiefs of Staff, he pointed out that Britain's proposal "suggests 'coordination' and 'agreement,' but as employed here the word 'coordination' means 'control' and 'agreement' means 'dependence.' . . . This attempt of the British, by reason of their physical control of

[10] These problems did not exist with the relatively new SOE.

territory and communication, to subordinate the American intelligence and counterintelligence service is shortsighted and dangerous to the ultimate interests of both countries."

As a result of his arguments, a new JCS directive on October 27, 1943 gave OSS full and unqualified authority to operate on the Continent, ETOUSA accordingly reversed its position, and the independence of American long-range espionage was assured. Rather than engage in destructive competition, the British yielded. OSS Special Operations (SO) and Counterintelligence (X-2) greatly strengthened their ETO and were given access to the extensive files which Britain had taken decades to develop. In turn, OSS provided funds, manpower, resistance supplies, three sub-chasers for Norwegian operations, and a squadron of Liberator bombers for airdrops to occupied countries. Thenceforth throughout the war American and British intelligence worked in productive though discreet partnership.

III

DONOVAN'S BELIEF that OSS would survive — "If we're right, we'll prevail" — had never faltered during the dark months of 1942. Even before the Joint Chiefs issued their authorization, he and his staff drafted General Order Number 9, drawing up an organizational chart for the agency and describing the functions of each operational branch and office of his entire command. Order Number 9 went into effect promptly upon receipt of the official JCS directive.

Colonel Donovan brought a trained legal mind to the task of organizing his fast-growing agency — OSS was to employ some thirty thousand people by the war's end — and set it up as he would prepare a trial case, with research experts to analyze the evidence and skilled assistants to conduct the prosecution. At the top of the chart were Donovan as director and Buxton as deputy director, and beside them were the Planning Group and the Planning Staff. Under Donovan were his three deputy directors, with staff but not command status, who were charged with the duty of coordinating the three main OSS functions: intelligence (research and analysis, secret intelligence, counterespionage, and collateral offices), operations (sabotage, guerrilla warfare, psychological warfare, and related activities), and schools and training. A chief of services supervised the work of the offices of budget, procurement, finance, and related problems. In addition, there were some eighteen essential offices which could not be assigned effectively to any subordinate command. Thus the Security Office reported directly to Donovan, since security involved all procedures and all personnel, regardless of rank. Other offices which served the entire organization were also placed under the director, including medical services, special funds, field photographic, communications, Navy and Army Commands which handled the administrative problems of OSS naval and military personnel, and a liaison office to maintain relations with other government agencies.[11] The functions of the principal branches were:

Research and Analysis (R&A) To produce the economic, military, social and political studies and estimates for every strategic area from Europe to the Far East.

Secret Intelligence (SI) To gather on-the-spot information from within neutral and enemy territory.

Special Operations (SO) To conduct sabotage and work with resistance forces.

Counterespionage (X-2) To protect our own and Allied intelligence operations, and to identify enemy agents overseas.

Morale Operations (MO) To create and disseminate black propaganda.

Operational Groups (OG) To train and supply and lead guerrilla forces in enemy territory.

Maritime Unit (MU) To conduct maritime sabotage.

Schools and Training (S&T) In overall charge of the assessment and training of personnel, both in the United States and overseas.

Not only did this departmentalization increase the agency's effectiveness, but it helped to maintain security. Each branch of OSS had its own secret file of information, which was available to members of other branches only on an official "need to know" basis. Donovan himself was not told the real names of some of his most successful agents, nor did he seek to learn them. Complete anonymity was the best safeguard against detection by the enemy.

Still there was considerable Washington opposition to certain collateral activities which OSS had been conducting, such as its Foreign Nationalities unit (FN). This branch, unlike almost every other unit in the agency except R&A, had its major activity centered in the United

[11] For complete organizational chart, see page 338.

States. Its function was to obtain political and other information from refugees, political escapees, or exiles from enemy or enemy-occupied countries. OSS would almost certainly have been denied this function, had it not been that the Secretary of State personally requested that it be continued, since political information gained from these exiles might be important both during and after the war, and could be made available to State without embarrassment. FN proved of great value to OSS intelligence and operational branches; the exiles usually had contacts in the enemy countries who were sympathetic to the Allied cause, and these contacts helped solve the difficult and dangerous problem of introducing agents into hostile territory.

The Maritime Unit (MU) likewise encountered some early opposition. The function of this unit was to develop the technique of clandestine infiltration by sea, and to execute maritime sabotage; and on the face of it this seemed to conflict with the prerogatives of the Navy. Nonetheless OSS received authorization to continue MU activities, and this unit performed a spectacular service by organizing a fleet of caïques to supply operations in the Middle East.

Just as Donovan's energy gave OSS its vitality, so the agency was buoyed by his fertile imagination. From the beginning, he had encouraged boldness and inventiveness in devising ingenious ways to harass the enemy; and any suggestion, however bizarre, was welcomed in the front office. "Go ahead and try it," he would nod. "We learn by our mistakes." No project was so implausible, no weapon so outlandish as to be discarded out of hand.

Someone might come up with the idea of making a land mine in the shape of camel dung, which members of a resistance group could plant on a desert trail. Donovan would order his researchers to explore the possibilities. Someone else might hit on the scheme of camouflaging a powerful explosive as a lump of coal, to be tossed into a passing coal truck and eventually shoveled into the fire box of a Nazi locomotive. Donovan would beam in approval: "Why not give it a whirl?" After all, he felt, it was no more fantastic than the other lethal inventions emanating from Dr. Lovell's Research and Development unit, sometimes referred to as the department of dirty tricks.

2

Dr. Stanley Lovell, in charge of the agency's calculated mischief, was a sunny little nihilist, his spectacles twinkling and his chubby face creasing with merriment as he displayed his latest diabolic devices. This simple candle could be placed by a female agent in the bedroom of an amorous German officer, Lovell chuckled, and would burn perfectly until the flame touched the high explosive contained in the lower half of the candle. This innocent-looking plastic cylinder called the Firefly, dropped furtively into the gas tank of a car by a Maquis filling-station attendant, would explode after the gasoline had swelled a rubber retaining ring. If the vehicle were a German tank — Lovell had to pause to wipe his spectacles and dab the tears of laughter from his eyes — the occupants would be cremated before they could open the escape hatch. This anerometer, a barometric fuse attached to a length of hose packed with explosive, could be slid into the rear of the fuselage of an enemy aircraft; at five thousand feet altitude, he explained gleefully, the entire tail section would blow off. This limpet, fastened by a powerful magnet to the side of a ship below waterline, would detonate when the magnesium alloy was eroded by salt water, long after the saboteur had left the area. It was used effectively by the Norwegian underground to sink Nazi troop-ships in the narrow fjords of Oslo and Narvik — Lovell doubled up and slapped his knees at the thought — and sent untold thousands of German soldiers to a watery grave.

One of Dr. Lovell's favorite products was "Aunt Jemima," a powdered form of TNT resembling ordinary wheat flour, activated by a time-delay detonator. If the Gestapo were suspicious, the flour could be kneaded into dough and baked into biscuits or bread which the agent could eat safely, though it was not advisable to smoke a cigarette immediately afterward.

Some R&D devices were so old that they were new again. A special shoe was prepared with a space in the sole to secrete messages, over which an upper sole was stitched and smoothed and stained at the edges — the same method employed by Nathan Hale to smuggle his maps of British fortifications out of New York. Another popular saboteur weapon was a four-cornered steel spike which would land on a highway or airplane runway with three prongs down and the fourth upraised, its sharpened point guaranteed to puncture the stoutest tire. Back in the American Revolution, these identical spikes, called "crow's feet," were scattered in the streets of Boston behind Howe's retreating army to discourage American pursuers.

Occasionally Dr. Lovell was carried away by his own enthusiasm. An OSS anthropologist reported that the Japanese were uniquely sensitive about the act of defecation, and considered any contact with fecal matter to be a disgrace. Inspired by this rare opportunity to make the Japanese lose face, Lovell directed his chemists to prepare a scatologic compound which exactly duplicated the consistency and odor of a loose bowel movement. This noisome chemical named "Who? Me?" was packaged in collapsible tubes and flown across the Himalayas to Chungking, where it was distributed to Chinese children in enemy-occupied cities such as Peiping and Shanghai and Canton. When a ranking Japanese officer strolled down the crowded street, the theory went, an urchin would creep up behind him and squirt a shot of "Who? Me?" onto the seat of his trousers, causing him to retire in malodorous confusion. How many Japs lost face could never be determined; but some skeptical OSS associates wondered why it was necessary to go to the expense of imitating human excrement and flying it halfway around the world, when the genuine article could be found anywhere in Asia in prodigal abundance.

It was Mrs. Eleanor Roosevelt, Lovell always insisted, who dreamed up the Bat Project, perhaps the strangest of all R&D ventures. According to her plan, a number of bats would be transported to Japan, armed with incendiary bombs, and released from an airplane or submarine. The bats would make for the eaves of the Japanese paper and bamboo houses and cling there until the delayed fuses fired, causing a conflagration which would wipe out the enemy city. The initial task was to acquire the bats. One of the project officers told me later that they first erected nets on top of a Manhattan hotel, but it turned out that New York bats were not the desired type. The operation was transferred to the

Carlsbad Caverns, where a number of bats were captured, chilled until they were comatose, and shipped in refrigerator trucks to an abandoned Western mining town which had been selected for the test. In the OSS equipment shed, tiny fire bombs were attached to the bodies of the frosted bats, they were revived and stowed in the bomb bay of an Air Force plane, and turned loose over the ghost town. Instinctively they homed in on the OSS shed and settled under the dry eaves, the officer concluded solemnly, and the resultant blaze destroyed all the experimental equipment and levelled most of the town. Mrs. Roosevelt was eventually persuaded to give up her idea.

An influential U.S. senator was responsible for a parallel venture, called the Cat Project. A constituent had pointed out to him that a cat hates water, and always makes for dry land. His suggestion was to sling a cat in a harness below an aerial bomb, with the mechanism set so delicately that the cat's least movement would direct the vanes of the bomb, and release the feline-guided missile over an enemy battleship. The startled cat would see the water below it, and struggle and claw to reach the one dry spot in sight. "We had to drop a cat in a harness," Lovell wrote, "to prove that the animal became unconscious and ineffective in the first fifty feet of fall."[12] The senator yielded, and Project Cat was duly scrubbed.

3

Inevitably rumors of such zany projects as "Who? Me?" and the incendiary bats began to travel the Washington cocktail circuit, and the isolationist press stepped up its ridicule of "Wild Bill" and his "cloak-and-dagger boys." Columnists referred sneeringly to the "amateur sleuths of the Donovan Committee, many of them former socialite hangers-on from the State Department." Newspaper editorials denounced what they described as the "astronomic waste of money by the boondoggling agency," despite the fact that the actual budget of America's worldwide intelligence service was extremely modest. From 1942 through 1945, excluding the salaries of members of the armed forces on active

12 Stanley Lovell, *Of Spies and Stratagems* (New York, 1963).

duty with the agency, and a substantial part of overseas logistics support, the cost of OSS averaged less than thirty-seven million a year.[13]

Colonel Donovan had no time to waste on his own defense. He was putting in a man-killing work schedule, taking no more than five hours of sleep a night, but he kept himself hard and trim. He had never lost his passion for physical conditioning, and his bathroom was fitted out like a gymnasium with barbells and wallpulls and a rowing machine. Despite all the pressure, he remained easily accessible, and could always find time for a leisurely chat with a World War I acquaintance in his map-lined office, or pause in the corridor to exchange greetings with an enlisted man standing guard at the door. Once a nervous staff assistant, discovering the Director talking to a bewhiskered little man with a German accent, broke in to remind him that he was twenty minutes late for an important meeting at the War Department. "This man is going to jump into Germany soon," Donovan told the aide. "The meeting isn't going anywhere."

With able staff support, perhaps best exemplified by Ned Buxton, Donovan was able to devote himself to the operational and policy problems of the various branches of OSS, and to check personally on their progress. Certain of his deputies felt that he should follow the chain-of-command principle and give more authority to his subordinates; and several leaders of what was referred to by a few of his staff as the "Palace Revolution" presented a written memorandum to Donovan recommending that he delegate complete command function to his deputy directors, and confine himself to making policy decisions. It was one of the few times that Donovan displayed anger. "If that's the way they feel," he told his executive officer, "then I've given them too much authority already." In a succinct reply to the authors of the

[13] "Donovan was the first man to whom Congress made a grant of twenty-five million dollars without requiring an accounting," Dr. Langer notes. "I recall the morning when the General announced this at a staff meeting, and at once turned a cold douche on our elation. This does not mean, he said, that a single dollar is going to be spent irresponsibly, because I know when the war is over this agency will be in a very exposed position unless its record is spotless. For this reason I have asked one of the leading New York accountants to join the OSS, and he will see to it that all expenditures are accounted for to me, even though I am under no such obligation to Congress."

memorandum, he stated that he could not make informed decisions without frequent firsthand contacts with the heads of his principal operating branches and the offices which reported directly to him, and that he would not entertain any more recommendations along this line. The "Palace Revolution" ended abruptly.

Donovan's decision was based on his conviction that the branch chiefs could not perform as effectively if they were denied direct and prompt access to the head of the agency. His availability and his constant probing not only kept subordinates on their toes, but served to inform him of what was going on in OSS both at home and abroad. When he was satisfied that a branch such as R&A was operating efficiently, he would never interfere. "If you run into any serious difficulties," he told Dr. Langer in 1943, "let me know. Otherwise I'll assume that things are going along as they should."

Donovan accepted no government salary from the time COI was formed in 1941 until the spring of 1943. President Roosevelt had written him that he was "entitled to compensation for actual and necessary transportation, subsistence, and other expenses incidental to the performance of duty," but he submitted a small expense account only once, and withdrew it immediately when the Budget Bureau informed him that it would have to be itemized.

For two years he remained a civilian; the title "Colonel" referred to his reserve status. Roosevelt had proposed making him a major general in 1941, to increase his effectiveness in dealing with American and Allied leaders, but had tabled the nomination when isolationist Congressmen threatened to block it. Again in 1942, after OSS was established, Roosevelt had attempted to arrange a promotion, and again the nomination was postponed.

It was not until April 2, 1943 that Donovan was made a brigadier general, and he was finally advanced to the rank of major general on November 10, 1944.

IV

DURING THE WAR an aide asked Donovan's longtime driver, Freeman, where to find the General. "I don't know where he's at," Freeman replied, "but I know that wherever at he is, that's where he want to be."

Donovan had feared that, as chief of OSS, he would be shackled to a Washington desk. Actually, he saw more varied action in World War II than he had encountered with New York's 69th. His staff lived in constant dread of being hauled out of bed in the middle of the night to accompany him on another whirlwind mission to Africa or London or China. He might visit a half-dozen countries between dawn and dark. A typical day's diary would read: "Bologna in Italy, to Munich in Bavaria, to Salzburg in Austria, to Patton's headquarters in Bad Nauheim, to Pilsen in Czechoslovakia, then in a B–25 that night to Paris."

As a harried staff member put it: "109 [General Donovan's code number] was a sort of one-man mobile unit. Space was no barrier to him — the Sahara Desert was a sand dune, the Himalayas were a bank of snow, the Pacific was a ditch. Circling the globe, he would catch up with time and pass it. We wouldn't have been at all surprised to see him leave one afternoon and return the previous morning." He realized how much the Gestapo would give to capture him, and he carried a K-capsule of deadly poison to be swallowed if he fell into enemy hands. But he wanted firsthand knowledge of OSS operations overseas and, equally important, he knew what his presence at a remote outpost meant to the OSS field personnel, who by the end of 1943 were scattered over all the strategic frontiers.

Associates claimed they could always tell when another Allied invasion was due by the General's abrupt departure from Washington. He wore three arrowheads on his European ribbon, signifying the major landings in which he participated. In July of 1943 his son David, a Navy lieutenant, was assigned to Admiral Hall's flagship *Samuel Chase* in Algiers. At the last minute, as they were about to cast off for the Anglo-American invasion of Sicily, word came from the fantail to hold everything, a general was arriving. There was a commotion on the pier below and David, glancing over the rail, saw his father pile out of a jeep and scurry aboard, accompanied by Lieutenant Ray Kellogg of John Ford's OSS field photographic unit. David has another distinct memory of General Donovan, clad in a borrowed pair of jungle trousers several sizes too big for him, clambering over the side on his way to the Sicilian beachhead. "Ray Kellogg followed right behind him," David recalls, "to help hold up his britches."

He was on an LST in January of 1944 with the first wave at Anzio. On June 6 he was aboard the *Tuscaloosa* at the Normandy invasion, wearing a woolen cap and nonchalantly munching an apple while the cruiser's big guns blasted the shore defenses. As he rode in on a landing craft with Colonel David Bruce, chief of OSS/Europe, Bruce groaned aloud at a belated realization. "I forgot to bring my K-capsule," he confessed.

"That's all right," the General shrugged, "I'll lend you one." He groped through the pockets of his uniform blouse, and his expression grew embarrassed. "I guess I forgot mine, too," he admitted, "But there's no need to worry." He patted Bruce's shoulder reassuringly. "If anything happens, I'll shoot you first."

On his way back to Washington after the Sicilian landings, General Donovan conferred with General Mark Clark at Fifth Army headquarters in Morocco, and offered to place his agency's resources at Fifth Army disposal for the coming invasion of Italy. It was decided to expand the OSS functions by adding operations specialists and research experts for tactical and strategic intelligence procurement, and the 2677th Special Reconnaisance Battalion (OSS), reorganized on a full

WJD (left) with General Mark Clark (right) at Fifth Army headquarters in Morocco, summer 1943. (WJD's belt was not regulation issue.)

military basis, was assigned to G-2, Fifth Army. During the Italian campaign, local agents were infiltrated almost daily through the German lines for tactical information, and trained units equipped with radios were dispatched on long-range missions deeper into enemy territory. The detachment was ordered to "brief combat intelligence teams, contact pro-American and anti-Fascist organizations, and recruit likely personnel for informers, *coup de main* groups, censorship work, guides, interpreters, translators, or leaders to be subsidized": the first time the new techniques of OSS support were employed directly by ground armies.

The decision to invade the Italian mainland had been reached after prolonged and heated debate. With the surrender of the German forces in Tunisia in May of 1943, and the capture of fifteen Axis divisions, the U.S. Joint Chiefs of Staff had renewed their pressure for a cross-Channel assault on German-occupied France. Prime Minister Churchill countered that the recent success in North Africa had exposed what he called, with both rhetoric and accuracy, the "soft underbelly" of Europe, and he insisted that the Allies should maintain their momentum in the Mediterranean. Roosevelt reluctantly acknowledged the logic of his argument, and the all-out attack on the German homeland was postponed for another year.

For a time, events seemed to justify Churchill's decision. Sicily and Corsica and the outlying islands fell to the Allies virtually without a struggle, due in part to previous OSS infiltration which had organized the local resistance, and early in September the Anglo-American forces established a successful foothold on the mainland at Salerno, near the tip of the Italian boot. On September 8, Mussolini's Fascist dictatorship toppled, the United States recognized the royal government of Victor Emmanuel, and his Prime Minister, Italian Field Marshal Badoglio, made haste to arrange the capitulation of the Italian Army. Hopes for a speedy Allied victory faded when the German forces, although deserted by their Axis partner, continued to fight on stubbornly, and the attack on the "soft underbelly" proved eventually to be the longest and bloodiest campaign of the European war.

While the Anglo-American armies moved slowly up the Italian

peninsula, contesting every mile with heavy losses, five OSS infiltration teams slipped into Naples harbor on small fishing boats. Two were repulsed by machine gun fire from German shore patrols, but the others succeeded in entering the captive city, carrying arms for Neapolitan patriots, and organized guerrilla resistance against the Nazis. As many as twenty line-crossings a day were carried out, and intelligence was radioed to Fifth Army to pinpoint Air Force bombing missions. When the Germans evacuated Naples on October 1st, the OSS teams and their Partisan followers greeted the American army of liberation with cheers and Chianti.

The Allied advance bogged down in December at Monte Cassino, where Field Marshal Kesselring's Tenth Army succeeded in halting the fourteen divisions of the American Fifth and British Eighth armies at the heavily entrenched Winter Line. To solve the stalemate, it was decided to launch a daring amphibious landing north of the Winter Line at Anzio, only thirty miles from Rome. Operation Shingle, as it was named, was conceived as a "cat claw" thrust with parachutists to seize the Alban Hills, a key height of land near Rome, and hold the ground long enough to cut communications and supplies for the German Tenth Army at Cassino. " 'Tis not intended to maintain these divisions for long over the beaches," Churchill cabled the Chiefs of Staff on December 26, "but rather to bring the battle to a climax in a week or ten days." The Shingle target date was to be on or about January 20, 1944.

A week before Anzio, General Donovan arrived unannounced at OSS headquarters in Naples, a dilapidated four-story palazzo requisitioned from an indigent Neapolitan duke. In its vast rococo rooms, radios and high-explosives mingled incongruously with the duke's gilded mirrors and heavy Victorian furniture, and the personnel feasted by candlelight on wines from their host's cellar and *fettucine* made with G.I. powdered eggs. The General joined them for dinner, and with instinctive courtesy insisted that Peter Tompkins, twenty-four-year-old chief of the Naples group, should preside at the head of the table. "You're the host," he said. "I'll sit at your right." Later, over coffee, he confided to Tompkins the purpose of his visit. It was expected that the coming landings at Anzio would result in the early liberation of Rome, the

General explained, and he desired someone to enter the occupied city, contact OSS secret radio *Vittorio* which had been operating in Rome since last October, and at a given signal institute sabotage and counter-sabotage measures to coincide with the Allied invasion. Filled with that sense of dedication which the General engendered in his men, Tompkins volunteered.

Donovan's selection was a shrewd one. Tompkins's parents had lived in Rome for years, he had spent much of his boyhood there, and spoke the language fluently enough to pass for an Italian. He had been working in the Rome bureau of the New York *Herald Tribune* before the war, and knew his way around the city "as well as any *trasteverino* born in the shadow of St. Peter's," he wrote in his autobiography.[14] Under the cover name of "Pietro," he was flown by OSS plane to Corsica, landed in a rubber boat at Fossa del Telfone pinpoint on the night of January 21, and was smuggled by car into Rome without detection. There he contacted "Coniglio," leader of the strategic intelligence team dispatched by the OSS Fifth Army Detachment in October, whose dark piercing eyes reminded Tompkins of a ferret, and a sensitive young Neapolitan agent known as "Cervo" who wore the uniform of a police lieutenant, complete with highly polished boots and official armband and revolver. It was Cervo who had brought the *Vittorio* radio up from Naples, and was charged with its care and concealment. Cervo invited Tompkins to hide out in his own apartment. "After all," he said, "who would expect to find an American agent in a Fascist policeman's bed?"

The following morning, January 22, Tompkins learned that an Allied assault convoy of fifty thousand men and five thousand vehicles had anchored off Anzio before dawn, and the troops had swarmed ashore without opposition. The invasion had caught the enemy completely off guard. In Rome the OSS countersabotage teams were readied to defuse the mines planted on the Tiber bridges, and initiate guerrilla activities against the Germans; and Tompkins waited impatiently for the signal over *Vittorio* to start their operations. The only message was a warning that the liberation of Rome would be temporarily postponed, and a top-

14 Peter Tompkins, *A Spy in Rome* (New York, 1962).

priority request for information on all German troop movements toward the beachhead.

Day after day passed without news of the expected Allied advance, and gradually the truth dawned on Tompkins: instead of the lightning "cat claw" thrust at the Alban Hills, General Clark's Anglo-American forces had inexplicably decided to dig in and consolidate their defensive position on the beach against a German counterattack. Long after the war it was revealed that Field Marshal Kesselring, upon learning of the Anzio landings, had exclaimed: "Only a miracle can save us now!" The miracle was Allied overcaution. The advantage of surprise was squandered, General Clark called off the plan to drop paratroopers who could have prevented the movement of enemy troops against the beachhead "lest it prematurely disclose the area of our main assault," and Anzio settled into a stalemate as complete as Cassino. Churchill cabled Field Marshal Viscount Alexander in disgust: "I expected to see a wildcat roaring into the mountains – and what do I find? A whale wallowing on the beaches."

For the next two months OSS radio *Vittorio* continued to supply detailed information on all the German units deployed against the Allied landing forces, identifying the Hermann Goering Panzer Division and elements of the 1st and 4th Nazi Parachute Divisions, and recommending railroad yards and main lines for bombing targets. The underground groups which Tompkins had alerted for countersabotage were transformed in February and March into a comprehensive intelligence network, deriving their information from the various political parties, from industrialists who still enjoyed German confidence, and from officers of the "Open City of Rome" staff, including one actually assigned to Kesselring's headquarters. The longer the Allies delayed at Anzio, the more tense the OSS situation in Rome became. Since the invaders had lost the initiative, Rome's Fascist police allied themselves more openly with the Germans, and the enthusiasm of the resistance groups began to fade as a result of the prolonged inaction and the lack of promised airdropped supplies of arms and food.

Elaborate precautions were taken to maintain the security of both *Vittorio* and a second clandestine radio transmitter which had been set up to handle the heavy flow of air traffic between OSS/Rome and the armies stalled on the Anzio beachhead. Cervo had concealed *Vittorio* on one of the numerous riverboats tied up along the Tiber, ramshackle wooden bathhouses on floating pontoons which were known as a favorite site for homosexual assignations and were usually left alone by the police. The riverboat he selected was almost opposite the Italian Ministry of Marine, whose radio signals would cover the weaker signals of the OSS station in case the enemy attempted triangulation. The other radio was hidden by an accommodating priest in a small church in the heart of Rome, and tapped out its code messages from the quiet penumbra of his sacristy. During a six-week period, the bulletins transmitted to Fifth Army totalled ninety-eight single-spaced typewritten pages, exclusive of tissue paper tracings of German insignia which were delivered to Cervo for transliteration to the base.

Inevitably the Allied delay brought disillusionment and defections. On March 13, OSS learned that its security had been blown by a radio technician, "Walter," who had entered the pay of the Germans to spy on resistance activities in Rome. Cervo and an orderly named Scottu sped by motorcycle to the riverboat to change the location of *Vittorio*, while Tompkins and his fellow agents waited in the apartment for his return. That evening the telephone rang insistently, and one of the agents answered, and hung up with a puzzled look. "Cervo's sister wants to know if you have bought her any honey," he told Tompkins. The others stared at their chief in sudden apprehension. "That was the conventional phrase we arranged for." Tompkins nodded. "They've got Cervo." In the shocked silence, the phone sounded again, two rings, a pause, and two more rings — the danger signal. Systematically they began collecting and burning all OSS messages and codebooks, armed themselves with hand grenades, and placed their automatics in readiness on the table, prepared for a last-ditch fight if Cervo, under torture, revealed their hideout.

Cervo never broke; though the others did not learn the full story of his capture until after a week of nerve-racking suspense. Alerted by the informer, a group of Fascist Republican Police had been waiting at the riverboat to seize Cervo and his orderly. They were taken to Via

Principe Amedeo 2, escorted to the top floor by armed guards led by Dr. Koch, noted as a torture expert, and thrown into separate cells. In an official report written after his escape, Scottu stated that "they started punching my chest, my jaw as if I were a punching bag. . . . At 2 A.M. the lieutenant [Cervo] was brought into our cell, bleeding from the mouth, nose, and with his face all swollen. He had lost several teeth." Cervo's first thought was to save the boy from further beating. "Receiving an order from him to confess to the fact that I knew him, I admitted the truth on this point, declaring myself to be his orderly."

Day after day the torture continued, but neither Cervo nor the orderly would reveal the names of their associates. On the 23rd, the fifth day after their capture, it was learned that some Partisans had thrown a bomb into a Rome side street called Via Rasella, which had killed thirty-two German MPs. Infuriated by the news, Koch and his Fascist inquisitors burst into the cell and "started to beat, kick and punch those present, covering us with spittle," Scottu reported. The lieutenant was interrogated alone for about twenty minutes, "coming back with his face disfigured, tottering and worn out. Walter, Cervo's former friend, punched him in the mouth. Blood flowed from the crushed lips and toothless gums. As he sat on the floor wiping the blood weakly, Walter, like a beast, raised his foot and brought it down with all the weight of his body, kicking him in the pubic region. The Lieutenant, at the end of his strength, cried 'Mamma, mamma, they've killed me.' "

Toward evening the turncoat Walter announced that the inmates of the cell were to be handed over to the Nazi SS, as part of the 320 civilians to be executed in ten-to-one retaliation for the 32 Germans bombed at Via Rasella. "Only the Lieutenant whispered words of encouragement to all. I helped him to the toilet, but he could pass only blood. Seeing us, Walter knocked us both to the ground." Cervo was carried bodily out of the cell and taken to Regina Coeli jail, but Scottu, arriving later at the same jail, was not among those selected for execution. Cervo and the other hostages were transported by truck to some catacombs near San Callisto, and were thrown into a cave and shot one by one in the back of the neck. When the victims were piled in a heap, the Germans exploded a number of mines, burying dead and dying under the collapsing walls of the cave.

The following morning a small paid announcement in a Rome newspaper's obit column stated that Cervo's parents, "torn with grief, request that their friends neither call nor send messages of condolence." The notice added discreetly: "At only twenty-three the life of a young lieutenant and doctor of law, a volunteer, wounded in action, and decorated, has most suddenly been extinguished."

Although Cervo's sacrifice had saved the lives of his associates, both the Germans and the Fascist police were now aware of the existence of the OSS group; and the members led a hunted life, hiding in garrets and cellar holes while waiting for the Allies to liberate the city. Complicating the situation was the increasing friction between Coniglio and Tompkins. Consequently the agents, resentful of each other, resorted to means of their own to transmit what was often duplicate intelligence. Coniglio sent his messages by courier to the north, to be relayed to Fifth Army by other OSS radios in Italy; and Tompkins, after the loss of *Vittorio,* made use of a British SIS circuit. Often the SIS set in southern Italy did not forward Tompkins's information until it was over a month old, and therefore useless.

Unable to contribute timely intelligence, Tompkins and his unit decided to organize patriot forces in Rome into secret brigades for the prevention of the German "scorched earth" program. In order to insure police cooperation, Tompkins had the wonderful audacity to issue a set of official orders to General Presti, head of the police forces in Rome, instructing him to maintain public discipline and prevent sabotage of buildings and utilities when the Germans departed. "The orders were written in official military form on paper headed 'United States Office of Strategic Services,'" Tompkins explained. "I then signed them 'OSS C.O. Rome Area' and affixed a special rubber stamp which I had had prepared for just such an occasion." When the Allies finally broke out of the beachhead at Anzio and the Germans evacuated Rome on June 6, 1944, all the major electric and telephone controls remained intact, and one of Rome's radio stations, preserved from destruction by Presti's police, broadcast the news of the Fifth Army's triumphant entry — the first Allied soldiers to occupy an enemy capital.

2

In October of 1944 Field Marshal Kesselring proclaimed a special week, from the 8th to the 14th, to be observed by all his troops in German-occupied Italy. "And what will be the nature of this week, Herr Marshal?" a staff general inquired.

"It will be known as 'Anti-Partisan Week,' " Kesselring growled, "and we will observe it by exterminating this guerrilla resistance once and for all. Our German Wehrmacht is being stopped by a shadow."

The shadow lay dark across the path of every retreating division as the Nazis moved northward through Italy, after the evacuation of Rome. It haunted the towns and hamlets they passed, poisoning their water, putting their trucks out of commission with emery dust concealed in the bearings. It struck silently in their bivouacs at night — the pad of feet, the gasp of a sentry garroted at his post. Land mines exploded along the line of march, snipers fired from ledges and faded away like phantoms, a key highway bridge crumbled before them in a cloud of smoke and flying chunks of concrete. Three survivors crawled out of the wreckage of a loaded troop train which had crashed through a weakened trestle into a chasm. Kesselring's own communication lines, repaired one day, were found cut in a dozen places the next. At the very moment that the Marshal was announcing Anti-Partisan Week to his division commanders, a mysterious blast in the power plant plunged the room into darkness, and Kesselring stamped back to his quarters with his speech unfinished.

The proud German army found itself on the defensive, fighting a force without substance. Sentries were ordered to walk in pairs, guards were doubled and redoubled. It was safer to risk the Allied Air Force in the daytime than to travel through the Partisan country at night. Whole battalions were pulled away from combat zones to hunt the elusive resistance bands. One company of picked troops scoured the hills for a week in search of a parachuted OSS radio team, and returned empty-handed with a third of their complement wounded or missing. Furious, Kesselring proclaimed that henceforth any Allied agent caught working with the Partisans, in uniform or not, would be shot on sight.

Threats and savage reprisals failed to cow the shadow army. Members of the resistance, taken prisoner by the Nazi SS, were castrated or had their eyes gouged out. Others were impaled on steel meat hooks and hanged in the village square, a popular form of SS torture. The Germans would tie a prisoner's hands, lift him off the ground, then lower him so that the two meat-hook points would penetrate the soft underside of his jaw, just inside the jawbones; and all the inhabitants of the village would be routed out at bayonet-point to watch the agonized writhings of the victim. Sometimes a prisoner would dangle alive for a day or more, until the thrashing of his body snapped the jawbone and forced the steel prongs into his brain.

Still the Partisans fought on, growing bolder and more numerous as Kesselring's forces reached North Italy, where anti-Fascist as well as anti-German sentiment was strongest. Many former Italian army officers joined the civilian resistance groups and imparted to them the formal organization of military units; and American operatives, parachuted or infiltrated by small boats along the coast, equipped and trained the Partisan bands, furnished them with G.I. uniforms dyed a dark green, and forged them into a powerful weapon which drove the Germans from whole sections of northern Italy. On certain segments of the fighting front, Partisan support made it possible for the thinly spread Allied forces to hold the lines.

One of the principal agents in the Spezia area was a frail Italian girl known as "Vera," who established contact with local guerrilla groups and arranged for repeated supply drops by parachute. On July 2 SS troopers broke into the room where she and her radio operator were making contact with the OSS base at Caserta. Vera tossed a couple of hand grenades, destroying the radio and killing two Germans, and escaped out of a window with the operator. She joined a patriot unit a few miles outside Florence, and within eight days had reopened communications with OSS.

When the general German retreat to the Gothic Line was at its height, in the summer and fall of 1944, several major Partisan groups deep inside northern Italy, supported by OSS with weapons and communication facilities, engaged in open combat with the Nazis. One of the principal uprisings was in the Val d'Ossola, where a large resistance group, led by OSS agent "Como," attacked German garrisons along the Lago Maggioro, hoping to clear the enemy from a stretch of the Swiss-Italian frontier. Marshal Kesselring committed two of his divisions to eliminate the Val d'Ossola bands, and they were bivouaced in the lakeside resort town of Cannobia. The Partisans notified OSS in Bern, Switzerland, that they could capture the town if they were supported by Allied air attacks on certain specified targets, including enemy barracks and boats being used as transports. Bern passed the word to Caserta, and on September 25 the Tactical Air Force bombed as requested. Como cabled OSS.

"The bombing was a complete success. Landing stages at Luino were destroyed and six lake steamers damaged at the pier. A large steamer carrying 500 Fascist troops was sunk . . . The bombing took place at the same time as our attack, the capture of Cannobia being successfully accomplished. The Partisans are now in control of the whole region."

The Germans, outraged at this blow to their prestige, mounted a heavy counterattack on Cannobia, and Como requested another airdrop of weapons and supplies. Since all Allied aircraft had been diverted to support the growing Warsaw resistance, it was impossible for the Air Force to comply. While the Partisans held off the German drive, Como made a personal trip to Switzerland, obtained a quantity of Swiss arms and ammunition, and loaded them secretly on a freight train. The Swiss border control discovered the contraband and threatened to confiscate it, whereupon Como took over the train, crashed it across the frontier into Italian territory, and distributed the precious weapons to the Partisans. The Swiss protested that his act was a flagrant infringement of their neutrality. To prevent further trouble with Switzerland, OSS spirited Como to southern Italy, where he was detained for the duration.

Supplementing the Partisan warfare, the Morale Operations (MO) branch of OSS conducted a campaign of "black" propaganda in an attempt to weaken the spirit of the German and Fascist Italian troops. A bogus newspaper, *Das Neue Deutschland*, purporting to be the instrument of a German peace party which aimed to liquidate the Nazis and end the war, was airdropped to resistance groups who smuggled it across

the lines. Copies of a forged military announcement by General Kesselring, stating that he was resigning his command because the "war is
lost in Germany," were disseminated by special "Sauerkraut" missions
in forward areas, and proved so successful that Kesselring found it
necessary on September 13 to deny authorship of the proclamation.
Even more effective with the Italian Fascists were "passes" from a self-
styled "Patriots' Committee," inviting the bearer to join the Partisans.
"Actually we didn't know whether the Partisans would honor the pass,"
an OSS field report admitted, "but we didn't give a damn; the idea was
to make the Italians completely useless to the Germans. The effect was
cumulative. Kesselring was forced to interlard his Fascist troops with
German units he badly needed elsewhere. When the Italians reached the
front lines, they deserted in whole platoons, armed with surrender
passes."

Distribution of these "black" propaganda items was often accomplished by carefully screened prisoners-of-war who were sent back, still
in German uniform, to the enemy lines. Another ingenious method
exploited the disruption of the German postal system due to Allied
bombing of the railways. Fake German mailbags were prepared and
filled with subversive letters stamped, postmarked, and inscribed with
real addresses taken from local directories. These bags were dropped by
the Fifteenth Air Force in strafing missions over marshaling yards and
railroad stations, in the hope that they would be picked up as stray mail
pouches lost from wrecked railroad cars, and would be sent on by
regular mail. There is no evidence that this device was ever detected.
The total of known desertions directly caused by MO subversion was
estimated at ten thousand, and the frequent and violent German reactions to MO "black" propaganda was an even more concrete measure
of its effectiveness.

Sometimes a Partisan area would be overrun by the Germans, the
leaders captured and executed, and the demoralized survivors sent
fleeing into the mountains. Then American OSS officers would drop
into the area to weld the scattered unit together again and lead it in
further sabotage efforts against assigned targets. General Donovan paid a
special postwar tribute to these men who "took some of the gravest risks

and performed some of the bravest acts of the war." Men with no previous experience in resistance, men like Captain Joseph Benucci or Captain Howard Chappell or Captain Roderick Hall, all handpicked to carry out resistance work in northern Italy. Their stories, strangely intertwined, are told here not because they are so extraordinary, but rather because they are so typical.

3

Donovan worked a kind of magic when he talked, and OSS field agents, infected by the General's confidence, would often volunteer without hesitation to carry out any hazardous duty he suggested. Captain Benucci said after his interview with Donovan: "He talked to me for half an hour, and I walked out of his office convinced that I could do the impossible."

Captain Joseph Benucci, twenty-eight, a railroad worker from Newark, N.J., had been chosen to lead an OSS sabotage operation in Italy called Mission Aztec. On October 13, 1944, with Sergeants Nick Gangelosi of Elmont, N.Y., and Sebastian Gionfriddo of Hartford, Conn., he had parachuted into the lower Alps north of Venice, a strategically vital area which lay astride the German route to the Brenner Pass and Austria. He had expected to find a large Partisan force awaiting him, but from the reception committee at the drop zone he learned that the Germans had struck just a month before and had killed over five hundred Partisans in a mass slaughter which had left only fifty effectives in the local underground, headed by a slight and neatly dressed Rome industrialist named "Antonio." Benucci would have to build his organization virtually from scratch.

By November 4, when Aztec received its first OSS supply drop, he had two hundred Partisans in his mountain hideout near Belluno, most of them members of the 7th Alpini Brigade and courageous fighters. The snow was already three feet deep, the temperature hovered around zero, and the encampment was badly in need of food. Accompanied by some of his best men, armed with automatic weapons, Benucci set an ambush for an enemy supply convoy. Mines blew the tracks off the vehicles, and the fifteen German guards were cut down by concentrated fire. Their booty was the payroll for the Nazi garrison at Belluno, abundant food and weapons, and, best of all, a month's cigarette rations. The Germans reacted promptly; an SS force swept the countryside, and captured several Partisans. Under torture they admitted Benucci's presence in the area, though they did not reveal his whereabouts, and the enemy put a price of five thousand dollars on his head.

Security was his prime concern. Antonio had warned him that the Partisan band was honeycombed with informers, ready to sell out their comrades to the SS for a reward. By great good luck, a young Italian woman was captured by the Alpini and brought before Benucci; her Partisan brother-in-law had been mysteriously fingered and hanged by the SS, and she was known to be sleeping with a German master sergeant in the village. Under pressure, she confessed that she was the paymaster for the local spy ring, and surrendered a ledger book with the names of all the traitors in the area. Thirty-three informers, many of them members of the Aztec group, were lined up along with the woman agent and shot by the Alpini. The following morning twelve more villagers left in haste. The betrayals abruptly ceased.

Other American volunteers were less fortunate. Captain Roderick "Steve" Hall of New Hampshire, a young geologist, had jumped from a Liberator bomber on August 2, 1944, the first OSS leader to drop in uniform into northern Italy. Working in the Val Cordovale area, he had directed a Partisan brigade for several months in demolition work. His radio operator was killed, and he arranged to send his intelligence to Mission Aztec for transmission to the OSS base at Florence. On two occasions Hall's trusted courier, a Swiss named "Tell," arrived to deliver the messages to Captain Benucci; but intuition warned Benucci to meet Tell at a point some distance from his own headquarters, on the opposite side of the River Piave. His suspicions of the Swiss courier were justified when Hall was betrayed to the SS in January and, although in uniform, was tortured and hanged.

His story was never fully known. Inquiries by OSS revealed that Hall had left his unit on January 26 to ski north alone for a sabotage effort near the Brenner Pass. The following day, while hiding out with a local priest in Ampezzo, he was seized by Fascist police and carried off to the torture chambers. After the war, an Italian doctor in Ampezzo disclosed a death certificate he had signed for one "R. G. Hall" giving the cause of death as "heart failure." The doctor confessed: "The Gestapo made me say that. All I saw was a body lying at the bottom of a cart. I noticed he had a rope around his neck."

Due to Benucci's precautions, the informer, Tell, had not been able to give the SS the location of Aztec headquarters; but he was able to furnish them with Benucci's name and rank, and an exact personal description. The Germans raised the reward for his capture to ten thousand dollars "dead or alive." For the rest of the Italian campaign, Benucci never remained in one spot for more than two days at a time.

On the day after Christmas, another OSS volunteer leader arrived: Infantry Captain Howard Chappell of East Cleveland, Ohio, a tall powerful blond of Prussian descent, former All-State football player and heavyweight boxing champion at Western Reserve University. Like Benucci and Hall, he had been selected personally by General Donovan for the mission. Chappell and his team, Corporal Silsby and T/5g Fabrega,[15] parachuted into the Aztec area near Belluno, and he spent several days with Benucci, being briefed on the territory he would penetrate. After some discussion, it was decided that Benucci would continue with the 7th Alpini and also take command of the leaderless Val Cordovale brigade. Chappell would assume command of the Mazzini and Tollot brigades, called the Nanette Division, which operated to the west near the city of Bolzano, headquarters of the Nazi SS troops in Italy.

The Nanette Division proved to be a Communist outfit, more concerned with future political developments than with the liberation of their country. The Nanette Division's local chief was "Mello," described by Chappell as "a pleasant character who, along with another Communist named De Lucca, schemed to have me murdered. Mello stole three plane loads of American equipment. One of his brigades had received from us clothing and forty Sten guns, which they buried whenever the Germans came near. They did no fighting."[16]

While carrying on their sabotage work, hiding in haystacks and

---

15 For Fabrega's story, see page 146.
16 William L. White, "Some Affairs of Honor," *Reader's Digest,* December, 1945.

bushes by day and striking at night, Chappell's unit picked up twenty-one American pilots, shot down behind the lines, and arranged for their evacuation to Yugoslavia. "When the parachutes landed," Chappell said, "my Partisans would try to get to them before the Germans or Fascists, who would kill our airmen on sight. The pilots usually drew their revolvers as soon as they scrambled to their feet, and it was difficult for the Partisans, few of whom spoke any English, to let the Americans know they were friendly. They brought in one pilot who told us that a couple of tough characters had come running toward him across a field, and he had whipped out his .45 and was about to knock them off when one began yelling. 'Jesus-Christ-Lucky-Strike-God-Damn-Chesterfield-Son-of-a-Bitch.' So the pilot put his gun away."

Word was received through the underground that the Fascists were gathering a large force in the area, equipped with machine guns and mortars, so Chappell moved his forces into another valley and dug in on the crest of a mountain. Over a hundred Fascist militiamen took over the tiny village of Chison at the foot of the mountain, cutting off their only source of food; and Chappell felt it was time for action. At midnight, twenty Partisans surrounded the Fascist garrison, fired a burst from a bazooka through a window, and called on the garrison to surrender. "A Fascist trooper came to the door to ask our terms," Chappell said, "but when one of our men advanced to talk with him the Fascist opened up with a machine gun, so we slammed all the rest of our bazooka rounds into the house. I'm sure no one escaped from it. We estimated the next morning that we had killed eighty."

Chappell knew the enemy would swarm like hornets in reprisal; and with added food supplies from Chison he and some thirty Partisans retreated to the highest mountain of the region, the Col de Moi, three thousand feet above the Po Valley, and hid in some shepherd huts on the crest. All that day the Fascists tried to storm the mountain peak, and were driven back with mortars and machine guns firing down on the successive waves. During the afternoon, the enemy rolled up cannon in an attempt to blast the huts off the mountain, but darkness fell before they got the range. That night the firing inexplicably ceased, and dawn revealed that the attackers had lost their nerve and pulled out, leaving their Fascist dead on the slopes. Later, rather than risk further casualties, they paid neutral civilians fifty lira for each body brought down for burial. Villagers counted over three hundred Fascists whom Chappell's small force had killed. Partisan losses were two dead and two wounded.

With Chappell's Mozzini and Tollot brigades harassing the enemy to the west, and the Val Cordovale brigade engaged in demolition activities to the north, the Germans were kept occupied all over the lower Alpine zone, unable to concentrate on wiping out Mission Aztec; and in February of 1945 Benucci decided to carry out his major sabotage assignment, the destruction of the important bridge across the Piave at San Felice. This bridge was midway between Belluno and Feltre, the two leading cities of the province, on the main highway which carried most of the German supplies to the fighting front. It was a three-hundred-foot, four-span structure of reinforced concrete, with guard posts at either end, situated only a mile from Belluno where the thousand SS troops had recently been augmented by fifteen hundred members of the German 20th Infantry, withdrawn from the combat zone for rest and reorganization. Another thousand troops were billeted at Feltre just south of the target. Benucci's saboteurs would have to operate in the very heart of the enemy country; but the Alpini remembered that a group of their comrades had been trapped on the bridge some months before by a German patrol which had slaughtered them to the last man, and they were eager for revenge.

Benucci, with Sergeant Nick Gangelosi and a Partisan engineer, crept to the edge of a wooded foothill, a hundred and fifty yards from the target, and made final plans for the demolition. They estimated that they would need forty men and four hundred pounds of plastic explosive to do the job. One two-hundred-pound charge would blast the buttress end of the bridge where it met the land, the other would be placed at the top of the first arch. A squad of assassins were to knock out the guards at each end of the bridge, and an ambush party would cover the demolition workers while they were setting the charges.

On the night of February 12 they carried the explosives down from their mountain cache and hid them in the patch of woods. "We planned to start working on the bridge at one A.M.," Captain Benucci stated to an OSS interviewer, Lieutenant Commander Kelly,[17] "at which time our intelligence had indicated we stood the best chance of avoiding detection by German traffic. About eleven P.M., Nick and I with thirty-five Partisans took up a position overlooking the bridge at the point where we had hidden the explosives. All of the men were well armed, and in addition we had four bazookas in case armored vehicles or tanks came out to interfere.

"At 12:30 A.M. I sent five of my most experienced assassins to take care of the southern guards. Twenty minutes later they flashed a signal to me, which meant they had wiped the guards out. Thirty seconds later a flash from the north side told me that things were under control there, too. I gave the order, and our Partisans picked up the explosives and sandbags and rushed onto the bridge. . . . Everyone worked fast, and in twenty minutes the last charges were laid, the last sandbags in place, and the whole thing wired together. I set the ten-minute time pencils, using a dozen to make sure. After a final check, I blew two blasts on my whistle and took off for the foothills.

"We all stopped about two hundred and fifty yards south of the bridge and waited for the explosion. It went up with a terrific roar. For a few seconds the span seemed to hang in the air, then collapsed into the river. When I saw that span go, I knew they couldn't repair it, and it was still down when the war ended."

While five hundred German SS with police dogs were scouring the countryside in search of the saboteurs, Benucci arranged for another meeting with Chappell. Both he and Chappell had been briefed at OSS training school that officers in the field should never risk a rendezvous, but they were anxious to coordinate their zone-wide operations. With his two sergeants and three leading Partisans, Benucci arrived at Chappell's secret command post near the town of San Antonio, and established his own headquarters in a small house about a thousand yards away. He and Chappell talked till four in the morning, and then Benucci ordered his sergeants and the three Partisans back to their temporary quarters, to send out the morning radio messages, while he remained to

[17] Lieutenant Commander Richard M. Kelly, "Operation Aztec," *Blue Book*, May, 1946.

enjoy a turkey which one of Chappell's contacts in San Antonio had furnished. "The turkey was cooking and we were shooting the breeze over some tea at about seven in the morning," Benucci's account continued, "when a young girl came running into our hut shouting: '*Tedeschi, Tedeschi, San Antonio!*'

"We weren't particularly alarmed at first, for we thought it was just a morning patrol, but we woke up Chappell's men and they began to bury the vital equipment, while I took a BAR and went outside with Chappell." From a small knoll, they spotted some Germans moving cautiously along a ridge to the west, and other groups working downhill toward them from the north and east. "Immediately we knew that we had been surrounded. We decided to make a break for it by following a creek south, the one direction that didn't seem to be covered, and our only hope of breaking out of the trap.

"We all took off at a run and started down the stream. The water was ice cold and knee-deep, which made it hard going. We managed to go about eight hundred yards before the Germans opened up on us with machine guns and automatic weapons from the ridges on either side and from our rear. . . ." Benucci waved four Partisans ahead of him up a small side-brook, while Chappell and the rest kept on going downstream. Suddenly he realized that he was near the temporary quarters where his sergeants had gone earlier to send the messages. Four Germans were running down the road toward the house, and he raised the carbine which he had been carrying and let them have half a clip.

"One of them fell, and the rest hit the dirt," Benucci went on. "This only took a few seconds, but it saved my life, because as I turned back to start following our four men up the side brook, I heard German voices and automatic fire just above me. I looked up and saw five SS men standing on the high bank, firing into the brook ahead of me. By some miracle they hadn't seen me, though I was only thirty yards away. I lifted my carbine and emptied the clip at the group. Three of them fell, one body tumbling into the brook just in front of me. The rest pulled back, dragging the other two bodies with them. From Chappell's direction I could hear a lot of firing.

"My carbine was useless, for I had no more ammo, so I threw it away. I still had my .45 and a hand grenade. . . . No matter what happened, I was determined not to be taken prisoner. I kept going up the brook, because there was no other place to go. Just as I reached the body of the SS man I had killed, I saw a place where the snow had drifted up against the overhanging bank. I dived into this cavity, scraped as much snow as possible up around me, and rubbed some clay from the bank onto my face and hands. I curled up and waited, scarcely daring to breathe. In one hand I had my .45 pointed out at the brook, and I held the ring of the grenade in my teeth so that, even if wounded, I could pull it out and take some of them with me.

"Just as I finished concealing myself, I heard German voices. While I crouched motionless, an SS lieutenant came to the edge of the bank above my head, and gave orders to two of his men, who waded into the stream and picked up the body. They were so close that I could nearly touch them, but their attention was concentrated on their dead comrade, and they didn't look at me. They retrieved the body and carried it away.

"All day long SS troops searched the area, and several other scouting parties waded up and down the brook. Fortunately they kept looking straight ahead. I lay there wet and freezing for seven hours until it was pitch dark and then rolled out of my hiding place, not knowing where to go. I was sure all my boys had been captured, and I knew such a trap could not have been an accident — someone had talked to the Germans. Driven by hunger, I made my way alone to the emergency quarters where we had buried some food and vitamins. As I crouched in the underbrush, I heard a voice inside the house — it was Nick! I hurled myself against the door, pounding it with my fists and shouting the password.

"They came tumbling out, the whole bunch of them, every single one safe. Nick kept shouting: 'But we thought you were dead!' I was all but carried into the house, and then I got the whole story. The bulk of the 7th Alpini had escaped the roundup and were concentrating in the Val Moral, though we had lost eighty-four Partisans in the fighting. They reported that Chappell and two of his men had been captured."

Captain Chappell, after leaving Benucci, had continued down the brook with his two companions, Corporal Silsby and Sergeant Eric Buchhardt of Summit, Ohio, an OSS medical technician who had parachuted into the area to treat wounded American airmen. Silsby and Buchhardt halted at a small waterfall, completely exhausted. Chappell took Buchhardt's arm and lowered him over the falls, and went back to help Silsby. A German patrol cornered and disarmed them, and marched them along the road toward an SS headquarters at Trichiana. Chappell watched for an opportunity and leaped off the road into a ravine, sliding and stumbling to the bottom. "I ran about four hundred yards," he said later, "and walked a mile, once encountering six Krauts. One shot me in the leg, which was good for five points on my discharge, and didn't bother me much. After getting away from them, I hid behind a boulder in the creekbed until dark."

The following morning, while searching for information about Buchhardt and Silsby, Chappell was recaptured by a member of a search party who thrust a gun in his back, ordered him to turn around, and marched him back up the creekbed toward the SS outpost. As soon as they were out of sight of the other Nazis, Chappell tackled the guard and silently broke his neck with his bare hands. He stuffed the body into a culvert, camouflaging it so it would not be detected. Knowing that the rest of the search party would start looking for him if he attempted to hide, he decided to brazen it out. "Ruffling my yellow hair to look as German as possible, I walked up the other bank of the creek, paying no attention to the Krauts on the knoll, and kept glancing right and left as though I were one of the search party. Passing within twenty yards of them in plain sight then, I kept straight on to a house, opened its door as if I was billeted there, and walked in."

The occupants, an old woman and two daughters, gave him hardboiled eggs and bread to stuff in his pockets, and one of the girls led him to a ravine where she thought he would be safe. That night he learned from Partisans that Sergeant Buchhardt was hiding in the home of a patriot in San Antonio, and he sent Buchhardt a message to meet him at some caves near the village of Dusoi which he knew would serve as a safe retreat. That night at the caves he found Sergeant Buchhardt, his left leg gashed and an ear torn off.

Both Chappell and Benucci ordered their Partisan followers to form small groups of three or four, make their way to a safer area, and wait for things to quiet down. Benucci went on the run with his two sergeants, changing their hiding place each night and never letting more than one or two people know their whereabouts. "Once the priest of the little town of Mel secreted us in the belfry of his church," Benucci recalled. "The town was full of Germans, and we watched them all day long while those bells rang right next to our ears." The whole German 20th Infantry Division joined the manhunt, and during the next few weeks several hundred Partisans were captured, the majority of whom were given the meat-hook treatment. One of those captured at San Antonio was a youngster named "Brownie," who had served as guide to Chappell. "When he refused to talk," Chappell said, "they took him into the public square, chopped off both hands at the wrists, and gouged out his eyes. Then they threw him on the pavement, and one of the troops mercifully shot him. Even the SS had some good guys."

On March 31 the 20th Infantry Division, now re-formed into the 26th Panzer Grenadiers, received emergency orders to leave at midnight for the Adriatic sector of the front, to repel an expected Allied landing. Benucci sent word to his scattered bands to dig out their arms and assemble every available patriot; and the Alpini resumed their sabotage operations, blasting ammunition dumps and destroying bridges and ambushing German patrols. In one action, they killed forty SS troops and took ninety prisoners, among them the notorious Lieutenant Carl, a leading SS torturer. "Later that night I heard that Carl had been killed while trying to escape," Benucci added. "Still later I heard that it had taken him eight hours to die. Knowing how many young boys he had impaled on meat-hooks, what he had done to American flyers, the number of Partisan girls he had sent to SS brothels, I made no further inquiries. It probably would not have done any good if I had. A lot of SS murderers were killed trying to escape."

In a ceremony at OSS headquarters in Washington, Captain Benucci was decorated with the Legion of Merit. On Benucci's strong recommendation, Sergeant Gionfriddo, his radio man, also received the Legion of Merit, and Sergeant Nick Gangelosi was awarded the Bronze Star. Captain Chappell, for his work in cutting off the German escape route through the Brenner Pass, was given the Silver Star, and Corporal Silsby and T/5g Fabrega, released from German prison camps after the war, received similar decorations. Captain Hall was posthumously awarded the Legion of Merit for "his remarkable bravery, resourcefulness and ability in keeping with the highest traditions of the Armed Forces of the United States."

All the presentations were made in person by General Donovan. The General did not know fear; but he knew courage.

V

GENERAL DONOVAN'S daily memorandum to the President used to arrive at the White House in the late afternoon. Roosevelt, who relished dark and devious intrigue, would drop all other business to read the latest OSS field reports, gathered from every combat zone.

Berlin. I enclose a group of recent photographs taken in the heart of Berlin, together with the following eyewitness description: "For months Berlin has been camouflaging its streets, squares, parks, and lakes to confuse Allied fliers. From the Brandenburger Tor, all of Unter den Linden is now covered with giant colored nets, under which the traffic moves, and the avenue itself is painted green, so that even in a full moon a pilot cannot observe the gleaming asphalt. The gilded Victory Pillar has been given a dull coating and disguised with artificial foliage, and an imitation gilded Pillar is being set up elsewhere to mislead enemy bombers. The Leitzensee has also 'vanished,' stakes being driven into the shallow lake-bottom and nets spread over these stakes about three yards above the surface, decorated according to the time of year with grass and flowers. A simulated "village" has been erected in the center of the lake, of painted canvas on thin laths. . . . To show British contempt for this German effort at camouflage, a single RAF plane flew over the wooden "village" last night and dropped one wooden bomb.

Rome. I had a private audience with the Pope last Wednesday. He discussed Communism and Russia, and I took up with him, at the request of Mr. Kirk, the question of the Japanese Embassy placing a radio-transmitter in the Vatican. . . . He expressed great interest in your reelection, and asked me to say to you that he sends "all my heart's affection."

Kunming. T. V. Soong believes that the Chinese do not plan to defend either Chang Tsau or Chang Tai. This means that the Japanese will have a virtually unimpeded advance along the railroad running from Hangkow to Canton, and will be able to complete their internal line of communication all the way from Korea to South China before the end of summer. It also means that the Chinese coastal provinces will be cut off from Chungking.

Norway. Subversion kits have been shipped into Scandinavia at the rate of 1000 a week since the end of May. These kits include 6 stencils, special clandestine paintbrushes, an envelope of sample poison pen letters, fake German newspapers, rubber stamps, and "black" propaganda distribution instructions.

London. An agent in Occupied France reports: "A Nazi detachment arrived at Oradour at ten in the morning of 10 June. It was market day, and many people from Limoges had gone there to get supplied. There was also a great number of children on vacation—a total of about 1200 persons. . . . On the pretext of searching for hidden munition depots, the SS Commander had the men shut up in three large barns, and the women and children in the church. The abandoned town was then pillaged. At two o'clock all the houses were set on fire, including the barns. The SS machine gunned all who tried to flee. At five o'clock the church was set on fire. Here again machine guns were used. Only one woman managed to escape."

Burma. The mystery of how the Japanese are concealing their fighter aircraft in North Burma was solved by a photograph seized from a captured enemy pilot, showing him standing beside his airplane. An OSS photo-technician enlarged the picture and discovered that, instead of building revetments, the Japs had dug holes to bury their planes and covered them with sod. The prisoner admitted that he was based at Meiktila, just south of Mandalay. A-2 of 10th Air Force reexamined previous aerial photos of the Jap base, and noted thirty suspicious shadows around the perimeter of the airfield and in a nearby clearing. A few days later, a flight of B-25's from Lower Assam bombed and strafed Meiktila, destroying most of the hidden fighters and relieving Jap pressure on our Hump transports.

France. In order to avoid German DF-ing [the direction-finding technique used to zero in on a clandestine radio transmitter], a

pair of agents in France hit on an ingenious device. They secured one
of the large hogsheads mounted on wheels which local wine-vendors
push through town, and inserted a partition halfway down the cask.
The lower half was filled with wine which could be drawn from a
bung at the bottom, and one of the agents concealed himself in the
empty upper half with his short-wave sending set. The other agent,
disguised as a peddler, moved from street to street while his teammate transmitted messages as long as the cask was in motion. If a
DF-ing truck approached, the peddler would halt, a signal to cease
sending. This team has been operating for months without detection,
forwarding intelligence to OSS/London on enemy troop movements
and pinpointing bomber targets.

Switzerland. A message just forwarded by OSS/Bern from a dependable informant deep inside Germany states: "With reference
to the rocket bombs, extremely secret information via Paris reveals
that the 'Gerade Lauffateratur' is produced in Gnydia, at the Askania
Works, also at the Krupp Works in Wuppertal. . . . In the neighborhood of Orlanuendo, a large airplane factory has been built underground. It was bombed on 29 June, but the raid did not cause much
damage and the plant will soon resume operations. Pursuit planes are
manufactured here, and possibly new secret weapons. . . . In comparison with the V–1, the V–2 model rocket travels through the
stratosphere, is radio controlled, and thus is a more accurate weapon
with longer range. This new model will be used by Hitler within 60
days at the outside."

Gradually, as the war progressed, OSS had developed a global intelligence network, unprecedented in American history. From the silent
buildings at 25th and E streets in Washington, a vast espionage web had
been woven around the world to the fighting fronts. Its sensitive strands
reached beyond the battlelines deep into Axis-held territory, probing
military secrets, vibrating to the least tremor of underground resistance,
tangling the enemy in its invisible pattern.

Theater by combat theater the web enlarged, as its loose skeins were
carried by the winds of war to new strategic areas. Prior to the invasion
of Africa, covert installations began to function in Casablanca and
Tangier and Algiers, later in Marrakesh, Rabat, Alexandria, Cairo. The
Italian campaign was served by forward units in the islands of Sicily and
Corsica, and on the mainland at Capri, Caserta, Bari, Naples, Rome,

Milan. By 1944 the clandestine web stretched from Norway and Denmark to Albania and Poland and Greece, to inconspicuous Spanish villas in Madrid and Lisbon and Barcelona, to Abadan and Istanbul and Baghdad. From the neutral capitals of Bern and Stockholm, from Copenhagen and Brussels and Antwerp, it spun its way stealthily into Austria and the German homeland.

Grosvenor Square in London had become in effect a secondary OSS headquarters when the agency's SI and SO branches transferred the bulk of their personnel overseas in order to mesh more closely with British intelligence, and training centers had sprung up throughout the British Isles from northernmost Scotland to the southern tip of England. Ancestral mansions and secluded country estates were taken over for sabotage schools, commando schools, and rest areas for agents brought back from grueling missions. When D-Day dawned, Anglo-American teams were already operating inside France at St.-Lô, Grandville, Ste.-Mère-Église. An OSS cell hidden in a modest apartment in Nazi-held Paris directed a string of substations in Toulouse, Dijon, Nice, Marseilles.

On the other side of the globe, the delicate filaments had penetrated the Far East from bases at Karachi and New Delhi and Calcutta in India, at Colombo and Kandy in Ceylon. There were active installations at Kunming and Chungking in China, performing reconnaisance for General Claire Chennault's 14th Air Force. OSS Detachment 101, billeted on a tea plantation in the Assam Valley, supported a complex of jungle outposts dotted over upper Burma, extending as far south as Lashio and Mandalay. Even the enemy stronghold of Thailand was infiltrated by a group of American agents secreted in the heart of Bangkok, who transmitted intelligence regularly until the Japanese surrender.

No one can even guess the actual size of OSS at its wartime peak. Over thirty thousand names were listed on the agency's roster; but there were countless Partisan workers in the occupied countries whose identities were never known, who were paid OSS money and armed with OSS weapons and performed OSS missions, yet for the most part were unaware that their direction came from Washington. Each field agent employed several local subagents, and they in turn recruited anonymous friends from the surrounding countryside, sometimes numbering in the thousands. One lone parachutist, Ernst Floege of Chicago, who dropped into the Héricourt district of France, wound up the war in command of an underground force of thirty-five hundred; another French-American agent named Duval organized and personally led an estimated seven thousand resistance fighters in the Lyons area. Altogether, the Maquis in France, the Kachin tribesmen in Burma formed a worldwide shadow army which served under OSS in close support of the Allied military effort, and which faded back into obscurity when the fighting ceased.

As the agency expanded, its functions grew more numerous and varied. "The Office of Strategic Services," General Donovan always emphasized, "means what its name implies: every service of a strategic nature, tried or untried, which may be useful to our Army and Navy and Air Force." In addition to its assigned tasks of intelligence-gathering and conducting unorthodox warfare, a new and highly important function emerged, quite unforeseen when OSS was formed; the rescue and evacuation of Allied airmen forced down in hostile territory.

2

A flier, by the nature of his mission, operates behind the enemy lines; and if he has to eject from his flack-riddled plane he is just another earthbound fugitive, moving cautiously by dark to avoid detection, traveling only a few miles a day, driven by hunger and fear. His shelter is a haystack or roadside culvert, his food a raw turnip dug from a farmer's field. Perhaps he lost his first-aid kit when he jumped, and the flak wound in his arm has become infected. Perhaps his hastily buried parachute has been discovered, and the Gestapo is hot on his trail. He has no knowledge of the local language or terrain, no plan of procedure, no one to whom he can turn for help.

As the 15th Air Force launched its one thousand plane raids on the Ploesti oilfields and other lucrative Balkan targets, Luftwaffe fighters and radar-guided missiles took an increasingly heavy toll of Allied aircraft. Bomber crews, debriefed on their return to base, reported seeing numbers of their squadron mates bail out of crippled planes over the mountainous interior of Yugoslavia. Ringed by the German occupation army, caught up in the political struggle between Partisans and Chetniks, the downed airmen's best hope of escape lay in contacting the OSS or British SOE agents working with the underground resistance.

Fifteen Reichswehr divisions, plus some hundred thousand native conscript troops, had been detailed to maintain order in the conquered country; and it was of prime importance to the Allies to keep these forces immobilized in Yugoslavia and prevent them from joining Kesselring's twenty-six divisions opposing the Anglo-American advance in Italy. As early as August of 1943, OSS agents led by Walter Mansfield and Louis Huot had parachuted into the rival Partisan and Chetnik areas, to organize the rough brigand bands and direct them in harassing tactics against the Germans. At first the Americans operated under control of British missions already in Yugoslavia; but General Donovan, on a visit to Cairo in November, 1943, established the right of OSS to function independently, though in cooperation with SOE. Supplies and weapons were dropped to the resistance forces by air, or transported by fishing boats from Italy across the hundred and fifty miles of stormy Adriatic to the Dalmatian coast.

Reports from these agents in Yugoslavia told of numerous American fliers hiding out in the rugged hinterland. A half-starved B–24 tail gunner, shot down in the first Ploesti raid, was discovered grubbing for food in a farmyard pigsty. Two fighter pilots were spotted in a convent when their broad-toed G.I. shoes protruded incongruously beneath the long black dresses supplied by the sisters. Five other injured airmen were found in a remote village in the Kukaricha Mountains, their shrapnel wounds being tended by loyal peasants. As the reports mounted, OSS/Bari suggested to General Nathan Twining, commander of the 15th Air Force, that a joint OSS-AF rescue project should be organized, utilizing the network of agents already behind the lines. With Twining's enthusiastic approval, escape maps were provided for each member of an air crew, pinpointing friendly areas and designating "safe houses" along the line of flight. Colored posters showing the markings of American aircraft and the uniforms and insignia of the airmen were distributed to the illiterate peasants. Air Force Rescue

Units, with OSS paratroopers dropped from Air Force troop carrier planes, contacted both Chetnik and Partisan headquarters and arranged for air evacuation. Over a hundred downed fliers were flown out successfully from hidden air strips that fall, despite the conflict brewing between the two opposing political factions.

By the end of 1943, a civil war was threatening in Yugoslavia. The Chetniks were led by General Draza Mihailovich, minister of war in King Peter's government-in-exile. Heading the Partisans was a Croat named Josef Broz (Tito), a Soviet-trained Communist, who was exploiting the opportunity provided by the war to wrest total control of the country. As the feuding worsened, the German menace was forgotten, and Tito's Communists engaged in open hostilities against the Mihailovich forces. Yugoslav fought Yugoslav with OSS-supplied weapons, and Allied agents, who were risking their lives to combat the Nazi occupation forces, found themselves pawns in the internal power struggle.

The dilemma was resolved at the Teheran Conference in December, 1943, when Winston Churchill decided that all aid would be withdrawn from Mihailovich and henceforth the Allies would back Tito. Churchill's own advisers warned him that Tito and his followers aimed to establish a Communist regime closely linked to Moscow; but the Prime Minister replied that no consideration of "long-term policy" should divert the Allied aim of "simply finding out who was killing the most Germans and suggesting means by which we could help them to kill more."[18] Roosevelt acquiesced, all support of Mihailovich was withdrawn, and OSS Captain George Musulin, leader of the AFRU mission to the Chetniks, was ordered to evacuate his entire party, including forty Allied airmen who had been cared for by Chetnik peasants. Learning that Mihailovich's supporters had located another twelve American fliers, Musulin radioed for permission to delay his departure until they could be rescued; but his request was denied by higher headquarters, and a carrier plane flew the party back to Bari.

Musulin was a hulking former University of Pittsburgh tackle, the

[18] General Albert C. Wedemeyer, *Wedemeyer Reports!* (New York, 1959).

son of immigrant Yugoslavian parents, whose knowledge of the Serbo-Croatian language had qualified him for his OSS mission. He had been welcomed enthusiastically by the Chetniks when he parachuted into their area, and had established liaison with the First Chetnik Corps, a ragged guerrilla group whose nondescript weapons ranged from rifles of the old Yugoslav army to mountaineer's axes and knives, but who had piled up a fabulous record of sabotage acts against the Nazi lines of communication. During the seven months that Captain Musulin worked with the Chetniks, he came to know the fabled General Mihailovich, with his Old Testament beard and incongruous steel-rimmed spectacles, hailed as the greatest underground fighter in all of Europe; and Musulin became convinced of the General's single determination to drive the Nazis from his country. When Musulin returned to Bari in May of 1944, he was outraged to learn that Tito had accused Mihailovich of collaborating with the Germans, and that American airmen were being briefed to bail out only in Partisan territory because the Chetniks would turn them over to the enemy for a price. He insisted that the Communist charges of collaboration were false, but he was helpless against the official policy laid down by London and Washington.

Late in June a message was picked up from General Mihailovich, stating that his forces were harboring another large group of American airmen, and offering to receive an evacuation unit and render them every assistance. His statement was supported by a personal broadcast in the clear on a rare frequency from one of the downed fliers, Lieutenant T. K. Oliver: "We are 250 American airmen, many sick and wounded, being cared for by Chetniks. Please notify 15th Air Force." To overcome any suspicion that his appeal might be sent by the Germans, or by Americans operating under German duress, Oliver interpolated his broadcast with intimate Air Force slang, and referred to certain distinguishing items of clothing, nicknames painted on planes, even details of the officers' club at Bari in order to establish authenticity. Through General Twining's efforts, high-level permission was given to send a rescue team, and Captain Musulin was put in charge of the "Halyard Mission" which would parachute into Chetnik territory, collect the stranded airmen, and arrange for their evacuation.

It was a perilous undertaking. The only communication with Mihailovich was a roundabout and tenuous radio link, which could easily
be intercepted by the Germans. A rendezvous had to be arranged
several days ahead, and there was no way of knowing whether the
enemy would overrun the drop zone in the meantime. The site was only
fifty miles from Belgrade, where a squadron of German night fighters
were based, and several Allied aircraft had been shot down recently in
the immediate area. Bad weather presented another hazard. Five times
during July the plane carrying the Halyard team to their pinpoint had
to abort because of fierce mountain storms, and twice it ran into a
barrage of German flak and barely made it back to base.

As the weeks dragged on, and mission after mission was scrubbed,
Musulin's frustration was matched by the impatience of the stranded
airmen, many of them sick or wounded. "It was way back in June when
our crew had to hit the silk," a B–24 pilot, Lieutenant Richard Felman,
told OSS interrogator Kelly later,[19] "and were found and brought
together by the Chetniks. One gunner had been killed when his 'chute
failed to open, and the Germans stripped his body and rolled it into a
ditch. After they left, the villagers gave him a decent burial and placed
fresh flowers on his grave every Sunday, at the risk of enemy reprisal.
They brought us his dog tags to send home. The Germans knew we were
somewhere in the area, and demanded that the local people surrender us.
When they refused, their village was burned to the ground. . . . Some
airmen in the group hiding with us had been down as long as five months,
but we all kept hoping our Chetnik friends could get word through to
Bari, although we knew that only Tito was receiving Allied support.

"Finally a message came back from base: 'Prepare reception for 31
July or first clear night following.' I don't need to tell you the lift that
gave us. General Mihailovich himself and about a thousand of his ragged
troops came to visit us at our encampment near a tiny airstrip the
Chetniks had built. He held a review in our honor, and told us through
an interpreter that his troops would be deployed over a twenty-mile

[19] Lieutenant Commander Richard M. Kelly, "Halyard Mission," *Blue Book*, August,
1946.

area around the airstrip, with orders to hold off the Germans at all costs while we were being evacuated."

It was not until August 2nd that the bad weather broke. "At 10:10 P.M. we heard the sound of engines in the distance," Felman continued. "We couldn't be sure it was an American plane, but at that point we were willing to risk anything, so we lit up the flares and the wind tee. . . . As the plane zoomed over our heads, we could see the big white star of the Air Force under the wings, and the most terrific cheer I've ever heard went up in those Yugoslavian mountains. Next thing we knew, Chetniks came running up, hauling packages of medical supplies and clothing which had been parachuted to us. Then I heard a tremendous commotion in the darkness, men and women and children shouting 'Captain George, Captain George!' With tears streaming down their faces, they were kissing and hugging a man in American uniform, one of the biggest chaps I'd ever seen. He walked over to us and put out his hand. 'I'm George Musulin,' he said."

The drop zone was at Pranjane, which Captain Musulin had visited frequently during his previous mission. An old friend with the First Chetnik Corps told him that twelve miles away, at the village of Chachak, there was a garrison of forty-five hundred German troops, and another garrison of two hundred and fifty were stationed on the other side of the mountain, only five air miles from the secret landing field. If the enemy attacked in strength with their superior armament, Musulin knew, the Chetniks would be forced to retreat through the mountains, and the injured American airmen could never survive such an ordeal. He would have to carry out the evacuation before the Germans got wind of their presence.

While the Halyard radio operator made contact with Bari and reported the team's safe arrival, the others set up an emergency hospital with the medical supplies, and an Italian doctor who had escaped from a prison camp in Belgrade took care of the sick. Musulin applied himself to the main problem, the enlargement of the airstrip to accommodate the rescue planes. "This strip — if you could call it that — was a small narrow plateau halfway up a mountainside," Musulin recalled. "It was only a hundred and fifty feet wide and some eighteen hundred long, with dense woods at the end of the runway and along one side, and a sheer drop on the other. By considerable work, we could improve it and lengthen it by about seventy-five yards, which would give us the absolute minimum for C–47 operations. The Chetniks supplied three hundred laborers, and sixty oxcarts were assigned to the task of hauling gravel and stones from nearby streambeds to extend the strip.

"What impressed me most was the truly amazing security of the Chetnik soldiers and peasants. The American airmen had been assembled from an area covering thousands of square miles, and everyone knew of their location. The Germans had tortured and killed villagers and destroyed homes, in an effort to learn where they were hidden. These poor people, who had been deserted by the British and American governments, and were under merciless attack from both the Germans and Tito's Partisans, would have received more money than they could ever dream of earning in their entire lives by turning over the fliers for reward; but not one American was betrayed. . . ."

By the 8th of the month, work on the strip was completed and a message radioed to Bari to start evacuation proceedings the following night. Six planes were requested, and Musulin ordered seventy-two airmen to be ready, the sick and wounded receiving the highest priority and the others selected according to the length of time they had been behind the lines. No distinction was made between officers and enlisted men. Everything was in readiness late on the afternoon of August 9th, and the Halyard team was placing flare pots to mark the strip, when they heard airplane engines in the distance. "I knew at once they were Germans," Musulin said, "and we took cover in the bushes, expecting to be strafed. Instead, a Stuka and two JU–52's buzzed the strip, and headed back toward their airfield at Kraljevo."

Somehow, whether by accident or by intercepting Halyard's radio messages to Bari, the enemy had penetrated their secret. It was too late to warn the base, Musulin realized; in all probability the rescue planes were already warming up on the flight line. Would the German night-fighters be circling in wait for their arrival? Were the nearby Nazi troops alerted for an attack on the weak Chetnik defenses? A check by a secret telephone line to Chachak reported no unusual activity by the

German garrison. Musulin decided to proceed with plans, and ordered the designated seventy-two airmen to assemble at the strip. A Chetnik soldier was stationed at each flare, ready to light it at Musulin's command, and his sergeant stood nearby with an Aldis lamp to blink the identification signal.

"Promptly at ten o'clock we heard airplane engines approaching," Musulin continued, "and the waiting airmen began to cheer — they recognized the sound of American planes. As they circled over for the first time, my sergeant blinked the codeword *Nan*, and received the correct reply *X-ray*. I gave the order to light the ground fires and shot up a green flare, our signal that the landings were to begin. . . . Everyone held his breath as the first pilot made his approach, and then gave it the gun and roared off, having overshot the tiny runway. The second plane made a perfect landing, and wheeled off the runway into a sloping depression to avoid the wings of the next plane, which missed it by inches as it turned to taxi. I could see that these night-landings were too dangerous, and decided to request the next rescue attempt at daylight tomorrow morning."

Only four planes had arrived — the other two had been forced to turn back because of engine trouble — and twenty-four of the waiting airmen were told they would have to wait until tomorrow. One pilot offered to fill up his plane with them, but Musulin persuaded him he would have trouble enough taking off with the twelve men assigned to his craft. Quickly the evacuees climbed aboard, stripping off their shoes and most of their clothing and tossing them gratefully to their Chetnik hosts, and the first plane roared down the strip. "We were all pretty tense," Musulin said, "but she took off without a hitch. The rest followed, one of them brushing a tree as he fought for altitude, but they all were airborne without incident. . . .

"Just before 0800 on the following morning, the tenth, we heard a tremendous roar in the distance. Our first thought was that it was another bombing mission on its way to some Balkan targets, but as the planes came closer, we recognized the unmistakable lines of six lovely C–47's, escorted by a swarm of P–51 fighters, and we realized the whole show was just for us. To team Halyard, to the airmen, to the Chetnik soldiers and peasants, it was the most inspiring sight we had ever witnessed. . . .

"The C–47's began to come in at five-minute intervals, and we sweated out each landing. The moment a plane rolled to a halt, it was surrounded by screaming women and girls, who showered the crews and the embarking Americans with flowers. The pilots were caught up in the excitement of the farewell, and I had trouble getting them to take off to clear the strip for other planes. Those pilots of the 60th Troop Carrier Command were the hottest fliers I've ever seen. Some of them even ground-looped in landing, to slow down and stop before they reached the end of the strip. In a half-hour, all six planes were loaded and away again, forming overhead into a clumsy V formation. With their fighter escort giving them cover, they dipped their wings in a final salute and headed back to base."

At nine o'clock a second wave of twenty-five P–51's escorted six more transports to the airstrip, and they evacuated another group of airmen without mishap. Within two hours, a total of 241 Americans had been taken off the "Missing in Action" list, as well as six British, four French, nine Italians, and twelve Russians. Evidently the fighters had done such an effective job of strafing that the Germans had dug in, and failed to observe the evacuation. The Chetniks continued to bring in additional airmen they had found, and on the nights of August 26th and 27th another fifty-eight were flown out safely. Altogether 432 Americans and 80 Allied personnel were evacuated over the summer, and Halyard Mission was awarded a unit citation by General Ira Eaker, air commander of the Mediterranean theater. The rescue operations terminated when Tito's Partisans drove the Chetniks from the Pranjane airstrip while they were preparing for still another evacuation.

Marshal Tito had been saved by Allied assistance when the Germans attacked his headquarters at Drvar with glider troops and armored columns, closing in on all sides. Answering his radio appeal for help, formations from the 15th Air Force had bombed and strafed the German troop concentrations until the Partisans were able to break through the encirclement, and he had conceded in an order of the day: "American and British prestige is now almost equal to that of the Russians." With the arrival of the Red Army in Belgrade, however, Tito's collaboration with U.S. and British officers abruptly ceased, and all OSS agents working with the Partisans were withdrawn. Yugoslavia ended the war as a Communist sphere of influence under Tito's complete control, the Chetniks were evicted from their ancestral land, and General Mihailovich, arraigned by Tito for "war crimes," was executed by a firing squad.

3

Of all the daily reports from OSS to cross President Roosevelt's desk, perhaps the most bizarre was General Donovan's memorandum of June 5, 1943:

> *Tibet.* We have received for you some tokens of esteem from the Dalai Lama of Tibet. These have been forwarded from Chungking by Lt. Col. Tolstoy and Capt. Dolan, two officers attached to OSS who were entrusted with your letter of July 3, 1942. The boxes contain a letter and presentation scarf; a framed picture of the Dalai Lama; four *tenghas* of gold brocade; three rare coins. In addition, there are some old and new Tibetan stamps for your collection.

Far-off Tibet had assumed a new strategic importance early in 1942. Germany was pushing inexorably eastward across Africa to Suez, and Japan was thrusting westward through Indochina and Thailand toward India. If the Axis pincers closed in middle Asia, this independent religious state in the heart of the Himalayas might become the only Allied access to the Orient. General Joseph Stilwell had taken his "hell of a licking" and retreated from Burma, leaving the ancient Burma Road in enemy hands. A goodwill mission to the Forbidden City of Lhasa, the high command felt, might achieve the double purpose of persuading the Dalai Lama of America's friendship, and of investigating the possibility of a new supply route through Tibet's mountain fastnesses to China.

Donovan had the man for the mission. Lieutenant Colonel Ilya Tolstoy, grandson of the Russian novelist and an experienced adventurer and explorer, was willing and eager to penetrate the mysteries of

the Forbidden City. Accompanied by Captain Brooke Dolan of Philadelphia, he flew to India in July of 1942, carrying a personal letter and
appropriate gifts from the American head of state to the holy ruler of
Tibet: a framed photograph of President Roosevelt inscribed to the
Dalai Lama, a portable radio, and an elaborately jeweled wristwatch
which told the hour, day, month, year, and current phase of the moon.
With a string of long-haired Siberian ponies and four Nepalese hired to
serve as guides and bearers, the little caravan headed northeast through
Nepal toward the cloud-packed Himalayan range.

The way to Shangri-La led over trails which in all probability had
never before been traveled by a Westerner. Flat-featured Mongolian
natives would surround them at each tiny settlement, plucking curiously
at their Occidental clothes and jabbering in an unknown dialect. Dragging a swarm of excited children who clung to either hand, the Americans would enter a stone hut, heated by an open fire of dried yak dung,
and sprawl on padded mats while their hosts proffered unleavened
barley bread and butter made from goat's milk and bitter tea sweetened
with salt. Word of their presence spread fast, and Buddhist priests from
the surrounding countryside would arrive on white donkeys to inspect
these strange visitors from another world. Tibet was a theocracy,
governed by ecclesiastical rulers under the deified Dalai Lama; the
villagers would step back as a spiritual leader passed, and suck in their
breath deferentially. The monks were attired in fur-lined maroon robes,
their trailing lengths gathered in a loop and held under an arm, and they
wore three-foot-high hats like terraced pagodas. Their long black hair
was wound around a carved bone ornament, and tied with a velvet
ribbon, and a single gold pendant dangled from the left ear. Their
attitude was friendly, but one monk who spoke a little Hindustani
warned Tolstoy that a party of Germans, attempting to cross Tibet
recently, had blundered into a religious ceremony and thoughtlessly
smoked cigarettes as they watched the rites. They had been stoned to
death.

The caravan skirted the base of 28,000-foot Mt. Kanchenjunga,
dwarfed only by the white summit of Everest, and started its slow climb
toward the Gopa Pass. Their native mountain ponies followed a narrow
manmade path of stone steps, hacked out of the side of an almost verti-

cal cliff; a rock dislodged by a horse's hoof might drop a sheer mile before they heard its echo. It grew bitter cold as they neared the summit, and they were glad they had exchanged their footgear for high Tibetan boots of black leather, lined with wildcat fur and shaped to fit either foot. They rested their horses frequently because of the lack of oxygen in the thin air, and sometimes the Nepalese bearers had to help them remount. At last they crossed the divide, and against the horizon, glinting in the white sunlight, were the gilded domes and spires of the Forbidden City.

Lhasa stands on an elevated plateau, in the center of a broad valley, and as they approached they could see innumerable paths leading down to the fertile lowlands where the inhabitants raised their food. Peasant huts dotted the valley, their dooryards spread with red peppers drying in the sun, and shaggy cattle eyed the visitors stolidly as they climbed to the plateau.

The holy city was enclosed by a massive stone wall, and they had to wait at the gates an entire week until a religious festival had been celebrated. Their entry was like a return to the fourteenth century, Tolstoy said. No wheels turned in the narrow winding streets, and the city had a strange cathedral hush. All the streets led to the Dalai Lama's red-and-white Potala, towering five stories above the other buildings — Tibetans believe that no human should be higher than the Lama — and its entrance was guarded by fierce mastiffs lunging at the end of their short chains.

Their audience with the holy ruler of Tibet was conducted with the utmost ceremony. Gifts were formally exchanged with lesser members of the household, even the Nepalese bearers trading presents with palace servants of comparable rank. Lining either side of the great hall as they entered were tall grim-faced monks, clad in layers of stiff gold brocade. A gong struck, the carved doors opened silently, and the two Americans were ushered into the throne room. Before them on an elevated teak-wood chair inlaid with gold was a boy of ten, with a sallow skin and dark intelligent eyes. Not a word was spoken as they approached the royal presence. A powerful six-foot-four monk handed Tolstoy a piece of black bread, a book, and a jeweled symbol, and he was led to the Dalai Lama, who took the sacred items from him, and gave him a white scarf woven of wood fiber, softer and finer than any silk. In return, Tolstoy presented the gifts from President Roosevelt.

The Dalai Lama inspected the photograph for a moment, and then murmured something. The huge monk leaned toward Tolstoy, and to his surprise, translated the Lama's remarks in flawless English. His Holiness had inquired as to the health of the President, he said. Tolstoy replied politely that the President was well, and the monk repeated his answer to the Lama, who nodded gravely but volunteered no further comment. Evidently the interview had been concluded. Servants began to pass bowls of rice and glasses of black tea — Tolstoy noticed that an official taster sipped the Lama's tea before it touched his sacred lips — and the English-speaking monk urged Tolstoy to throw a pinch of rice over his shoulder for luck. Abruptly a yellow-robed acolyte in the doorway uttered an enormous bellow, signifying that the audience was over. As Tolstoy left the throne room, he stole a glance over his shoulder, and noted that the Dalai Lama was putting on his wristwatch, an indication that the goodwill mission had succeeded.

At the doorway, Tolstoy paused to thank the monk for his kindness. "Where did you learn to speak English?" he asked. "At Rugby," the monk replied, and closed the door.

They lingered in the Forbidden City another week while the women of Lhasa prepared four gold-embroidered *tenghas*, gifts from the Lama for President Roosevelt. After a farewell banquet of mutton and exotic sweetmeats and a potent barley beer called *chung*, the caravan set out across unexplored Eastern Tibet toward Chungking, studying the potential route for a military road and noting on their map the sites of possible airfields. The area was infested with bandit tribes, and the travelers wore American flags sewed conspicuously on their jackets and kept their carbines handy. Late in May of 1943, ten months after their departure from the States, they arrived at Kangting, China, and were flown the rest of the way to Chungking. General Stilwell wired his personal congratulations, and on their return to Washington General Donovan awarded Tolstoy and Dolan the Legion of Merit.

The clandestine web had spun another sensitive strand to the Far East.

4

OSS had established its initial link with Asia as early as the spring of 1942, when the agency was still known as COI. The project had taken shape after the failure of General Joseph W. Stilwell's Burma campaign, which had ended in "Vinegar Joe's" ignominious withdrawal to Assam. A prime factor in his defeat, Donovan recognized, was Japanese fifth column activity — the jungle ambushes and surprise night attacks which had demoralized Stilwell's troops and sapped their strength. Donovan proposed to match the Japanese in their irregular warfare by organizing a guerrilla unit to conduct similar espionage and sabotage operations in support of the Allied forces — unprecedented in OSS, in fact the first such unit since Washington's Rangers.

The immediate problem was to find someone qualified to handle this unique project. Donovan's attention was called to a former Los Angeles police officer named Carl Eifler, who had served with the Mexican Border Patrol and later as deputy director of customs in Honolulu. He had dealt with Chinese and Japanese smugglers and knew the Oriental mind, and his determination and raw courage made him a natural for the job. A hasty check revealed that Eifler had just been called up for active duty as a captain with the 35th Infantry Regiment in Hawaii. His transfer to OSS was promptly arranged, and he was ordered to report to the headquarters at 25th and E.

Carl Eifler was a great bear of a man, 250 pounds of lithe muscle, whose merest whisper was a bellow. He had boxed professionally, was skilled in jujitsu, flew his own plane, and entertained the stubborn belief that nothing was impossible, a trait which General Donovan admired above all others. His first choices for the new unit were Captain John Coughlin, also of the 35th Regiment, a West Pointer whose level-headedness was an effective foil to Eifler's ebullient enthusiasm, and Captain Ray Peers, another Regular Army officer and an excellent administrator, who was later to head the detachment when Eifler was invalided home. By careful interrogation and flashes of intuition — one of his most capable recruits was discovered during a casual conversation in a Baltimore bar — Eifler soon filled his assigned quota of twenty-five officers and enlisted men, each adapted in his peculiar way to the operation ahead. Supplies were procured, ranging from jungle sleeping bags and mosquito nets to demolition materials and jeeps, and late in May the secret unit embarked for India.

OSS Detachment 101 — although it was number one of its kind, they felt a larger figure would lend them more prestige — had originally been assigned to conduct paramilitary operations in China, but General Stilwell had other ideas. He was in urgent need of all possible help in his pending campaign to retake northern Burma and establish an overland supply route from Ledo on the Assam-Burma border, through the Hukawng Valley and southward to the key city of Myitkyina (Americanized as Mishina) and thence east through Bhamo to join the old Burma Road at the Chinese border.[20] Stilwell's operational directive to Detachment 101 was specific: to deny the Japanese the use of the Myitkyina airfield, through sabotage of enemy communications and supply lines, and to give direct tactical support to American air and ground forces in the theater. Vinegar Joe, his eyes snapping behind steel-rimmed spectacles and his long cigarette holder tilted at a challenging angle, concluded the interview with Eifler tartly: "The next thing I want to hear out of you are some loud booms from behind the Jap lines."

The detachment established its base camp on an isolated tea plantation at Nazira, Assam, in the heart of Kipling's *Jungle Book* country. Tigers prowled the perimeter of their compound, and the British plantation manager suggested pleasantly that they'd best shut their doors and windows at night; the ruddy cobras had a way of slipping inside and curling up in a chap's bed, you know, or a vampire bat might puncture the jugular of a sleeping victim and he would bleed to death without awakening. The camp had an informal air — standard 101 attire con-

---

[20] Without British and Indian support, Stilwell had not the capacity to do this. In fact, this campaign never looked as if it would get off the ground until SEAC was formed in the fall of 1943. At no time did the United States have more than one regiment operational in Burma — first "Gallahad" (Merrill's Marauder's), which was succeeded by "Mars."

sisted of British ammunition boots, a pair of shorts, and a broad-brimmed campaign hat with a jaunty feather — but there was nothing casual about Eifler and his staff as they worked long hours in the monsoon heat, perfecting plans for infiltrating American-led guerrilla teams into the interior, and training their Kachin levies in harassing tactics to drive the estimated million Japanese troops out of Burma.

It was a David and Goliath task, and only the jungle cunning of the native volunteers made it feasible. The Kachins are squat and blocky Asiatics, their hair matted and their teeth black from chewing betel nut, who inhabit the heavily wooded ranges around Myitkyina and along the upper Irrawaddy River. Descended from the hill people of the Himalayas, they possess the fierce pride of mountain men, and for centuries have fought to preserve their independence from the Rangoon government. They viewed the other Burmese tribes, the Japanese, and the British with an equally jaundiced eye; but between them and the Americans there developed a mutual regard and understanding. The men of 101 respected their native allies as invaluable comrades-in-arms; and in return the Kachins gave them their wholehearted loyalty.

This kinship with the Americans stemmed in large part from the previous efforts of a fabulous missionary-priest named Father James Stuart, who for nine years had roamed the wild Naga Hills, a battered Gurkha hat shoved back on his head and a .45 hanging from his belt, talking the Kachin language with a thick Irish brogue. At Myitkyina he had seen his parish tortured and killed by the Japanese, and had led the remnants of his devoted congregation north to the refugee camp at Sumprabum, where he told the Japanese major bluntly, "I want medicine and food. I'm taking care of these people." Even the enemy did not dare refuse him. Father Stuart joined Detachment 101 as liaison with the Kachins, recruiting the natives and also advising OSS on tribal eccentricities and taboos.

The Kachins had few superiors as jungle fighters. They seemed to be able to smell Japs; they would follow the faintest tracks through the dense bamboo thickets, and their keen senses would tell them the size of the enemy detachment and where it was going. If they were in doubt at the junction of two trails, they would toss a hair onto the ground and take the direction it pointed, and for some reason it was always the right one. They taught their American comrades to eat termites and small white bees, and to kill wild pigs with a concealed crossbow and tripline, a technique they also employed in warfare. Their favorite weapon was the dreaded *panji;* two-foot bamboo slivers sharpened to a needle point and fire-hardened, which they planted on either side of the trail, slanting in the direction of an approaching enemy patrol. When the column was ambushed, the Japanese would dive headlong into the thicket and impale themselves on the hidden spikes.

As the guerrilla units completed their training, they were parachuted to strategic outposts in north Burma, directed by two advance bases code-named Forward and Knothead. Supplies for these remote posts were slow in arriving from Washington, and the scarcity of available aircraft made airdrops so erratic that the whole program was threatened. 101's problem was solved when General Donovan, accompanied by Navy Captain John Ford, showed up without notice at Nazira on a personal tour of inspection behind the lines. Donovan climbed into the detachment's single-engine airplane, an unarmed L–5 called the Gypsy Moth, and Carl Eifler flew the chief of American wartime intelligence over the uncharted jungle, hugging the treetops to avoid detection by enemy fighters, and landed on an improvised rice-paddy strip at Knot-head, a hundred and fifty miles inside Jap-occupied territory. The staff at 101 was considerably relieved when the General returned safely at sunset after having talked at length to OSS Major Vincent Curl and his Kachin headmen, with Father Stuart acting as interpreter. Not only did Donovan's surprise visit behind the lines have an enormous impact on field morale, but he sent off some blistering cables to Washington demanding immediate shipment of the needed supplies. Added aircraft were procured from Tenth Air Force, 101's monthly appropriation was raised to $100,000, and its personnel, depleted by malaria, was reinforced by replacements from the States.

Now General Stilwell began to hear booms loud enough to satisfy his critical ears. Some twenty field stations were established along a 600-mile front, and the feats of the Kachin jungle fighters won the admiration of the hitherto skeptical theater command. Railroad lines were interdicted, bridges blown, and hit-and-run attacks kept the enemy in a

WJD with Colonel Carl Eifler, Detachment 101, Burma.

constant state of confusion. In a single daring assault, the guerrillas forced five thousand regular troops of the Japanese 56th Division to retreat 170 miles to the south. 101-trained Kachins formed an advance screen for General Orde Wingate's Chindit strike in February of 1943. They covered the slow progress of the Army engineers along the route of the new Ledo Road. When the solid canopy of jungle foliage made Tenth Air Force reconnaisance impossible, native scouts provided the only means of spotting lucrative targets: a camouflaged Japanese ammo dump, or a cleverly constructed bridge whose surface was a couple of inches under water to make it invisible from the air. Powerful waterproof radios, designed by OSS for the monsoon weather, maintained contact between the forward bases and Nazira, employing a code made up of Kachin words which the Japs could never solve.

From one of these outposts near Bhamo came a laconic message, signed by a native agent known as Betty: "I have three Japanese captives, including one officer. When can you come get them? Recommend action earliest possible date as enemy patrols one mile away." Japanese prisoners were invaluable for OSS interrogation, and the following morning two L–1's took off for Betty's position, eighty-six miles behind the enemy front. When they reached the rendezvous, they could see only a brush-covered field with a Buddhist pagoda at the far end; but by the time they had circled to fly over it again, the brush had miraculously disappeared, a windsock was up, and natives were setting out white marker stakes and the safe-to-land panel. As the planes bumped to a halt, a bullock cart emerged from a clump of bamboo, hauling the three prisoners bound hand and foot, with bloody bandages around their heads. The cart drew up to the planes, and the two sergeant pilots waited uncertainly.

"Suddenly I felt somebody tugging at my sleeve," Sergeant Trifletti said later, "and there was a slim young native with an almost girlish face, who said in perfect English with a slight Oxford accent: 'I'm Betty. One would never suspect I was an agent, would one?'" Betty apologized profusely for the prisoners' battered condition. "They resisted arrest strenuously and fought with their fists," he explained to Trifletti, "so it was impossible to avoid banging them about a bit."

Trifletti asked how many other Japanese were in the area. "Oh, I should estimate there are perhaps seven thousand in the immediate vicinity," Betty sighed. "Sometimes I get very lonely here, seeing nothing but Japs." The sergeants wasted no time loading the prisoners into their planes, and took off at full throttle. As they circled over the field, they saw the earlier phenomenon in reverse: all traces of the strip had disappeared in a few seconds, and there was only a brush-covered field, with the lone figure of Betty waving them a courteous farewell.

Dozens of these secret landing strips were hacked out of the jungle, on isolated mountain plateaus or river deltas to which sick and wounded could be floated on rafts; and over two hundred American airmen, forced down in northern Burma, were rescued by Kachin scouts and evacuated by 101 liaison planes to India. In the Army hospital at Chabua, I remember hearing the story of one Air Transport Command sergeant, radio operator on a C–87 which was lost in bad weather on its return from China. Their fuel tanks were empty, he told me, and the pilot gave the order to hit the silk. As the sergeant bailed out, the slipstream caught him and flung him back against a horizontal stabilizer, breaking both arms and cutting a deep gash in his forehead. His next conscious memory was of opening his eyes and looking up bewildered at the ground overhead. Then he realized that he was dangling upside down from a tall mahogany tree, wrapped tightly in the tangled shroud lines of his parachute. Blood from the gash in his forehead dripped steadily onto the jungle floor a hundred feet below.

Three members of his air crew were standing in a group at the foot of the tree, discussing him. He could hear what they were saying, but he was too weak from loss of blood to shout. Evidently his crewmates had tried in vain to climb the smooth trunk of the tree to release him. There were Japanese in the vicinity, they could tell by fresh spoor in the trail, and enemy patrols would soon be scouring the jungle for possible survivors of the wreck. They could not leave the sergeant like this, to starve or still worse to fall into enemy hands. There was only one thing to do.

The sergeant tried to protest, but he could only groan. As though in a nightmare, he watched his crewmates break off three straws. The man who drew the short straw took a .45 from his holster. The helpless sergeant heard the dry click of the hammer as it was pulled back; and then he heard another sound, the rustle of vines and pad of bare feet. A searching party of Kachins, alerted by the crashed plane, went to work swiftly, felling a second tree against the towering mahogany, and scaling it like monkeys to the base of the branch from which he was hanging. They tossed a loop of rattan around the branch and pulled it toward them, and he felt himself being cut free and passed from hand to hand gently to the ground. That night he was given emergency first aid at a 101 forward base, and the following morning an L–1 flew him to Nazira.

Reports from intelligence agents in the field revealed that the Japanese had failed to supply any medical aid to the natives in the territories they occupied; and Detachment 101 decided to capitalize on this neglect. It happened that Commander James Luce, in charge of the advance base Forward, was a skilled Navy surgeon. Extensive medical supplies were flown to Fort Hertz and moved overland to his base, and by Christmas of 1943 a bamboo hospital and surgical clinic and dispensary had been completed. The response of the natives to their first white doctor was overwhelming, Commander Luce reported, even though their reactions were quite a surprise to the Western mind. "The Kachins were at first cautious and then fascinated by medical procedures," his dispatch read, "but remained suspicious until the beneficial results were observed, and then came in such numbers that it was almost impossible to handle all of them. They accepted medical care in a very matter-of-fact manner, evidently feeling that it was no more than right that we Americans, who had come to live with them, should render whatever aid we could."

After Lord Mountbatten became Supreme Allied Commander, Southeast Asia, he conceived the idea of a special striking force, which General Marshall authorized at Mountbatten's request to give the United States at least a token force to fight alongside the million men of other nationalities under Mountbatten's direct command. This elite unit came to be known as Merrill's Marauders.

Early in 1944 General Frank D. Merrill and his Marauders, battle-hardened veterans of the South Pacific fighting, struck out across

Burma toward the Myitkyina airport, from which Jap fighters were taking a heavy toll of transports flying the Hump. Hundreds of miles of leech-infested jungle lay in their path; streams had been swollen to torrents by the monsoon rains; the muddy trails led up mountains so steep that their mules could not get footing, and the weary troops had to push the rumps of their pack animals to the summit. Every foot of their epic march through Jap territory was covered by 101 natives who provided flank security, scouted the enemy ahead, and warned them of any ambush. Guided by the uncanny jungle knowledge of a Kachin chief named N'Naw Yang Nau, they skirted Jap patrols by little-known paths through the Naga Hills, crossed traveled highways without detection, and forded rivers on native-built bamboo suspension bridges. Once an under-strength Marauder battalion was cut off and surrounded by Japanese troops, who held them besieged for almost two weeks. OSS Lieutenant Tilly, head of a Kachin band called "The Lightning Force," hammered the enemy so viciously from the rear that the trapped battalion was able to escape and rejoin the main column.

As the Marauders neared Myitkyina, a special task force under Colonel Charles Hunter was organized for a swift thrust to take the airfield by surprise. Simultaneously two advance units from Forward, led by Commander Luce and Lieutenant Gerry Larsen, struck at the Jap supply lines from the south and northeast. So effective were their guerrilla attacks, a command report stated, that "enemy reinforcements headed for Myitkyina were halted and finally diverted from their objective." As N'Naw Yang Nau directed Hunter's meager forces toward the airfield, he was bitten in the heel by a poisonous snake; but he insisted on leading them on horseback, his sagging body strapped into the saddle. Stealthily the Marauder group crept through thick brush to the very edge of the Myitkyina strip, and the burst of automatic weapons was the first knowledge the Japs had of their presence. The garrison quickly surrendered, the airfield was secured, and Colonel Hunter cabled Ray Peers at 101: "Thanks to your people for a swell job. Could not have succeeded without them."

Although the primary contribution of the detachment was in support of ground operations, it provided services to the U.S. air units which they considered "indispensable." Tenth Air Force estimated that 101 scouting units contributed eighty-five percent of their intelligence on enemy air strength, bombing targets, and escape routes or safe areas for downed aviators, as well as all-important damage assessments after a mission. An A-2 report dated August 14 stated that "1000 Japs, with considerable stores, were located by 101 agents in Moda . . . an inconspicuous Burmese town which hitherto had been disregarded and never photographed. Fighters, loaded with demolition and incendiary bombs, attacked the town at once. Subsequently 101 radioed that enemy casualties totaled 200 Japs killed, and a dump filled with ammunition and arms had been completely destroyed."

By 1945, when the Allies broke the final Japanese grip on northern Burma with the capture of Bhamo and Lashio, Detachment 101's original quota of 25 had expanded to 566 Americans and almost 10,000 native levies. Meanwhile, Stilwell's 3,000-man "Mars" force had been augmented by the 25,000-man 36th Division, which included one Indian and two British brigades under the command of the redoubtable Major General Frankie Festing. Mountbatten also had two Army corps operating in the neighboring Central Front and another Army corps on the Arakan Front. During their three years of guerrilla operations, they had accounted for 5,447 known Japanese dead and twice that number estimated killed or wounded, at the cost of only 18 American and 184 native lives. Colonel Peers recalls that General Stilwell, dubious of their casualty figures, once asked a Kachin Headman how he could tally the dead so accurately. The Kachin opened a bamboo tube tied to his waist, and dumped a number of objects like dried prunes on Stilwell's desk. "What are those?" the startled General asked. "Japanese ears," the Kachin said. "Divide by two, and you know how many killed." Stilwell never questioned the native battle statistics again.[21]

The semiautonomous OSS Detachment, the first United States unit to form an intelligence screen and to organize and employ a large guerrilla army deep in enemy territory, accomplished what the Chiefs of Staff termed "one of the most difficult and hazardous assignments that any

[21] W. R. Peers and D. Brelis, *Behind the Burma Road* (Boston, 1963).

military unit has ever been called upon to perform." In 1946, the detachment was awarded a Presidential Distinguished Unit Citation, and the commendation, signed by General Eisenhower, concluded: "Under the most hazardous jungle conditions, Americans of Detachment 101, Office of Strategic Services, displayed extraordinary heroism in leading their coordinated battalions of natives to complete victory against an overwhelming superior force. [From 8 May to 15 June, 1945] they met and routed 10,000 Japanese throughout an area of 10,000 square miles, killed 1,247 while sustaining losses of 37, demolished or captured 4 large dumps, destroyed the enemy motor transport, and inflicted extensive damage to communications and facilities." Even Vinegar Joe Stilwell, never given to lavish praise, went so far as to admit that "services rendered by 101 . . . were of great value."

When the detachment was dissolved at the war's end, the men of 101 desired to express their gratitude to the courageous native volunteers who had contributed so signally to the Burma victory. From Nazira they radioed a message to Army headquarters in New Delhi: "Recommend gallant Kachin leaders be awarded citation, medal or other recognition." Unfortunately the officer who received the message failed to realize that in cables the comma is usually designated by the letters CMA; and Delhi, anxious to comply with the OSS request, tried in vain to find a CMA Medal among the U.S. Army decorations. Rather than disappoint 101, a hundred special medals were struck off — handsome silver emblems dangling from green ribbons, bearing on their face the peacocks of Burma and the cryptic initials CMA.

101 was equally nonplussed when the medals arrived. They had arranged a formal ceremony that afternoon to present their tributes to the Kachin chiefs, and some solution had to be found. OSS met the crisis with characteristic ingenuity. At the appointed hour, the native leaders stood in solemn formation to receive that rarest of American medals, the Civilian Military Assistance award.

VI

HITLER'S MECHANIZED *blitzkrieg* across Europe had brought millions upon millions of civilians under Axis domination. In past invasions, the populace of a captured country had remained supine under the conqueror's heel, disorganized and easily suppressed if they tried to rebel; but in World War II, thanks to such technological advances as the portable radio and the long-range airplane to parachute supplies and weapons and trained leaders, they became a highly effective supporting arm of the Allies, a development which the German occupation had not anticipated. The Maquis of the French underground constituted a secret weapon as revolutionary as the atom bomb, and in its way as devastating. "In no previous war," General Eisenhower said after V-Day, "and in no other theater of this war have the resistance forces been so closely harnessed to the main military effort."

The Maquis — the name derived from a low dense undergrowth on Corsica called *maquis* in which bandits and fugitives would hide from the police — was a nondescript army, made up of refugees from every walk of French life. There were farmers, students, brokers, wine merchants, ministers. A dispossessed aristocrat from Paris, a butcher fleeing Nazi labor conscription, a former captain of the French Army escaped from a prison camp, a peasant who had killed a German looter and was in hiding from the Gestapo. These outlawed and hunted men who asked to join the underground often posed a problem for the ill-equipped and undernourished guerrilla bands — another mouth to feed, another pair of feet to find shoes for — but they never turned away a volunteer who might aid in the common struggle against the Nazi invaders. Their uniforms were tattered farm clothes; they had all but forgotten such luxuries as clean sheets and coffee and sugar; they depended on England and America for their arms, for strength and hope.

It takes a gun and shoes to make a fighting man. Day after day the Maquis groups would hug their clandestine radios, waiting for the BBC broadcast from London which would alert them to the next supply drop. The signals came on three successive days. Their first notice would be a prearranged message: "Suzette has hung her washing out to dry."(The operation will take place Saturday at the designated time and place.) The following day BBC would insert among its announcements a cryptic sentence: "There are red flowers in the forest." (The drop will be made tomorrow night as planned.) On the third day, as they crowded around their tiny RBZ set in a forest hideout, they would hear the final confirming message: "Snow will fall in early December this year." (Everything is in order, the drop will take place as scheduled.)

An hour before the supply plane was due, the local reception committee would outline the field with flashlights sunk in the ground, so that only a pilot directly overhead could see the beams, and a man would lie in readiness beside each buried light. The rest of the group would post themselves around the perimeter of the drop zone as sentries in case the operation was raided by the Germans. When they heard the aircraft approaching, they would snap on the flashlights just long enough for the pilot to make a practice run over the field. The lights would be put out while he circled, and turned on again as the plane came over on its drop-run. The moment the parachutes opened, all lights would be extinguished, and the Maquis committee would swarm over the dark field to pick up the containers as they landed. They would rush with them into the woods, and guards would stand over the precious pile as they unpacked American or British army shoes, food, medical supplies, W/T radio sets, and grenades and tommy guns and rifles.

The Maquisards were fascinated by the American weapons. Their arms were mostly old fieldpieces from prior European wars, and they would fondle and caress the modern carbines, load and swing them to the shoulder, finger the bolt with quiet anticipation. One OSS officer who had parachuted to aid the resistance rested his own carbine against a tree for a moment while he helped the group bury the empty containers. He noticed a young Frenchman pick up the rifle and start away with it. The boy turned at his shout, and explained that he would bring it back immediately, he merely desired to get the feel of it. He returned it that night, and the American officer noticed that the clip of the rifle was empty. "I tried it on a couple of Germans," the young Maquisard said apologetically. "It sights very well."

The women would gather up the red and yellow and green parachute canopies and carry them home. They did not dare make them into dresses, but they could use them for underwear. It was the only luxury they knew. Before the war was over, most of the Maquis women were wearing bright-colored silk lingerie concealed under their drab peasant skirts.

With each successive air drop, the Maquis fighting potential increased. Heretofore the lack of gasoline had forced them to depend for transportation on antiquated and unreliable charcoal-burning vehicles known as "gazogenes"; but now they could use their newly acquired weapons to ambush German trucks carrying gas or raid an enemy fuel dump. As their mobility increased, their guerrilla operations grew bolder and more varied. Weather spotters radioed regular data to Allied Air Forces in England. Resistance units staked out minefields in front of the Allied advance, removed booby traps from railroad stations or post offices, even liberated villages occupied by the enemy. Fifty Maquisards, residents of Nazi-held Angoulême, crept into town via the sewage system, and an imaginative parish priest provided the means of distributing the weapons they had brought for their fellow townsmen. "Looking extremely solemn and chanting Latin incantations," an official account stated, "he led a mournful funeral procession to the cemetery, where a coffin was interred with much loud weeping. During the night the coffin was dug up again, and the arms it contained were passed out to the citizens." The entire German garrison was wiped out.

Maquis hatred for the Nazis was surpassed only by their bitterness toward the *milice*, Vichy French sympathizers who worked with the Gestapo against their own countrymen. In the department of Cher, Lieutenant Robert Anstett reported to OSS, a young *milicien* was picked up by the Maquis on suspicion, and confessed that he was an agent for the Germans. "He asked to see me before his execution," Lieutenant Anstett said, "and told me he would like permission to command his own firing squad, in order to show the villagers that he was a real Frenchman and could die like one. I recommended to the Maquis leaders that he be granted his request. They agreed, and I went to the village square that afternoon to witness one of the most extraordinary spectacles I'll ever see. It was midsummer, and the prisoner was stripped to the waist. Calmly he drank his wine and smoked his last cigarette, which the custom of French justice prescribed for doomed men. Then he called the firing squad to attention, and made a little speech in which he admitted his crime and asked for forgiveness of his neighbors. He took his position against the wall of a building, looked straight at his twelve executioners and, without a tremor in his voice, gave the commands: 'Ready! Aim! Fire!' The bullets ripped into his body and he fell dead, a brave but misguided man who had been a victim of Nazi propaganda. The crowd was hushed, a final token of respect."

The gratitude of the French underground toward the Americans, who had given them their chance to fight back effectively after four years of German occupation, was overwhelming. Navy Lieutenant Mike Burke, now president of the New York Yankees, was a member of an OSS Jedburgh team which parachuted into the Vosges Mountains just after D-Day; he said the Maquisards threw their arms around him and kissed him when they recognized his uniform. "It was miserably cold that night," Burke told me, "and there was only one little shed in the woods where we were hiding. All three of us had waterproof sleeping bags, and they didn't have so much as a blanket to spread over them; but they insisted that we should sleep inside. We couldn't refuse because it would hurt their feelings. It started raining after we turned in, and an hour or so later I heard the door creak open. A shivering Frenchman, soaked to the skin, snuggled down beside us to keep warm. Another crept in out of the rain a few minutes later, and then another, and pretty soon the whole group was inside the shed, steaming in the close atmosphere and snoring so loud we couldn't sleep. They'd kicked off their shoes, and we had to hold our breath, and now and then we'd feel an arm flung across us like a child's embrace. But we didn't move. We knew those skinny little guys were enjoying their first relaxed night's rest because we were there, and we were glad to be lying beside them."

The night after their arrival, the Maquis chief escorted the Jedburgh team to his secret headquarters in a forest two kilometers out of town, where a banquet had been prepared in their honor. It was not much of a banquet. The table was a single plank resting on two logs, and the feast consisted of a couple of snared rabbits simmering in an iron stewpot. An eighty-year-old citizen had hobbled up from the village to cook the meal. He was too old to fight the Germans, but he wanted to do something. They all waited formally until the guests unclasped their knives and speared some chunks of rabbit, and then the hungry Maquisards dug in ravenously, gouging bread from a long loaf to mop up the gravy, sucking the bones dry. The old man kept looking at him, Burke noticed; and suddenly great tears began to roll down his seamed cheeks.

"To think," he said brokenly, "to think that General Eisenhower thought enough of our little village to send an American officer here to help us."

At the Quebec Conference in the late summer of 1943, Secretary of War Stimson and Generals Marshall and H. H. Arnold and Admiral Ernest King — with, for once, the firm backing of President Roosevelt — obtained the agreement of the Prime Minister for a cross-Channel strike, code-named Overlord, as the major Allied effort in 1944.

Target date for Overlord was set for May, though the actual landings at Normandy, which Churchill had predicted would be determined "mainly by the moon and the weather," did not take place until June 6. With D-Day established, OSS/London embarked with British SOE on a joint Anglo-American enterprise, designated Special Force Headquarters (SFHQ), which would organize all underground resistance in

France in support of the forthcoming invasion. Their program called for large-scale paramilitary activity, aided by a maximum delivery of arms and supplies, which would culminate in an all-out Maquis attack on the Germans on D-Day. Once the landings had been made, the resistance forces would create chaos behind the enemy lines, disrupting communications, ambushing troops and convoys, blocking all escape routes, and conducting anti-scorch measures to prevent the demolition of key installations by the retreating Nazis. To integrate this Free French uprising with the advance of the Allies, a number of three-man SFHQ teams called Jedburghs would be trained and dropped, in uniform, into France and Belgium and Holland after D-Day to direct the underground army.

At Milton Hall, an Elizabethan manor house some hundred miles north of London, was assembled a heterogeneous group of 240 volunteers: American and British and French and Belgian and Dutch, Army and Navy and Marine, officers and enlisted men, all living and learning the tactics of unorthodox warfare in a staid atmosphere of oak-beamed halls and Cromwellian armor. Paratrooper boots thudded from a training harness onto the neat lawns, and men practiced silent killing in the sunken gardens. From the croquet pitch came the crackle of small arms or the louder explosion of Sten guns and Enfields, and the acrid smell of burnt powder blended with the traditional odor of boxwood and roses. Demolition charges shook the far end of the golf course, and a hand-powered wireless set — everyone had to master the Morse code — stuttered day and night in the paneled library.

The Jeds were taught to jump at an RAF school at Ringway, located in a sheep pasture in the rolling downs country near Manchester. They dropped from war-weary Sterling Bombers, ten men to a plane, five forward and five aft of the Joe-hole. The first jump was made in pairs, to avoid fouling; the second was in strings of five; on the third jump all ten men descended together, while a British jump-instructor on the ground coached them over a bullhorn: "Get your knees together, Number Two!" "Pull down those front riders, Five!" "Always come in for a forward landing." The final lesson, a night drop under combat conditions, concluded their three-day course. Some hardened Fort

Benning paratroopers with the Jedburghs were astounded; back at Benning it was six weeks before your first jump.

Gradually the trainees grew better acquainted, and individual teams began to form. At the outset these teams had been assigned by the colonel in charge, but it was decided that the partnerships made by mutual consent were more efficient in combat. After a preliminary courtship period, shy and rather self-conscious, an American and a Frenchman would decide to become "engaged," and their "marriage" was duly solemnized in the following day's orders. A radio operator, usually an enlisted man, would be invited to join the team, the trio would be given their own code name — Dauntless, Harvard, Argonne — and henceforth they would work and eat and live together in a tight-knit comradeship on which their very lives might depend. Sometimes, after a marriage, the members of a team would realize that they were incompatible and apply for a divorce; but it was better to find out at training school than in the field.

In May of 1944, the first Jedburgh teams were sent to North Africa, to be parachuted into southern France. During June, six more teams were dropped behind the lines in Brittany, from which they radioed vital intelligence to the Normandy beachhead. By the end of August, after General Patton's breakthrough, all the remaining Jeds had jumped into France or the Low Countries, to gather about them their own little armies of Maquis and lead them in hit-and-run forays, the basic strategy of guerrilla warfare. "*Surprise, mitraillage, évanouissement,*" the Maquis called it; surprise, kill, vanish. Of the eighty-two Americans who participated in the Jedburgh operation, fifty-three received the Distinguished Service Cross, Croix de Guerre, Legion of Merit, Silver or Bronze Star, or Purple Heart — claimed to be the highest percentage of citations awarded to a single group in the entire war.

Danger was always a fourth member of a Jedburgh team, and each man carried an undated death warrant in the pocket of his jumpsuit. Frequently a unit would be overrun by the enemy, and only their survival training at Milton Hall enabled them to hide out for long periods without food or shelter until they shook the Gestapo off their trail. One Jed, hounded by German searchers, spent ten hours in a bog with nothing but his nose above water. Another team was ambushed, the radio operator killed, and the American officer and his French teammate cornered at night in a scrubby woodlot. The Germans set fire to the underbrush, and guarded every exit with machine guns. The Allied officers covered their faces with wet socks against the smoke, and waited their chance. A small cloud over the moon gave them a precious few moments to slip across an opening to a deep drainage ditch and scuttle out of danger.

Captain Paul Cyr of Vermont, operating with a Jed team in the heavily fortified Loire Inférieure, rescued several British and American pilots who had crash-landed in the vicinity, and his Maquis associates guided them safely to Allied territory. Cyr knew that the Gestapo had an accurate description of him, and it would have been the better part of valor to depart with the fliers, but he had wind of an important prize. Through a woman member of the underground who was employed as a charlady in the German headquarters, he managed to obtain a photostatic copy of the Nazi plans for the defense of that strategic coastal area, including the fortifications of St.-Nazaire. Realizing their immediate value, he resolved to deliver the plans in person to Eighth Army headquarters, made his way through the German front lines, and handed them to the astonished Assistant Chief of Staff G-2. Cyr was recommended for the Distinguished Service Cross, but he was not on hand to receive the award. He had already started back through the German gauntlet to rejoin his teammates, and lead the Maquis forces in the coming attack on the Loire.

It took a special difference in a man, a kind of fundamental oddness, to volunteer for a Jedburgh mission. He had to have cool courage, of course, resourcefulness, high motivation, sometimes a touch of sheer bravado. There was Captain Douglas Bazata, who dressed in peasant clothes and escaped across a field surrounded by Germans by creeping on his hands and knees, ostensibly picking mushrooms. Ahead of him stood a stolid German guard, his legs spread wide apart. Yielding to an irresistible impulse, Bazata crawled right between his legs and disappeared into the woods.

Or twenty-three-year-old Edwin Poitras of Lowell, Massachusetts,

Navy Sp/1c, who tucked his bell-bottomed trousers into jump-boots and joined a Jedburgh team as a radio operator. The Liberator carrying this novice paratrooper on his first mission was shot down, but Poitras managed to jump clear, the sole survivor. He located the Maquis leader to whom his team had been assigned, but the safe house in which he hid that night was dynamited, and he had to flee to the hills. From his cave shelter, he directed the Maquis in guerrilla operations, and after the war he was awarded the Navy Cross. I asked him how he won it. "One day I drove into town to get some cigarettes," he replied casually, "and a carload of Gestapo chased the truck I was in and opened up with submachine guns. I put a live grenade into an empty briefcase and tossed it out, and they stopped to pick it up. Maybe they thought it was my codebook or something, but anyway there were four very dead Gestapo a moment later."

2

The American Joint Chiefs proposed to support the Normandy operations with added troop landings in southern France, termed by Eisenhower essential to the eventual assault on Germany itself. British leaders had opposed the idea, and suggested instead an attack on Austria through Trieste and the Ljubljana Gap of Yugoslavia which Churchill, with his penchant for anatomical metaphors, called "a stab in the Adriatic armpit." Churchill was moved by more than military considerations. By 1944, he was feeling an increasing alarm over the spread of Soviet power, and one purpose of his Ljubljana plan was to beat the Russians to Vienna; but the United States declined to go along, partly because of the logistic difficulties involved in an Istrian campaign, and partly because of President Roosevelt's indifference to postwar political problems. After some debate, the southern France invasion, called Anvil, was launched on August 15, and the Allies moved quickly from the beachhead up the Rhone Valley to draw the noose around Germany tighter.

Anvil's outstanding success was greatly aided by superior intelligence concerning the German system of defense along the Mediterranean shore of France. OSS agents infiltrated from Algiers as early as 1943 had informed the Anvil Planning Staff about the enemy's coastal emplacements, minefields, entanglements, roadblocks, antiaircraft guns and searchlights, as well as camouflaged pillboxes and antitank walls and underwater obstacles such as mines and blockships. One of their most valuable services lay in identifying faked German installations, dummy casements made of stucco or wooden guns placed on a breakwater to divert attention from the real guns hidden a short distance away. In the seventy days between Overlord and Anvil, OSS Secret Intelligence (SI) furnished map coordinates of enemy fuel depots containing at least five million gallons of gasoline, twelve large ammunition dumps, and forty-five transport bottlenecks for Eighth and Fifteenth Air Force bombing. Allied plans for a frontal attack on Marseilles and Toulon were abandoned when SI warned that both port cities were heavily defended.

Two days before D-Day, an OSS observer bicycled from Cannes to Hyeres for a last-minute survey of the target area, and cabled the exact calibers and coordinates of enemy gun emplacements to intelligence officers aboard General Alexander M. Patch's command ship. Urgent inquiries by Seventh Army invading forces were relayed via Algiers to agents in critical tactical areas, and responses returned promptly by the OSS network, including a report on anti-parachute pickets at Le May where American paratroopers were scheduled to drop. After the landings, SI operatives behind the German lines continued to transmit on-the-spot tactical intelligence, tailing German panzer units day after day and reporting every detail of their size and position. The long-lost SS Das Reich Division was located by an agent named "Durants" who flashed word to OSS Algiers that the division was traveling north from Bordeaux along Highways 20 and 126. In one hour and forty minutes from the time Durants tapped out his message, it was relayed to SHAEF Headquarters in London, and bombers were on their way to work the two highways over.

A Seventh Army G-2 Summary report on Anvil acknowledged that "D-Day dispositions of German troops confirmed advance information in every particular," and credited OSS sources with 79 percent of all battle order data. In a letter to Russell Forgan on May 31, 1945, General Eisenhower paid tribute to the Jedburgh-led Maquis army of France: "I consider that the disruption of enemy rail communications, the harassing of German road moves, and the continual and increasing strain on the German war economy and internal security services throughout Europe by the organized forces of the resistance played a very considerable part in our victory."

VII

As the agency's overseas operations multiplied, before the success of Anvil, its organization became more complex; and General Donovan found it increasingly difficult to keep himself informed, make policy decisions, direct both his Washington headquarters and his branch headquarters overseas, and at the same time maintain his essential personal relationships with high-ranking American and Allied military commanders and government officials. General Magruder, deputy director of intelligence, suggested the formation of an executive office and a secretariat, similar to that of the Joint Chiefs of Staff, to handle the avalanche of official mail and cables which buried the director's desk each morning, and to answer the branch chiefs' requests for approval and incessant cries for help. Now the director would have more time for other pressing duties.

It was a long day. Donovan usually rose about six A.M., and devoted an hour to calisthenics and his daily massage. At eight he breakfasted at his Georgetown home with a few selected guests, discussing urgent business, while his driver Freeman waited at the wheel of his black limousine parked at the door. Shortly before nine, he drove to OSS headquarters at 25th and E, arriving just in time for his regular nine o'clock staff meeting, held in the special conference room of the administration building. During the meeting, which might last from a half-hour to an hour, Donovan briefed his principal staff and branch chiefs on information of general importance, and called on them for any comments or reports which should be considered by the whole group.

By the time the director returned to his own office, his overnight mail and cables would be sorted and arranged on his desk, with comments and recommendations from the executive office such as: "Copy of this cable has gone to Chief SI. He is handling. Recommend we send copy to Chief SO since it concerns Project Pincers." "This plan will require attention of Planning Group and JCS approval. We are preparing draft of necessary papers." "This suggestion might violate Geneva Convention. General Counsel will have memo for you on this later today."

Thus General Donovan could see quickly whether the volume of communications was being handled to his satisfaction, and make any necessary corrections or request more information or order different action. Then he was ready to proceed with a full morning of conferences within or outside the agency, interviews and inspections, and meetings with theater commanders and American or Allied diplomats. Often he would bring the conferees back home with him for lunch, to continue their talk; and again at dinner — Mrs. Donovan does not recall that he ever ate alone — he would entertain important admirals and generals for private discussions. Frequently he would return to OSS headquarters after dinner to put in several more hours at his desk. His day seldom ended before midnight, when he would retire to spend another couple of hours reading Dr. Langer's latest R&A estimates and economic reports, or lie awake weighing some grave decision he would have to make in the morning.

When an overseas project entailed considerable risk, it was the director's lonely task to decide whether to take the chance. As he said to his executive officer once: "We're in a business where we have to gamble. Even though it appears that the odds are ten to one against us, we still should go ahead if the rewards of a possible success outweigh the costs of a possible failure."

2

One such gamble was Donovan's decision to utilize the labor movement in occupied Europe. All French labor unions had been broken up by the Nazis, their skilled workers conscripted for German war production and their leaders forced to flee to England. The disbanded International Transport Workers Federation, whose affiliated branches included every railroad, trucking, inland barge, airplane, and maritime facility in France and the Low Countries, offered a potential underground network which could be exploited for espionage and demolition efforts in support of the Allies. If the union leaders hiding in London could contact their former members now working as Nazi slave laborers and direct them in slowdowns and sabotage, General Donovan believed, labor could furnish another effective means of hampering Hitler's transport system and crippling his war machine.

At his request, the National Labor Relations Board in Washington supplied personnel familiar with the union structure overseas, and a Labor Desk was formed early in 1942, headed by George O. Pratt, general counsel for NLRB, and Major Arthur J. Goldberg. In London they established cordial relations with refugee union officials from France and Belgium and Holland. Although some of the organizations with which the Labor Desk dealt were Communist, OSS carefully refrained from politics. Funds were provided to supply food and clothing for the destitute families of men who had taken to the hills to escape the German labor draft, and to support others who quit their jobs and became Allied agents.

Gradually a mysterious shortage of production workers began to develop throughout Europe. Expert technicians failed to answer the morning roll call. A wave of absenteeism produced bottlenecks in Nazi transportation, and backlogs of critical airplane engines piled up in railroad yards and sidings. Truckloads of "Rush" materials would arrive inexplicably at the wrong destination. Stacks of half-finished boosters waited on the assembly line for weeks because the remaining parts were delayed in shipment. Freight trains carrying tanks and guns to the front were derailed when a switch was left open.

Labor saboteurs worked deviously to escape detection. Sand was mixed with lubricating oil, or fine steel fragments were tossed into gears. The bearings of a brand-new truck would burn out for no apparent reason. While the Germans were laying a concrete floor in a factory, a Belgian worker reported, the concrete was reinforced with irreplaceable precision instruments which were dropped surreptitiously into the wet forms while the Nazi superintendent's back was turned. "That was probably the most expensive factory floor in Europe," the worker added. A French civil engineer revealed another ingenious method of silent destruction. "Let's say an eccentric cog was being manufactured. The blueprint man would design it with the hole only an eighth of an inch from the rim. We worked with under-tolerance, so that items could not be retooled. Then the machinist would shift the hole even closer to the edge, to make sure the cog would break when it was in operation. The plant inspector always passed the finished product." He smiled. "I know; I was the inspector."

Intelligence on German supply depots and cargo loadings was furnished regularly by the labor underground. Their on-the-spot reports of mass shipments of war materials, analyzed by OSS R&A, with information from other sources, helped to forecast military plans of the enemy. Hidden factories manufacturing synthetic rubber or ersatz steel were pinpointed for Air Force targets. The SKF ball-bearing plant in the heart of Paris could not be bombed from the air without endangering the lives of thousands of French civilians living in the vicinity. A worker with nineteen pounds of smuggled explosive stayed at his bench a little late one night, and the plant was out of commission.

One labor agent, former member of an Austrian union, made the first contact with POEN, the anti-Nazi resistance in his own country. He traveled from Switzerland to Austria in an OSS-supplied uniform of a German first sergeant, and returned with a file of strategic intelligence, including information on fifteen defense plants which had not yet been spotted for air attack. En route from Vienna, on a train crowded with German military personnel, he was ordered by a Nazi major to check the credentials of every other soldier on the train. The bogus sergeant, his own pockets filled with counterfeit papers, tried to beg off, but the major told him curtly not to talk back. Dutifully he investigated the entire trainful, and discovered to his surprise that most of them were deserters, heading in the wrong direction to evade the war. He turned in a couple, he said, just to make the major happy.

The problem of disrupting the German communication system in at least one area of France was solved by a pair of French telephone workers, who offered their services to a Jedburgh team in the Châteauroux area south of Paris. Their method of sabotage was simple, one of them explained, and pointed to the other: "I cut; he feex." The first worker, a company inspector, would travel around the country in his official car, clipping the wires at several key points. On his return to the office, he would solemnly report the breaks to his partner, who would take his own time about repairing them. Due to their intimate knowledge of local installations, they managed to keep the German telephone service continuously out of order for a year without arousing suspicion. As an added contribution, the two workers stole wire and instruments and set up a secret system for the Jedburgh unit, enabling them to maintain a constant surveillance of enemy troop movements through messages phoned from their outposts.

Germany itself was weakened by the growing labor resistance. Eighty separate operational points were established within the Reich, including Munich and Berlin. Workers were subsidized even in the closely guarded Krupp factories of the Ruhr, and wavering Nazi sympathizers induced to change their jobs or plead illness. In anticipation of D-Day at Normandy, a seventy-five-year-old former chief of the local Transport Workers Federation slipped through the German defense lines and alerted his dock workers who had fled to the hills to avoid Nazi conscription. As soon as the Allied troops landed, the French longshoremen returned to their jobs, and supply ships were unloaded in record time. When General Patton's spearhead reached the Rhine, members of the suppressed bargemen's union were ready to assist in the crossing. Hitler's strong-arm efforts to drive organized labor underground turned out to be one of his gravest mistakes.

3

X-2, the supersecret counterespionage branch of OSS, had sent small groups of field personnel with the advancing Allied armies after the Normandy landings, to protect OSS sources of information behind the German lines and to help in the examination of captured documents and agents in order to piece together the overall pattern of enemy intelligence. One forward group arrived in Paris on August 25, 1944, before the Germans had been completely cleared from the city, and set up headquarters for all X-2 operations in France, including a special countersabotage unit. During the Wehrmacht drive toward Liège and the Meuse, about one hundred Nazi sabotage and subversion experts trained by Skorzeny, chief of the Reich's sabotage section (Abwehr II), were infiltrated into Allied territory dressed in American uniforms. Nearly all were apprehended (they had no dog tags), and by September X-2/Paris had in hand six enemy agents operating as playbacks under OSS control.

One of the most valuable prisoners was a German noncommissioned officer, who was given the X-2 code name of "Juggler." Because of his two years with Abwehr II and his contacts with German intelligence personnel, Juggler was able to supply X-2 with an impressive mass of detailed notes on the Nazi sabotage organization, including extensive records which he had removed from the files of the Abwehr's Paris headquarters. He made repeated journeys with OSS officers to locate some of the thousand sabotage dumps left in France by the German armies, and was so helpful to the Allies that several captured German agents confessed they had been sent to assassinate him.

"Hoch," who had been left behind in Paris by the Germans as a "sleeper" agent, gave himself up to X-2 on August 28, three days after the city was liberated. X-2 plans to exploit him as a playback were thwarted when Hoch was murdered by French civilians, taking justice into their own hands for his past betrayals of their friends and relatives. An American sergeant thereupon took over the operation of Hoch's radio set, explaining to the German base that the changed "fist" was due to a fictional accident to the dead agent's right hand. A French intelligence officer checked the new messages for correctness of idiom and tone. Although the Germans were not completely fooled, three Abwehr paymaster agents were picked up, all of whom had been sent to determine whether Hoch was a double agent. Each carried two hundred thousand francs to give him if he proved genuine.

Another Abwehr agent named "Chariot," a Spanish national living in Cherbourg, was captured shortly after the Allied invasion of France, and became the first American case to be run on the Continent. Like most of the German agents who were caught, Chariot agreed at once to work under control. Contact with his base was established on July 25, and Chariot was almost continuously on the air for more than nine months until the German surrender. The notional employment of Chariot presented to the Germans was made as convincing as possible. He informed his base that he was working as an interpreter in an American port office, and could supply information gained from direct observation of the harbor, actually no more than could be seen by any German reconnaisance plane. The material he forwarded, furnished by X-2, consisted of censored facts which, by omissions, were made purposely misleading to the enemy. At German request, the captive playback made several notional trips around the Gotentin Peninsula to report on specific targets. In all, Chariot sent 238 messages to the Abwehr concerning this strategic area, containing only that information which the Allies considered safe or advantageous for the Germans to know. His false reports on American naval strength in Cherbourg discouraged U-boat attacks on incoming convoys in adjacent waters. So skillfully was Chariot handled, postwar interrogation revealed, that the Germans considered him one of their best stay-behind agents in France.

On the night of October 26, 1944, a Luftwaffe plane carried out the double mission of supplying beleaguered German forces on the French coast and parachuting en route a Vichy French agent and W/T operator. Their assignment was to procure intelligence on Allied troop identification in the Verdun area, to report their findings by W/T, and to return across the German lines as soon as their mission was completed. The two agents were captured within a few hours of landing and turned over to X-2, and both agreed to transfer their affiliations. Since the information-gathering French agent would be merely an encumbrance in a controlled W/T operation, it was decided that "Spook," the code name given the radio operator, would report to the Abwehr that he had not seen his companion after the jump and presumed that he had been killed or captured.

Spook was installed in the 12th Army Group Interrogation Center jail in Verdun, and managed to make contact with his base on November 4. A logical explanation was given the Germans that Spook had encountered difficulties after parachuting, in order to explain his eight-day delay in reporting. Hoping to gain a counterintelligence advantage out of the case, Spook was instructed by X-2 to ask the Abwehr for the easiest escape route across the lines when he returned. The Germans unsuspectingly proposed to Spook several alternative routes for his passage, which were communicated at once to Third Army, and steps taken to tighten security controls at these points. To prove Spook's good faith, it was decided to have him notionally attempt to return by one of these routes; and the local American intelligence officer at St.-Avold, through which he would pass, cooperated in simulating Spook's arrest and escape. Although the actual capture was not enacted, the 80th Division public address system at St.-Avold announced the seizure and disappearance of an alleged enemy agent, whose description tallied with Spook's in every detail.

After allowing sufficient time for Spook notionally to make his way back to Verdun, he sent a bitter message to his base, reporting his failure and berating the Germans for their inefficiency in choosing escape routes. The base offered abject apologies, and to soothe his feelings instructed Spook to establish himself in the important Metz area, where he arrived just in time for the Battle of the Bulge. Metz was a most critical point along the lateral lines of Allied communication, and an uncontrolled German spy might observe the overall American plan of unit shifts as it unfolded to meet the Ardennes crisis.

So pleased were the Germans with Spook's tactical information that Hitler awarded him the Iron Cross — the first of three Iron Crosses which OSS-controlled German agents received for their outstanding "services" to the Reich.

4

There were few conventional Mata Haris in World War II, those seductive blondes of spy fiction whose amorous caresses coax military secrets in the intimacy of a boudoir or a drawing room on the Orient

Express. Espionage was a business; and the success of a female agent depended, not on glamour, but on her steel nerves and serene indifference to danger.

The men of the Maquis did not have a corner on courage. Equally valiant were their anonymous womenfolk who moved back and forth through the lines, singly or in pairs, to procure combat intelligence. They attracted less suspicion than the men, who were likely to be halted and searched by the SS, and by mingling with the German officers in cafes were often able to extract valuable information. Traveling afoot or on bicycles, they would transport radios and other agent equipment in a market basket which, if it had been opened by the Gestapo or the French *milice*, would have spelled certain death. Fearless women like the nameless young Maquisard who stood at a road junction during the German retreat and coolly misdirected a fleeing Nazi battalion into an Allied trap. Or Madame Andrée Goubillon, whose husband had been imprisoned by the Germans and who managed their small cafe in Paris throughout the occupation. Her cafe became a permanent letter drop for spy messages, and she fed and sheltered no less than twenty-one OSS agents during the war, concealing their incriminating W/T sets in her cellar. Or Maria Dulovitch, a Czech girl who walked barefoot in midwinter through miles of enemy territory to guide four downed fliers through the lines to safety. She refused any monetary reward, but admitted that she longed someday to study in an American university. General Donovan arranged personally for her education at Vassar.

Or the widowed Italian marchesa, a white-haired aristocrat, whose ancestral *palazzo* in southern Italy was taken over for a German communication center. The marchesa was permitted to live in one small wing of her home. An OSS agent, disguised as her hump-backed gardener, made his way past the sentries at the gate, and installed a tiny induction microphone with a threadlike wire powerful enough to pick up enemy conversations in the adjoining rooms and monitor telephone messages to forward operational posts. The agent, bent and hobbling to simulate the crippled gardener, would return at regular intervals to pick up the intelligence she had gathered and forward it to OSS headquarters. When the Allies landed at Salerno, her house became the focal point of the entire German communications system; and the marchesa sent word to the Fifteenth Air Force that it was such a vital target that it must be destroyed. Piling her personal belongings in a donkey cart, she drove past the German sentries and into town. The following morning a wave of Liberator bombers from Sicily blasted her home into ruins.

Sometimes a woman agent would be captured by the Gestapo, and left to waste away in the living death of a Nazi concentration camp. It was on a visit to Dachau, during the waning days of the war, that General Donovan found OSS agent Adrienne, who had parachuted into her native Belgium some months before and vanished without a trace. Adrienne had been an attractive brunette, her curling hair worn in a long bob and her white teeth flashing when she smiled. Now her head was shorn of hair, and all her teeth had been extracted by sadistic guards so that the once lovely face sagged grotesquely over her gums. Her blue eyes stared blankly from sunken sockets as the General bent over her cot. He arranged for her to be flown to the best hospital in England, and later she returned to Belgium; but the horror of her experience had unbalanced her mind. A year after the war she hanged herself from a rod in her clothes closet.[22]

A few captives escaped. Jeanette, a French housewife and the mother of two children, had already performed two OSS missions behind the lines, but offered herself for still another drop in the Gerardier region near the Vosges Mountains. She was betrayed by a German sympathizer planted within the resistance forces. After a week of grilling, she was thrown into a Gestapo jail to await more exquisite torture. Jeanette noticed that when the guard entered her cell each day with food, he always shoved open the heavy iron door with a violent thrust of his shoulder. An escape plan formed in her mind. With a piece of broken glass she had secreted, she cut her scalp so that it bled profusely, lay on the floor with her head toward the door, and awaited the guard's arrival. Believing that he had cracked her skull when he flung the door open, he had her limp form carried to the prison hospital, from which she

[22] Robert Alcorn, *No Bugles for Spies* (New York, 1962).

managed to slip away at night and make her way back to the Allied lines. She volunteered for another mission as soon as the gash in her scalp had healed.

General Donovan took a very particular pride in the women of OSS, mothers or grandmothers, prominent social leaders or the wives and friends of G.I.s in service. Some worked selflessly as secretaries and file clerks and office assistants, keeping the machinery of the agency running. Others volunteered to infiltrate enemy territory by boat or parachute, to locate potential drop fields and rally the resistance forces. One of these, Virginia Hall, was the first civilian woman in World War II to win the Distinguished Service Cross. Although she had lost a leg in a motor accident, she received special permission to parachute with her artificial limb tucked under an arm so that it would not be damaged while landing. In a memorandum to President Roosevelt accompanying the DSC recommendation, Donovan wrote:

"Despite the fact that she was well known to the Gestapo from a previous mission, Miss Hall voluntarily returned to France in March 1944 to assist in sabotage operations against the Germans. Through her extraordinary courage, and despite her physical handicap, Miss Hall, with two American officers, succeeded in organizing, arming, and training three Free French battalions which took part in many engagements with the enemy and performed numerous acts of sabotage, resulting in the demolition of bridges, destruction of supply trains, and disruption of enemy communications. As a result of blowing one bridge, a German convoy was ambushed and during a bitter struggle 150 Germans were killed and 500 captured. In addition, Miss Hall provided radio communication between London Headquarters and the resistance forces in the Haute-Loire Department, transmitting and receiving operational and intelligence information. This was a most perilous type of work, due to the danger of enemy DF-ing, and it was frequently necessary for Miss Hall to change her location in order to avoid detection." General Donovan added a suggestion to the President: "Inasmuch as an award of this kind has not been previously given to a woman during the war, you may wish to make the presentation personally."

Another distinction, though less enviable, was achieved by Gertrude

Legendre, who was the first American woman captured by the Germans. Mrs. Legendre was a noted sportswoman and big-game hunter who had roamed the world in search of trophies; but in Paris her love of adventure lured her into disaster. She had served in OSS, and one weekend she and an Army officer, an old friend from the States, borrowed a jeep and set out for a firsthand look at the front lines beyond Luxembourg. Confused by the fluid military situation, the joy-riding jeep blundered into German territory, the officer was wounded by machine gun fire, and Mrs. Legendre was taken prisoner. Fortunately she was wearing a WAC uniform, prescribed for all American civilians in Paris, and the Germans did not realize that their prize was an ex-member of OSS with access to highly sensitive material. Mrs. Legendre was moved from jail to jail across Germany, but with nerve and cunning she managed to conceal her intelligence connections. After six months, she leaped from a prison train during a switching operation when it backed for a moment across the Swiss border, and made her way to Bern. She was flown back to Washington in deep secrecy, lest the news of her escape should provoke German reprisals against other Allied captives.[23]

General Donovan's favorite woman spy — and whenever he recalled her story he would break into one of his rare fits of laughter — was an American expatriate in her seventies, the widow of a wealthy French count, who maintained an apartment in wartime Paris and a handsome château in the countryside. Because of her social position and her long residence in France, she was allowed by the Germans to move back and forth freely; and OSS persuaded her to smuggle messages to secret X-2 operatives on her visits to the city. One hot August day, traveling to Paris on a crowded and stifling train, the perspiring countess felt the need to go to the lavatory. Like all toilets on French trains, particularly during the occupation, the facilities were anything but clean, and she took the precaution of spreading her morning newspaper over the toilet seat before settling herself. She emerged from the lavatory just as the train was halted at a German checkpoint, and the passengers were

[23] Gertrude Legendre, *The Sands Ceased to Run* (New York, 1947).

herded into the station for a routine inspection, the men in one room and the women in another.

She resigned herself to this delay as one of the inconveniences of war, until a burly female in Nazi uniform ordered the women to strip to the buff. The countess was a lady of austere mien, accustomed to her privacy, but her protests fell on deaf ears. In considerable embarrassment she removed all her clothes, even her shoes and stockings, and joined the group of naked country women who were being scrutinized one by one. As the female inspector circled her, the countess heard her utter an exclamation of triumph. She was forced to bend forward, hands on knees, while the excited German tried to read the reversed print from the newspaper which had been transferred onto her damp behind. With the aid of a mirror from the washroom, the inspector painstakingly copied down the morning news inked on the countess's rear, convinced that she had discovered a new method of secret communication, and hurried from the room to present the evidence to her commanding officer. After an interval she returned crestfallen, and sullenly ordered the passengers to dress again and board the train.

The countess's ruffled dignity was balanced by a vast relief. In all the excitement the Nazi inspector had overlooked the OSS messages hidden in the lining of her handbag.

VIII

Asia was the forgotten front of World War II. Churchill and Roosevelt had agreed as early as 1941 that Hitler's defeat was their paramount objective, and the campaign against Japan was assigned secondary priority in the strategy of the Combined Chiefs of Staff. Consequently the bulk of Allied men and material was committed to a victory over Germany, and until that occurred the military forces in the Orient were depleted and starved for supplies. Since no bases of operation against the Japanese homeland remained in Allied hands within the range of available aircraft, they were forced to rely on heterodox efforts to harness native resistance in the enemy-occupied lands of the Far East.

This would have seemed a natural sphere of opportunity for OSS; but General Donovan ran into an unexpected block. Despite the clearly demonstrated value of OSS in the African and French invasions, the U.S. Army and Navy commanders in the Pacific never responded to formal requests by the agency to operate in their areas of jurisdiction. Early in 1944, en route to General Douglas MacArthur's headquarters to seek a better understanding, Donovan paused at Pearl Harbor and arranged with Admiral Nimitz and his staff for one Strategic Services officer to be assigned to CINCPOA, restricted to Honolulu; but Mac-Arthur refused to accept any OSS-trained personnel unless they lost their identity with the agency and were transferred bodily to his command.

Later that year, as his much-publicized return to the Philippines drew near, MacArthur found himself in dire need of information on the landing beaches, local food supply, and transportation facilities. Overlooking his previous position toward OSS, the agency's Research and Analysis Branch collected quantities of facts and figures from American businessmen with interests in the Philippines, and forwarded their surveys to MacArthur's planning staff. So valuable were the R&A findings that MacArthur's chief of G-2, Brigadier General Charles Willoughby, flew to Washington and personally called on Dr. Langer and requested twenty of his best men to work directly at MacArthur's headquarters. "At first I thought the ice was finally broken," Dr. Langer said later, "but then Willoughby added that we must give them up completely and MacArthur would take them over." Donovan understandably declined;[24] and thereafter in the war, save for a small OSS maritime unit which participated in underwater demolition action with Nimitz's fleet and another group which delivered special OSS weapons to Tenth Army for the Okinawa invasion, OSS was never authorized to operate in the Pacific island-hopping campaign.

General MacArthur's intransigence is difficult to explain. His personal relationship with Donovan was cordial, they had served together in the Rainbow Division during the First World War, and both were highly decorated heroes. Donovan entertained the deepest regard for MacArthur's brilliance as a military strategist, and never offered any reason for his adamant opposition to OSS; but members of the agency had their private theories. Some speculated that Willoughby, anxious to insure full credit for his intelligence unit, feared that "Wild Bill" would grab the spotlight. Others held that MacArthur, a West Pointer and firm believer in the chain of command, objected to the presence of a uniformed civilian acting independently in his theater. A few intimates, who knew Donovan's own determination, suspected that it was the

[24] This was not due to the unwillingness of OSS to send its trained personnel to MacArthur's theater. All OSS units and personnel in *any* theater of war were by JCS order under the direct command of the theater commander, who could use OSS personnel as he saw fit. However, General Willoughby's proposal went far beyond the JCS order: any personnel sent to MacArthur's theater would cease to be part of the integrated worldwide effort that OSS had been directed to perform.

inevitable clash between two strong personalities, equally fixed in purpose.

General Donovan was never one to be deterred by what he considered an unreasonable attitude. He believed that his agency had a vital function to perform in the Far East, and that OSS had already demonstrated the validity of his concept that good intelligence must be the product of a worldwide effort. (Agents deep inside Germany were supplying some of the most important information about Japan.) Since he was not allowed to approach the enemy from the Pacific, Donovan obtained permission to move eastward through the China-Burma-India Theater (CBI), and strike at Japan by way of occupied Southeast Asia.

Operating in Japanese-held territory posed an unprecedented problem. The linguistic and cultural affiliations with Europe did not exist in the Orient, and the difference in race made it all but impossible for a Caucasian to circulate unnoticed behind the enemy lines. Whereas an American agent could live off the land in France or Italy, the impenetrable jungle with its malarial swamps and monsoon heat threatened his very survival. Even more impenetrable were the politics and tangled jealousies of the CBI command. Strained relations had long prevailed between the U.S. forces in India and British civilian and military authorities; and OSS faced the open hostility of the Royal Indian Army and the British espionage organizations in the theater, particularly SOE. Perhaps Britain was already aware that the jewel of India was working loose from its setting in the imperial crown, and the antagonism toward OSS reflected a basic misgiving about American activities among the subject peoples in her wavering Far East empire.

So badly had Anglo-American relations deteriorated in CBI by 1943 that the Combined Chiefs decided at the Quebec Conference in August to superimpose an overall control in that troubled theater. China was made a separate command, the U.S. Army and Air Force coming under General Stilwell who was in a position to coordinate their movements with Chinese forces by being appointed Chief of Staff to the Chinese Supreme Commander, Generalissimo Chiang Kai-shek. A Southeast Asia Command (SEAC) was formed, with Admiral Lord Louis Mountbatten, then Chief of Combined Operations, and a cousin of the King, as the

Supreme Allied Commander, with an integrated Allied Headquarters Staff and U.S. General Albert C. Wedemeyer as Deputy Chief of Staff.

Before the Quebec Conference was over, he had worked out an agreement with Admiral Mountbatten, permitting the agency to continue the comparatively small scale of operations which had been possible up to then, but above all to expand OSS strengths and operations in the Southeast Asia theater very considerably. Admiral Mountbatten conceded OSS the right to gather strategic intelligence independently through its own agents as required by U.S. interests. In return, General Donovan agreed that Admiral Mountbatten should coordinate all clandestine activities in his theater and accepted the setting up of "P" Division of SEAC under Captain Garnons-Williams of the Royal Navy, with Lieutenant Commander Ed Taylor of the United States Navy as his deputy. After about fifteen months Taylor was succeeded by Lieutenant Colonel Harry Berno; both were nominated by General Donovan. The British SIS and SOE had liaison officers with "P" Division as well as OSS. This organization for coordinating clandestine activities was made possible by the great personal friendship between General Donovan and Admiral Mountbatten.

On a personal visit to India in November of that year, Donovan took the further step of creating a new OSS unit, designated Detachment 404, which would handle all Southeast Asian operations (except in North Burma where 101 remained semiautonomous) subject to Mountbatten's approval. When the Admiral moved his SEAC headquarters from New Delhi to Kandy in Ceylon, Detachment 404 dutifully joined the military migration.

Ceylon, lying off the southern tip of India, was an enchanted island, a startling contrast to the grime and misery of the mainland. Wild elephants roamed its jungles, occasionally challenging a passing jeep, and leopards slunk under red-flowered rhododendrons the size of maple trees. Admiral Mountbatten established his command post in the center of Kandy's celebrated orchid gardens, doubtless the most exotic headquarters of World War II; and OSS set up shop nearby, with training camps for native agents at Galle and Clodagh and a maritime unit at Trincomalee on the Bay of Bengal.

Here at Trincomalee the war seemed far away and unreal. Tropical fish flashed in the blue lagoon beside the base, the rocks offshore were studded with tiny sweet oysters, and a tribe of uninhibited monkeys swung by their tails from the rafters of the mess hall, occasionally interrupting a meal with a sudden squirt from overhead. The war came a little closer one idle evening when Dillon Ripley, chief of 404's X-2 branch, invited me to accompany him on a jungle jeep ride. Ripley was a noted ornithologist from Yale, and was in search of a rare species of brown owl. Somehow he lost his way in the maze of elephant trails, and we blundered into a secret training compound filled with trigger-happy recruits from Senegal. A blinding spotlight shone in our eyes, and we heard the ominous click of rifle bolts above the Senegalese sentry's bellowed "Hult!" With scientific detachment, Ripley rose to his feet in the open jeep and explained matter-of-factly: "American officers hunting owls." Thereafter I stayed close to base.

For all its natural charm, Ceylon proved logistically the worst site that could have been chosen for OSS headquarters. Not only was Kandy some eighteen hundred miles from the main supply ports and service bases in India, but air transportation was woefully inadequate. Eventually the MO branch, due to lack of printing and paper facilities on the island, had to move its operations to Calcutta, and X-2 transferred its own branch headquarters to New Delhi. The activities of the Maritime Unit (MU) were curtailed by a lack of suitable craft to cross the stormy Bay of Bengal for infiltration of the Burmese coast. Natives for behind-the-lines operations were so difficult to recruit that 404 resorted to a modern version of blackbirding — kidnapping prospective agents on some enemy shore at the point of a gun, and offering them the alternative of joining OSS at high pay or spending the rest of the war in an internment camp. Curiously, although agents obtained under duress often proved worthless, not one case of treachery was ever recorded. Since many of these primitive tribesmen were illiterate, wooden scale models of Japanese radar and communications equipment were used as visual training aids, and in the field they were able to recognize Jap radar posts and produce relatively high-grade intelligence.

In spite of its handicaps, the agency's remotest detachment could boast of one spectacular achievement — the prolonged secret collaboration with the heads of an enemy-held country which OSS/404 conducted in Siam.

2

The Siamese call their country Muang Thai, which means Land of the Free People — the name "Siam" is a foreign corruption, as unintelligible to the Thais as "China" is in Chinese. And Thailand, as Siam became known during the war, has always been fiercely independent. The little nation, about the size of France, is situated between Burma and Cambodia, extending down most of the tapering Malay Peninsula; and in 1941 it lay helpless athwart the Japanese march southward toward Singapore. Betrayed by its pro-Axis defense minister, Marshal Pibul Singgram, Siam had yielded to the Japanese invaders the day after Pearl Harbor, and Marshal Pibul had issued a declaration of war against the Allies which the United States, with remarkable foresight, had chosen to ignore. Thereafter the conquered nation had lapsed into silence, swallowed as completely as the licking green flames of jungle had consumed the ancient temple of Angkor Wat.

R&A experts in OSS were convinced that Siam's submission was only a surface gesture, that there must be some latent resistance in this freedom-loving land which had always been antagonistic toward the Japanese. Seni Pramoj, the young aesthete and watercolor painter who had been Siam's minister to the United States before the war, had remained in Washington to organize a Free Thai movement, and Siamese students with scholarships at Harvard or Stanford or MIT had quit their classrooms to enlist in the Free Thai Army. OSS, though it had no idea at the time how they might be used, had worked with the minister to set up a training program and instruct these Thai volunteers in the technique of infiltration and communication, should the opportunity to penetrate their homeland ever develop.

It developed with dramatic suddenness early in 1943 when two Thai businessmen from Bangkok arrived without notice in Chungking, China, after crossing the mountains and jungles of northern Siam, and identi-

fied themselves as representatives of a potential resistance group inside
the country. To OSS interrogators in Chungking, they revealed that the
leader of the Thai underground was none other than the Regent Luang
Pradit Manudharu,[25] who had secretly repudiated Marshall Pibul's col-
laborationist policy, together with many other high officials and cabinet
members. The two Thais were promptly flown to Washington, and
General Donovan learned for the first time of a covert conspiracy
against the Japanese, headed by Regent Pradit and including the chief of
police, the ministers of the interior and of foreign affairs, anti-Pibul
officers of the armed services, and many leading civilians. Countless
patriots in Siam were eager to serve as guerrillas under the direction of
OSS, and the intelligence services of the government offered in effect an
SI network.

Now at last General Donovan had the key to Siam's back door. Led
by OSS Lieutenant Colonel Nicol Smith, author of *Burma Road* and
long familiar with the Orient, twenty-one trained Thai scholars, many
of them Ph.D.'s and Phi Beta Kappas, left Washington in the summer of
1943 and flew to Szemao in southern China. Five were selected to make
the first infiltration attempt, and after lengthy negotiations with the
Chinese they started down the cobblestone trail to Cheli on the Yunnan-
Burma border, disguised as Chinese merchants. Tiny compasses were
hidden in the buttons of their coats, and OSS-developed demountable
radio sets were wrapped in waterproof blankets and stored at the
bottom of the wicker hampers on their pack mules, concealed under
ostensible items of trade: safety pins and needles, small mirrors, spools
of thread, blue cotton cloth, and quinine pills. Each man carried two
thousand dollars' worth of gold Indian *tolas* and Yunnan dollars in a
hollow leather belt around his waist. General Tai-li, Chiang Kai-shek's
intelligence chief, had promised them every assistance; but for some
unexplained reason the party was held up for months at the border by
Chinese troops, and returned to Szemao in April of 1944, defeated and
discouraged.

At this frustrating moment in the mission, Colonel Smith received

[25] Also known as Pridi Panomyong Manndharu.

unexpected assistance from a remarkable Chinese Catholic priest, chaplain of the 93rd Chinese Division. Father Jean Tong, once amateur boxing champion of China, had been educated in Shanghai and later in Switzerland, spoke nine languages, and was well acquainted with the natives along the border and the little-known headhunters of the remote Wa states. At Smith's offer of a thousand silver dollars to build a new church, Father Tong agreed to guide the party on their second attempt to enter Thailand.

From Cheli they traveled a couple of hundred miles down the wild Mekong River, abandoned their canoes, and set out on foot across the unexplored Yunnan jungles, struggling through the downpours and flash floods of the tropical monsoon season. Father Tong had expected that the journey would take two weeks; it lasted eighty-seven days. Their tender feet, accustomed to the sidewalks of Harvard Square, were soon lacerated and bruised, and leech bites started festering sores. Often berries and roots were their only food. All came down with malaria, and one nearly died of dysentery. Two members of the group, separated from the others, were captured by a Jap patrol and murdered for their gold.

Father Tong left the remainder of the party at the Siamese border, to return alone to Szemao. As soon as they crossed the frontier they were taken into custody by the Thai police, whose chief was number-two man of the underground, and conducted secretly to Bangkok. There they languished until a team of Thai students, trained by and operating from OSS in Kandy, were sent into Bangkok. Their leader, "Ben," knew Luang Pradit; in a personal interview, he convinced him of the eagerness of OSS to help. "Ben" was given a radio set obtained from one of the Thai operatives from China, and using his own special crystals, "Ben" first flashed word to Detachment 404/OSS in Kandy that OSS personnel and aid would be warmly received.

Luang Pradit was given the improbable OSS code name of "Ruth," which became so well established that it was used regularly in official United States communications. One of Ruth's first requests was for American representatives to visit Bangkok in order to work out a closer liaison. Chosen for this mission were Major Richard Greenlee, a former associate in Donovan's New York law firm and chief of SO at 404, and Major John Wester, who had spent many years as an engineer in prewar Siam and had escaped from a Jap internment camp to join Detachment 101.

After a long night flight over the Gulf of Siam in a Catalina flying boat — the only aircraft with sufficient range — the two officers were set down at a prearranged rendezvous off the Siamese coast, and transferred to a government customs launch for the remaining trip to Bangkok. Major Greenlee's report was somewhat bitter about this launch; the antiquated engine had a habit of breaking down at inconvenient moments, he recorded, and once they drifted helplessly right under the guns of a Japanese minesweeper. It was noon when they arrived at a wharf in Bangkok Harbor and were hustled into a waiting car, given gaudy hats and native shirts to wear over their uniforms, and driven in broad daylight through the streets of the capital city, occupied by some seven thousand enemy troops. Major Greenlee said it gave him quite a turn to look out of the car window at a Japanese soldier on a bicycle, peering incredulously at the first Americans to enter Siam since its capture. Nothing happened; evidently the soldier was afraid he would lose face if he reported such a preposterous story.

They were quartered in one barred and shuttered room of a government house near the Regent's palace in the heart of the city. "Our dinner that night was positively amazing," Greenlee recalled. "It began and ended with iced beer. On the table were roast duck, freshwater prawns fixed in many fashions, salad, curried beef, dried fish, and of course, the ever-present rice soaked with hot sauces. The feast concluded with coffee, large bowls of fresh bananas, and delicate segments of Sum O, the Thai improvement on grapefruit."

Life in Bangkok was not all iced beer and duck. After his first flush of enthusiasm at their warm welcome, Greenlee began to detect certain serious flaws in this seeming OSS bonanza. Luang Pradit was already under suspicion, both by the Japanese occupation commander and the wartime dictator Pibul. The underground forces available were illequipped and untrained in the technique of gathering and evaluating intelligence. Furthermore, OSS was not dealing with an ordinary resistance group but with the leaders of a sovereign state, determined to obtain for their country the greatest possible benefits at the least cost. While there was no reason to doubt the anti-Japanese sentiment of Regent Pradit, he was primarily concerned with the interests of Siam, and was inclined to postpone direct action and follow a wait-and-see policy in order to avoid enemy reprisals.

Because of Siam's potential importance to OSS and the necessity of tying in such actions as a national uprising with the Allied war plans, Greenlee was exfiltrated and flown back to Washington, and OSS headquarters secured the full approval and support of the U.S. State Department and the Joint Chiefs of Staff. All phases of future operations in Siam were carefully coordinated by General Donovan, and OSS was authorized by the Joint Chiefs to proceed with its program, but to operate under the Regent as chief of all the country's clandestine activities. No attempt should be made to create a separate American organization, Greenlee was warned, and the greatest care should be taken to avoid stirring up the Siamese against the British. To make full use of the underground potential, it would be essential to have additional liaison officers and instructors not only in Bangkok but scattered at strategic points in the hinterland.

Major Greenlee returned to Bangkok in April with Captain Howard Palmer, a Siam-born son of American missionaries, as a replacement for Major Wester, whose long confinement had brought on a nervous collapse. (Tension was an OSS occupational disease.) Month after month the members of the mission had to eat and work and sleep in a single ten-foot-square room, rocked by occasional Allied bombings, cringing at every footfall in the corridor outside the door. From their window they could see Jap patrols constantly pacing the street below. At night they conferred behind drawn blinds with loyal Thai army officers, in daily contact with the Japanese, who informed them of the latest enemy plans, recent transfers of troops across Siam, or concealed supply dumps for Allied aerial attack. Their intelligence was radioed back to Ceylon from the transmitter concealed in the city police station, where the steady flow of routine police messages made Jap DF-ing difficult. The first B–29 raid, which battered enemy defenses around Bangkok, was pinpointed on the basis of their intelligence.

As more and more American personnel arrived in Siam, it was decided to move the mission headquarters to more secluded quarters in a residential area of Bangkok, and a Thai colonel offered to drive the OSS officers to their new home. "He was very proud," Captain Palmer reported, "because the Army chief of staff had loaned him his own car for the occasion. To get to our place, we had to go through the main downtown district of Bangkok, and at the busiest intersection, with a Jap MP directing traffic, the horn of the car got stuck. The remainder of our journey was as secret as Mayor LaGuardia going to a fire. We tried to persuade the colonel to stop and yank the wires, but he was too panicky and confined his efforts to begging the horn in a low undertone to please be quiet. We howled through the city, trying to look inconspicuous, and luckily the horn gave out just before we arrived at the new residence."

In the summer of 1945, Lieutenant Colonel Nicol Smith traveled to Bangkok to relieve the ailing Greenlee. OSS had secured the use of a remote airfield at Pukeo in the hilly jungle country of north-central Siam, where C–47's from India or southern Burma could make dawn landings without enemy detection. Smith landed and changed planes at this secret runway, and flew in a four-seater Fairchild to another Thai-controlled strip, only half an hour's hop from the Don Muang field at Bangkok. While waiting to complete the last leg of his trip under cover of darkness, Smith noticed a file of naked white men trudging over the crest of a hill. "They're from an Australian prison camp," a Thai official explained. "Officers and men are stripped naked and made to work every day in the broiling sun at hard labor. We smuggle food to them whenever we can."

The eastern side of the Don Muang airport was used by the Japanese, and the western by the Thais; and the little Fairchild, painted conspicuously with Siam's symbolic white elephants, made a direct landing without circling. "The field was so small that, as we taxied in, we could hear Japs singing in their barracks," Smith wrote.[26] "As soon as we came to a final stop, Thai maintenance men swarmed about us like bees, and we were wheeled into a hangar and the door closed. In the pitch

[26] Nicol Smith and Blake Clark, *Into Siam* (New York, 1946).

blackness, I was led through a side door and whisked into a secondhand Dodge for the ride into town. We passed numerous Jap pillboxes, skirted the Internee Camp, and turned into a dark driveway and halted at the Palace of the Roses, once the residence of the traitorous Marshal Pibul, now the sumptuous OSS headquarters in Bangkok.

"No secret agents trying to deliver a country from oppression ever enjoyed such palatial living quarters. The paneled reception hall of the mansion was a solid mass of inlaid carved roses, the magnificent drawing-room carpet was of rose design, and the ceilings of the seven spacious bedrooms were painted with flowers. The fragrance of real roses from the garden permeated every room of the Palace. Pibul's former bedroom had been converted into a radio station, his study was devoted to encoding and decoding messages, and in what had been his office six powerful hundred-watt transmitters were on the air almost continually." As a final unlikely touch, Smith said, their meals were served by a deaf-and-dumb servant named Bai, who entertained the guests during dinner by touching his head to the floor and standing on his thumbs.

By the end of the summer, twenty-eight Americans and scores of Ceylon-trained Thais had parachuted into Siam, and more than three thousand resistance troops were under arms. Supplies were airdropped regularly, as many as five drops being made in a single night. Sometimes the planes were attacked by Zeroes; five Americans died in one crash. As guerrilla camps began to dot the interior, Japanese suspicions mounted. In a surprise raid on a radio station, an OSS sergeant was killed and three other officers and enlisted men wounded by an enemy patrol. Although a steady stream of intelligence flowed in from the field, the Bangkok headquarters remained the center of the network. On one occasion two Siamese travelers, just returned from Tokyo, furnished a detailed account of the fire-bomb damage and chaos in the Japanese homeland, and described a mob attack on a high-ranking staff officer in Tokyo after a B-29 raid. Their information, forwarded to OSS/Washington, foreshadowed the inevitable enemy capitulation.

The secret Thai resistance helped in other ways. Three enemy deserters, a rare intelligence find, were captured in a small village and flown outside for interrogation. "They were in M.P. uniforms and heavily armed," a Thai general told Smith. "We traced them to a barn and burned a few Korat joss sticks, the fumes of which will make a man sleep so soundly that he can be carried off like a meal-bag on the shoulder." Smith asked the formula for this Thai secret weapon. "Very simple," the general replied. "Pulverized bones of eels and the red-backed Korat toad found only in one section of Siam."

Round-the-clock weather reports and opportune targets for bombing were sent to the Tenth and Fourteenth Air Forces, and their radioed requests for information were answered promptly. A personal message from General Chennault asked OSS to search for one of his outstanding AVG pilots, Lieutenant William McGarry, who had crashed on the Burma-Siamese border in midsummer of 1942. His fighter plane had been seen to settle in a spreading banyan tree, and other members of the flight reported that it had not caught fire; and Chennault had a hunch that McGarry was still alive in some internment camp. A description was flashed from Kunming to all OSS field units, and wily Thai scouts began a systematic combing of all prison compounds. McGarry was located at last in a crude jungle stockade. The Thai guards, members of the underground, informed the Japanese commandant that the American pilot was very ill, then reported his death, and buried an empty coffin. That night they slipped McGarry out of the prison camp, emaciated and half blind, and Chennault sent a special plane to fly him back to Kunming.

In mid-1945 the Japanese became aware of the underground conspiracy, though they did not know its extent, and the enemy commander warned Luang Pradit that they had definite information that C-47s were dropping men and supplies in the north. Rumors of an impending assassination of all resistance leaders filled Bangkok, and the Regent expected hourly that the Japs would declare martial law and disarm the Thai army and police. Pradit made plans for a coup d'etat against Marshal Pibul to be timed with an Allied invasion — he claimed that two divisions would be sufficient — and asked for Admiral Mountbatten's support, as he was now taking orders from him as Theater Commander. Through OSS he also asked Washington to support his request. However, Admiral Mountbatten had to turn down his request for the time being, as his forces could not give the support asked for until after his invasion of Malaya (Operation ZIPPER) timed for August. The Supreme Allied Commander and Washington both urged the Regent to remain underground and keep up his deception. To the end of the war, Siam feigned obedience to the Chinese, while keeping the Supreme Allied Commander supplied with excellent intelligence and serving as America's best listening post in the Far East.

3

If Asia was a neglected theater of war, China was the end of the line. Because of the Allied Germany-first strategy, Britain and Russia were receiving full American support, in comparison with the mere trickle of supplies that reached China. Although Generalissimo Chiang Kai-shek had rejected Japanese peace feelers after Pearl Harbor, and Free China had remained on the side of the Allies, his voice in their counsels was given only polite attention. The Generalissimo was not invited to the Casablanca Conference in January of 1943. Later that year Chiang met with Roosevelt and Churchill at Cairo,- but their ready promises of increased aid were as readily forgotten. With her sea lanes cut off by the Japanese, and the land route through Burma in enemy hands, the isolated nation was left depleted and vulnerable.

Part of China's difficulty was due to Chiang's own devious nature. He was a fine-boned graceful man with a shy smile and shrewd calculating eyes, a curious admixture of ruthlessness and reticence. Accustomed to covert intrigue, he had neither the talent nor taste for the open brawling and bluster of international diplomacy. Whereas General de Gaulle had shouldered into the Casablanca meeting and loudly proclaimed that Free France had the right to participate in all Allied high-level discussions — it was Churchill's blunt objection which marked the opening rift in Anglo-French relations during the war — Chiang was relegated to a minor role, and was looked on with suspicion. The American theater commander, General Stilwell, referred to the Generalissimo contemptuously as "the peanut" and accused his Nationalist government of refusing to fight, ignoring Chiang's claim that he had sacrificed the flower of his army against the Japanese at Shanghai in 1937 and was no longer capable of his former military effort. France had gone down to defeat six weeks after Germany launched her offensive, the Generalissimo argued; in 1941, after seven years of war, China had not yielded.

Chiang was called a dictator, a profiteering war lord, the head of a graft-ridden government which sought American weapons and supplies only to maintain itself in power. Certainly the charges had substance but it should be recognized that Chiang was forced to defend himself on four fronts: against the Japanese invaders; against the corrupt provincial officials in his own political family; and finally against the Chinese Communists in the north, who were more concerned with overthrowing the Nationalist regime than with fighting the common enemy. Mao Tse-tung's Eighth Route Army never took part in any major engagement of the Sino-Japanese War, and Mao revealed his actual aims as early as 1937 when he instructed his followers: "Our fixed effort should be divided into seventy percent expansion, twenty percent dealing with [Chiang's] Kuomintang, and ten percent resisting Japan. . . . The first objective is to show our outward obedience to the Central Government as camouflage for the development of our party. While waiting, we should give the Japanese invader certain concessions . . . until we are ready to take the counteroffensive and wrest the leadership from the hands of the Kuomintang."[27]

Like Mihailovich and Tito in Yugoslavia, both Chiang and Mao were more concerned with their future power struggle than with the immediate threat of Japan. Many American observers, aware that the Generalissimo was hoarding Allied supplies for his own use in China's coming civil war, concluded that Chiang was not to be trusted, and advocated instead the support of North China. "Vinegar Joe" Stilwell expressed open preference for the Communist regime in Yenan which he termed "China's last best hope." American correspondents were outraged at the corruption and widespread poverty under Chiang's dictatorship, and described Mao's followers in contrast as "agrarian re-

[27] Freda Utley, *Last Chance in China* (New York, 1947).

formers" — overlooking firsthand reports by the United States Observation Group in Yunan concerning the machinations and subversion of the northern Chinese by Mao and Chou En-lai and other Red leaders. State Department representatives in Chungking likewise took the side of the "agrarian reformers" and John Davies wrote in a dispatch to Washington that if the United States were to transfer its "allegiance from the Kuomintang to Communist China, we shall have aligned ourselves behind the most coherent, progressive and powerful force in China."

Such was the tangled situation which OSS met when it sought to operate from Chinese soil against Japan. The first OSS mission, Detachment 101, had been originally intended for Chungking, but was diverted by Stilwell on its arrival and ordered to give him tactical support in his Burma campaign. Further attempts to gain a foothold in China were frustrated by the Nationalist government's refusal to permit a foreign intelligence service to function independently. Chiang's internal security and counterintelligence were conducted by a clandestine Bureau of Investigation and Statistics under the inscrutable General Tai Li, sometimes called "the Chinese Himmler." The only U.S. intelligence organization allowed in the theater was Navy Group China, headed by an ambitious naval officer, Captain M. E. (nicknamed "Mary") Miles. With the personal blessing of Admiral King, Miles had effected a close and confidential relationship with Tai Li and his secret police,[28] and he was not about to surrender his own sovereign rights to a rival American group.

In an effort to solve the impasse and establish OSS in China, General Donovan acquiesced to a tentative agreement in January, 1943, which named Captain Miles as chief of OSS activities in the theater. A special agency was formed, designated the Sino-American Cooperative Organization (SACO), with General Tai Li as director and Miles as deputy director. It soon developed that, under SACO, even a nominal independence was denied OSS. Tai Li, suspicious of any OSS involvement in internal Chinese affairs, reported the information gathered by his Gestapo directly to Miles, who in turn withheld it from OSS until he was

[28] Vice Admiral Milton E. Miles, *A Different Kind of War* (New York, 1967).

sure it had been cabled to the Navy Department first. When OSS asked Tai Li for copies of the reports given to Navy Group, the General offered the polite excuse that the Chinese did not use carbon paper.

Stalemated in its attempt to initiate U.S. intelligence procurement through SACO, blocked at every turn both by Tai Li and by Navy Group which consistently sided with him, OSS found another means of achieving an independent status in China, although not yet developing the full scope of the agency's paramilitary and research facilities. In December 1943 General Donovan and Dr. Langer of R&A conferred in Chungking with the tough leathery commander of the Fourteenth Air Force, Major General Claire L. Chennault, former head of the volunteer Flying Tigers and idolized by the Chinese. The only U.S. combat command operating throughout China, Fourteenth Air Force was badly in need of a widespread tactical intelligence service to pinpoint enemy targets such as troop concentrations and supply dumps. Under cover of Chennault's command, a joint OSS-Fourteenth Air Force unit was formed in April, 1944, with the unwieldy name of 5329th Air and Ground Forces Resources and Technical Staff (AGFRTS), referred to as "Agfighters," or more popularly, "Agfarts." Personnel representing the major OSS branches were attached to the Fourteenth Air Force, and General Chennault's prestige in China was so great that neither Tai Li nor Miles was able to oppose the unit when it undertook its own intelligence operations.

AGFRTS succeeded where SACO had failed, and its results were almost immediately apparent. OSS agents, infiltrated behind the lines, constituted a wide clandestine network which supplied both Air Force Headquarters and the Pacific Fleet with daily weather and meteorological data. On-the-spot radio coverage of Yangtze River traffic and coastal and rail shipping enabled Chennault's fliers to hit "hot" targets with maximum efficiency, and R&A target analysis and assessment of bomb damage aided Chennault greatly in planning future attacks. Six months after it was established, the major part of Fourteenth Air Force tactical intelligence was credited to the new unit.

The situation of the Chungking government had become extremely critical by the summer of 1944. China's campaigns had been marked by a

WJD with General Claire L. Chennault (left), Chunking, December, 1943.

series of military disasters, including the defeat of seven hundred thousand Chinese troops by an enemy force of one hundred thousand. The successful use by the Japanese of well-trained fifth-column forces posed an increasingly serious threat. Adding to Chiang Kai-shek's problems, General Stilwell's feud with both the Generalissimo and General Chennault had become so bitter that the harassed Chiang was forced to ask President Roosevelt for his recall. On October 31, "Vinegar Joe" was replaced by Lieutenant General Wedemeyer, who was transferred from Admiral Mountbatten's staff in Ceylon to assume command of the China theater. In a memorandum to the White House, General Donovan reviewed the past difficulties encountered by OSS in performing its principal function in China: collecting information necessary both for the defeat of Japan and for making informed decisions on ultimate peace settlements in the Far East. He suggested to the President: "Now is the time to make OSS in China directly responsible to the U.S. commanding general and to service him and his subordinates, as well as General MacArthur and Admiral Nimitz."

At last, after two relatively unproductive years, OSS/China emerged as an independent agency operating directly under the commanding general, charged with the coordination of all U.S. clandestine operations in the theater. In January, 1945, General Donovan personally went to the field to complete the reorientation of OSS installations in Chungking and Kunming.[29] One of Wedemeyer's first decisions was to relieve Captain "Mary" Miles of control and place both Navy Group and AGFRTS under the theater commander — an arrangement that Donovan had proposed as early as 1942. Colonel Richard Heppner, head of OSS/SEAC, became the Strategic Services chief in China, and was invited to attend weekly meetings of General Wedemeyer's committee which formulated theater policy; and for the first time OSS was authorized to organize resistance activities, to conduct intelligence and sabotage, and to equip and direct special commando groups in support of the Chinese armies.

OSS/China moved promptly to take advantage of its new directive.

[29] From Kunming, Donovan flew on to Kandy to visit Admiral Mountbatten at his Supreme Headquarters.

WJD with General Albert C. Wedemeyer, De-tachment 202 in China, January or February, 1945.

OSS/China. Colonel Rucker's Chinese paratroopers during a practice jump near Kunming.

The first paratroopers in Chinese history were trained by the veteran Lieutenant Colonel Lucius Rucker at an area near Kunming. The paratroop school was 6,400 feet above sea level, and in the thin air the rate of descent was abnormally fast; but the Chinese took their bumps with good humor. When one of them landed with a jarring thud in a cabbage patch, he would roll over and hold his sides with laughter. The only hitch in Rucker's rapid-fire training program came when the first ninety paratroopers were graduated from jump school. A national holiday was declared to commemorate the important date, stores and business establishments were closed, and celebrations of the event consumed several valuable days. Thereafter Rucker did away with graduations.

These commando units, usually accompanied by an American operator, leaped into action without delay. Seventeen combat teams nipped savagely at the Japanese flanks in the enemy drive down the Liuchow corridor. They virtually surrounded Canton, and in Swatow the Jap commander declared martial law because guerrilla activities led him to believe that an armed uprising of the populace was imminent. The most spectacular demolition job by the Chinese commandos was the destruction of the key three-mile bridge across the Yellow River west of Kaifeng, called by the Air Force "the hottest target in China." Led by Major Paul Cyr — the same Cyr who had earlier won the Distinguished Service Cross for his exploits with the Maquis in France — an OSS team parachuted into the Kaifeng area, and Cyr made plans for his sabotage assignment. "Soon after dark on August ninth," Cyr wrote,[30] "our rivermen crawled down through the grass to their hidden boats and loaded the demolition charges aboard, with 100-foot fuses which would burn, even under water, for twenty-five minutes. . . . Each pier of the bridge consisted of six steel tubes filled with concrete, laced together with structural steel, which had saved the span many times from our bombers. Agile as monkeys, the saboteurs swarmed up the bridge supports, passing seventy-two-pound packets of explosive from one to another quickly and noiselessly." A Chinese major lit the fuses, paused

[30] Major Paul Cyr, "We Blew the Yellow River Bridge," *Saturday Evening Post,* March 23, 1946.

calmly to see that they were burning properly, and then dropped into the boat with Cyr and they sculled ashore.

"We didn't have an electric detonator for exact timing," Cyr continued, "but we got a train just the same. It puffed onto the bridge just as we reached the bank. The locomotive was almost across when all hell broke loose. Six cars crumbled and the locomotive slid back into the hole where the inshore pier had been. The other cars were stopped right over another mined pier, in perfect position. Jap soldiers were everywhere, nineteen carloads of them. As they screamed and scolded and asked questions about the delay, the second charge went off, then another and another. The rest of the train, the soldiers, and that whole section of bridge vanished into the swirling river." Enemy casualties in the single operation were estimated at one thousand.

When the Japanese drive threatened the city of Chungking, and members of the American Embassy were quietly advised to evacuate their families, OSS-trained teams directed the efforts of Chiang's forces to hold their positions, constructed roadblocks to help stem the enemy advance, and boobytrapped buildings abandoned by the Chinese. A single team cut telephone and telegraph lines in 156 places, dynamited seven bridges, and removed 524 sections of track from the Canton-Hankow railroad, wrecking one troop train and stalling three others which were subsequently destroyed by air assault. Equipped with VHF radios, two OSS privates sighted a large enemy cavalry unit approaching the river near Yiyang. An urgent message, first in code and then in clear text, brought Fourteenth Air Force fighter-bombers to attack the Japanese while they were in midstream, and native estimates placed the enemy dead in the thousands. Two days afterward, one of the same privates radioed that enemy troops were crossing the Siang River in sampans. The message was received by Fourteenth Air Force planes which were already airborne, and they proceeded at once to the target. The sampans proved to be double-decked troop barges, and Chinese sources reported that at least twenty-five barges had been sunk with heavy losses.

Sometimes the Japanese would try to jam the radios of Chennault's fighter planes by cutting in on their wave length with loud music. The pilot of a Mustang, tuning in on his radio on the way to work over an enemy headquarters, was greeted by the lilting melody of the "Blue Danube Waltz." Nonchalantly he barreled down the Jap company street, rocking his wings in time to the music and firing rhythmic bursts from his machine guns to accent the soft strains of Strauss: "Da da da, da dee! (Brp, brp, brp brp) da da da, da *dee!* (Bur-r-rrrp, brp brp)."

Communist North China, with its access to Manchuria and Korea, was a vital intelligence area. In July, 1944, an American mission designated "Dixie," which included a number of OSS men among its personnel, was permitted to enter Yunan in order to obtain Japanese order-of-battle information, train counts on the highly strategic North China rail lines, and data on enemy counterintelligence units in China. In return, the Communists demanded a full supply of American military equipment. Chungking objected violently to giving the Communists any weapons which might be used against the Chiang Kai-shek regime after the war, and President Roosevelt decided that lend-lease material could not be used to arm the Communists unless and until they acknowledged the Nationalist government of the Republic of China.[31] The Dixie mission was withdrawn, and Mao's antagonism toward the United States was further aggravated.

Any doubts that the Red Chinese were merely "agrarian reformers" were resolved when General Wedemeyer held a private discussion with Mao Tse-tung and Chou En-Lai at his home in Chungking. In answer to the General's probing questions, Mao declared flatly: "Chinese revolution is an integral part of world revolution against imperialism, feudalism, and capitalism."[32] Still the State Department advisers in Chungking urged the United States to "have no qualms in abandoning [Chiang] in favor of the progressive — Communist — forces" in the north. Their advocacy of the Red Chinese riled the short-tempered American ambassador Pat Hurley, a former cowpuncher from Oklahoma who delighted in giving a Comanche Indian war whoop whenever he entered a conference room, and he insisted that Davies and John Service and two

[31] Donald Lohbeck, *Patrick J. Hurley* (Chicago, 1956).
[32] General Albert C. Wedemeyer, *Wedemeyer Reports!* (New York, 1959).

other embassy advisers be recalled.[33] During the later Amerasia scandal in Washington, Service was arrested on the charge of having given secret government reports to the Communists, prompting a characteristically distorted column by Drew Pearson which repeated the popular cliché that the "so-called Chinese Communists" were "actually an agrarian party," and insisted that "the USA is backing the wrong horse in China." While we may forgive these early Communist apologists for their lack of foresight — a number of ranking officials in America were equally misled — the fact remains that their support of Mao, however sincere, served to aggravate Chiang still further, and OSS was forbidden to operate in North China and Manchuria.

The result was a crucial gap in U.S. intelligence coverage. OSS penetration of Manchuria inevitably would have revealed the weakness of the vaunted and largely mythical Japanese Kwantung Army — an army which the wily Stalin claimed was being held in check by Russian troops, and which he used as a bargaining point at the Yalta Conference in 1945. Because of America's lack of knowledge to the contrary, Stalin's bluff won the Yalta poker game.

---

[33] "It may be that Davies' pervasive conservatism [today] is an unconscious atonement for the error that he did make in assessing the Chinese years ago. 'My mistake in 1944 was in saying that the Chinese Communists were democratic,' he once admitted in a conversation. 'I confused the popularity of the Communists with democracy. In the war against the Japanese, the Chinese Communists were a popular regime. They had a democratic facade. As in so many revolutions, the leadership betrayed the people.'" — Look, March 4, 1969.

IX

COMMUNICATIONS ARE THE VERY ESSENCE of behind-the-lines espionage. Unless the infiltrated agent can transmit his information back to head-quarters while it is still timely, his effort is largely wasted. In occupied France, it was possible for OSS teams to operate bulky radios from safe houses, shifting them frequently to escape German detection; but penetration of the Greater Reich presented problems which nullified all previous techniques. A hostile population and tighter security controls made a W/T set, with its codebooks and aerials and power supply, dangerously conspicuous to carry around and extremely difficult to hide; and the Gestapo's efficient direction-finding methods added to the peril of radio transmission in the German homeland.

The need for a viable solution to these problems of communication was no more urgent than in the fall of 1944, following the Battle of the Bulge. And the solution may best be given in the words of William J. Casey, then Chief of SI for OSS/ETO:

"I suppose we all think our own operation was particularly striking. I have always thought that one of our most impressive achievements was starting in a brand new business in October, or so, of 1944, sending some 200 men into Germany and getting all but a dozen back safely. The SHAEF assessment had been that we would win the war in France. When the Allied forces stalled at the Aachen-Colmar, we had to put together a German operation around a very tiny nucleus. By the time the Ardennes offensive revealed how badly we missed the kind of deep reports on movements through rail centers we had had in France, we were ready to send Polish, Belgian and French teams to the major cross-road cities of Germany with WT or Joan-Eleanor sets. During the January–April period, we sent over 100 such teams. To avoid losing time waiting for moon periods and since the Allied command had given OSS SI top priority, we developed a technique of radar-controlled blind drops and put it into operation. The radar-equipped planes were based near Liège and commanded by Elliott Roosevelt. We were getting advice from ground to air one night on where our bombers could find a major troop or supply concentration. It would be bombed the next night. The third night we'd get a ground to air report on the success of the bombing mission."

The development of the communications device known as "Joan-Eleanor" (J-E), enabled an agent on the ground to talk directly to a specially equipped plane flying overhead at as much as thirty thousand feet. Since a J-E weighed only four pounds and used small long-life batteries, it was easier to transport and conceal, and its high frequency and vertical cone-shaped directivity virtually defied enemy DF-ing. The danger of mistakes in transmission was minimized by having the agent in two-way voice communication with an OSS operative overhead, who could request repeats or clarifications on confusing points, and in turn give the ground agent spot briefings. Most important of all, a volume of data could be exchanged in a few minutes which might require days or even weeks of periodic W/T transmission.

To fly these J-E missions, the tail sections of three British Mosquitoes were remodeled to accommodate the J-E operator and his equipment, as well as a complete oxygen system, secondary intercom, direction indicators, and emergency lights. Fourteen J-E ground agents were parachuted in November, 1944, to Berlin, Stuttgart, Regensburg, Munich, and other points in Germany, and to the heavily defended Low Countries. Some were killed, others smashed their sets on landing and disappeared without a trace; but the four missions which established contact proved so valuable that they more than made up for the failures.

The first J-E equipped agent to operate on the Continent was "Bobby," a very religious young Hollander who had escaped in a small boat to England, and who begged OSS for a chance to return to his native land and work against the Germans. On November 10 he jumped from a Liberator bomber in the vicinity of Ulrum, Holland, to lay the foundations for an underground railroad along which other agents could be infiltrated. After an interval of several anxious weeks, a J-E plane, circling over a fixed rendezvous, heard Bobby's polite voice: "I am quite all right, and ready to receive my friends one mile north of the eleventh position," a signal that he had completed arrangements with the underground for further agent drops. He added confidently: "I have a car now, and I need two sets of automobile tires 16×25 and 17×50."

The voice contacts continued through the winter, and Bobby, in his courteous and precise speech, delivered important information on German preparations to blow the dams and flood the Polder River, enemy troop movements at Arnhem, and results of Allied air raids on the Gaarkeuken docks. Then, early in February, he was seized by the Gestapo, the victim of a mistake in identity which, ironically enough, saved his life. Another Bobby in the same area, a former British agent who had "turned" and betrayed a number of Dutch resistance workers to the Germans, was marked for assassination by the underground. Confusing him with the OSS Bobby, the Dutch were on their way to kill him when they were arrested by the Gestapo, who learned the hideout of their intended victim and took him into custody. Bobby realized that there had been an error, and decided that his only chance lay in playing out the turncoat's role. He feigned hatred for the underground which had ordered him murdered, explained that he had turned against the Allies because they had never paid him, and volunteered to work for the Germans as a double agent. His manner was so sincere that he convinced the Gestapo, and on February 10 they began playing back Bobby, feeding him false military information to deliver over his J-E set.

While four Germans stood over him with drawn pistols to prevent any trickery, Bobby made contact with a J-E plane overhead, and complained that it was late in arriving at the rendezvous: "It's cold as hell waiting down here." The use of profanity, so alien to Bobby's nature, was his ingenious means of warning OSS that he was operating under duress as a playback. "Don't take so goddamned long next time." He repeated the German information, requested a supply drop, but added:

"No damned friends." The J-E operator who recognized the profanity as a control signal, gave no sign of concern. "Sorry about the delay, Bobby," he apologized. "We'll be damned sure it doesn't happen again."

SI/London worked with X-2 in following the standard procedure for protecting a captured agent, giving him misleading intelligence and dropping occasional supplies to persuade the enemy that he was worth more to them alive than dead. So completely was the Gestapo taken in that, after two months of J-E contacts, they arranged for Bobby to return to London with a secret proposal. If representatives of OSS would meet with the Gestapo, he was authorized to offer, the Germans would turn over all the intelligence they possessed on Japan, in exchange for a promise by OSS to persuade the Allies to withhold any aid to Russia. Passports and photographs and a Gestapo pass were prepared; and Bobby, as a final gesture of cooperation, informed his captors that the Allies were planning an invasion of Holland in the vicinity of Friesland. At a time when Germany needed all her resources to defend the West Wall, three Nazi paratroop divisions were moved to Friesland where they waited in vain for the notional landings.

On May 3 Bobby was escorted across the minefields by a German SS officer. They shook hands, Bobby returned his Gestapo pass, and set out alone toward the Allied front lines, waving a white handkerchief and smiling broadly.

An even more successful J-E mission was "Chauffeur," a pair of Belgian agents who dropped into Germany near Regensburg on March 31, carrying both J-E and W/T equipment. This double communication was an excellent precaution in case of a shift in their pinpoint due to enemy concentration in the assigned area. With rare good luck, the Chauffeur team discovered a dairy which employed ten Belgian and French POW's, and the agents obtained the support of all the workers, including the non-German manager. In a silo of the dairy they set up the first W/T set to communicate out of Germany proper. Using the milk delivery trucks, they moved freely around the country, gathering intelligence on enemy defenses and target locations. One of the agents met a French girl, forced to work in a German brothel, and she consented to draw her amorous customers out on troop movements and other military subjects. For four days, the agent sat in a closet in the girl's busy bedroom, taking notes on the indiscreet conversations he overheard. In a J-E contact in April, he gave the location of the German General Staff as a precision target: "The General Staff is at Regensburg, Hotel Du Parc, Maximilianstrasse, the street facing the station, first house on the left."

Only one U.S. team penetrated Berlin itself. Mission "Hammer" consisted of two Czech Communists recruited by the OSS Labor Desk in London. Equipped with cover and documentation identifying them as Czech toolmakers fleeing before the Russian advance, they parachuted blind on March 2, 1945, to a field near Alt Friesack, some fifty kilometers northwest of Berlin, walked to the nearest railroad station, and took a train to the German capital. There they proceeded to the home of the parents of one agent, and his sister and brother-in-law joined them in collecting intelligence, talking to soldiers in the bomb-wrecked city, or visiting military areas and industrial plants. As one of the agents was returning home with a satchel full of incriminating maps and reports, he was stopped by an SS guard, who found his false papers satisfactory but demanded to look in his bags. The agent opened the sack of dirty laundry he always carried, and the guard did not search further — a fortunate matter for all concerned, since it was a standard agent custom to cock his pistol while shuffling for papers. After a successful aerial contact on March 28, the J-E operator reported to OSS/London:

"Hammer stated that the Klingenberg power plant on Rommelsberg Lake was fully functioning and was furnishing electric power to factories. . . . He added: 'We need medicine that soldiers can take in order to become ill, four pistols and three knives, also food stamps or paper on which stamps can be forged. Please give our regards to our wives and children.' Hammer ended up by saying that the city railroad [Stadtbahn] was the only system of transportation in working order in Berlin, that if it could be knocked out all traffic in the city would stop. He also located the position of the main post office and telegraph office, and reported one freight yard full of 26 freight trains and 18 passenger trains."

On April 24, the Russians came upon the Hammer team fighting to prevent some thirty Wehrmacht troops from blowing a bridge outside Berlin, and the mission was evacuated safely.

The most effective team to operate in Austria was "Greenup," led by Sergeant Frederic A. Mayer of Brooklyn, a German-born OSS paratrooper who dropped with two other skiers into the mountainous Tyrol region of West Austria. Two pairs of skis were lost on the drop, and his companions floundered and crawled through the deep snow while Mayer skied ahead, dragging the Greenup equipment to a mountain resort. Friends received the team and helped install their radio, and contacts in neighboring villages supplied them with intelligence which refuted the rumor that the Nazis were preparing a final defense in the "Redoubt." Mayer signaled to OSS the arrivals of Mussolini and Daladier and the establishment of Himmler's headquarters in the area, and reported that the Germans had been timing the Fifteenth Air Force bombings of the Brenner Pass and were running their rail schedules accordingly. The Air Force varied the timing of its raids, and repeatedly produced train wrecks which blocked the vital pass.

In Oberpfuss, a suburb of Innsbruck, Mayer obtained a German officer's uniform and fake papers indicating that he was under hospitalization. He set up a network of anti-Nazis, who gave him details of enemy freight and troop movements and factory production, which he relayed regularly to OSS/Italy. The Germans caught up with him at last when one of his own assistants, a black marketeer, betrayed him to the Nazi police. Handcuffed, he was taken to a Gestapo jail for "special questioning." For four hours they beat him about the body and head, "making a pulp of his face" and bursting an eardrum with a blow from the cupped hand of a torture expert. Mayer stuck to his cover story until he was confronted with the traitorous assistant, but though he had to admit he was an American he refused to reveal the location of his two OSS confederates.

Now the infuriated Gestapo really went to work. They doubled Mayer over an iron bar placed between his trussed arms and knees, hung him upside down from the ceiling of his cell, and poured water up his nostrils and into the ear which had been perforated in the earlier beating. After six hours of torture, the police dragged him half-conscious to the suburb where he had lived, and began a house-to-house search. They found the secret hideout, but his companions had fled, and the Gestapo's renewed beatings and kickings failed to break Mayer's silence.

It was the Germans themselves who finally cracked. The local Nazi leader, astonished that this young American had withstood two days of steady torture without confessing, concluded that Mayer must have knowledge of the imminent arrival of Allied troops. He arranged a meeting between Mayer and the Tyrolean district gauleiter, Herr Hofer, who agreed to enter into surrender negotiations. Mayer managed to slip word through the underground to his radio operator, who notified OSS headquarters of the German offer.

As the U.S. forces approached Innsbruck, Mayer learned that the wavering gauleiter had changed his mind and was about to broadcast an appeal to his district, urging a last-ditch stand. Mayer hurried back to Hofer's office and persuaded him that resistance would be hopeless; and that afternoon the people of the Tyrolean district were told by their gauleiter that Innsbruck had been declared an open city. Sergeant Mayer formally interned Hofer and other leading Nazis in a farmhouse, left his radio operator in charge of a German police guard, and drove calmly through the advancing lines to meet officers of the 103rd Division and inform them that Innsbruck had surrendered without bloodshed.

2

In the capitals of three neutral countries, Turkey and Sweden and Switzerland, OSS performed the most difficult kind of positive intelligence work. Whereas normal agent operations involved sending observers to a target area to collect information which could be seen or heard, espionage in Istanbul or Stockholm or Bern required an indirect and discreet approach to a few highly placed members of the target community. Their high-level intelligence was of a type which could rarely be obtained by agents operating on a lower echelon, and by coupling it with specific messages from the field OSS was able to piece together a complete picture of affairs in the enemy homeland.

Istanbul provided an unparalleled opportunity for gathering intelligence on Central and East Europe. Through Turkey traveled the main body of Jewish refugees fleeing the Nazi regime, and a stream of businessmen and government officials passed back and forth constantly. Some seventeen foreign intelligence services were active in Istanbul, not only German and Italian and British but also Japanese and Chinese and Russian, and the neutral city teemed with professional informers. Provided OSS activities were not directed against the Turks themselves, the Turkish police were willing to coopcrate in every way, even supplying the Istanbul mission with hotel and border registrations.

From a contact in the Rumanian Embassy, OSS procured copies of all the political and economic reports pouched from the Rumanian Foreign Office. Another contact supplied the Reich's secret Telegram Address-buch, listing addresses of all German firms. A local newspaper reporter, turned undercover agent, furnished information on Rumanian oil developments and output, which culminated in the Ploesti air raids. An Austrian corporation manager volunteered details on Nazi synthetic rubber production, and gave the fuel and construction details of the V–2 rocket, its exact size and speed and range, and the locations of various plants manufacturing or assembling the new secret weapon.

An ingenious representative of OSS/Istanbul managed to engage in private conversations with Franz von Papen, Germany's minister to Turkey, regarding the possibility of a negotiated settlement of the war. When these conversations were duly reported to President Roosevelt and the JCS, OSS received peremptory orders to instruct its representative to break off all contact with von Papen at once. Whether Roosevelt feared that the Russians, already highly suspicious of American motives, would find out and make a separate peace with Germany, OSS was never told; but the possible path to an early termination of hostilities was abandoned. The eventual penetration of OSS/Istanbul by Hungarian double agents and the notorious female spy, Mrs. Hildegarde Reilly, ended the mission's usefulness.

Stockholm, like Istanbul, offered a neutral base close to German-controlled Europe. In the congenial atmosphere of Sweden's friendly capital, OSS personnel chatted freely with sailors and travelers from Norway and Denmark and Germany. Agents attached as vice-consuls in the three main ports lining the Kattegat sea lane between Denmark and Sweden were able to secure spot intelligence on German traffic to and from Norway. By interviewing leaders of transport workers in these ports, an R&A unit in Stockholm obtained proof that the movement of Nazi troops and matériel was far greater than the German-Swedish agreement allowed, and in late 1943 the Swedish government, confronted with the facts, suspended its permission for German troops to travel through the country.

As the eventual Axis defeat became more obvious during 1944, Swedish cooperation with the Allies improved, and agents along the Norwegian border were able to dispatch supplies across the frontier to Norwegian guerrilla groups. An outstanding espionage accomplishment was the exposure of secret ball-bearing shipments to Germany, long a prime objective of the strategic bombing program. A worker in the SKF shipping office in Goeteborg, refusing any payment, furnished OSS with exact statistics on the export of ball-bearings, tools, and machinery, far in excess of the figures the Swedish government had given to the Allies; and the United States extracted an agreement from Sweden to halt all ball-bearing sales in the future. Another OSS agent from Washington, code-named "Red," posed as a Swedish oil dealer, and in October, 1944, he arranged to be conducted on a week's tour of the synthetic oil industry in Germany, visiting and inspecting many plants and reporting his findings to British and American experts.

The crafty Finnish Intelligence Service in Stockholm generally played a double role, selling information to Axis and Allied espionage services alike. From the Finnish military attaché, OSS purchased some excellent German and Russian battle order reports, and also learned for the first time that the Finns had broken and sold to Axis powers the U.S. diplomatic code. Finland's naval attaché made an even more significant sale. In 1943, OSS bought from him a complete description of the Red Navy, providing what the British Admiralty estimated as ninety-eight percent of all Anglo-American knowledge of Russian sea power. The British rated it as "the find of the year."

Switzerland, due to its long record of neutrality, was the spy center of World War II. With strict impartiality, the thrifty little country served as a sort of honest curb broker in European intrigue, and Bern, its capital, became the leading international exchange for espionage and counterespionage dealings of all the belligerent powers. Throughout the war, undercover agents and diplomats without portfolio rifled one another's luggage, tapped each other's telephones, planted dictaphones under their own beds, and shadowed themselves in endless circles around the revolving doors of Bern's leading hotels.

Bern's role of intelligence broker was nothing new. Switzerland had been host to spies in every European war since 1618, and had learned to content itself with a fair commission, and shut its eyes to certain fast transactions that took place under the counter. It was common gossip in Bern that the Gestapo and the Italian SIM had sought to keep the Countess Ciano from entering Switzerland, and had tried to confiscate the personal papers of her slain husband; but the closemouthed Swiss kept to themselves the story of how the Axis managed to steal Ciano's revealing diary, only to have the British SOE steal it back. The fact that Allied "black" propaganda — counterfeit Nazi newspapers, handbills, papers forged with Hitler's official seal — were smuggled across the border into Germany was likewise no secret; nor were the Swiss unaware of Britain's "Atlantic Radio" which pretended to be a Freedom station somewhere inside the Reich, and was accepted as authentic by much of the German population. Only if a bucket-shop manipulation became too brazen did the government take countermeasures. When the German Legation installed a powerful radio transmitter in the center of Bern, the Swiss jammed it by increasing the legation's electric voltage, and then tactfully hinted to Germany's envoy that it might be just as well if it were not put back into operation.

In this world's market of cloak-and-dagger operations, the Office of Strategic Services conducted a brisk business of its own. Allen Dulles, a prominent New York lawyer who was well acquainted in Switzerland, was selected by General Donovan in May, 1942, to set up an OSS mission in Bern. He arrived at the border the day after the Germans moved into southern France and closed the entire Franco-Swiss frontier, and it was only through the connivance of anti-Vichy French guards that the prospective mission chief was spirited across in time to escape internment.

An office was opened in a building occupied by OWI, where OSS could enjoy diplomatic immunity, and meetings with subagents were held after blackout in Dulles's own residence, free from enemy or Swiss surveillance. Auxiliary bases were soon established throughout Switzerland, and courier service to these outlying posts was arranged through the American Legation. Since all telephones were tapped by the Swiss, messages to Washington and London had to be sent in code by commercial telegraph channels. The task of enciphering and deciphering the daily mass of reports swamped the mission's small staff, but relief came from the skies. As American airmen made forced landings in Switzerland, permission was obtained to attach a number of downed aviators to the legation staff, and they worked for OSS as cipher clerks on a 24-hour shift.

After the liberation of Corsica in October, 1943, a complicated but nonetheless reliable scheme was worked out to get pouch material through to London. Maps and drawings and the full texts of reports were microfilmed in Bern and sent to Geneva, where they were given to a locomotive engineer on the Geneva-Lyons run. The film was hidden in a secret compartment built over the firebox, so that if the train were searched by the Germans the engineer could open a trapdoor at the bottom of the compartment and the film would be destroyed in the flames. At Lyons the film was turned over to a courier, who took it by bicycle to Marseilles, and delivered it to the captain of a fishing boat bound for Corsica, where it was picked up by a plane from Algiers and flown to London. This roundabout method continued until November 1944, when a clandestine radio post was established in Bern.

The most productive of all Bern's contacts, called by Allen Dulles "not only our best source on Germany but undoubtedly one of the best secret agents any intelligence service ever had,"[34] was established in August, 1943. The volunteer agent, code-named "Wood," held a most confidential post in the German Foreign Office in Berlin. He had

[34] Allen Dulles, *The Secret Surrender* (New York, 1966).

entered the foreign service before Hitler's rise to power, and from the beginning had been hostile to the Nazi regime and refused to become a party member; but because of his abilities he was rapidly promoted to a position in the Foreign Office which gave him access to top-secret information. What he learned only increased his determination to oppose the Nazis, and he secured permission to make a trip as official courier to Bern, where he contacted OSS. Wood brought with him several classified cables which had crossed his desk, and copious notes he had made in Berlin. At his first meeting with Dulles, he offered to copy all significant messages henceforth, and either bring them himself or send them to Bern by a trusted intermediary.

For several months, Wood managed to travel to Switzerland every few weeks, bringing cables by the pound which he had personally packaged and sealed in the Foreign Office. Toward the end of 1944, because of the increasingly difficult conditions in Berlin, he was furnished with an OSS camera to photograph his documents and send the rolls of microfilm to OSS in an envelope addressed to an imaginary Swiss sweetheart. With the help of an Alsatian doctor, Wood's photographing was done in the basement of a hospital in Berlin, frequently by flashlight during the recurrent air raids. Once Himmler arrived unexpectedly at the Foreign Office and requested a document which was at that very moment being filmed. Wood, notified at the hospital, rushed back to his office and pretended to pull the paper out of his files while actually extricating it from his pocket.

As Allied interests shifted to the Far East, information from the German air attaché in Japan became increasingly desirable. Since OSS/Bern had no means of passing to Wood the urgent request from Washington, Dulles hit on the simple idea of sending him a postcard from the fictitious Swiss sweetheart. On the reverse of an Alpine scene was an innocent message, stating that one of her friends was managing a gift shop selling Japanese trinkets and had found a considerable market for them but, alas, her friend could get them no more. In view of Germany's close ties with Japan, was it possible to procure any of this Japanese material in Berlin? The tip was all that Wood needed, and his next batch of film contained dozens of up-to-date reports direct from the German Embassy in Tokyo.

Over a period of a year and a half, Wood furnished more than sixteen hundred true readings of cables from the Foreign Office as well as from some forty German diplomatic and consular missions, including extensive data on the German secret service in Spain and Sweden and Switzerland, and information revealing Nazi espionage activities in England. A cable delivered by Wood gave Dulles the first clue to the noted Nazi spy "Cicero," who was serving as valet to the British ambassador in Istanbul.

In addition to Wood, OSS/Bern established direct contact with one of the chief Abwehr officers in Switzerland, Hans Gisevius, vice-consul with the German Consulate General in Zurich. As proof of his good faith, Gisevius handed Dulles the text of several telegrams sent to Washington by the American Legation in a code which the Gestapo had broken. One of these enemy-deciphered messages described the political situation in Italy, and mentioned that certain leading Fascists, including Mussolini's son-in-law Ciano, were possibly open to approaches from the Allies. The intercepted telegram had been shown to Hitler, who promptly forwarded it to Mussolini, and a few days later Ciano was removed from his position as Italy's foreign minister. To have ceased using the code abruptly would have aroused German suspicions, but thereafter the American minister employed it only for innocuous reports or misleading information.

It was through Gisevius that OSS learned the names and plans of high-ranking German generals and anti-Nazi officials involved in the plot to overthrow Hitler, to which OSS gave the code name "Breakers." For eighteen months preceding July 20, 1944, Bern was kept informed of the assassination plans, and notified Washington that the conspirators hoped to cooperate with American forces in a mass uprising against the Nazi dictator. Washington replied that under no circumstances would America act unilaterally without the consent of her Russian ally, a condition which the German resistance would not accept. Gisevius took part in the abortive *putsch* on the twentieth, escaped the Gestapo dragnet after its failure, and for six months remained concealed in Berlin. To help protect him, OSS circulated a rumor that he was hiding in Switzerland, and the Gestapo combed the country in vain. At last, with a complete set of false papers prepared by OSS/London, Gisevius escaped to Bern in January, 1945.

Bern received a constant flow of intelligence from other sources. Important German industrial centers were penetrated, and detailed information was forwarded to Washington regarding Nazi aircraft production, including the first jet planes. OSS in Switzerland also reported the midget or "beetle" tank, a year before it made its appearance at Anzio; and the earliest inkling of the V–1 came from a Swiss industrialist, who informed Dulles in February, 1943, that Germany's secret weapon was some sort of aerial torpedo. In May OSS learned that a new heavy missile employing the rocket principle was already in limited production somewhere in Pomerania. At the end of June, an Austrian source pinpointed the assembly plant and testing ground at Peenemünde, which was raided by the RAF. Hitler's timetable for "Program A-4," as the Germans called it, was set back six months, and the first V–1 did not appear over England until June, 1944.

An outstanding Swiss physicist provided OSS with the startling news that his fellow German scientists were working on atomic development. The Manhattan Project in the United States was so secret at the time that Bern was not even asked to explore the matter further. The only indication that Dulles's cable had caused quite a flap in Washington was the immediate instruction to reclassify it top secret, followed by an urgent request for the addresses of a long list of German nuclear physicists. Ascertaining that the headquarters of German atom-splitting activities had been moved from the Kaiser Wilhelm Institute in Berlin, OSS determined the new location of the laboratory through the telltale postmarks of letters mailed to the Swiss scientist from little towns close together in a significant cluster. A quick investigation satisfied U.S. atomic experts that the Germans were far behind in the race.

No other endeavor by OSS/Bern, however, equaled the secret negotiations called "Sunrise" which aimed at the surrender of all the German armies in Italy. Countless lives would have been spared by this early termination of hostilities, had it not been for an offhand statement made by President Roosevelt at the Casablanca Conference in French Morocco.

3

When Roosevelt and Churchill met at Casablanca in January, 1943, the war moved irretrievably from the control of the military to the control of the politicians. At a fateful press conference, without the advance agreement of his Chiefs of Staff, the American President announced that the Allies demanded nothing less than unconditional surrender by the Axis. Though Roosevelt explained later to Churchill that he did not mean "the destruction of the population of Germany and Italy and Japan" but merely of their leadership which had brought on the war, his proclamation stiffened the enemy's will to resist, and forced even Hitler's enemies to continue fighting with the courage of despair, conceivably lengthening the war by as much as a year. The doctrine of unconditional surrender also precluded any possibility that an anti-Hitler coup might succeed in time for the Germans to lay down their arms while the Russians were still short of the Vistula River. Not only did Roosevelt's policy play directly into Stalin's hands, but it postponed the proposed capitulation of the German forces in Italy until May 2, 1945, almost at the end of the war in Europe.

OSS/Bern had urged Washington repeatedly that extensive results might be obtained by following up Allied military successes with secret surrender missions to wavering German generals. During the early months of 1944, Dulles had reported evidence of a real opportunity to drive a wedge between the Hitler-SS group and the old-line German leaders. Full information was forwarded on the plot against Hitler, and on disloyalty in the higher ranks of the Wehrmacht and the Abwehr; but the JCS, tied by the Allied unconditional surrender policy, offered no encouragement to any effort to split the Germans. General Omar Bradley, in command of 12th Army Group, endorsed an OSS suggestion to induce certain pliable German generals on the West Front to defect, but again Washington deferred the project until it was too late. The Battle of the Bulge, spearheaded by SS panzer divisions, confirmed the final seizure of control by the Nazi party. Most of the generals who might earlier have been willing to surrender, including Rommel and

Schwerin, had been executed or had committed suicide, and were replaced by fanatic Nazi followers of Hitler.

On February 25, 1945, a Swiss intelligence officer conveyed word to OSS/Bern that an anti-Fascist Italian industrialist in Milan, Baron Luigi Parilli, wished to establish contact with the Allies on behalf of Nazi General Karl Wolff. A meeting was arranged, and Baron Parilli told Dulles that Wolff, anxious to end an increasingly futile struggle, was ready to negotiate the capitulation of all German and Fascist forces in northern Italy. Dulles warned Parilli that Allied policy required unconditional surrender, but suggested that Wolff might give evidence of his sincerity by arranging the release of two prominent Italians held by the Gestapo.

Three days later, Dulles was summoned to a hospital in Zurich. There he found the two Italians, Ferruccio Parri, resistance leader and later Italian Prime Minister, and Major Antonio Usmiani, one of the key OSS agents in Milan. They told Dulles that they had been led from their cells without a word, shoved into a car, and driven behind drawn curtains through the night. They had assumed they were being taken to an execution area, like so many of their fellow prisoners, but instead they had been ushered across the Swiss border, still without a word of explanation, and set free. Not only had Wolff met the first test; as added indication of his good intentions, Parilli informed Dulles that the General himself would come to Switzerland to discuss the surrender terms.

Still Dulles suspected a Nazi trick. Before involving the Allied High Command, he arranged a private meeting with Wolff in his own home. Wolff was a volatile, sharp-featured German, a wealthy exquisite who fancied himself a connoisseur of art. It was this aesthetic urge, he explained to Dulles, that had prompted him to appropriate the priceless collections of the Uffizi and Pitti galleries as well as King Emmanuel's coin collection. He confirmed his understanding that only an unconditional surrender would be accepted by the Allies, and stated that he believed his superior, Field Marshal Kesselring, could be won over to this position. He further asserted that he was acting entirely independently of Himmler.

Dulles was noncommittal; but as soon as the interview was concluded he informed General Sir Harold Alexander at AFHQ of Wolff's offer, adding that he had checked many of Wolff's claims and found them authentic. Alexander sent two officers, U.S. Major General L. L. Lemnitzer, his deputy chief of staff, and British Major General Terence Airey, head of G-2, as authorized emissaries to conduct further exploratory conversations. An OSS representative, David Crockett, accompanied them. They arrived incognito in Switzerland, wearing the G.I. uniforms and dog tags of two OSS sergeants, and hid in Dulles's home until the next rendezvous with Wolff on March 19 in a remote villa on Lake Maggiore near Locarno. The two Allied officers were introduced to Wolff as military advisers; their actual names and ranks were not revealed.

Wolff had discouraging news to report. An informer had told Himmler of the release of the two Italian prisoners, he said, and Himmler had telephoned Wolff and ordered him not to leave his post under any circumstances. The Gestapo had located Wolff's wife and children and confined them on Wolff's estate at St. Wolfgang in the Tyrol for, as Himmler ominously phrased it, safekeeping. Field Marshal Kesselring, Wolff's accomplice in the plot, had been transferred abruptly from the Italian command to the Western Front — Hitler's own airplane had arrived to take Kesselring to his new post — and he had been replaced by Colonel General Heinrich von Vietinghoff. Wolff requested another two weeks, during which he would try to win von Vietinghoff over to the unconditional surrender agreement. He promised to rendezvous with the emissaries again on April 2. To maintain dependable contact in the interim, Wolff offered to hide an OSS radio operator in Milan.

Chosen for this unenviable assignment was a young Czech, known only as "Wally," who had escaped from the Nazi concentration camp at Dachau to join OSS. He had been trained at the radio school at Bari, and was at an advance outpost near Strasbourg when Dulles's request for a German-speaking operator was received. With his radio and ciphers, Wally was smuggled into Milan and lodged with Wolff's aide, SS Lieutenant Guido Zimmer, at 22 Via Cimarosa in the center of the city. Surrounded by SS troops who would have cut his throat on sight, he remained operated in Zimmer's home and kept up regular contact with OSS on a prearranged signal plan. One of his messages gave the location of von Vietinghoff's headquarters, an obvious invitation by Wolff to bomb it in hope of forcing his dilatory senior officer into a decision, and in the ensuing air raid von Vietinghoff nearly lost his life. Wally also radioed that Mussolini was in Milan, lodging only a few doors away, but asked that care be taken not to hit the Zimmer residence nearby.

Late in March Wally reported the disturbing news that the April rendezvous would have to be postponed. Marshal von Vietinghoff was hesitant to accept the Allied surrender terms, particularly since most of his staff were ardent Nazis and still confident that Hitler would produce a secret weapon to turn the Allied tide. Even a personal plea from General Kesselring, which Wolff had obtained after a special trip to the Western Front, failed to overcome von Vietinghoff's doubts. On April 17 Wally sent an even more disheartening message. Himmler had ordered Wolff to Hitler's headquarters, and Wolff, after stalling as long as possible, had flown to Berlin. Feeling that the cause was hopeless, AFHQ recalled its emissaries, and on April 21 Washington instructed OSS/Bern in the most definite terms and from the highest authority to break all Sunrise contacts.

At this dark moment when the negotiations seemed doomed to failure, another message was received from Wally. Generals Wolff and von Vietinghoff were prepared at last to meet the Allied demands. The following day, Baron Parilli arrived in Switzerland with details of this unexpected turn of events. Wolff had seen Hitler in his Berlin air-raid shelter, together with Der Führer's closest associates, Himmler and Gestapo Chief Kaltenbrunner. Hitler was pasty-faced, shaking visibly as he talked, and apparently incapable of grasping the military situation. His two aides, Wolff observed, were equally unnerved. Himmler urged Hitler to take a plane to Berchtesgaden, but Der Führer, with a sudden unreasoning fear of flying, insisted on staying in Berlin. Intermittently, during the argument, Himmler and Kaltenbrunner berated Wolff for his treacherous negotiations with the Allies, but Hitler stared emptily at the concrete walls of the bunker and seemed unaware of what was being said. Emboldened, Wolff put on a defiant front and stated to Hitler that if his action had been dishonorable he was ready to be executed by a firing squad. Hitler did not answer, his knuckles drumming on the side of his cot as he mumbled disconnected phrases: Germany must hold out two months more; by that time the Allies would be split; then he would join the side which made the best offer. Himmler and Kaltenbrunner began to argue with him again, and Wolff, unnoticed, rose to leave the room. He had a last glimpse of Hitler sitting on the edge of his cot, his head sagging forward and his fingers combing slowly through his graying hair. He made no move to return Wolff's farewell salute.

On April 23, Wolff and his adjutant and an envoy from von Victinghoff arrived in Switzerland to sign the surrender agreement, but Dulles informed them that orders from Washington expressly prohibited any official contact with the German delegation. After waiting several days in Lucerne, Wolff delegated authority to his adjutant to sign if Washington changed its mind, and departed for Italy on April 27, fearing that his return might be cut off at any moment. In Cernobbio, Italian Partisans surrounded the villa where he had taken refuge for the night and made him a prisoner. Wolff managed to get word by telephone to Dulles, and Donald Jones of OSS, who had been working with the Partisans, hurried to Cernobbio to plead for Wolff's release. The car was fired on at a roadblock, and Jones jumped out and stood in the glare of his own headlights in hope that the excited peasants would recognize him. The firing ceased, and Jones proceeded to Wolff's villa. Wolff, dressed in civilian clothes, was driven safely to his new headquarters in the summer palace of the Duke of Pistoia at Bolzano.

On that same day, April 28, OSS/Bern was authorized by Washington to resume the surrender negotiations, and Wolff's two associates were flown to AFHQ headquarters at Caserta. Communications with Wolff had become crucial, and Wally was moved to Bolzano, hurried past suspicious SS guards surrounding the palace, and taken to a small room on the third floor which had formerly served as a linen closet. The following night, while Wally waited at his radio behind locked doors, a flight of American bombers attacked Bolzano, killing several German staff officers. Wally could hear angry voices in the corridor outside his room, and a fist hammered on the door. If one more bombing took place, he was told, he would be shot without trial. Wally warned OSS that a bomb had landed only fifty meters from the headquarters building, and if the Air Force did not cease its raids, he added plaintively, *"Wally ist verloren!"*

On May 1 the long-awaited message arrived from Caserta, stating that the surrender papers had been signed and a cease-fire should be ordered by Wolff at noon on the 2nd. As Wally was taking down the message, low-flying Allied planes once more attacked Wolff's headquarters. Wally remained in his vulnerable third-floor hideout, preferring the falling bombs to the fury of the troops below.

For the next twenty-four hours, Wally's life hung in the balance. Himmler sent Nazi General Schulz to replace von Vietinghoff, but Wolff, alerted in time, locked the successor in a bomb shelter and cut the telephone and telegraph wires to Berlin. At one in the morning, eleven hours before the cease-fire order was to be given, Gestapo Chief Kaltenbrunner learned of Schulz's kidnapping and ordered the arrest of Wolff. Wolff tried to escape, but a crowd of SS storm troopers was gathered in the palace courtyard. He rushed back indoors, ordered up seven tanks to dispel the troopers, and surrounded himself with trusted soldiers of his own Elite Guard. At dawn, the suicide of Hitler was officially announced. Wolff persuaded the commander of the storm troopers that the death of Der Führer relieved him of his oath of allegiance; and at noon on May 2 all hostilities in northern Italy ceased.

The Sunrise negotiations, hampered by the unconditional surrender formula, had dragged on for almost two months of needless bloodshed before they were concluded, only five days before the final ceremony of capitulation at Eisenhower's headquarters in Rheims. Meantime the Soviet armies had won the race to Berlin and raped the city, and Stalin had broken his Yalta promises by the swift subjection of Rumania and Poland. Churchill had pleaded for the Allied liberation of Prague, which he said "might make the whole difference to the postwar situation in Czechoslovakia"; but Harry Truman, who had succeeded to the Presidency after Roosevelt's death in March, declined the suggestion for deeper American involvement in Central Europe.

The effect of Roosevelt's pronouncement at Casablanca was even more tragic in the Far East. The Emperor realized that Japan's situation was hopeless, and in July of 1945 Tokyo requested Soviet mediation to bring the war to an end, though it added: "So long as the enemy demands unconditional surrender, we will fight as one man." At Potsdam, however, Truman reiterated that Japan must yield to Allied demands for total capitulation or face "the utter devastation of the Japanese homeland," a decision which left Tokyo's leaders with no choice but to continue the struggle. The result was the catastrophic flash over Hiroshima on August 6 which ushered the world into the atomic age.

X

BY THE EARLY SUMMER of 1945 it had become clear that the surrender of Japan was imminent. Some twenty thousand American and Allied prisoners-of-war and fifteen thousand civilian internees were being held in enemy camps, which OSS agents had located at scattered points from Manchuria and Korea south to Indochina; and the Allied command was deeply apprehensive that the defeated Japanese might revenge themselves on their captives or cut off all food supplies and leave them to starve when the troops withdrew.

General Donovan moved fast. Some nine volunteer Mercy Teams were mounted in China in mid-July, to be parachuted to prisoner-of-war centers before the end of hostilities. Each team included an interpreter, a radio operator, an agent who had kept in clandestine touch with the assigned prison camp, and a doctor for inmates in need of immediate medical attention; and carried five hundred pounds of medical supplies, powdered milk, dehydrated soup, and vitamins. Their mission was to insure proper protection for the prisoners, prevent forced marches or other mistreatment, and clear suitable airfields for their prompt evacuation.

No one knew how the Japanese would react to this unprecedented rescue project, and as a precaution the plan involved five stages. First a secret contact would determine the number and condition of captives in each camp. Then leaflets would be dropped, notifying the Japanese that the OSS teams were arriving for purely humanitarian reasons. Next the parachutists themselves would jump to the camp site, followed by a drop of additional supplies as needed, and the final step would be the arrival of hospital planes to bring out the released prisoners.

On August 15, the first four Mercy Teams assembled at the Sian base to board planes furnished by the Fourteenth Air Force: Mission Magpie to operate in the Peking area, Duck in Weihsien, Flamingo in Harbin, and Cardinal in Mukden. Mission Flamingo was canceled at the last minute, because Harbin was under Communist control and no clearance with the Russians could be arranged. The others landed successfully; and in a compound near Peiping Mission Magpie found Commander Winfield S. Scott, commander of naval and marine forces at Wake Island on December 8, 1941, and four fliers from the Doolittle raid who had been kept in solitary confinement since their capture, one of them almost dead from beriberi.

Japanese reactions to these mercy missions was varied. A message to Chungking from Lieutenant General Takahashi, in charge of the Japanese garrison of north China, stated that the teams that arrived in Peking and Weihsien were receiving the "courteous protection" of the Imperial Army and had been put up at the best hotels. On the other hand, a transport plane that landed at the Canton strip, amid the fire of anti-aircraft guns in the surrounding hills, was detained for five hours and then asked to leave to avoid "provoking an incident." Another plane, planning to set down at an airfield in Indochina which had been designated by the Japanese, found the runway obstructed, and proceeded to the Gai Lam airdrome near Hanoi, where a crowd at the edge of the field could be seen waving in friendly greeting. As the plane taxied to a stop, however, it was surrounded by truckloads of belligerent Japanese soldiers and tanks. The flight crew set up Browning automatics under the plane's wings and prepared for defense; but the crowd around the field, who turned out to be Indian troops captured in the fall of Singapore, formed a protective cordon around the plane and pushed back the armed Japanese when they tried to approach. The bewildered commander, who had not been briefed by his superiors, was finally persuaded to order his men back, and the Mercy Team proceeded to the Hanoi prison compound.

The riddle of the USS *Houston,* lost without a trace in the Battle of the Java Sea in February, 1942, was solved when almost half of her crew was discovered in a Japanese prison camp in Thailand. The first hint of any survivors of the missing ship had come a few months after the battle, when the commander of a Japanese aircraft carrier mentioned in a broadcast from Tokyo that he had seen prisoners from the *Houston* in one of the "southern countries" under Japan's control. "Those that are hard to handle," the admiral boasted, "are severely beaten with rope used by sailors. Because of the pain, the lazy Americans continue to work with expressions of suffering on their faces." Thereafter their fate remained a mystery until the summer of 1945, when two emaciated Navy enlisted men staggered into one of the OSS guerrilla camps in Thailand, escorted by members of the Thai underground, and stated that they had escaped from the Petburi prison camp near Bangkok where several hundred of their crewmates were still alive after three years of disease and torture. An OSS Mercy Team parachuted to the camp with doctors and food supplies and an Army cook, and late in August, 315 *Houston* survivors boarded hospital planes for Calcutta, many of them wearing their original khaki drill uniforms, carefully darned and patched, which they had saved for such an occasion.

Mission Cardinal effected the most dramatic rescue. When the team landed at Mukden, chief industrial center of Manchuria, they were interned by the Japanese who explained that the area was under Communist control and they could not act until the Russians gave permission. On August 21 the Soviet government grudgingly agreed to let the U.S. proceed with the prisoner evacuation. In a small camp at Sian, a hundred miles northeast of Mukden, the Mercy Team found sixty-two-year-old Lieutenant General Jonathan M. Wainwright, hero of Bataan and Corregidor and the highest ranking Allied prisoner of the Japanese, as well as General Edward M. Percival, former British commander at Malaya, Sir Benton Thomas, former governor of Malaya and the Dutch governor-general of the Dutch East Indies.

General Wainwright and his party were not flown out for a week, due to Russian reluctance to allow American operations in their zone of activity. His plane was the last to leave Mukden; Mission Cardinal was withdrawn following Soviet protests to Washington, and the remaining prisoners were held until the formal surrender of Japan. Wainwright emerged from the rescue plane at Chungking, lean and gaunt and permanently deafened by explosives at Corregidor, but holding himself rigidly erect with the aid of two canes. Having feared for three years that he would face a U.S. court-martial for the capitulation of his forces in the Philippines, his voice broke as he expressed to reporters his gratitude that "the American people have accepted my dire disaster with forebearance and generosity which are perhaps unique in the experience of any defeated commander." Later President Truman presented him with the Congressional Medal of Honor.

One of the members of the Cardinal Mission was OSS Captain R. F. Hilsman, Jr., who had joined Detachment 101 in Burma, after being wounded at Myitkyina with Merrill's Marauders, and led a team of Kachin jungle fighters for a year. His father, Colonel Hilsman, former commander on Negros Island, had surrendered to overwhelming Japanese forces two months after the fall of Corregidor; and young Hilsman, convinced that the Colonel was still alive somewhere in Manchuria, requested permission to join the Mercy Team which parachuted into Mukden. At Hoten prison camp, amid conditions of unbelievable filth and suffering, he found Colonel Hilsman lying on a wooden cot, staring at him blankly. To persuade his father that this was not a delirious dream, Captain Hilsman began chatting about his own experiences in Burma and mentioned that his Kachins had killed three hundred Japanese without suffering a single fatal casualty. "When Dad sat up and contradicted me," he said, "I knew he was all right."

On another mercy mission a young OSS lieutenant, John Birch, was senselessly slain by a group of Chinese Communists who blocked his way to the prison camp. Though Birch himself had no violent right-wing views, the name of this early martyr to Communism was appropriated years later by America's extremist right-wing political society.

2

Opposition to OSS by the rival service intelligence departments and the FBI had been largely contained during the war, though it was

Lieutenant General Jonathan M. Wainwright (seated, left), after rescue by OSS Mission Cardinal, August, 1945.

evident that Washington jealousies still simmered beneath the surface. Occasionally the undercurrent of hostility broke through in a deliberate bureaucratic delay or a snide newspaper comment that "for a six-month period, the travel expenses of the Office of Strategic Services, or as the Bureaucrats would say, the OSS, amounted to $328,949, an amount which would purchase 221 field ambulances." Both President Roosevelt and General Donovan were well aware that the end of the war would bring an open attack on the temporary agency; and on October 31, 1944, the President asked Donovan to give consideration to the structure of a permanent intelligence service for the postwar period. Two weeks later, on November 18, Donovan submitted a "Memorandum for the President," a duplicate of which was delivered to the Joint Chiefs of Staff. In accordance with practice, the JCS made a limited number of copies, classified top secret and stamped with their reference number, which they distributed in turn to the intelligence community.

In his covering letter, General Donovan stated that "when our enemies are defeated, the demand will be equally pressing for information that will aid us in solving the problems of peace," and proposed a long-range plan wherein intelligence control in peacetime would be returned from the Joint Chiefs of Staff to the supervision of the President. He suggested that an advisory board should be established within the new agency, including the Secretaries of State, War, Navy, and pointed out: "You will note that in this plan coordination and centralization are placed at the policy level, but operational intelligence (that pertaining primarily to departmental action) remains within the existing agencies concerned. The creation of a central authority thus would not conflict with or limit necessary intelligence functions within the Army, Navy, Department of State or other agencies."

He attached a lengthy draft directive, which provided that the organization would go under the Joint Chiefs of Staff in time of war, as was the case with OSS, and specified that the postwar agency "shall have no police or law-enforcement functions, either at home or abroad." His letter concluded: "There are common-sense reasons why you may desire to lay the keel of the ship at once. . . . We have now in the Government the trained and specialized personnel needed for the task. This talent should not be dispersed."

General Donovan was an early riser; and it was shortly after five A.M. on February 9, 1945 that he opened his morning copy of the Washington *Times-Herald* and read the front-page headlines: "Donovan Proposes Super-spy System for Postwar New Deal." The article, written by Walter Trohan and appearing simultaneously in the isolationist Chicago *Tribune* and the New York *Daily News*, began: "Creation of an all-powerful intelligence service to spy on the postwar world and to pry into the lives of citizens at home is under serious consideration by the New Deal. The Washington *Times-Herald* and the Chicago *Tribune* yesterday secured exclusively a copy of a highly confidential and secret memorandum from General Donovan to President Roosevelt, proposing to set up the super-spy agency. . . . Also obtained was a copy of an equally secret suggested draft of an order setting up the general intelligence service, which would supersede all existing Federal police and intelligence units, including Army G-2, Navy ONI, the Federal Bureau of Investigation, the Internal Revenue Agency and the Federal Communications Commission.

"Under the draft order," Trohan's article continued, "the director of the super-spy unit would have tremendous power in being charged with gathering and sifting intelligence for the White House and all Federal agencies. It is possible, under such an order, for him to determine American foreign policy by weeding out, withholding, or coloring information gathered at his direction. The spy director . . . might employ the FBI on some tasks and charge the G-men not to report to J. Edgar Hoover, their chief. . . . The unit would operate under an independent budget and presumably have secret funds for spy work along the lines of bribing and luxury living described in the novels of E. Phillips Oppenheim." The article then proceeded to quote verbatim General Donovan's top-secret memorandum and the appended draft directive, explaining carefully that the classified documents "were never officially in possession of this newspaper. They were copied by its representative on paper belonging to the Chicago *Tribune*."

Colonel Doering, executive officer of OSS, was awakened before daylight by an outraged phone call from the General. Donovan informed him of the flagrant breach of security and said, "Ole, I want you to find the source of this leak. See the Director of Naval Intelligence, the Chief of Staff G-2, and the Secretary of the Joint Chiefs of Staff, and report back to me by nine o'clock." Doering dressed hurriedly, and was waiting at the office of the DNI when the DNI arrived. While they were talking, the deputy DNI burst into the office with a copy of the morning *Times Herald* and, before he saw Doering, blurted, "Who in hell let this out?"

Promptly at nine, Doering reported to General Donovan and stated his personal belief that neither the Army nor Navy had tried to scuttle the postwar plan by slipping it to the opposition press but that the Secretary of the JCS had informed Doering that they would immediately make their own investigation. At noon that same day, word was received from the JCS that the White House had ordered the whole matter to be tabled, since it had become so politically controversial. The source of the leak was never revealed.

During the ensuing public furor over the disclosure, some newspapers rose to the defense of the proposed peacetime agency. The New York *Times* suggested that the antagonism to it was due to "competition among government services for control and direction of its operations," and political columnist Frank R. Kent openly blamed "absurd misconceptions and bureaucratic jealousies . . . which distort the facts and misrepresent the purpose"; but the reactions of some anti-New Deal Congressmen, who would seem to have scanned only the headlines, were vehement. Walter Trohan gleefully described in a subsequent article the "prompt congressional denunciation of the adoption of Gestapo, Nazi secret police, and Ogpu [sic] Russian secret police, methods in the United States," and quoted Representative Shafer of Michigan: "This is another indication that the New Deal will not halt in its quest for power. Like Simon Legree it wants to own us body and soul. . . . I'm for toleration at home and abroad." In view of the aroused opposition, President Roosevelt pulled in his horns for the time being, and advised General Donovan that he would wait out the storm and submit the proposal to Congress at a more propitious moment.

The moment never came. On April 12, 1945, while General Donovan was in Paris, he learned of the sudden death of the President from Colonel Russell Forgan. Forgan vividly recalls the deep emotional impact the news had on Donovan. For several hours thereafter, Donovan talked

with Forgan of his long and close association with the President, and
the disastrous consequences for the country he feared would result from
Roosevelt's death. This was one of the few occasions in Donovan's
career when he betrayed grief or emotion to his associates.

BOOK FOUR
1945-1959

Memo to the President

I

THE RIVERSIDE SKATING RINK on Rock Creek Park Drive, at the foot of the hill below the Washington headquarters of the Office of Strategic Services, was filled with a strangely subdued crowd that night of September 28, 1945. Although they had all belonged to the same organization, security had been so tight during the war years that many of those present met each other for the first time, and there were surprised greetings between friends: "I never knew you were in OSS." The majority of the audience was in civilian clothes, for the war was over now; some had already been separated from the service, others were remaining on duty only until the agency could be liquidated following President Truman's executive order issued after the Japanese surrender.

A table stood at the end of the polished floor, banked with flags and a military guard of honor, boots polished and rifles at parade rest. Behind the table were seated some of the leaders of the agency: Colonel Doering, now assistant director, Brigadier General John Magruder, head of intelligence, Colonel Ned Buxton, deputy director, and General Donovan. On behalf of the General's associates in OSS, Ned Buxton paid a brief tribute:

"In matters which affect our sentiments as sincerely, it is hard to find adequate expression. Let me say as simply as I can that we are very proud to have stood with the General at Armageddon. At the outbreak of global war, he was given a fantastic assignment — to create and operate a secret intelligence agency after the enemy had erected his barbed wire and contrived every conceivable scheme to make himself impregnable. The General founded the organization; he formulated the program; he devised the tactics; he penetrated the barriers. He personally attended the invasions.

"History will know and record only in part the value of that service.

"As the perilous years passed, he extemporized; he devised; he asked for the improbable and confidently achieved it. Inspired by his personality and his vision, thousands of devoted people took the uneven odds. They killed or were killed alone or in groups, in jungles, in cities, by sea or air. They organized resistance where there was no resistance. They helped it to grow where it was weak. They assaulted the enemy's mind as well as his body; they helped confuse his will and disrupt his plans.

"And with it all, the General assembled the brains to evaluate and the competence to estimate the material that flowed back from a thousand vital sources, dealing with the enemy's capabilities and intentions and morale, both military and civilian, the bottleneck targets, and the web of diplomatic intrigue. General Donovan, all of us, whatever our role, whatever our individual spot in the pattern of your unprecedented task — we esteem it a very great privilege to have served our country under your banner.

"You were a legend of gallant combat leadership in the First World War. It would seem that a very full and honorable lifetime of unique experience and training had unconsciously prepared you for your role in World War Two.

"To the director of OSS, the General, whose duties are about to terminate, we offer our salute, and hail and farewell. To Bill Donovan, the man, our friend, we say — au revoir, good luck, and God be with you."

General Donovan rose, and faltered a moment. His associates thought he looked old. The usually ruddy face was pale — he had not slept much the past week since the President's order was received — and his eyes were red-rimmed and swollen. It had not been easy to contemplate the dissolution of an organization built over four dedicated years. He straightened with a conscious effort, and began speaking in the familiar soft but firm voice which an amplifier carried to every corner of the hushed arena:

At the OSS dinner at Riverside Skating Rink, September 25, 1945. (left to right): Otto C. Doering, Jr.; John T. Magruder; WJD; and Ned Buxton.

"We have come to the end of an unusual experiment. This experiment was to determine whether a group of Americans constituting a cross-section of racial origins, of abilities, temperaments and talents, could risk an encounter with the long-established and well-trained enemy organizations.

"How well that experiment has succeeded is measured by your accomplishments and by the recognition of your achievements. You should feel deeply gratified by President Truman's expression of the purpose of basing a coordinated intelligence service upon the techniques and resources that you have initiated and developed.

"When I speak of your achievements, that does not mean we did not make mistakes. We were not afraid to make mistakes because we were not afraid to try things that had not been tried before. All of us would like to think that we could have done a better job; but all of you must know that, whatever the errors or failures, the job you did was honest and self-respecting.

"Within a few days each one of us will be going to new tasks, whether in civilian life or in government service. You can go with the assurance that you have made a beginning in showing the people of America that only by decisions of national policy based upon accurate information can we have the chance of a peace that will endure."

It must be conceded, in fairness to Harry Truman, that he had never been taken into the full confidence of President Roosevelt. Their relationship was less than full or intimate; and, deliberately or due to carelessness, he had failed to brief his Vice-President on the dangers of an intelligence gap in the dawning atomic age. Whether it would have saved Donovan's plan for a centralized and independent postwar intelligence service is questionable. Truman was a practical politician; and he saw OSS as a political liability because it gave the opposition, both extreme right and extreme left, a chance to attack the administration. The cry was on to cut the military expenditure, to disarm, to bring the boys home. Roosevelt might have refused to yield to public pressure, but Truman could not count on the same support of the American people.

General Donovan had realized, when Roosevelt died, that he faced a lonely fight to keep the United States from reverting to the state of woeful ignorance which had existed before Pearl Harbor. In a sense, he was the victim of his own wartime policy of tight security. Unlike other Washington agency heads, Donovan had held no press conferences and issued no handouts. Indeed, OSS never had a public relations office.

With the war's end, however, OSS could no longer hope to maintain absolute security with respect to its demobilized personnel. To be sure, a program had been instituted within OSS to debrief personnel. (It proved particularly useful in evaluating the accuracy of Dr. Murray's assessment methods.) This did not solve the problem of unwanted publicity, however, and Donovan, in a memo to the JCS, recommended that the Public Relations Office of the War Department undertake the task of declassification. The JCS, in reply, instructed OSS to undertake its own declassification.

Now OSS opponents seized the opportunity to charge that "Wild Bill" was indulging in vainglorious publicity. In a final attempt to salvage his proposal for a peacetime agency, the General resolved to offer his resignation from government service. He was the personal target of much of the hostility toward OSS, he felt, and was repeatedly accused of seeking to build a future power organization for his own ends. Convinced that the only way to silence his critics was to eliminate himself — a course which President Lyndon Johnson was to follow two decades later — he sent a letter on August 25 to Harold B. Smith, director of the Bureau of the Budget, in which he declared that "I wish to return to civilian life. Therefore, in considering the disposition to be made of the assets created by OSS, I speak as a private citizen concerned only with the security of his country."

It was a fatal concession. Once the General had withdrawn from the arena, there was no one of sufficient stature left to battle for his program. The Bureau of the Budget, which should never have been allowed to make basic policy decisions, threw its prestigious influence into the balance against OSS. Only General H. H. Arnold of the Army Air Forces, who like Donovan had struggled to establish the independence of his organization during the war, had the courage to stress in his final report that "it will be suicidally dangerous to depend on military attachés and casual sources of information regarding foreign states" as the nation's sole guard against "surprise weapons and surprise attacks."

The new President, inexperienced and under enormous pressure, had no time to weigh his decisions; and he had developed a habit of shooting from the hip. On September 20, 1945, without consulting Donovan or the Joint Chiefs of Staff, Truman handed down his edict terminating OSS as of October 1st. To soften the blow, he wrote Donovan thanking him for "the capable leadership you have brought to a wartime activity . . . which will not be needed in time of peace" and assured him that "the postwar intelligence services of the government are being erected on the foundation of the facilities and resources mobilized through the Office of Strategic Services."

Truman's assurances came to nothing. OSS was dismembered; its Research and Analysis branch was assigned to the State Department;[1] Secret Intelligence (SI) and Counterespionage (X-2) were absorbed by the War Department under the title of Strategic Services Unit.

Only after the integrated mechanism of OSS had been scrapped, and the majority of its trained personnel, who would have liked to continue, had drifted away in disgust, did the truth dawn on Truman that he was no longer able to obtain overseas information of the type available during World War II. As General Donovan had predicted, a critical intelligence gap had developed, leaving the United States far behind the other major powers. So urgent was the need for knowledge that in January, 1946, at far greater expense and effort than would have been necessary if Donovan's advice had been followed, Truman set up an intermediate National Intelligence Authority, made up of the Secretaries of State, War, and Navy, and the Chief of Staff to the President. Under this agency was a so-called Central Intelligence Group (CIG), headed by Rear Admiral Sidney Souers, an acquaintance of Truman's from Missouri whose intelligence background consisted of a tour as

---

[1] It was the Bureau of the Budget, prompted by Secretary of State Byrnes, which insisted on putting R&A in State, on the theory that the department did not have a research branch and needed it badly. At Secretary Byrnes's request, Dr. Langer came to State in 1946 for six months, to set up the intelligence unit, but the regional desks were not particularly interested at the time.

deputy director of ONI and who is said to have been instrumental in persuading Truman to set up the NIA and the CIG. He was to be succeeded less than six months later by Lieutenant General Hoyt Vandenberg, a capable Air Force strategist but equally lacking in intelligence experience, who in less than a year returned to the Air Force.

Weakened by these rapid changes in command, racked by endless arguments over its authority and responsibility, the stopgap CIG so deteriorated that Admiral Souers seriously considered turning its functions over to the FBI — a move which conceivably could have resulted in the very Gestapo which Donovan's critics had feared. "This country would in fact have what only such nations as Germany, Spain and Russia have heretofore boasted," Joseph and Stewart Alsop pointed out in their syndicated column, "a secret service with the responsibility for both foreign espionage and internal security, and with the power of internal arrest. . . . It was for this precise reason that the forceful J. Edgar Hoover was excluded, in the original executive order prepared by the chiefs of the State and War and Navy Departments, from any participation in the central intelligence agency."[2]

Although General Donovan had returned to his New York law practice, he continued to warn that the present U.S. intelligence system was dangerously weak. He had never recommended that OSS itself should be continued after the war — the agency had been infiltrated by too many emergency appointments who might represent a security problem, and he was equally aware that a peacetime intelligence agency must be organized and operated in a wholly different fashion. But he perceived, as few other Americans saw so clearly, the need for permanent and first-rate intelligence "in this imperfect world, as yet ruled by power and swept by passion and ambition." He wrote: "If we Americans know and are able to evaluate properly the comparative resources, production, manpower, and political outlook of a neighbor, we should be able to measure the friendship or enmity of that neighbor. If we know the true state of morale of our allies and the structure of their economies, we can plan our own security with confidence. . . . For peace-

2 Washington *Post*, April 29, 1946.

time it was urged that OSS be replaced by another central intelligence service appropriate to our position as the world's greatest power and having at its organizational fingertips all the information affecting the American position everywhere and anywhere. Instead there has emerged a makeshift intelligence service, honoring in the breach every principle learned so painfully under fire. The new National Intelligence Authority is . . . a committee, the first duty of whose members is to their respective departments. Intelligence is a full-time job. How can we expect to get an efficient service based upon such an administrative fallacy?" Again he recommended that the agency "must be independent of other departments in the government" and "the director should be a civilian appointed by the President."[3]

The solution came in June, 1947, when Congress passed the hotly debated National Security Act, probably the most far-reaching defense legislation ever enacted in peacetime. A new National Security Council was established; the feuding War and Navy Departments were brought together under a joint Department of Defense; General Hap Arnold's dream of a separate United States Air Force was realized, though after his retirement; and General Donovan had the satisfaction of seeing his proposal accepted at long last with the creation of an independent Central Intelligence Agency (CIA) on September 18, just two years after the farewell gathering of OSS at the Riverview skating rink.

The Central Intelligence Agency was the direct outgrowth of Donovan's World War II organization, and was based on fundamental OSS principles. Following the General's recommendation, the director of CIA became the coordinator of the total United States intelligence effort. The new agency was removed from military control and placed "under the direction of the National Security Council" to "correlate and evaluate intelligence relating to the national security, and provide for the appropriate dissemination." Again in line with the Donovan proposal, the act specified that the CIA would "have no police, subpoena, or law enforcement powers, or internal security functions." Thus the

[3] *Life,* September 30, 1946.

other agencies would continue to produce intelligence to satisfy their special needs, and the FBI would retain its vital and jealously guarded responsibility for detecting subversive activity within the United States; but the CIA director would be permitted to inspect all the intelligence of the other government departments, and also "perform, for the benefit of the existing intelligence agencies, such additional services of common concern as the National Security Council determines can be more efficiently accomplished centrally."

General Vandenberg had left CIG to assume the duties of vice chief of staff under General Spaatz, and later to command the newly formed U.S. Air Force; and his successor, Rear Admiral Roscoe Hillenkoetter, became the first director of the Central Intelligence Agency. In October, 1950, the Admiral moved on to a Korean combat naval assignment, and was replaced by General Walter Bedell Smith, Eisenhower's former chief of staff in Europe and later ambassador to the Soviet Union. A man of direct action and a brilliant organizer, General Smith shook the soporific CIA awake. Implementing the January, 1949, report of a joint study group established by Truman on February 13, 1948, he trimmed out much of the deadwood, changed or eliminated duplicate functions, and initiated a CIA junior officer training policy. His reforms, coming at a crucial time in CIA history, laid the groundwork for today's agency.[4]

Still the feeling persisted that the head of Central Intelligence should be a civilian. Although the Security Act provided that the director, if a military man, would be "subject to no supervision, control, restriction or prohibition" by the armed services, nevertheless it was only human nature for him to have certain allegiances and ties to his own branch of the service. If he were not at the end of his professional career, he would eventually return to active duty, and his actions while with CIA

[4] One of General Smith's first acts was to invite Dr. Langer to return to Washington and set up a national estimating branch for CIA, thus perpetuating what Dr. Langer considers one of the greatest accomplishments of R&A during the last year of the war when OSS was asked to estimate the strength of the Soviet Union, both economic and military. "This is the heart of the whole business," Bedell Smith told Langer. "If we can't give the government the very best in the way of national estimates, all the rest of our activity is of little value."

would be remembered in deciding on a promotion. The joint study group had been highly critical of the fact that most of the key positions in CIA were held by military personnel on a limited tour of duty, and there were increasing grumbles in the press. The *Atlantic Monthly* noted that there had been four heads of intelligence, all military, in the few years since the war; and Hanson Baldwin, writing in the New York *Times*, insisted that the "CIA should be headed by a civilian, not by a military or naval man as its previous directors have been. Its senior executives and office chiefs should also be largely civilian."

General Smith left CIA in January, 1953, to become Under Secretary of State in the new Eisenhower administration, and the President began casting about for a civilian replacement. All signs seemed to point to Donovan, because of his long experience and broad knowledge of the intelligence task. Intimates knew that Donovan's heart was set on the appointment, and since he was a close associate of Eisenhower — he had been one of the first to suggest that Ike should run for President — they were sure that he would be selected. A mutual friend offered to broach the matter to Eisenhower privately, in case he were not aware of Donovan's desires; but the General's pride would not allow himself to be put in the position of begging for consideration. He would prefer to sit in New York and wait.

Late in January President Eisenhower announced that Allen Dulles, brother of his Secretary of State and deputy director of CIA since 1951, was his choice for the new director. Although General Donovan was still consulted unofficially, and Allen Dulles, who called him "the father of American intelligence," could come to him at any time for advice, he never again held a position of influence in public life.

II

THE ENERGY that had driven General Donovan all his life still needed an outlet, and he was not content to assume the role of an elder statesman, excluded from the nation's councils, sidelined and inactive. His experience as head of OSS had convinced him of the real and present dangers of the Cold War; and the same voice which had alerted the country to the Nazi peril in the Thirties was raised again in the late Forties to sound what he considered an even more urgent alarm.

As a private citizen, in speeches and broadcasts and articles, he seized every opportunity to stress the need for a counteroffensive by the free world against postwar Communist aggrandizement. At a bankers' gathering in Philadelphia, at a Veterans of Strategic Services convention in Milwaukee, at the opening of a Red Cross drive in Rochester, at a Columbia alumni dinner in New York where he was awarded the Alexander Hamilton Medal for distinguished public service, he hammered home his message: That since 1945 Stalin had been waging covert aggression against the United States, that the Kremlin was infiltrating spies and operating open and undercover propaganda in the battle for men's minds. Reiterating the prophetic entry in his Siberian diary in 1919, he warned that the only way to avoid a shooting war was to take the initiative in the current subversive war.

The real strength of the Russian fifth column, he stated in a radio broadcast, "lies in its worldwide organization, highly developed techniques and communications, and rigid discipline. . . . We must integrate our own unorthodox resources as we have unified our conventional services. Economic, political and psychological countermeasures, pulled together under centralized direction, with a well-conceived strategic concept and the recruitment of the best brains and most courageous spirits," might succeed in breaking through the Iron Curtain to reach the working classes of Russia. "No dictator dares move if uncertain of his own safety at home," he concluded. "Our greatest ally therefore can be the Russian people."[5]

His concern over the Soviet threat had been growing over the past years. "I think the biggest mistake I made during the war was that I was not tougher on Communism," he confessed to an associate a year after the dissolution of OSS. The agency had worked with the Communist underground in Nazi-held Europe because the Red membership was already organized and trained in subversion and sabotage. Long before the outbreak of hostilities, many of its leaders had attended the Lenin School in Moscow, with the eventual aim of overthrowing the governments of the non-Communist nations. Donovan did not doubt that after Hitler's defeat they would revert to their original purpose; but OSS was not a policy-making organization, he stressed repeatedly, and with Russia as a co-belligerent it was his duty to cooperate in the common objective — the earliest possible defeat of the Axis.

In Yugoslavia OSS had given aid both to Tito and to Mihailovich, until ordered out of Mihailovich's territory. In Indochina the agency had delivered some material to Ho Chi Minh, in the belief that he would continue to fight the Japanese forces; but, contrary to claims made later by the French press, it was not of such nature or amount as to have made the slightest difference in the ultimate defeat of the French at Dien Bien Phu. Although OSS security checks had revealed that a number of prospective trainees, due for overseas guerrilla assignment, had previously fought as volunteers on behalf of the Spanish Loyalist cause, primarily in the Abraham Lincoln Brigade, Donovan had not felt at the time that, without other evidence of active Communist sympathy,

[5] Mutual Broadcasting Company, 1948.

and recognizing their anti-Fascist motivation, this was sufficient reason to reject them.

Donovan's practice of trying to utilize the Communist resistance had been shaken by several wartime incidents. When OSS representatives serving in Yugoslavia came into contact with the Russians in the closing months of the war, one of the Russians' first demands was that the markings on boxes of supplies for Tito, which showed that they came from the U.S., should be removed. The Soviet comment was: "We don't need you any more." OSS Major William V. Holohan, head of a team which had parachuted behind enemy lines in Italy late in 1944, was murdered because he refused to turn over OSS money to local Communists. His alleged killers were two members of his own unit, Aldo Icardi and Carl G. LoDolce; the latter confessed and then retracted his confession. They were tried in Italy, but with no results, since the allegations came only after they had been discharged from military service, and the United States disclaimed jurisdiction.

Still General Donovan sought to support in every way the national policy of improving America's relations with the Soviet Union, and in 1944 he proposed an exchange of missions between OSS and the Russian intelligence service, MVD. Some of his staff voiced misgivings that the presence of an MVD mission in the United States would enable the Russians to conduct espionage or subversive activities in this country. Donovan replied that since they were probably going to spy anyway, it would be preferable to have an official mission on which we could keep an eye and with which we could deal. With the approval of the Joint Chiefs of Staff, Donovan flew to Moscow, and, after discussing the problems involved with the American ambassador, he went to the headquarters of the dreaded MVD, a headquarters seldom visited voluntarily by an outsider.

He was admitted to a windowless room, and found himself seated at a conference table opposite a group of MVD officials. Behind them, a strong light shone directly in Donovan's face. After formal greetings were exchanged, Donovan remarked mildly: "Now, gentlemen, since we're all in the same profession, I think you can dispense with that bright light behind you. We've used it, too, but usually with suspected agents, not with equals." There was no comment, but the light was turned off at once.

General Donovan proceeded to state his proposal, and a detailed discussion ensued regarding the exchange of missions: the number of personnel, their categories and functions, even the transfer of such devices as plastic explosives and other special weapons developed by OSS, about which Donovan was certain the Russians already had full knowledge. Donovan left Moscow with every indication that the proposed exchange would be acceptable to the Soviets, and returned to Washington to set up the mission. The personnel had their travel orders cut and were about to leave when word came from the JCS that the White House had ordered the project canceled.

It was not until Stalin broke the promises he made at Yalta by annexing Poland, and opened a savage political offensive against the West, that Donovan became convinced that the Communist drive for world domination foredoomed a lasting peace. He read with dismay the agreement at Potsdam which divided up the city of Berlin, and perceived that in their effort to appease Russia the Allies had neglected to provide a neutral zone of a hundred miles around the city, as R&A had recommended — an oversight which resulted in one of the main sources of Cold War tension.

"Only now in America and in Europe are we awakening to the hard fact that the Stalin challenge to our world is indistinguishable from the Hitler challenge — except that the Stalin attack is more thorough and more ruthless," he wrote in 1948 after the Soviet seizure of Czechoslovakia.[6] "For a long period our political and military leaders were susceptible to the suggestion that Stalin was becoming more cooperative and that all would be well if we were patient and understanding. In our desire to get along with the Soviet Union, and in our almost abject effort to placate her, we yielded on terms and accepted conditions in which we did not believe. . . . Today Communist deeds as well as words testify that they still insist upon violent struggle as Marx and Engels did a century ago.

[6] William J. Donovan, "Stop Russia's Subversive War," *Atlantic Monthly*, May, 1948.

"We are against an enemy who is in this for keeps," he continued. "We can expect no mercy, we can expect no rules. . . . Each day hundreds of Soviet radio transmitters, the guns of the psychological war front, aim into every part of the world a salvo of doubt and suspicion and hostility against the United States. In his speech at Chicago, Secretary of State Marshall called this 'a calculated campaign of vilification and distortion of American motives in foreign affairs.' . . . Steadily and ever faster the Soviet subversive war has eaten into our strength in Southeastern Europe, the Middle East, China, and Korea, wherever our interests have been in conflict with those of Russia. Our bastion of Western Europe is being disintegrated by an invasion which we have up to this moment let go by default. A study of the tactics employed in Rumania, Bulgaria, Poland, Albania, Yugoslavia, Hungary, and Czechoslovakia is like a study of a battlefield. . . . Our real danger lies in the fact that if we permit Russia to outmaneuver us, to seize bases important to us, to penetrate our inner defense under a strategy of disunity, the day may come when, if we should feel it necessary to fight, we should not be able to get on our feet to do so."

He added a further warning. Russia "has the biggest stockpile of information of any nation in the world," he told a New York *Times* interviewer, "but they lack a strong evaluating machine because they have not an adequate number of informed persons in their country who understand other countries." Ignorance of the true motives of the United States, he pointed out, had resulted in the suspicion and intrigue which could lead to open war.

Although Donovan no longer had any official status, he continued to travel abroad in his latter years to keep abreast of political developments on the Continent. As chairman of the American Committee for a United Europe, he worked closely with Paul Henri Spaak, Prime Minister of Belgium, who described Donovan as "one of the most faithful defenders and one of the most strenuous pioneers" in the effort to build a consolidated organization of free nations against the mounting pressure of Communism. He was an early advocate of the Marshall Plan, though he warned that it should not be regarded as "a kind of economic Maginot Line which is automatic in its resistance and its effectiveness." After it was revealed that Soviet spies had secured the atomic secrets, he told intimates: "There isn't going to be any shooting war for a long time, because the Reds are winning what they want without shooting. . . . The newest weapons are falling before the oldest one of them all — subversion. It is time to stop wondering if we will win the next war and find out why we are losing the one we're in."

They were frustrating years. His warnings failed to stir the public, his speeches and articles were played down by the press as the individual opinions of a private citizen. Once he had had direct access to the President; now his audience might be a Junior Chamber of Commerce meeting or a Women's Republican Club luncheon. General Donovan realized that he needed an official rostrum from which to convey his views to all the American people. Although he had never been successful in seeking an elective office, he agreed readily when New York Republican leaders asked permission to propose him as candidate for United States senator during Governor Thomas E. Dewey's campaign for reelection in 1950. His name was never submitted to the convention. *Newsday* quoted "party bigwigs" as stating that Dewey personally had blocked the nomination because he "resented such a strong personality as Donovan in his political family, and was definitely afraid that Donovan might overshadow him."

Whatever the reason, it was the General's last fling at politics. He was called on only once more, in the early 1950's, for a brief and final appearance on the national scene.

2

Events in Southeast Asia had taken an ugly turn by 1952. Communist expansion, pushing southward after the collapse of Free China, posed a definite threat to Thailand. Former Regent Luang Pradit, who had worked so closely with OSS during the Japanese occupation, had gone to Red China where he was reportedly making plans for a Communist upheaval in his own country to put himself back in power. Thousands of Red Chinese trained guerrillas were already being slipped across the Thai border.

WJD on vacation in Bermuda, 1949.

General Donovan had maintained an active interest in Far East problems. As early as 1950, on his return from a seven-week business trip to China and Southeast Asia, he urged that America should assert its leadership in that vital area, containing a quarter of the earth's population, and buttress Indochina as the key to Malaysia and Thailand. "Russia's timetable of conquest has been stepped up in an endeavor to take full advantage of the momentum from her speedy victories in China," he told reporters when his ship docked. "Non-Communist Asiatics want to be on our side, but only if we're safe to be with — if we can be relied upon to stick with them when the going gets bad."[7]

On May 15, 1953, while the General was on a visit to Norway, he received a cablegram from General Walter Bedell Smith, Under Secretary of State: "Extremely urgent return immediately (repeat immediately) for conference Washington." Two days later he reported to the State Department, and Smith confided that there was "a tough dirty job" to be done, and stated: "I am authorized by the President to offer you the Ambassadorship of Siam."

Donovan accepted. On May 19 he wrote Smith, expressing his gratitude at being "entrusted with so important a mission in these critical days," and explained: "From the enemy's point of view, the problem involves a single geographic unit — including Burma, Thailand, Indonesia, French Indochina, Hong Kong, the Philippines, Formosa. Within this frame, the tight organization of local Communists permits the enemy to coordinate and operate through a unified command. From our point of view, the geographic unit is broken up into several centers of political power with varying capacities and speeds of reaction, further divided by a feeling of competition with one another. The situation, therefore, has to be commanded, not negotiated, into unity. . . . At least for the moment, the initiative is with the enemy. Response to that challenge will require 'irregular' improvisation."

In a subsequent letter to President Eisenhower on June 3, Donovan reported that he and Smith had discussed "the means to be taken in doing the job. Bedell suggested that I put on paper what I thought

[7] New York *Times*, February 19, 1950.

would be constructive and necessary. In substance I said [that] I assume the President will issue a Directive which would include:

"In case of necessity, the resumption of (my) military in addition to diplomatic status.
"The designation by me of a staff of at least twelve members.
"The right to travel to such areas as in my discretion seem necessary and proper in the accomplishment of that task assigned to me.

"I then further suggested that if the President wished, he could by Executive Order and without confirmation by the Senate designate me a 'Personal Representative of the President of the United States.' "

Donovan had hoped that as personal representative he could work to coordinate the countries in the geographic unit favorable to the United States, and he realized that this would be impossible if he bore the title of ambassador; but Eisenhower tactfully turned down his suggestion and replied to Donovan on June 9: "When Foster [Secretary of State Dulles] and I were considering the difficult situation in Southeast Asia and particularly its possible intensification as the result of events in Korea, we agreed that Thailand was a key point which might be made a bastion of resistance. One of the immediate desirable moves . . . was to send as Ambassador to Thailand a man with particular experience, knowledge and background who, while serving as chief of the diplomatic mission, would also quietly coordinate the existing means for psychological and economic operations, increase their effectiveness, and possibly prepare them for broader use. You are the man best qualified to do this. However, I want you to do it in the capacity of an Ambassador, under the direction of the Secretary of State, and within the State Department channels of control. I have strongly affirmed the responsibility of the Secretary of State in the field of foreign policy, and want to maintain his position there."

The new ambassador received an affectionate welcome from the Thais, who remembered Donovan as one of their best friends in the West, and he threw himself into his task with the same unsparing drive he had shown during the war. Despite the enervating climate, he traveled everywhere in Thailand, talking with Buddhist leaders, with schoolmasters, with politicians, with farmers and fishermen. He made several arduous trips to Burma and Indochina and India. Through local radio facilities he broadcast speeches by the President, he informed Eisenhower, "to make clear to the people that you are aiming at peace, and in further support of that aim we are undertaking a drive on public health throughout the entire country."

He was seventy-one, and his ceaseless activity in the monsoon heat was beginning to tell on him. When I saw him at the Embassy in Bangkok in 1954, he seemed to me thin and drawn. The temperature was well over a hundred that day, but he had chartered a plane to fly his hard-working Embassy staff to the Angkor Wat in Cambodia, and he insisted on accompanying them, though he was too exhausted to explore the fabled ruins. He had agreed to serve as ambassador for twelve months; and as the end of his year approached, he wrote President Eisenhower tendering his resignation. He sent the letter to be delivered to the White House by a mutual friend, Marcellus Dodge, and asked him to explain confidentially to the President "why I cannot accept an additional period of service in my present capacity." It was more than health which forced him to terminate his tour of duty. "You may, if you think it necessary," he added to Dodge, "show him my financial status which clearly indicates the compelling reasons necessitating my return to private practice."

President Eisenhower accepted his resignation with "extreme reluctance, for I am aware of the drive, energy and devotion which has characterized your service. Your accomplishments on this assignment reflect a broad comprehension of the complex factors so influential in the molding of our policy toward the free nations of Southeast Asia."

Donovan returned to America late in 1954, exhausted from his mission, but he could not relax. At the request of the American Bar Association, he took on the chairmanship of a special committee to study the administration of criminal justice. When Hungary rebelled against Soviet domination, he flew to Europe to work with the Hungarian refugees, and organized a campaign to raise a million dollars for relief. He refused to spare himself, and the signs of weariness were becoming more apparent. Personal tragedies added to his burden. One of his grandchildren died of accidental poisoning, and his son's wife, whom he adored, succumbed in 1955 to an incurable illness.

The indefatigable spirit was plainly flagging. In 1956 he suffered a slight stroke, though his rugged constitution seemed to weather the blow at first. For weeks he did not mention the attack, and appeared at his Wall Street law office daily; but associates could see that his once incisive mind was clouded, and he was so feeble and uncertain of step that he had to take a partner's arm when they walked to lunch. At last he bowed to the inevitable, and secluded himself in his apartment on Sutton Place.

In the spring of 1957, following another stroke, his law partner George Leisure informed President Eisenhower that the General was not expected to live much longer. On April 2 the President awarded him the National Security Medal, America's highest civilian honor, with the signed citation:

> Through his foresight, wisdom, and experience, he foresaw, during the course of World War II, the problems which would face the postwar world and the urgent need for a permanent, centralized intelligence function. Thus his wartime work contributed to the establishment of the Central Intelligence Agency and a coordinated national intelligence structure. Since the creation of the Agency, he has given to it generously of his experience. . . . In 1953 and 1954, as Ambassador of the United States to Thailand, he served in this important diplomatic post with the same tireless energy and skill he had shown in his wartime service. Both in public and in private life he has made outstanding contributions to the security and defense of his country.
>
> — DWIGHT D. EISENHOWER.

On the same day that the National Security Medal was presented, I went with Otto C. Doering to the Sutton Place apartment to congratulate General Donovan. He was lying in bed, the medal pinned to his pajama top. "General," Doering reminded him, "do you realize you are the first American to receive all of the nation's top honors?" Donovan turned his head away. "Oh no, Ole, please," he protested.

3

During my visit to Donovan's apartment that afternoon in 1957 — it was the last time I saw him — I realized how little I knew, how little anyone really knew, of the General. Even now as I approach the end of this biography, after reading all his personal diaries and letters and interviewing his family and closest associates, I still wonder what the qualities were which made him unique.

Today the revisionist public is tired of heroes, the military heroes who win wars or the political heroes who lose them. Donovan was another kind of hero. His courage in combat during the First World War was a legend, but he had no love of battle. He participated in most of the landings during the Second World War, he exposed himself heedlessly, because he felt a recurrent need to take risks in order to justify asking others to do the same. "It isn't how brave you were yesterday," he told me once in a moment of revealing frankness, "it's how brave you are today." His coolness under fire — not only in war but in government service — was the result of stern self-discipline. Caught between the attacks of the extreme right and the extreme left, he forced himself to remain objective and calm.

Though Donovan craved success, he refused to achieve it by courting favor. Some scrupulous sense of dignity balked at using Irish blandishment or what he called "genuflecting" — he said the word with scorn — in order to ingratiate himself with his wartime superiors. He never was on intimate social terms with the President or the Chiefs of Staff, and no personal note was permitted to creep into his official correspondence; in every letter I have read, he states his case factually, even bluntly, and avoids unctuous phrases to gain his point. That same reluctance to indulge in campaign oratory or glittering campaign promises was his political undoing. Because of his unwillingness to compromise with the voters, he never won an elective office.

All his life Donovan was driven by a vast inner restlessness, but through his rigid control of himself he was able to channel his energy to positive and patriotic ends. He was at his best under stress. He worked relentlessly, and he expected the same of his subordinates. If one of them proved unable to carry out a task, Donovan never blamed him; he simply changed the man's assignment, and found someone else for the job. His staff could rely on him for support, provided they had done their best, and he was not dismayed by setbacks. "If we're wrong, the sooner we find it out the better," he would say. "If we're right, we'll prevail."

His forceful nature was balanced by a quick and intuitive understanding. During occasional weekend visits to his 500-acre Chapel Hill Farm in Berryville, Virginia, he would enjoy the company of his five grandchildren. David's youngest daughter, four years old, was the butt of persistent teasing by her older brothers and sisters, who told her that the bear rug in the living room was alive and would eat her. She lived in mortal terror of the rug until her grandfather took her on his knee one afternoon and explained how he had shot the bear himself on a hunting trip in Canada, and had brought home the hide to make a soft rug for her to walk on. Now he was giving the bearskin to her for her very own, he said, and she could decide whether her brothers and sisters would be allowed to step on it.

The very qualities which made him a leader also served to set him apart. It is significant that Donovan had no cronies, no bosom companions. The fact that he surrounded himself with people, that he seemed to enjoy the confusion and conflict of opinions, might indicate a natural gregariousness; but it might as easily have been a compensation for his essential loneliness. He was always a little withdrawn, amiable but somehow aloof, dwelling in an austere and humorless world of his own. He denied himself the ordinary pleasures, he did not smoke or drink, he played squash not for the sport but to keep himself in physical condition. The hunting trip to Canada was one of the few vacations that associates ever knew him to take.

His sole relaxation lay in reading, constantly seeking new challenges and new concepts. His intellectual curiosity was insatiable. One Sunday morning during the war, he picked up Dr. Langer on his way to OSS headquarters, and during their conversation in the car Langer remarked that a topic under discussion had been mentioned back in Greek times by Thucydides. The General asked eagerly: "You don't happen to have a copy with you, do you?" Dr. Langer explained that he seldom carried Thucydides around. "Then let's buy one," he persisted. Langer reminded him that the Washington bookstores were closed on Sunday. "Well, maybe it's in paperback," Donovan said, and for the next hour they drove from one drugstore to another in vain search for a paperback edition of Thucydides.

He had neither arrogance of power nor of intellect. Some opponents claimed his unpretentiousness was an affectation, but the humility was genuine; I was convinced of that when I saw his honest distress at being congratulated on the National Security Medal. After his death Allen Dulles called him "one of the great men of our time," and I could almost hear Donovan's voice protesting: "Oh no, Allen, please." In a speech accepting the annual William J. Donovan Award at a Veterans of Strategic Services ceremony in 1966, Admiral Louis Mountbatten stated: "This man wasn't just a great American, he was a great international citizen, a man of enormous courage, leadership, vision . . . and I doubt whether any one person contributed more to the ultimate victory of the Allies than Bill Donovan."[8]

Perhaps it is still too early to assess his place in history. But I think what General Donovan would like most to have history say of him is this: that he believed in his country, that he was willing to die for it, that he sought to achieve for it the best he could in a lifetime of disciplined and imaginative and unflagging effort.

Donovan's strength had been failing steadily after his second stroke, and in 1958, at the personal intervention of President Eisenhower, he was moved from New York to Walter Reed General Army Hospital in Washington. There he lingered for almost a year. Some days his mind would be as keen as ever, other days it would blank out and he would lie staring dully at the ceiling. A few weeks before his death on February 8, 1959, he was invited by Larry Houston, his former associate in OSS and

[8] See Appendix, page 345.

now general counsel for the Central Intelligence Agency, to view the full-length oil painting of himself which had just been hung in CIA's main corridor.

Donovan was helped into civilian clothes, and they drove in silence to the agency headquarters in Virginia. He made his way feebly on Houston's arm to the room in which the portrait was hung and halted before it.

The empty eyes came into focus on the erect figure in Army uniform, the twin stars of rank on each shoulder, the banks of bright ribbons with the blue Medal of Honor at the top. This was the Donovan who had commanded his troops in battle at St.-Mihiel and the Argonne Forest, who had led OSS through the Second World War, who had served his country above and beyond the call of duty. The bowed head came up, the jaw hardened, the sagging body stiffened to attention. Straight as a soldier, the General about-faced and strode down the corridor and through the foyer, and climbed without help into the car.

His eyes were fixed ahead as they drove to Walter Reed, and he asked Houston for a pad and pencil. He began: "Memo to the President . . ." and then his writing trailed and the pencil dropped from his limp fingers. The eyes were empty again. He had left the living past, and was back in the unreal present.

APPENDICES

A. Executive Order Designating a Coordinator of Information, July 11, 1941.

By virtue of the authority vested in me as President of the United States and as Commander in Chief of the Army and Navy of the United States, it is ordered as follows:

1. There is hereby established the position of Coordinator of Information, with authority to collect and analyze all information and data, which may bear upon national security; to correlate such information and data, and to make such information and data available to the President and to such departments and officials of the Government as the President may determine; and to carry out, when requested by the President, such supplementary activities as may facilitate the securing of information important for national security not now available to the Government.

2. The several departments and agencies of the Government shall make available to the Coordinator of Information all and any such information and data relating to national security as the Coordinator, with the approval of the President, may from time to time request.

3. The Coordinator of Information may appoint such committees, consisting of appropriate representatives of the various departments and agencies of the Government, as he may deem necessary to assist him in the performance of his functions.

4. Nothing in the duties and responsibilities of the Coordinator of Information shall in any way interfere with or impair the duties and responsibilities of the regular military and naval advisers of the President as Commander-in-Chief of the Army and Navy.

5. Within the limits of such funds as may be allocated to the Coordinator

of Information by the President, the Coordinator may employ necessary personnel and make provision for the necessary supplies, facilities and services.

6. William J. Donovan is hereby designated as Coordinator of Information.

Franklin D. Roosevelt

THE WHITE HOUSE

B. *Military Order Establishing the Office of Strategic Services, June 13, 1942.*

By virtue of the authority vested in me as President of the United States and as Commander-in-Chief of the Army and Navy of the United States, it is ordered as follows:

1) The Office of the Coordinator of Information, established by order of July 11, 1941, exclusive of the Foreign Information activities transferred to the Office of War Information by executive order of June 13, 1942 shall hereafter be known as the Office of Strategic Services, and is hereby transferred to the jurisdiction of the United States Joint Chiefs of Staff.

2) The Office of Strategic Services shall perform the following missions:

a) Collect and analyze such strategic information as may be required by the United States Joint Chiefs of Staff:

b) Plan and operate such special services as may be directed by the United States Joint Chiefs of Staff.

3) At the head of the Office of Strategic Services shall be a director of Strategic Services who shall be appointed by the President and who shall perform his duties under the direction and supervision of the Joint Chiefs of Staff.

4) William J. Donovan is hereby appointed as Director of Strategic Services.

5) The Order of July 11, 1941 is hereby revoked.

Franklin D. Roosevelt
Commander-in-Chief

THE WHITE HOUSE
June 13, 1942

C. *Organization of the Office of Strategic Services*

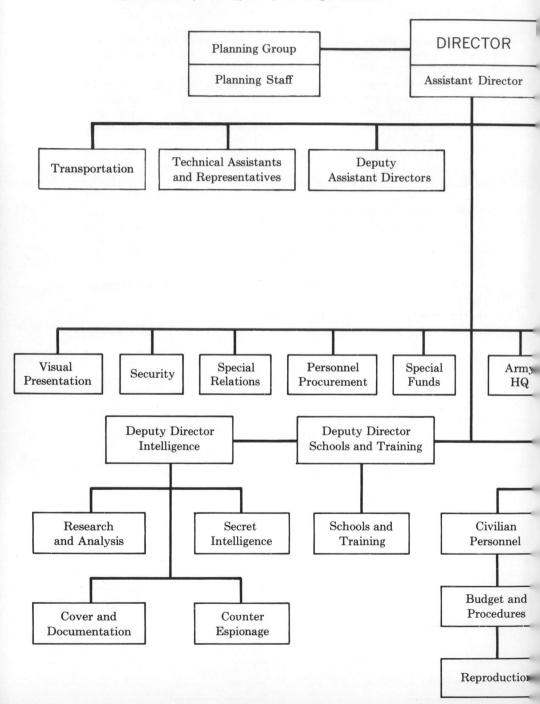

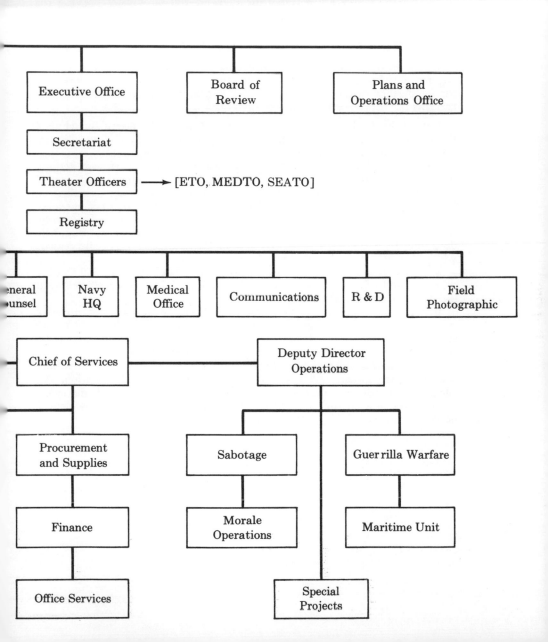

Executive Office

Board of Review

Plans and Operations Office

Secretariat

Theater Officers → [ETO, MEDTO, SEATO]

Registry

General Counsel

Navy HQ

Medical Office

Communications

R & D

Field Photographic

Chief of Services

Deputy Director Operations

Procurement and Supplies

Sabotage

Guerrilla Warfare

Finance

Morale Operations

Maritime Unit

Office Services

Special Projects

D. *Donovan's Memorandum for the President, November 18, 1944.*

Pursuant to your note of 31 October 1944 I have given consideration to the organization of an intelligence service for the post-war period.

In the early days of the war, when the demands upon intelligence services were mainly in and for military operations, the OSS was placed under the direction of the JCS.

Once our enemies are defeated the demand will be equally pressing for information that will aid us in solving the problems of peace.

This will require two things:

1. That intelligence control be returned to the supervision of the President.

2. The establishment of a central authority reporting directly to you, with responsibility to frame intelligence objectives and to collect and coordinate the intelligence material required by the Executive Branch in planning and carrying out national policy and strategy.

I attach in the form of a draft directive (Tab A) the means by which I think this could be realized without difficulty or loss of time. You will note that coordination and centralization are placed at the policy level but operational intelligence (that pertaining primarily to Department action) remains within the existing agencies concerned. The creation of a central authority thus would not conflict with or limit necessary intelligence functions within the Army, Navy, Department of State and other agencies.

In accordance with your wish, this is set up as a permanent long-range plan. But you may want to consider whether this (or part of it) should be done now, by executive or legislative action. There are common-sense reasons why you may desire to lay the keel of the ship at once.

The immediate revision and coordination of our present intelligence system would effect substantial economies and aid in the more efficient and speedy termination of the war.

Information important to the national defense, being gathered now by certain Departments and agencies, is not being used to full advantage in the war. Coordination at the strategy level would prevent waste, and avoid the present confusion that leads to waste and unnecessary duplication.

Though in the midst of war, we are also in a period of transition which, before we are aware, will take us into the tumult of rehabilitation. An adequate and orderly intelligence system will contribute to informed decisions.

We have now in the Government the trained and specialized personnel needed for the task. This talent should not be dispersed.

William J. Donovan
DIRECTOR

TAB A

Substantive Authority Necessary
in Establishment of a
Central Intelligence Service

In order to coordinate and centralize the policies and actions of the Government relating to intelligence:

1. There is established in the Executive Office of the President a central intelligence service, to be known as the _____, at the head of which shall be a Director appointed by the President. The Director shall discharge and perform his functions and duties under the direction and supervision of the President. Subject to the approval of the President, the Director may exercise his powers, authorities and duties through such officials or agencies and in such manner as he may determine.

2. There is established in the _____ an Advisory Board consisting of the Secretary of State, the Secretary of War, the Secretary of the Navy, and such other members as the President may subsequently appoint. The Board shall advise and assist the Director with respect to the formulation of basic policies and plans of the _____.

3. Subject to the direction and control of the President, and with any necessary advice and assistance from the other Departments and agencies of the Government, the _____ shall perform the following functions and duties:

(a) Coordination of the functions of all intelligence agencies of the Government, and the establishment of such policies and objectives as will assure the integration of national intelligence efforts;

(b) Collection either directly or through existing Government Departments and agencies, of pertinent information, including military, economic, political and scientific, concerning the capabilities, intentions and activities of foreign nations, with particular reference to the effect such matters may have upon the national security, policies and interests of the United States;

(c) Final evaluation, synthesis and dissemination within the Government of the intelligence required to enable the Government to determine policies with respect to national planning and security in peace and war, and the advancement of broad national policy;

(d) Procurement, training and supervision of its intelligence personnel;

(e) Subversive operations abroad;

(f) Determination of policies for and coordination of facilities essential to the collection of information under subparagraph "(b)" hereof; and

(g) Such other functions and duties relating to intelligence as the President from time to time may direct.

4. The _____ shall have no police or law-enforcement functions, either at home or abroad.

5. Subject to Paragraph 3 hereof, existing intelligence agencies within the Government shall collect, evaluate, synthesize and disseminate departmental operating intelligence, herein defined as intelligence required by such agencies in the actual performance of their functions and duties.

6. The Director shall be authorized to call upon Departments and agencies of the Government to furnish appropriate specialists for such supervisory and functional positions within the _____ as may be required.

7. All Government Departments and agencies shall make available to the Director such intelligence material as the Director, with the approval of the President, from time to time may request.

8. The _____ shall operate under an independent budget.

9. In time of war or unlimited national emergency, all programs of the _____ in areas of actual or projected military operations shall be co-ordinated with military plans and shall be subject to the approval of the Joint Chiefs of Staff. Parts of such programs which are to be executed in a theater of military operations shall be subject to the control of the Theater Commander.

10. Within the limits of such funds as may be made available to the _____, the Director may employ necessary personnel and make provision for necessary supplies, facilities and services. The Director shall be assigned, upon the approval of the President, such military and naval personnel as may be required in the performance of the functions and duties of the _____. The Director may provide for the internal organization and management of the _____ in such manner as he may determine.

E. *President Truman Disperses the Office of Strategic Services, September 20, 1945.*

My dear General Donovan:

I appreciate very much the work which you and your staff undertook, beginning prior to the Japanese surrender, to liquidate those wartime activities of the Office of Strategic Services which will not be needed in time of peace.

Timely steps should also be taken to conserve those resources and skills developed within your organization which are vital to our peacetime purposes.

Accordingly, I have today directed, by Executive order, that the activities of the Research and Analysis Branch and the Presentation Branch of the Office of Strategic Services be transferred to the State Department. This transfer, which is effective as of October 1, 1945, represents the beginning of the development of a coordinated system of foreign intelligence within the permanent framework of the Government.

Consistent with the foregoing, the Executive order provides for the transfer of the remaining activities of the Office of Strategic Services to the War Department; for the abolition of the Office of Strategic Services; and for the continued orderly liquidation of some of the activities of the Office without interrupting other services of a military nature the need for which will continue for some time.

I want to take this occasion to thank you for the capable leadership you have brought to a vital wartime activity in your capacity as Director of Strategic Services. You may well find satisfaction in the achievements of the Office and take pride in your own contribution to them. These are in themselves large rewards. Great additional reward for your efforts should lie in the knowledge that the peacetime intelligence services of the Government are being erected on the foundation of the facilities and resources mobilized through the Office of Strategic Services during the war.

Sincerely yours,

Harry S. Truman

F. *Remarks of Major General William J. Donovan, U.S.A., Director of Strategic Services, at the Final Gathering of OSS employees, September 28, 1945.*

Men and Women of OSS:

We have come to the end of an unusual experiment. This experiment was to determine whether a group of Americans constituting a cross section of racial origins, of abilities, temperaments and talents could meet and risk an encounter with the long-established and well-trained enemy organizations.

How well that experiment has succeeded is measured by your accomplishments and by the recognition of your achievements. You should feel deeply gratified by President Truman's expression of the purpose of basing a coordinated intelligence service upon the techniques and resources that you have initiated and developed.

This could not have been done if you had not been willing to fuse yourselves into a team — a team that was made up not only of scholars and research experts and of the active units in operations and intelligence who engaged the enemy in direct encounter, but also of the great numbers of our organization who drove our motor vehicles, carried our mail, kept our records and documents and performed those other innumerable duties of administrative services without which no organization can succeed and which, because well done with us, made our activities that much more effective.

When I speak of your achievements that does not mean we did not make mistakes. We were not afraid to make mistakes because we were not afraid to try things that had not been tried before. All of us would like to think that we could have done a better job, but all of you must know that, whatever the errors or failures, you have done an honest and self-respecting job. But more than that, because there existed in this organization a sense of solidarity, you must also have the conviction that this agency, in which each of you played a part, was an effective force.

Within a few days each one of us will be going to new tasks whether in civilian life or in governmental work. You can go with the assurance that you have made a beginning in showing the people of America that only by decisions of national policy based upon accurate information can we have the chance of a peace that will endure.

G. *Donovan's Decorations and Awards*

DEPARTMENT OF THE ARMY
Office of the Adjutant General
Washington, D.C.

The records show that Major General William J. Donovan, o 102 383, USAR (Hon-Res) is entitled to the following decorations and awards:

Decorations

Medal of Honor per War Department General Orders Number 56, dated 30 December 1922. Presented 8:30 P.M., 18 January 1923, at the 69th Regiment Armory, New York City by Major General Robert L. Bullard, USA.

Distinguished Service Cross per War Department General Orders Number 99, dated 1 November 1918 for an act of heroism performed on 28–31 July 1918 and presented 7 September 1918

Distinguished Service Medal per War Department General Orders Number 43, dated 23 October 1922. Presented 9 December 1922 at Buffalo, New York, by B. R. Wade, Lieutenant Colonel 28th Infantry, Commanding

Distinguished Service Medal (First Oak Leaf Cluster) per War Department General Orders Number 9, dated 25 January 1946

Purple Heart with one bronze oak leaf cluster for wounds received in action on 29 July 1918 and 15 October 1918

National Security Medal, awarded by President Eisenhower, presented in New York City, 2 April 1957

Service Medals

Mexican Border Service Medal
World War I Victory Medal with five battle clasps
Army of Occupation of Germany Medal
American Defense Service Medal
American Campaign Medal
Asiatic–Pacific Campaign Medal with arrowhead and two bronze service stars for participation in the Central Burma and China Offensive campaigns
European–African Middle Eastern Campaign Medal with arrowhead and two silver service stars (in lieu of ten bronze service stars) for participation in the Rome-Arno; Central Europe; Ardennes-Alsace; Normandy; Rhineland; Northern France; Southern France; Algiers-French; Morocco; Sicily and Anzio.
World War II Victory Medal
Armed Forces Reserve Medal with one ten year device

Unit Award

Distinguished Unit Emblem with one bronze oak leaf cluster

Foreign Decorations

CHINA: Special Collar Order of Yun Hui

FRANCE: Légion d'Honneur, grade de Commandeur
  Croix de Guerre with Palm
  Croix de Guerre with Silver Star

CZECHOSLOVAKIA: War Cross 1939

NETHERLANDS: Order of Orange Nassau with Swords, degree of Grand Officer

BELGIUM: Grand Officer of the Order of Leopold with Palm
  Croix de Guerre 1940 with Palm

ITALY: Order of the Crown, Cavalier of Grand Cross
  War Cross

GREAT BRITAIN: Order of the British Empire, Knight Commander

NORWAY: Royal Order of Saint Olav, Commander Cross with Star

BIBLIOGRAPHY

In addition to the material in General Donovan's files, the following works have proved useful in providing further information:

Primary Sources

Blum, John M., Bruce Catton, Edmund S. Morgan, Arthur M. Schlesinger, Jr., Kenneth M. Stampp, C. Vann Woodward. *The National Experience.* New York, 1963.

Donovan, William J., and Edgar Ansel Mowrer. *Fifth Column Lessons for America.* American Council on Public Affairs, Washington, D.C., 1941.

Duffy, Francis P. *Father Duffy's Story.* New York, 1919.

Dulles, Allen. *Secret Surrender.* New York, 1966.

———. *The Craft of Intelligence.* New York, 1963.

Howe, DeWolfe. *Oliver Ames, Jr., 1895–1918.* Boston (privately printed), 1922.

Hyde, H. Montgomery. *Room 3603.* New York, 1963.

Kent, Sherman. *Strategic Intelligence.* Princeton, N.J., 1949.

Langer, William L., and Everett Gleason. *The Undeclared War.* New York, 1953.

OSS Assessment Staff. *Assessment of Men.* New York, 1948.

Peers, William R., and Dean Brelis. *Behind the Burma Road.* Boston, 1963.

Pogue, Forrest C. *George C. Marshall,* Vol. II. New York, 1965.

Roosevelt, Elliott (ed.). *The Roosevelt Letters.* New York, 1950.

Sherwood, Robert E. *The White House Papers of Harry Hopkins.* New York, 1948.

Smith, Nicol, and Blake Clark. *Into Siam.* New York, 1945.

Tompkins, Peter. *A Spy in Rome.* New York, 1962.

Wedemeyer, Albert C. *Wedemeyer Reports!* New York, 1958.

Wilson, Hugh R. *Diplomat Between Wars.* New York, 1941.

Added Sources Consulted

Alcorn, Robert. *No Bugles for Spies*. New York, 1962.
Alsop, Stewart, and Thomas Braden. *Sub Rosa*. New York, 1946.
Farago, Ladislas. *Burn After Reading*. New York, 1961.
————. *Secret Missions*. New York, 1946.
Foot, M. R. D. *SOE in France*. London, 1946.
Kirkpatrick, Lyman B., Jr. *The Real CIA*. New York, 1968.
Legendre, Gertrude S. *The Sands Ceased to Run*. New York, 1947.
Liston, Robert. *Spies and Spying*. New York, 1967.
Lovell, Stanley P. *Of Spies and Stratagems*. Englewood, N.J., 1963.
McLachlan, Donald. *Room 39*. New York, 1968.
Miles, Milton E. *A Different Kind of War*. New York, 1967.
Montagu, Ewen. *The Man Who Never Was*. Philadelphia and New York, 1954.
Moss, W. Stanley. *Ill Met by Moonlight*. New York, 1950.
Oblensky, Serge. *One Man in His Time*. New York, 1958.
Wighton, Charles, and Gunter Peis. *Hitler's Spies and Saboteurs*. New York, 1958.
Wilhelm, Maria. *The Fighting Irishman*. New York, 1964.
Willoughby, Charles A. *Shanghai Conspiracy—The Sorge Spy Ring*. New York, 1952.
Zacharias, Ellis M. *Behind Closed Doors*. New York, 1950.
————. *Secret Missions*. New York, 1946.

ACKNOWLEDGMENTS

THIS BIOGRAPHY of General Donovan, and the story of the Office of Strategic Services which he conceived and led in World War II, is based in large part on the General's unusually comprehensive files and personal diaries and letters, most of which are made public here for the first time. For her confidence in entrusting me with these hitherto private papers, and giving me complete freedom to prepare the General's life story without any restriction or veto, I am deeply grateful to Mrs. Ruth Donovan; and I should like to take this opportunity to acknowledge my added indebtedness to Mrs. Donovan and her family, and to the Reverend Vincent Donovan, for supplying me with many intimate recollections and anecdotes.

My particular thanks also to O. C. Doering, Jr., law partner of General Donovan for a quarter century and successively general counsel for OSS, chief of its Secretariat, and executive officer, who gave so generously of his time to amplify and improve my manuscript as it progressed, to contribute recollections out of his own firsthand experience, and to set down authentic details of the agency's organization and operation, which I have quoted extensively in this book.

To Dr. William L. Langer, Coolidge professor of history at Harvard University, former head of the Research and Analysis Branch of OSS and until recently a member of the President's Foreign Intelligence Advisory Board, who read the first draft of my manuscript and offered invaluable corrections and suggestions.

To Lord Mountbatten of Burma, a close personal friend of Donovan's, who, as one of the four members of the British Chief of Staff's Committee, so greatly helped Donovan in the early stages of the formation and operation of OSS, and who, as Supreme Allied Commander, South East Asia, accepted and gave full support to OSS activities in that area. While assuming no responsibility for the content of this book, Lord Mountbatten has generously set the record straight on a number of important issues.

To William J. Casey, former Chief of Special Intelligence, OSS/ETO; to

Albert E. Jolis, SI branch OSS/ETO, who served with Casey in organizing the infiltration of SI agents into France and Germany; and to J. Russell Forgan, Deputy Chief and then Chief of OSS/ETO.

To George Leisure, Carl Newton, Ralstone Irvine, Thomas McFadden and David Teitelbaum, Donovan's senior law partners, for their advice and assistance; to Walter Pforzheimer of Washington, D.C., for his generous help; to General Philip Strong, who gave me access to his own intelligence library; to the staff of Baker Library at Dartmouth College for their un-failing cooperation; and to Morris W. Watkins of the Columbia Alumni Federation and to the Columbia University Archives for supplying details of Donovan's undergraduate days as well as a collection of his public ad-dresses.

More personally, my thanks to Norma Bouchard of Hanover, N.H., for her patience in transcribing the taped recordings of countless interviews, and typing and retyping and re-retyping this manuscript; to Professor Her-bert F. West of Dartmouth, who suggested its title; to Richard W. Ridgway of Cody, Wyoming, and John Borden of Liberty, N.Y., for their loyal as-sistance as research associates on my project; to Dorothy Olding of Harold Ober Associates, as always, for her encouragement and penetrating criticism during the book's long period of gestation; and finally to Llewellyn Howland III of Little, Brown and Company, who first conceived the form of this biography and whose sustaining enthusiasm and brilliant editorial direction were of more help to me than I can adequately express.

INDEX